BLOOD OATH

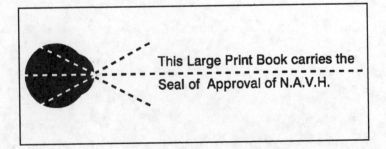

BLOOD OATH

MELISSA LENHARDT

WHEELER PUBLISHING
A part of Gale, a Cengage Company

Farmington Hills, Mich • San Francisco • New York • Waterville, Maine
Meriden, Conn • Mason, Ohio • Chicago

LIBRARY OF CONGRESS CIP DATA ON FILE.
CATALOGUING IN PUBLICATION FOR THIS BOOK
IS AVAILABLE FROM THE LIBRARY OF CONGRESS

ISBN-13: 978-1-4328-4198-0 (hardcover)
ISBN-10: 1-4328-4198-X (hardcover)

Published in 2017 by arrangement with Redhook, an imprint of Orbit, a
division of Hachette Book Group

Printed in Mexico
1 2 3 4 5 6 7 21 20 19 18 17

For Mark, who was the first to believe

■ ■ ■ ■

PART ONE:
THE MURDERESS
AND THE MAJOR

■ ■ ■ ■

CHAPTER 1

We smelled him first.

"Hail the camp!"

His appearance was no more or less disheveled and dirty than the other men who happened upon us, but his stench was astonishing, stronger than the smoke from the fire that lit his grimy features. His was not a countenance to inspire confidence in innocent travelers, let alone us. The left side of his face seemed to be sliding down, away from a jutting cheekbone and a brown leather eye patch. When he spoke, only the right side of his mouth moved. Though brief, I saw recognition in his right eye before he assumed the mien of a lonely traveler begging for frontier hospitality always given — and often regretted.

"Saw your fire 'n' hoped to share it with you, if I might."

"Of course, and welcome," Kindle said.

"Enloe's the name. Oscar Enloe."

"Picket your horse, and join us."

"Already done. Picketed him back there with yours. Nice gray you got there. Don't suppose he's for sale."

"Not today."

Enloe glanced around the camp, a dry, wide creek bed with steep banks, which offered a modicum of protection from the southern wind gusting across the plains. Our fire flickered and guttered as Enloe sat on the hard, cracked ground with exaggerated difficulty and a great sigh. He placed his rifle across his lap and nestled his saddlebags between his bowed legs.

"Well, it figures. Every time I see a good piece of horseflesh he's either not for sale or I don't have the money. Turns out it's both in this case." Enloe's laugh went up and down the scale before dying away in a little hum. His crooked smile revealed a small set of rotten teeth that ended at the incisor on the left side. He removed his hat and bent his head to rustle in his saddlebag, giving us a clear view of his scarred, hairless scalp. I cut my eyes to Kindle and saw the barest of acknowledgments in the dip of his chin. His gaze never left our guest.

Enloe lifted his head, expecting a reaction, and was disappointed he did not receive one. I imagine he enjoyed telling the story

10

of how he survived a scalping, since so few men did so. I was curious but held my tongue, as I had every time we met a stranger. Tonight silence was a tax on my willpower, the strongest indication yet I was slowly coming out of the fog I'd been in for weeks.

Enloe pulled a jar out of his bag. "Boiled eggs. Bought 'em in Sherman two days ago. Like one?" He motioned to me with the jar. I shook my head no.

"Dontcha speak?"

"No, he doesn't," Kindle said.

"Why not?"

"He's deaf."

Enloe's head jerked back. "Looked like he understood me well enough."

"He reads lips."

"You don't say?" Enloe shrugged, as if it wasn't any business of his. "Want one?"

"Thank you," Kindle said.

Enloe opened the jar, fished out a pickled egg with his dirty hands, and handed it to Kindle, along with the tangy scent of vinegar. Kindle thanked him and ate half in one bite. "What's the news in Sherman?"

"Where'd you come from?" Enloe shoved an entire egg into his mouth. I watched in fascination as he ate on one side and somehow managed to keep the egg from falling

11

out of the gaping, unmovable left side.

"Arkansas. Heading to Fort Worth."

"Fort Worth?" He spewed bits of egg out of his mouth. Some hung in his beard. "Ain't nothing worth doing or seeing in Fort Worth. Wyoming's where the action is."

"I'm not much for prospecting. Looking to get a plot of land and make a go of it."

"This here your son?" Enloe's eye narrowed at me.

"Brother."

"Well, bringing an idiot to the frontier ain't the smartest thing I ever heard. He won't be able to hear when the Kioway come raiding, now will he?"

"I've heard tell the Army protects the settlers."

Enloe laughed derisively. "Fucking Army ain't worth a tinker's damn. Except those niggers. Now, there's the perfect soldier. Those white officers order them to charge and they do 'cause they're too stupid to do anything but blindly follow orders. Can't think for themselves. Redskins mistake it for bravery and won't go up against them." The corner of Kindle's eye twitched, and I knew it took great resolve to not contradict Enloe.

Enloe brought out a bottle of whisky, pulled the cork, and drank deeply from the corner of his mouth. "If you're expectin' the Army to protect you, better turn right around and go back to Arkansas." He narrowed his eyes. "You're awfully well-spoken for an Arkansan."

"Our mother was a teacher."

He nodded slowly. "Suppose you've heard about the excitement in Fort Richardson."

"No."

"Surely you heard about the Warren Wagon Train Massacre? You do got papers in Arkansas, dontchee? Suppose not many a you hillbillies can read it." I doubted Oscar Enloe knew a *G* from a *C*.

"We heard about it," Kindle said. "Did they catch the Indians?"

"They did. Sherman himself, though it was pure luck. The redskins were at Sill, bragging about it. Well, Sherman didn't give a damn about the Indian Peace Policy and arrested 'em. Shocked he didn't put 'em on trial right there and tighten the noose himself. They sent them to Jacksboro to stand trial. One of 'em tried to get away and was shot in the back. One less redskin to worry about, I say. Other two were convicted, 'course." Enloe held out his whisky. "Want some?"

Kindle refused. I held out my hand. Enloe ignored my knobby fingers wrapping around

13

the bottle, foreign to me even now, weeks later, and turned his attention to Kindle. I drank from the bottle and held the rotgut in my mouth, barely resisting the urge to spit it into the fire. It was whisky in name only. The liquid scorched my throat as I swallowed, burned a hole in my stomach. I held the back of my hand to my mouth and saw Enloe watching me with a knowing smirk. Keeping my eyes on him, I drank another swallow, didn't wince as it made its way down, and kept the bottle. I only hoped it would numb the pain before Enloe tried to kill us.

Kindle didn't move, flinch, or take his eyes from Enloe. His rifle lay on the ground next to him, out of reach. Neither moved. "You'd think the massacre and hanging Injuns would be enough to be going on with, but that ain't even the most interesting story outta Jacksboro," Enloe said.

"No?"

"Jacksboro was overflowin' with people there celebrating, wanting to see those two redskins hang. Gov'nor killed their fun, staying their execution. I imagine they've turned their attention now to the fugitives."

"Fugitives?"

"The Murderess and the Major, that's what the newspaper's calling them. Catchy

14

name, at that."

"Never heard of 'em."

"Woman who survived the massacre, turns out she's out here on the run. 'Course, she ain't alone in that, is she? Heh-heh. Supposed to have saved the Major right after the massacre, but we have it from his nigger soldiers so it's probably a lie."

I bristled and drank more of Enloe's whisky to avoid speaking.

"Yep, she killed a man in New York City. Her lover, they say, and I believe it. Just like a woman, she lured the Major into fallin' in love with her. He threw his career away to go off an' save her from the Comanche, and then sprung her before the Pinkerton could come take her back to New York."

Enloe put a finger against one nostril and shot a stream of snot onto the ground. "Some think they headed north to the railroad, or maybe south to Mexico. The Pinkerton thought they stayed in the tent city sprung up outside a Jacksboro for the trial. Tore it to pieces one night, searching. Torched a few nigger tents for the hell of it. He's mad 'cause he was in town that night."

"What night?"

"The night they escaped. I heard tell he decided to go whoring instead of taking the Murderess into custody as he shoulda. He

15

tore through the tent city like the devil. 'Course, nothing came of it. The Major ain't stupid."

"You know him?" Kindle said.

"Nah, but I heard of him. Has a scar down the side of his face, said to be given to him by his brother in the war."

"The Pinkerton go back East?"

"Can't very well without his prisoner, now can he?"

I glanced at Kindle, whose expression was closed. Enloe pulled a plug of tobacco from his vest pocket. He tore off a chunk and chewed on it a bit, his gaze never wavering from us. He spit a brown stream into the fire. The spittle sizzled and a log fell. "Wouldya lookit?" He laughed up and down the scale again. "Kinda hot out for a fire."

"Thought I'd make it easy for you to find us."

"Didja now?"

"You've been shadowing us for three days. You aren't as good as you think you are."

"Well, I found you, didn't I?"

"Oh, you weren't the first," Kindle said. Enloe's smile slipped. "And, you won't be the last."

In a smooth, easy motion, Enloe leveled his gun at Kindle. "I seem to have caught you without your gun handy."

16

"True. What made you come into Indian Territory? Alone."

"Who said I'm alone?"

"My scout."

"What scout?"

"The one who's been shadowing you for three days. Where's the Pinkerton?"

"I —"

I heard the tomahawk cut through the air the second before it cleaved Enloe's skull cleanly down the middle. Blood ran crookedly down his scarred head, like a river cutting through a winding canyon. He tipped over onto his side.

I drank his whisky and watched him die.

CHAPTER 2

Clutching the whisky bottle to my breast with my knotted fingers, I stared at the dead man while the words of my Hippocratic oath ran through my mind.

I will take care that they suffer no hurt or damage.

Little Stick, our Tonkawa scout, placed his foot on Enloe's shoulder and pulled the ax from Enloe's head with a sucking, wet squelch. The Indian threw the saddlebags across the fire to Kindle, who rifled through them searching for loot. I thought of my indignation with the Buffalo Soldiers looting after my wagon train was massacred, shook my head, and chuckled.

"What?" Kindle said.

Enloe's dead eye stared accusingly at me. "Nothing."

"Laura." Kindle touched my shoulder, and despite myself, I flinched. He removed his hand. "He would have killed me and

18

taken you."

"Five men in seven days." I turned to Kindle. "Did you know I've never lost five patients in my *life*?"

"No."

"Here I sit, watching a man bleed to death and doing nothing. If my profession wasn't lost to me because of this" — I lifted my disfigured hand — "it is because I have so thoroughly broken my oath, I cannot call myself a physician."

"Oaths mean little on the frontier. Here it's all about survival. Kill or be killed."

"What a nihilistic life we will lead."

"It's better than being dead."

I watched Little Stick rifle through Enloe's person, searching for trinkets to trade or possibly give to his family as gifts. "His horse is good enough," the Indian said. "We can trade him at the next camp we come to."

"How much longer until we reach your tribe?" Kindle asked.

"Four days."

I stiffened, the thought of hiding out in a camp of Indians no more reassuring to me seven days on than it was when Kindle told me.

After we escaped Jacksboro, Kindle and I rode hard all night and most of the next

19

day, until we arrived at what remained of the ruined Army camp on the Red River. Six weeks had passed since the Comanche abducted me from the camp and killed all the soldiers escorting me to Fort Sill. With the influx of travelers for the trial of Big Tree and Satanta, the ruins had been scavenged until there was nothing left but a broken wagon and empty crates.

I had pulled my horse to an abrupt stop and stared at the wreckage. "We're heading north?"

Kindle reined his horse back to me. He gave his horse his head and rested his hands on the saddle horn. "Northeast. To Independence, Missouri."

I narrowed my eyes. "Through Indian Country?"

Kindle nodded slowly.

"No. Absolutely not."

"Laura, I expect a dozen or more men left Jacksboro this morning, on our trail. The last place they expect us to go is through Indian Country."

"It's the last place I want to go."

"Most will expect us to head to the railroad in Fort Worth. Sherman, maybe. A few will head south to Austin. But my picture will be all over the papers, and yours as well. Every railroad station in the state will be on

20

high alert for us. The only direction that's less likely than north is west, through the Comancheria."

My head throbbed behind my eyes. "What's in Independence?"

"Options. The railroad east or west. The Oregon Trail. The river to New Orleans. We can go wherever you want from there."

"How are we going to get across Indian Country without being scalped or kidnapped?"

Little Stick emerged from the darkness, as if cued by a stage director.

"You cannot be serious."

"We cannot do this alone, Laura. Little Stick will scout for us, ahead and behind. He will be with us little, only at night camp."

I shook my head and looked away, trying to hide my tears of fear and frustration.

"Laura. We need another man, another gun, another person to take a watch at night."

"I can shoot."

"And very well. But, do you know how to speak Comanche? Cheyenne? Ute?" I shook my head. "Me, either. He will translate for us. He will be a modicum of protection from other Indians."

"A modicum?"

"The Tonkawas don't have many Indian

21

friends these days."

"Lovely."

"He's scouted for the Army for years. We can trust him."

I sighed. "You can trust him. I'll trust you."

And, so here we were, seven days later, with five dead men and Little Stick grabbing the ankle of the last to drag him off to God only knew where.

"Wait." I walked around the fire and removed Enloe's eye patch. I washed the blood off with the leftover rotgut and handed it to Kindle.

"No one's looking for a bearded Army officer with an eye patch."

He stared at the bit of leather with distaste. "I suppose you're right."

I held the whisky out to Little Stick. He took it with a nod of thanks and set to his task.

"Don't worry," I said. "There isn't enough for him to get drunk on."

Kindle nodded, and with a half smile said, "You're warming up to him."

"No, I'm making sure he has no incentive to kill me, rape me, or turn me in. If a couple of sips of rotgut will buy another day of safety, I guess it's a good bargain." I took the eye patch from Kindle. "Here, let me." He held the patch against his eye while I tied the leather strings behind his head. He adjusted it and said, "How do I look?"

With his salt-and-pepper week-old beard obscuring his scar, hat flattened hair, and face smudged with dirt, it was difficult to see the man I fell in love with. "Disreputable."

He donned his hat and pulled it low. His one eye was barely discernible beneath the brim, waking the memory of a man staring at me across Lost Creek. I removed his hat. "Too much like your brother."

Slowly, Kindle removed the bit of leather. His brother's ghost descended like a curtain. John Kindle — or Cotter Black as he was known west of the Mississippi — couldn't have separated us more completely if he was physically between us, grinning and laughing at how his plan to make me and his brother suffer had worked so perfectly.

Little Stick returned, holding a long, headless snake in his hand. "Dinner," he said. The dead snake twisted and squirmed in the Tonkawa's hand, and I tried not to vomit.

"Will it ever stop moving?"

Chunks of the skinned snake lay on a flat rock in the middle of the fire, twisting back and forth, though it was long dead and cooked through.

"When it gets to your stomach," Kindle said. "Maybe." Little Stick chuckled and bit into the piece he held.

I covered my mouth and pulled a piece of hardtack from my saddlebag. I longed for Maureen's thick, savory Irish stew, for the warmth of our New York kitchen, for the sound of her humming her favorite tune as she worked, sometimes singing the Gaelic words softly to herself. I would stand in the hallway and listen, knowing she would stop as soon as I entered the kitchen, look up, and after a brief expression of irritation at being interrupted, her face would clear into a smile, and she would sing the stanza she made up for me.

I stared at the snake meat Kindle held, meat I'd skinned, gutted, and cooked while he'd taken care of the horses. Little Stick watched, giving me suggestions as my stiff fingers fumbled with squirming snake. My first human dissection came to mind: standing around a body as our professor cut into the dead man's chest, the two male students next to me fainting, and the other students expecting me to follow. Instead, I stepped toward the body, kept my hands grasped lightly in front of me, and stared resolutely at the incision. The idea that six years later I would be using my surgical skills for my survival rather than another human being's was absolutely unfathomable.

What a young, ignorant, innocent girl I had been. My experiences posing as a male orderly in the war had hardened me, but nothing prepared me for the West. The frontier had been an abstract, a myth of towering, noble men cutting a trail for civilization created by newspapermen to sell broadsheets, a dream of a better life dangled to poor farmers, the promise of a new start. A promise I bought into only too eagerly, a dream shattered on the banks of the Canadian River, and a myth crushed beneath brutality on a scale unimaginable in the civilized parlors of the East.

"Laura?"

I lifted my gaze to Kindle. "Hmm?"

"Are you sure you don't want some? Cold camp the next two nights."

"No, thank you."

Little Stick finished off the whisky and tossed the bottle into the fire. "We will come to the forest soon. Better game. Less exposure."

I closed my eyes and sighed. "Trees. How I've missed trees."

From the waist down, Little Stick dressed

as an Indian: deerskin pants, breechclout, and moccasins. Over his bare chest he wore a multicolored gentleman's waistcoat that must have been splendid when new, but was now faded from exposure. The lines and swirls tattooed dark on his face were terrifying in the firelight. Strips of his long hair were braided with cloth and tied with metal trinkets and beads. My eyes were always drawn to the silver thimble on a thin strip of hair braided with yellow calico, and I couldn't help wondering what woman had died so Little Stick could adorn his hair.

A mostly empty bandolier crossed his chest from left to right and he wore a Colt Walker on his left hip, gun handle pointing forward. An Army kepi embroidered with a horn rounded out his eclectic attire. He was dirty and stank and reminded me of things I longed to forget. But he showed a deference to me — almost a gentleness — I couldn't understand and did not want.

As he did every night, Little Stick nodded to us, turned, and walked away from the camp. Kindle kicked dirt over the fire, extinguishing it, though a few embers peeked through. Bright stars speckled the moonless carpet of dark sky above us. I wondered if tonight would be the night Kindle would reach for me to quiet my

26

growing worry that Cotter Black's words had been prophetic.

Kindle sat next to me, close enough to feel his energy, though not close enough to touch. He smiled faintly. "Feeling okay?"

I nodded. Lying to Kindle was easiest when I didn't speak. "Will they ever stop coming?"

"Eventually."

"I should go back."

"It is too late for that."

"Five men, Kindle, dead because of me."

"The world will not miss those five men."

"Possibly."

None of the dead men would have fit the stereotype of noble frontiersman the Eastern papers pushed. They were all cut from the same dirty mold, with a decided air of desperation hovering around the edges. I'd seen many more men of their ilk while in the West than honorable men. I sat next to one of the few of the latter.

I pulled my knees close and rested my forehead against them. I inhaled deeply, lay my cheek on my knees, and watched Kindle. He leaned back on one elbow, a leg extended toward the smoldering embers, the other bent and holding up his other arm. He rolled a twig of sage in his fingers, brought it to his nose, and inhaled deeply.

He closed his eyes and smiled ever so slightly, his face relaxing from the tension of the trail into the countenance I knew so well from Fort Richardson.

He opened his eyes, glanced at me, and covered his embarrassment with a chuckle. He held out his hand and I leaned forward to sniff. The sage's woodsy, slightly lemon scent brought a smile to my lips as well.

"Calming, isn't it?" Kindle said.

"Yes."

"Indians use it for cleansing ceremonies. They also use it for a variety of ailments. Mostly stomach troubles."

"Do they? And how do you know so much about it?"

"I've spent almost six years in the West. You pick these things up."

"What's a cleansing ceremony?"

"Different tribes have different names and traditions, but they're generally the same. When a boy is old enough, he is sent on a vision quest. He's sent out into the wild alone to commune with the spirits, to get direction. Often times, a boy is given his adult name based on the vision received."

"Is that how Little Stick got his name?"

Kindle laughed more heartily than he had in weeks. "No. He was given his name at birth and never outgrew it. It isn't an exact translation." Kindle raised his eyebrows and I understood.

"Heavens. Poor Little Stick." I couldn't repress a giggle.

"It hasn't kept him from having two wives and six children." Kindle waved away Little Stick's inadequacies. "But, before a brave leaves on his quest, he's cleansed in a sweat lodge ceremony." He held out the sage branch. "That's where the sage comes in."

"Have you seen one?"

"No." He scratched at his beard.

"Does it itch?"

"No, but I can't seem to get out of the habit of scratching it."

"Do you want me to shave you?" His eyes met mine, and I knew he remembered the night I had shaved him at Fort Richardson, how the world outside fell away. I longed to return to that moment, to do things differently, to make different decisions so we wouldn't end up in Indian Country, a degraded woman and a disgraced Army officer.

"When we reach Independence."

I reached out and touched Kindle's hand. The jolt of electricity I'd felt when I shaved him was there, though faint, buried beneath shame and guilt. Kindle had given me so much and sacrificed everything to save me, and what had I done for him? The one thing I could do for him, he refused to consider. "I have ruined your career and your future. If we return, you could restore your good name, be dishonorably discharged."

"My good name?" He laughed bitterly and pulled his hand away.

"Very few people know Cotter Black was your brother. Even so, no one will hold him against you, especially since you went after him."

"There's so much you don't know about me, Laura."

"There is nothing you could tell me that would make me think less of you."

He met my gaze, and though I could barely see his eyes in the darkness, I could feel their intensity. "I wouldn't be so sure."

"Tell me."

"No."

"Don't you trust me?" When he didn't answer, I dropped my gaze. "I see."

I stood and smoothed my blanket on the ground, folded it over for cushioning, and lay my head on my saddle, keeping my back to Kindle and the deadened fire. I tried to imagine myself in my bedroom in New York City, my head on a down pillow, sleeping under a blanket stitched together by Maureen. Outside, the lamplighters would be walking on their stilts, lighting the streets for the night. A heavy medical tome would sit on my bedside table, a bookmark saving my place for the next evening or whenever I had a chance to pick it up again. There could be a knock at the door any moment, with Maureen coming to tell me a servant was at the back door, asking for the doctor to come quick.

An owl hooted in the distance. I stared at the bank of the river. It could have easily been the riverbed where the Comanche stopped the first morning after they captured me. Where they spent hours raping and beating me, laughing and talking as they waited their turns. The memory was with me constantly, brought forth in a dozen ways. The sound of running water. The thunder of horses' hooves. Laughing. Crying. Kindle's grunt when he heaved a saddle on a horse. The clink of the trinkets in Little Stick's hair. Little Stick. The stench of unwashed men. Kindle pulling away from my fingers lightly touching his hand.

I lived in a constant state of terror and despair, a scream of frustration always at the back of my throat wanting desperately to be free. I hugged myself to stop the shaking I knew would come despite the warm weather and the residual heat from the dying fire, as the longing for and revulsion of Kindle's touch warred within me.

CHAPTER 3

East of the Wichita Mountains the plains undulated and rolled off toward the forests and river valleys feeding the Missouri and Mississippi Rivers. The swells and valleys of the small hills did little to break up the monotony of traveling across featureless plains with buffalo grass so tall it grazed our horses' bellies. The constant motion of the buffalo grass, as well as the searing heat of the midday sun and the dry, hot wind blowing from the west, brought on a severe case of nausea. I could hardly remember a time in the last three months when I hadn't been stricken with either nausea or a headache. I pulled my hat down low on my forehead, drank from my canteen, and kept my complaints to myself. Kindle could do nothing; there wasn't a tree to rest under in sight.

"What is that song?" Kindle asked.

"Hmm?"

"The song you are humming? What is it?"

"It's a song Maureen used to sing to me when I was a child. An Irish song. My earliest memory of her was her teaching me the song."

"She raised you?"

"From the time I was five. My mother had died the same year."

"Do you remember her?"

"No. Just Maureen. The boat she came over on was struck with typhoid. My father went to help when it docked and found Maureen trying to nurse the entire third class by herself. She was barely sixteen. Lost her entire family." I shook my head and laughed. "My father hoped she would become his nurse but she vowed to never do it again. So she became my nanny and our maid." I held my hand out to Kindle and he took it. "She was sick for the entire voyage to Galveston. Her refusal to sail for California is what put us on the wagon train across Texas."

"I suppose I should thank her for it."

I thought of the mass grave Kindle's Buffalo Soldiers dug for Maureen and the victims of the Kiowa massacre I survived. "I wish you could. She would love you." I squeezed his hand and released it. "Tell me about your war after Antietam."

I met Kindle for the first time outside a makeshift Union hospital on the edge of the Antietam battlefield. Posing as a male orderly because I had been refused as a nurse for being "too handsome," I was throwing an amputated limb onto the shoulder-high pile outside the hospital when I saw Kindle sitting against a tree, drunk. Furious, I stalked over to him to get his name and report him for drunkenness. When I saw his face sliced open from temple to jaw, I took it upon myself to suture his wound. Helping Kindle was what convinced me to spend the next eight years fighting to become a doctor. I knew little of Kindle's life in the ensuing eight years.

"I tried to find you," Kindle said.

"My father was wounded by a Confederate soldier when he tried to help him on the battlefield," I said. "He wasn't going to be able to perform surgery for months so we moved him back to New York. The other doctors with our regiment wanted me to stay, but my father outed me as a woman so I wouldn't be able to."

"I can imagine how you reacted."

I steered my palomino, which I'd named Piper, around a prairie-dog hole and chuckled. "Poorly, I grant you. But, at least I wasn't there when you arrived."

"Why's that?"

"The letter we received in condemnation of my working on you was angry enough. I can't imagine I would have lived through the ire in person."

"The doctor I spoke to was impressed with the work. He hardly believed you had done it."

"To him I was a baby-faced seventeen-year-old boy."

"Instead you were a baby-faced twenty-three-year-old woman." He glanced at me from the side of his eyes.

"I am not going to tell you how old I am."

"Why not?"

"Because you are changing the subject. Where did you go after Antietam?"

"Why?"

"Look around. There's nothing interesting to talk about, and I want to know more of you. We know little of each other's background."

Kindle flipped his eye patch up and rubbed his left eye. "I hate this thing."

"Leave it up. We will see people from miles away. After Antietam."

"I went to Boston to be with Victoria."

A pang of jealousy shot through me, though Kindle's wife was long dead. I knew almost nothing of her, save what Kindle's

36

brother had told me when he held me captive in Palo Duro Canyon, and I wasn't sure how much of his perspective I should trust. The words were out of my mouth before I realized. "What was she like?"

"Nothing like you," Kindle answered immediately. He pursed his lips. "I take it back. You are two of the most stubborn women I've ever known."

"You say it as if it's a character flaw."

"It's not the most attractive trait in a woman."

"You seem to be attracted to it."

Kindle's mouth quirked up into a wry smile. "Point taken."

"If I wasn't stubborn, I wouldn't have been at Antietam to sew up your face. You would have been maimed for life. I also wouldn't have completed medical school and saved your life on the prairie, twice in one day."

"Don't look so smug."

"I operated on you in the middle of the smoldering ruin of my wagon train with a storm on the horizon. And I operated on you at the fort with Sherman himself holding a lantern and glaring at me. I believe smugness is warranted."

He raised his hands in surrender. "You've made your point. I love stubborn women.

Happy?"

I grinned. "Immensely." Our horses went down through a dry wash and up the other side. "When you returned, how long had it been since you'd seen her?"

"Almost a year. I didn't stay long."

"Why? I would think with such a severe wound they would have given you desk duty."

"They tried. I wanted to be in the field leading my men." He cleared his throat. "The day after Gettysburg, I received word she died."

"William, I'm so sorry."

His mouth tightened and he stared resolutely at the horizon. I was silent, waiting for him to say more about her, but he did not. "After, I was transferred west, to Fort Lyon in Colorado territory. The Indian problem hadn't stopped because we were at war with the South."

It was on the tip of my tongue to ask why a West Point graduate such as he would be transferred out of the fighting when we crested a hill and he stopped. "Go back." Kindle turned his horse and galloped down the back of the hill. I followed.

When I caught up he'd dismounted, pulled a spyglass from his saddlebag, and gone back up the hill. I dismounted, tied

38

our horses together, and quickly picketed mine. The last thing we needed to do was chase our string across the plains.

I crawled up next to Kindle and lay on my stomach. "The horses are tied down." In the distance I saw a dust cloud spanning the northeast. Kindle handed me the spyglass.

I positioned the eyepiece. "What is it?"

"Army patrol."

"Why didn't Little Stick warn us?"

"I told him to follow and watch for bounty hunters."

I handed the glass back to Kindle. "What are we going to do?"

He stared for a long time, letting the patrol come closer for a better view, I supposed. He let the spyglass fall from his face, took his hat off, and wiped his forehead with his sleeve.

"Is it Mackenzie?"

"No."

He stared into the middle distance, considering our options. Showing the letter from Colonel Ranald Mackenzie in Kindle's inside pocket would do us no good. Admitting who Kindle was would reveal my identity and put me on the first train to New York. Plus, chances were the letter had been forged by the colonel's sister, Harriet Mackenzie, who helped us escape Jacksboro. It would need to be used hundreds of miles away, where confirming its veracity with the colonel would be too difficult. Last we heard, Mackenzie was patrolling Indian Territory. We'd been lucky not to come across him.

Kindle pulled Enloe's eye patch down. "The officer looks young, too young to recognize me."

"What about the soldiers?"

"Guess we will see how good of a disguise the beard and eye patch are."

We mounted up and rode below the hill for a mile before dipping down into a dry wash and following it north. It leveled out onto the plains about a half a mile southeast of the supply train. My hope we were far enough away and behind to be ignored by the patrol was soon dashed when two outriders spun away from the wagons and galloped toward us. We pulled up and Kindle held up his rifle, to which he'd tied a white flag.

"It's a sergeant and a lieutenant," Kindle said. He bit off a hunk of tobacco looted from the third bounty hunter and quickly worked it into a large mass in his right cheek opposite his scar and eye patch.

"That's good, isn't it?"

"I hope so." He spit a stream of tobacco on the ground. "I hope I don't fall off my horse."

"Why would you?"

"Chewing tobacco makes me sick. Always has." Kindle continued to work the plug, turning paler by the second beneath a fresh sheen of perspiration. "Let me do the talking, Laura," Kindle said, voice low. The sergeant reined his horse in about ten yards from us but the lieutenant rode practically up on us. I heard Kindle curse beneath his breath and knew he recognized the soldier.

"Lieutenant," Kindle said, with a pronounced Texan accent.

The lieutenant and sergeant made an interesting pair. The officer was small, almost boyish, with a wispy red mustache and a sunburned face. The soldier was stout, with a barrel chest and a thick neck. Though covered with a wool uniform coat and leather gauntlets, it was easy to see his arms were powerful and muscular. The soldier looked off into the distance around us, searching for more travelers, while the lieutenant asked in a haughty voice, "What is your business here?"

"Traveling north."

"Why?"

"Following the trail of the Murderess and

the Major."

"Who?"

"You ain't heard of 'em?"

"No."

"Some Yankee woman doctor on the run. They caught up with her at Richardson. She's the only survivor of the wagon train massacre back in May." Kindle spat some juice on the ground. "Where'd you come from to have not heard it? 'S all over the country."

"I've heard of her. When we left Sill, she was under guard at Richardson."

"Whatchew been doin'?" Kindle said.

"Searching for whisky traders. We hear they have a camp somewhere nearby. A base of operations where they cut the whisky, then break off in small groups to sell it. Have you seen anything like it?"

"No, sir. Came up from Sherman. Haven't seen anyone."

"You said the Murderess and the Major?"

"The woman convinced an Army major to help her evade the law. They left Jacksboro about a week ago. Bounty hunters all over the country looking for 'em. Pinkerton, too."

"Who was the Army officer?"

"Kindle."

"William Kindle?" The sergeant spoke up.

"Ah, you're messing with me."

"Nope. He broke out of the brig, then sprung the murderess. No one realized they were gone for almost a day, what with Satanta and Big Tree in Jacksboro. You know Kindle?"

"Served with him. At Washita."

Kindle spat on the ground and grunted. "Wouldn't be bragging about it."

"I ain't."

My horse shifted on his feet and threw his head, as if feeling my tension, and made the officer take notice of me. "Who's this with you?"

"Brother. He don't speak. Deaf and dumb."

I held the lieutenant's gaze, but he lost interest in me quickly. He turned his attention back to Kindle. "What'd you say your name is?"

"Didn't. But, it's Oscar Enloe."

"What makes you think the fugitives went this way?"

"Gotta go through Indian Territory to get to the railroad, dontcha? Well, if there's nothing else, we're gonna be heading on."

The lieutenant tipped his hat. "Be careful. We got some unhappy Indians around here. And, they're drunk."

My stomach twisted.

"I ain't ever met a happy Indian. But, thanks for the tip all the same," Kindle said.

The lieutenant reined his horse around and rode off to the column. The sergeant stayed put, watching us. Kindle and I reined our horses east and rode off at an easy walk. The wind buffeted us and almost blew my hat off. I grabbed it at the last minute and chanced to look over my shoulder at the retreating soldiers, but the sergeant sat his horse, watching us go.

When we were far enough away I said, "You think he recognized you?"

"Yes. His name is Jones."

"Will he turn us in?"

"I don't know."

When we'd ridden slowly for a mile, we kicked our horses into an easy gallop. We alternated between a gallop and a walk, giving them time to recover before kicking them into a lope again. We didn't stop until the setting sun was low on the horizon.

CHAPTER 4

"Do you say I'm deaf and dumb because you don't trust me to speak?"

After riding hard all day and half of the night, we happened on a clear spring amid a copse of cottonwood and hackberry trees. We judiciously watered our horses to keep them from foundering, picketed them, and made a cold camp beneath the largest cottonwood. A quarter moon hung in the starry sky.

Kindle didn't respond and I continued. "It cannot be because I sound too much like a woman."

I dug a stick into the cool, muddy ground and didn't look at Kindle. I'd hoped with time my voice would return to normal, but it had been weeks since Cotter Black punched me in the throat. My voice had always been more alto than soprano, but now my low voice would crack unexpectedly. I sounded like a young boy whose voice was changing.

"I'm more familiar with this world. It's safer if I do the talking," Kindle said. "Why don't you get some rest. I'll take watch."

I tossed the stick into the pool. "When will Little Stick catch up to us?"

"I'm not sure. We rode hard but he can ride faster than we do. The morning, probably."

"I can take a watch. You need to rest, too."

"I'm fine. Go on. Rest."

Without argument, I rolled out my blanket, lay down, and curled into a ball. I heard Kindle's steady breathing, frogs croaking on the edge of the spring, the whisper of buffalo grass waving in the breeze, and my own heartbeat throbbing in my ears. I would pretend to sleep for a while, then make Kindle give me the watch. Why did he insist on taking everything on and letting me do nothing? Did he think me so useless? Or was he merely trying to protect me? Take care of me?

Of course I knew the answer. He was trying to do both. The question I couldn't answer was what drove him? Guilt? A sense of honor? Or love?

I squeezed my eyes tight and tried to focus on what we had before: tending to Kindle at Fort Richardson as he healed from two serious wounds, talking late into the night, falling in love, making love in the small fort library and again on the trail the night before we separated. How complete I'd felt in his presence, the way he'd said my name as we made love.

Catherine.

A rough voice in my ear, a knife held to my throat.

He won't touch you now you've been fucked by Indians.

The smell of laudanum and the soft voice of a dear friend.

I've taken care of it for you.

I jolted awake and sat up. Kindle sat a few feet away, cradling his Spencer repeating rifle and watching me. Kindle didn't move to comfort me, merely sat and watched me. "Bad dream?"

I clutched at my chest and thought of Cotter Black whispering vile lies about me into Kindle's ear, and then doing the same about Kindle into mine, and didn't answer.

Across the pond, pale light was cresting the eastern horizon. I'd slept longer than I intended. Little Stick was nowhere to be seen. "Will you please rest? I am awake now."

He walked to me and held out his hand. I took it and stood. He handed me his rifle, but didn't let go of my hand. He massaged my healing fingers, one at a time, bent them gently into a fist and repeated the action. "How do they feel?"

"They ache."

"Does this help?"

"Yes. Where did you learn it?"

"From a doctor, as a child." He continued before I could ask more. "What were you dreaming about?"

"Antietam."

He knew I was lying. He released my hand, lay on my blanket, and tilted his hat over his eyes.

"I'd love some coffee when I wake."

I glanced down at his half-covered face and saw him peeking from beneath the brim with a smirk.

"You trust me to make the fire without you?"

"It's a gamble, I admit."

I kicked his boot and went to gather firewood.

Ten minutes later I was rubbing a fire stick between my palms, hoping the soapwood would spark the tinder of leaves and grass quickly. I squeaked in excitement when the tinder caught and glanced over my shoulder to make sure Kindle hadn't heard it. He hadn't moved, and his face was slack in sleep. I leaned over and blew on the small flame and fed more leaves and grass into the blaze until it was going strong.

When the coffee was on the fire, I took the gun with me to relieve myself near the picketed horses. I led them to the stream, let them drink, and picketed them amid fresh grass. I walked up a small rise and gazed across the plains. I could see miles in every direction. There was no sign of Little Stick, or anyone else. Kindle and I could be the only two people on earth.

I returned to Kindle, who was snoring lightly. His face in repose was the face I fell in love with: clear, honorable, without the tension and worry I saw in every line while he was awake. I longed to reach out and touch him, to run my finger over the beard hiding the scar on his cheek.

I turned away and tried to erase the mortifying memory of the last time I had reached out to him. Intimacy had been the last thing on either of our minds our first days out of Jacksboro. At our first opportunity to talk, to take stock of where we'd been and where we were going, Kindle retreated into himself with barely a glance in my direction.

Stories of women who were abducted by Indians and then rescued, only to be shunned by friends, family, and society played constantly in my mind. During the first two hectic days of running, had he had time to think of what I endured, of the shame that covered me like a pox? Was his polite distance born of duty and responsibility, of respect for what I'd been through, or of disgust?

The idea of freeing Kindle when we arrived wherever it was we were going was dismissed as soon as it came to mind. Though I'd ferociously guarded my independence in New York City, the thought of being alone in the West terrorized me. There were too many dangers, too many men who would do me harm and take advantage of me. Without my profession, I couldn't survive. I'd flirted with destitution before my practice flourished in New York. Treating prostitutes had saved me. Now I would be fit only for the other side of the bed. If my history with the Comanche became known, even that avenue would be closed to me.

I needed Kindle to survive. His protection, his expertise, his strength. What did I offer him? Clever conversation and intelligence? Stubborness? The latter two were hardly enough to satisfy a man. The former could be bought along with a warm body and a soft bed. The idea of Kindle finding consolation with another woman haunted me and pushed me to bridge the distance between us.

The first night Little Stick had stood watch, I placed my blanket on the ground next to Kindle and lay down. He didn't move, though his breathing was not deep enough to make sleep believable. I waited, and still he didn't move. I lifted his arm, pillowed my head on his chest and rested my hand on his stomach above his belt. I didn't look at him. I couldn't lest he see my humiliation at stooping to sex acts to secure his loyalty. His shallow breathing confirmed my suspicion; he was awake.

He grasped my wrist before my hand slid halfway beneath the waist of his britches. "This might be the only chance to sleep for days."

I waited and hoped for a kind word, a re-assurance, something, anything to make me believe his love for me was as strong as it had been before. When he remained stiff and silent, I rose, took my blanket to the other side of the fire, and spent a sleepless night crying quietly. My dream of a marriage of equals full of playfulness and passion faded, only to be revived the next day with the easy companionship and flirty banter that had sparked our love affair at Fort Richardson. At night, the distance returned. Our relationship swung like a pendulum from hope to despair and back again.

A frog splashed into the pond and jerked me to the present: the smell of coffee, Kindle asleep. The sounds of Indian whoops made me flinch, grasp my gun, and rush up the bank. The horizon was as clear as it had been moments earlier. I rubbed my forehead, breathed deeply, and tried to forget.

Physically I was almost healed from the degradation the Indians had put me through on the banks of the Canadian River. I flexed the fingers of my right hand. Kindle's massage had helped. Dr. Ezra Kline had done an admirable job of breaking and resetting them. Though I might not ever be able to perform delicate, internal surgery, they would be sufficient to remove bullets, stitch up knife wounds, and deliver babies — the types of complaints I was likely to see the most in the West anyhow.

Despite riding astride since that morning on the Canadian, my pudenda had healed, though they had lost most of their sensitivity. A blessing or a curse? Would it return once I got out of the saddle? I didn't know.

My hand went to my abdomen.

I've taken care of it for you.

Ezra had taken care not only of my broken hands and other outer injuries, he had also terminated my pregnancy. I squeezed my eyes shut at the memory of his expression as he told me once I woke from a laudanum-induced unconsciousness. He had not asked if I wanted it, only assumed the baby was the result of the Comanche's abuse. There was a good chance he was right. But there was also the possibility it had been Kindle's baby he had aborted, though Ezra couldn't have known. I told myself it was the correct decision, that I would have asked him to do it, or done it myself, as soon as I knew I was with child. I only had to imagine the horror on Kindle's face at seeing the culmination of Cotter Black's revenge in the face of a half-Comanche baby to know Ezra had made the right decision. When I dreamt of the baby, though, it had Kindle's eyes.

The sun was fully over the horizon now and sweat popped out on my upper lip. The cool water of the pool enticed me. I couldn't remember the last time I had a bath. My breathing quickened. What if someone were to ride up? I would be naked and vulnerable. Should I wake Kindle to keep watch? I searched the horizon again, saw nothing and no one. Kindle snored slightly, and his face had the slack expression of one in a deep sleep. He'd slept so little since we left Fort Richardson I was loath to wake him. I decided to be quick about it, and stay within easy reach of the bank and my rifle.

With my back to Kindle's sleeping form I placed the gun on the edge of the water and quickly shed my pants and shirt. I unlaced the corset I'd been wearing upside down to flatten my breasts. I removed it gingerly and somewhat painfully. The whalebone ribs left deep lines on my skin. I lifted my breasts and squeezed them, relieved to feel like a woman again, if only briefly. Goose bumps raced across my body when I stepped into the cool water. I inhaled sharply and glanced over my shoulder at Kindle, who was dead to the world. I walked farther into the pool, mud squelching through my toes, wondering idly if there were snakes nearby, when the bottom fell out of the world and I submerged.

The cold water rushing over my body was glorious. I broke through the surface, soaking wet and laughing. Kindle stood on the bank, eye patch flipped up on his forehead, half-awake, gun drawn, looking around for danger. When he saw me in the middle of the pool, laughing, he looked angry at first, then his face cleared. "Taking a dip?"

"A bath, actually. Though I don't have soap. I didn't mean to wake you. It's deep in the middle."

"Of course it is. It's a spring."

"Ah. Right. I checked the horizon before I got in. No one and nothing. See for yourself."

Kindle holstered his Colt, picked up the rifle, walked up the rise, and was gone. I leaned my head back into the water and ran my hands through my shorn hair. Kindle'd taken a knife to it our first day, so I could pull off the ruse of being a man more easily. I closed my eyes, leaned back, and floated, thinking of how wonderful it felt: cool water beneath me, the sun warming my chest and face, the only sound the water flowing through my fingers as my arms moved lazily back and forth, keeping me afloat. I smiled and was almost content for the first time in months.

I opened my eyes. Kindle watched me from the bank, eye patch over his left eye, the rifle held lightly in his hand. I treaded water and waited for him to say or do something. When he didn't, I sat up, keeping my nakedness submerged.

"Did you see anyone?"

"No."

"Are you well rested?"

"Enough."

"The eye patch is growing on you, isn't it?" I said.

"No, but now that I've used it, I'm committed to wearing it."

He didn't move, but his eye flicked down to the water.

"How long did you watch me?"

"Not long enough."

"Yet, still you stand on the bank." I held out my hand.

Without taking his eye off me, he put the gun on the bank, removed his boots, and walked into the pool fully clothed. He stopped and tensed. "God Almighty, that's cold."

"You'll get used to it."

He stepped forward cautiously. "Are you going to tell me where —" With a shout, he dropped into the pool. When he came up I saw a glimpse of Kindle as a child. Carefree, happy, and laughing.

"Right there," I said.

He splashed my face and treaded water a few feet from me.

"Have I told you about how I met General Sherman?" I asked.

"No."

"He was bathing. In the middle of a creek, naked as you please. He asked me to throw him his soap. I think he assumed I would have bad aim and he would be forced to stand up and show off his assets."

"And did you have bad aim?"

"No. I plopped it right in front of his face."

Kindle grinned and inched closer to me. The water was crystal clear, giving him an unrestricted view of my entire body, but he kept his eyes steadily on my own. "We shouldn't stay in here too long. You'd be surprised how quickly a man can cross the horizon."

I nodded. "I miss your scar."

"The eye patch doesn't make up for it?"

"No." Tiny droplets of water clung to Kindle's beard. With a hand shaking from the cold as much as nerves, I reached out to touch him but pulled my hand back, the sting of rejection too fresh. Kindle's penetrating gaze never left my face.

"Tell me plain," I said. "Are you with me out of a sense of obligation?"

"Obligation?"

"I cannot bear your pity."

Kindle turned his head away, his jaw working, pain clear on his face.

"Your brother said —"

His head snapped forward. "Whatever he said was a lie."

"Was it? Why don't you want me?"

57

"Is that what you think?" I didn't answer but kept my eyes squarely on him. His voice thick with emotion, he said, "I don't deserve to be with you. I brought it all on you, and I'll never forgive myself for it."

My stomach seized. I wasn't sure I was ready for Kindle to take me, but surely the anticipation of the event was worse than the act itself. Get it over with. Secure his love and loyalty and move on.

I reached out and touched his face. He grasped my hand and kissed my palm, and I was in his arms. He kissed me like a drowning man hungry for air. His lips and tongue were so familiar I almost forgot where it was leading.

He turned me around so I faced away, wrapping his arms around me. He ran a finger along the corset grooves lining my breasts. "You have your own scars."

"They will heal."

"I'm not talking of these." His finger traced my nipple before cupping and gently squeezing my breast. His other hand slid down my stomach and between my legs. Kindle's breathing quickened as his fingers stroked me tentatively. I closed my eyes and thought only of Kindle, of the first time he touched me, of the passion he ignited in me at Fort Richardson. Or tried to.

Kindle stilled and I opened my eyes. Four men on horses were on the rise above the pool, watching.

"Don't stop on our account," one of the men said. "Though, if you ask me, she don't look like she's enjoying it overmuch."

CHAPTER 5

"She's my wife. I'll do with her what I
please."

Kindle's voice was harsh, but his arm
moved across my chest, shielding me from
the strangers' eyes. Below the surface, he
squeezed my hip in warning.

"As I said, don't mind us." The man on a
blaze-faced sorrel twirled his hand in the
air. "Please, continue."

"We don't care for an audience."

"Then you shouldn't have tried for a poke
in the best watering hole for thirty miles."

The men dismounted and led their horses
to the pond to drink. The speaker squatted
down next to his horse's head and studied
us with pale blue eyes. His face was long
and thin, made more pronounced by the
blond bushy mustache and narrow beard
hanging off the center of his chin. His
companions were a varied lot. A rope-thin
Mexican wearing a sombrero, a portly

ginger wearing a derby, and a soft, thickset young man whose pants were being held up by red suspenders, most likely in an effort to distract from his noseless face. My shock and revulsion must have shown because the leader spoke. "She don't like people staring."

"She?" I said.

The man paused briefly and continued. "Her name's Tuesday, 'cause we rescued her on a Tuesday."

"From where?"

"A small band of Kiowas, up off the Canadian. They were taking her to Fort Scott to ransom her back. Not before they tortured her a while. She got the last word, though, didn't you Tuesday?" The girl nodded with a sadistic smile.

"Taught us all a good lesson, didnit, boys?"

"Sí."

"Ja."

"What lesson?"

The blue-eyed man grinned. "Ain't nothing more terrifying than a vengeful woman."

"Enough talking," Kindle barked. "Move on so we can get out."

"Get out. We ain't stopping you."

Kindle turned us around and said in my ear. "Walk out, get dressed, and don't act

61

embarrassed."

I did as he said. The heat was a relief after the cold water of the spring. Water streamed from Kindle's wet clothes as he put his gun belt on. He picked up his rifle and faced the four strangers across the pond while I dressed with my back to them as deliberately and unhurriedly as I could. "Let me do the talking this time," I said.

He looked at me from the side of his eyes and dipped his chin in assent. I inhaled and turned to the strangers, with a wide smile. "Would you like to join us for breakfast?"

The leader rose slowly. "What are you cooking?"

I laughed, somewhat nervously, and walked around the pool and across the stream feeding it. "Good question. What do you have?"

The four strangers looked at one another in confusion. "You invited us, lady," the man in the derby said.

"Yes, and I would love to treat you, but, you see, we aren't very good at this."

"At what?"

"Running from the law. Before we get all into that, we must make introductions. I'm Charlotte. This is my savior" — I placed my hand on Kindle's arm and stared up at him lovingly trying to think of a name — "Oscar." I turned my attention to the strangers. "We've met Tuesday, of course. Lovely to meet you, dear. How dreadful about your nose." I waited for her to say something, but she merely glared at me. Without taking my eyes from her, I said to the leader, "Doesn't she talk?"

"The redskins took her tongue, too," the derby-hatted man said.

"Oh." I almost lost my composure but held on to the vain, vapid persona I hoped would distract and disarm this group. "I'm so sorry," was all I could manage.

I focused on the derby-hatted man next to Tuesday. "Kruger," he said.

"Cuidado," the Mexican said.

The leader removed his hat — "Charlie Bell" — and with a sweeping bow — "at your service."

I placed my hand on my chest and twittered. "How gallant."

Kindle glowered at Bell, either perfectly in character or perfectly suspicious.

To pull this off, I hoped it was both.

I chewed and swallowed the buffalo jerky Charlie Bell gave us for breakfast. "How delightful compared to the cold meal and raw prairie chickens we've been eating. Our guide refused to let us light a fire, saying it would draw attention."

"Who's your guide?" Bell asked.

"Oh, some Indian Oscar knew from the Army. The younger son of a renowned scout, wasn't he, darling?"

Kindle grunted.

"I'm not chastising you, darling. He was the best we could get on such short notice. I am so pleased to be away from my horrible husband, I hardly care we've been abandoned in the middle of Indian Territory by our scout."

"Where are you headed?" Kruger asked.

"To the railroad. We thought going through Indian Territory was terribly clever. Why would we head this way instead of south? From Sherman. That's where we've come from. Martin, my husband, is a cattleman. Or at least he wants to be. He's having a hard time of it. Not many Southerners are interested in helping a Yankee get a toehold into their business. Of course, he took his frustrations out on me." I clutched at my throat with my damaged hand and swallowed thickly. "That is why I sound like this. Martin is a big man, strong. One night, while he was taking his marital pleasures against my will, he grabbed me by the throat and squeezed." I mimed the action, seeing not my imaginary husband, but Cotter

Black's expression of pure pleasure and the light of evil in his eyes as he punched me in the throat.

My audience waited expectantly. I dropped my hand and continued. "I thought I was dying, but I only passed out. He finished his business, I suppose, and I woke up alone, unable to speak. That was when Oscar said we were leaving."

"I would've killed him, first," Kruger said.

"Oh, I had a difficult time keeping Oscar from doing just that. But he finally understood us being together was more important. As fate would have it the murderess escaping from Jacksboro happened about the same time, so a wife running off with a cowboy barely made a ripple in the papers."

"How 'bout that, two couples running from the law, and through the same country," Bell said.

"Isn't it a coincidence? We were afraid Martin might send someone after me, which is why I'm wearing men's clothes." I touched my short, damp hair. "Martin cut my hair when he thought I was flirting with one of his business associates. It was one of his least violent punishments, so I didn't mind overmuch. I was only trying to *charm* the man, after all. I find Texans are much more amiable to Yankee women than men.

I'd heard about Southern chivalry, of course, but was surprised to find it still intact after the war." I sighed. "I miss my hair much more than I miss Martin. I think it's a rather fetching style — it's much less hassle which is good for a woman on the run, it turns out — but Oscar says he's anxious for it to grow back."

"Don't seem to me Oscar says much," Bell said.

"She's telling the story good enough. She gets anything wrong, I'll correct her."

I prattled on. "Martin didn't send anyone after me. Not that we can tell. 'Course, the bounty hunters looking for the murderess sure have. We've had a heck of a time explaining ourselves. Turns out the murderess is known for dressing like a man. Why in the world she'd choose to do it, I'll never understand. Though wearing pants makes riding easier. I'm sure you agree, Tuesday." The silent woman's glare didn't alter. I smiled — vacuously I hoped — and said, "You've heard our story. What's yours? Are you chasing the fugitives?"

"We're up here killing Indians," Bell said.

The smile froze on my face. I laughed, but cold fingers of fear tickled the base of my spine. "You're joking, of course."

Cuidado, taciturn to this point, said,

66

"Never joke about killing," and crossed himself.

"Haven't you heard?" Bell said. "Sherman's advocating the extermination of the Indians. We came up here to do our part."

"These Indians are peaceful. They've stopped fighting," Kindle said.

Kruger barked out a laugh. "Dey use the Territory as a safe haven to raid into Texas."

"Ain't no such thing as a peaceful Indian," Bell said.

Kindle stared hard at the four strangers with an expression full of hatred. "I've heard of you."

Bell's ebullient expression didn't reach his eyes. "And, what have you heard?"

Kindle narrowed his eyes. I could tell he was evaluating his odds. He might get one shot off, but they'd spread out enough that there was no way he'd get all four. I realized Tuesday was gone at the same time I heard her behind me. Kindle must have heard her, too.

"Hear you're a better friend than enemy."

"And, what do you and Charlotte here want to be?" Cuidado and Kruger lazily pulled their guns. I didn't need to see Tuesday to know hers was out and trained on me.

Kindle held out his hand. "Friends."

CHAPTER 6

When Bell told Cuidado to stay behind and wait for Little Stick, Kindle told him it was a waste of his time, that we suspected our guide had taken our money and deserted. Since I appeared to have botched my chance to get us out of a tight spot, I remained silent. Kindle saddled our horses, and in the ruse of checking my saddle, said in an undertone, "Keep up the act, but be careful what you say."

"Have you heard of them?"

"No. But, I know Bell's type."

"Which is?"

"Big hat, no cattle."

"What about Little Stick?"

Kindle exhaled sharply. "He's a good tracker; he won't be caught unaware." Though his voice was confident, his expression was worried.

He boosted me into the saddle and winked at me. How he could possibly wink at me in a time like this, I had no idea.

Tuesday rode next to me and, of course, didn't say a word. Kruger rode behind and Kindle and Bell rode next to each other in front. I did as Kindle asked and kept up the act. It wasn't much of an act, truth be told. I had lived eight years in England, and had learned the art of meaningless conversation at the knee of my aunt Emily, who was the absolute master. My cousin Charlotte — my current namesake, as it were, would think throwing in with four killers all a great adventure, no doubt — and I had watched many a duchess's eyes glaze over with boredom after spending fifteen minutes in my aunt's presence. By my estimate, it took twenty minutes of me talking about the weather, the flora and fauna, living in England, quizzing Kruger on Germany and asking him nonsensically if he'd ever met the king and didn't he know they were related to the British royal family and I'd actually danced with the Prince of Wales (he wasn't very good, of course, but one had to pretend otherwise), then my father had lost his fortune and I had to come home and . . .

"Does she talk this much all the time?" Bell asked Kindle.

"Yes."

"Are you talking about me, darling?"

"You're driving him batty, Lottie. Shut up."

"Excuse me for trying to keep my mind off killing."

Bell craned his neck to look over his shoulder at me. "You've never killed a man?"

I thought of Cotter Black jerking and falling forward, blood and brain matter spewing out the front of his head. I almost laughed at poor Charlie Bell. He thought I was a complete fool. Little did he know I would have no qualms about killing him if it came down to it.

"Heavens, no. I know it doesn't appear so, and I wouldn't blame you for mistaking it, but I was born to money. This is all foreign to me. Oh, I thought it would be a great adventure when Martin told me his plans when we were courting. The reality has been a shock. Before you get any ideas about ransoming me, my family is destitute and Martin doesn't appear to care a wit where I am. How many men have you killed?"

"Men or Indians?"

"I know they are savages, but they are men, at least."

"I don't want to leave out the women and children." He lifted a strap, which hung from his saddle horn. Both edges were nocked almost completely. He fingered the small space at the bottom that was uncut. "I'm gonna need a new strap after the next raid, if I'm lucky." He let it fall and continued. "The Indians call it counting coup. They attach scalps to a pole and carry them around. Some of the tame ones carry a pole with feathers, so as to not offend the Quakers. But it stands for the same. White scalps."

"And redskin," Kindle said.

"You an Indian lover?"

"I know they scalp their red enemies, too."

"More white nowadays, no thanks to the Army. What'd you do in the Army?"

"Chase Indians without finding many. Too much fatigue duty on the fort so I left. We don't want to go this way," Kindle said.

"Why not?"

"We came across an Army patrol yesterday. They were heading east, chasing some whisky traders. Best to go north, I think."

"Oh, do you?"

Kindle shrugged. "Go where you want, but if you don't want to run into the Army, I'd go that way."

"Maybe we'll go west, toward Sill and the Wichita Mountains. I bet we could find some Indians there."

I only generally knew where we were and where we were going, but I knew for certain we did not want to go in the direction of Fort Sill.

"Ja, but they won't be drunk Indians," Kruger said. "They're easier to kill."

Kindle spat a stream of tobacco juice. "You're the leader. Go where you want. But I don't particularly want to come across the Army again. I'm afraid someone recognized me."

Kruger spoke up. "Is that bad?"

"I mighta killed a man before I left."

Bell smiled. "I thought you had it in you." He nodded to Kindle's gray. "How long you had this horse?"

Kindle shrugged. "Awhile."

"I knew a man who had a horse like this."

"More than one gray in the world."

"You kinda remind me of him. In the eyes."

Kindle spit again and glared at the man. "You don't say."

"He was a mean motherfucker."

"More than one mean motherfucker in the world."

I grimaced at the language, though I should have been used to the version of Kindle I observed around strangers. His switch to harsh and uncompromising no longer surprised me, and I realized it never should have at all. There had been flashes of this side of him at Fort Richardson — his full-throated defense of his men looting my ruined wagon train, his reaction to my lone excursion to town and drinking with the laundresses, his rage at his brother in Palo Duro Canyon. But, I'd preferred to focus on his gentler side, his tenderness, flirty conversation, and honor. The farther we traveled in Indian Country, the more I appreciated the fact he could be both. I knew he would go to any lengths to protect me one minute, and take me in his arms and comfort me the next.

Bell nodded. "Yes, there is. Well, as your luck will have it, we are going north. Northwest, in fact, to meet some friends. As a mark of good will for our new companions, we will give Fort Sill a wide berth. But we have nothing to fear from the Army. We're making their job easier."

"By killing women and children?" I said.

"The Army's killed their fair share of Indian women and children. Ain't that right, Oscar?"

Kindle nodded. " 'S right."

"Then you won't have any compunction when the time comes."

Kindle chewed his wad of tobacco and

stared straight ahead. "I don't have any compunction about killing who needs killing."

"Good to hear," Bell said. "Good to hear."

The tall flowing grass of the plains was gradually replaced by short, stubby trees that gave way to taller hackberry, cottonwood, and a few oaks. I knew we would reach water soon, but wasn't expecting the water to hug the base of a towering wall of red rock. Water seeped from the top of the wall in three places and trickled down into the pool below. A camp of tents and wagons was set up in a half moon along the bank, with the central area full of three or four cook fires and men ambling around. The horses picketed to the east of the camp were being guarded by two heavily armed men.

I stopped my horse and tried to catch my breath. In my mind's eye saw Cotter Black falling forward onto the red dirt of the canyon, a smoking gun in my hand.

Kruger slapped my palomino on the rump as he rode past. She jumped forward, almost sending me to the ground. Terrified, I gathered her up and shouted at Kruger. "Keep your hands off me."

His brows furrowed. "I didn't touch you," he said, and kept riding. Tuesday watched me over her shoulder as she rode off with Kruger. Bell seemed oblivious.

My horse danced, feeling every bit of my anxiety. The sound of a splash made me jump, and sent my horse into a circle. I patted her neck, to reassure myself as much as my mount, and shushed her. "Easy girl."

Someone whooped in the distance. I squeezed my eyes closed and felt the weight of a man pinning me to the ground, ripping at my clothes, felt my legs being forced apart, my arms pinned wide.

I flinched and opened my eyes. A bearded man had edged his horse up next to mine. His leg pressed against my own as he steadied us by holding on to my saddle horn. "What's the matter?" I clutched at my throat and stared at Cotter Black in terror. "Laura?" His voice was gentle and questioning, his eyes full of concern.

Kindle. I closed my eyes and covered my mouth while the last six weeks rushed through my mind in a blur. Cotter Black was dead. I killed him in Palo Duro. Kindle would protect me. I was safe.

"What's wrong?" Kindle's voice took on a note of exasperation. Was he so oblivious he couldn't see the similarities to Palo Duro and how this might bring up ugly memories?

Angry, I kicked my horse forward and didn't answer.

We unsaddled our horses and led them to the water to drink. We kept our voices low so we could talk without being heard.

"What's the matter?" Kindle said.

I narrowed my eyes and stared at him. His eyes darted around the camp, taking stock of our surroundings, before settling back on me. His gaze was tense, impatient, calculating, focused on the problem at hand, not on what happened weeks ago and hundreds of miles away.

I reached down and pulled a clump of prairie grass from the ground. "Nothing." I rubbed Piper's sweaty back with the grass and kept my face averted from Kindle to hide my tears. Kindle cursed softly under his breath, moved beside me, and stilled my hand with his own. I rested my cheek against my horse's neck, taking comfort in her warmth and smell. She stomped her back foot and swished her tail against the flies swarming around us.

"Laura."

Piper's tail swatted me in the face. I lifted my head, ran my hand beneath my running nose, and kept rubbing my horse down. "Do you think Bell knows who we are?" Kindle didn't answer immediately. I glanced up.

"Do you?"

He exhaled sharply. "Unless he's a complete idiot, which I'm not ruling out as yet. He brought us to a camp with other men who will want the reward, which makes me think he's not the sharpest knife in the drawer. But, I think he recognized my horse."

I remembered the first time I'd seen Kindle's gray across Lost Creek. Though I didn't know it then, the man who held the reins was Kindle's brother.

"Do you think this is what's left of Black's gang?"

Kindle shrugged. "Could be, though I can't imagine my brother having much patience for a big-talking ass like Charlie Bell. More like a smaller gang with delusions of grander things."

"Is this the camp the Army's looking for?"

"Yep. See those pots? They're making rotgut in it."

"Am I the only woman here?"

"Besides Tuesday, probably."

I scoffed. "She hardly looks like a woman."

Kindle tried to hide his smile. "I agree, but you do know you're dressed like she is."

"And you know Bell and Kruger saw every inch of me this morning."

Kindle pulled me into a gentle embrace.

"Don't worry. I won't leave your side."

My stomach fluttered at the feel of his breath on my ear. I placed my forehead on his shoulder and leaned into him. His arms tightened around me.

"I apologize for this morning," he said.

I leaned back to see his face. "Why? I invited you in."

"You don't need to give yourself to me until you're ready. I know what you went through."

I swallowed and couldn't meet his gaze. I appreciated the sentiment but didn't believe him. He couldn't know what I went through. To him, to society, I'd been degraded. No one dared say the word, which accurately described the terror, pain, and humiliation I endured for hours. No one dared let themselves imagine what it was like, how I relived it every hour of every day. I should be thankful Kindle wasn't like most men, that his brother's prediction he would never want to be with me had been wrong.

A new thought entered my mind. "How do you know?"

"What?"

"How do you know what I went through? Have you seen, or . . ."

He pulled away slightly, but I held fast.

"It was done," he said, "but not by my men, and not by me."

"Where?"

"Washita." He looked over my shoulder, and now he did extract himself from my embrace. "Bell."

"You two are always at each other, aren't ya?" Bell leered at me. "Lottie seems like the type who wants to be loved instead of fucked. We can probably find a tent for you. Picket your horses. Quinn wants to meet you." He walked off.

My fingers itched to pull my gun and put a bullet in the back of his head. As if sensing my thoughts, Kindle put out his arm to hold me back. "My guess is you'll have your chance sooner rather than later."

We picketed the horses and found Bell talking to a man who was indiscernible from any other frontier opportunist — bearded, dirty, and greedy — with one significant difference: he was a midget. To make matters worse, he had shockingly orange hair, an apple-red face, and his neck was peeling like a snake shedding its skin.

Bell made the introductions. The midget's — Quinn — gaze traveled up and down my person with an amused expression. "Well, you wear men's clothes a damn sight better than Tuesday does."

79

I gave Quinn my best smile and tried not to stare offensively. "Why, thank you, Mr. Quinn."

"Just Quinn. No need for formality out here." He narrowed his eyes at Kindle. "I didn't catch your last name."

"I didn't give it. No need for formality out here."

Quinn grinned and shrugged, bested with his own turn of phrase. "Charlie here tells me you've run off from your husband."

"That's right."

Quinn pursed his lips and nodded. "From Sherman?"

"No, from Philadelphia. We'd been in Sherman a short time."

"Long enough to meet Oscar here. Lucky you."

With an adoring expression, I threaded my arm through Kindle's. "Every day I thank God for sending him to me. I think he might be the last honorable man in the West." I turned my attention back to Bell, then Quinn. "I haven't met anyone to challenge the belief yet."

Quinn's red, bushy eyebrows shot almost up to his hairline, which was unnaturally low. "Well, then. I suppose we know where we stand, don't we, Charlie?"

"I suppose so."

"Help yourself to food and drink. Don't drink this shit." Quinn waved at the pot of liquid behind him. "The good stuff is in Chilvers's tent. He's the oaf. You can't miss him."

I peeked into the pot. It smelled horrid. "What's in it?"

"Whisky, water — mostly water — molasses, red pepper, chewing tobacco for color, and we finish it off with gunpowder."

"Gunpowder?"

"Gives it a pop." He laughed at his own joke. "Redskins don't know any better. One time, I accidentally gave one buck a bottle of the good stuff and he almost scalped me. Thought I was cheating him." He patted his head. "I have to play fair with 'em or I'll be scalped for sure. My red hair never ceases to amaze them." He stirred the whisky concoction with a board and inhaled deeply. "Almost ready." He lay the board across the top of the pot. "Now normally I'd be worried bringing a woman into camp with all these men. Whisky traders are a sorry lot. Not as bad as buffalo hunters, but pretty damn close. But the men are sated right now. They shouldn't give you any trouble. Stay close to her, all the same," he said to Kindle.

"What about Tuesday?"

81

Quinn laughed. "She won't let anyone but Kruger get within ten feet of her. Chilvers learned the hard way, let me tell you. Why don't y'all rest in my tent? Or fuck. It's been a while since you've had four walls, if you ever have. It's the second tent from the end down yonder." He turned his back and walked off with Charlie Bell, dismissing us.

I should have been worried about Quinn, Bell, and the situation we were in, but when I saw the cot in Quinn's tent, all the worries flew out of my brain. I lay on the cot and groaned. "Am I really going to not have to sleep on the ground? This might be heaven."

"Don't get too comfy, Marie Antoinette."

"They know who we are, don't they?"

"Probably."

"Then we're safe. They won't get the reward if they kill us."

"You, but there's no reward for me."

I sat up. "You don't think they'll kill you."

"Not if I can be useful for them."

"How?"

"Protect them from Army patrols."

"Can you?"

Kindle shrugged. "Maybe. But I can make them believe it." He hung his hat on a peg on the center pole, spread a buffalo robe on the ground next to the cot, and lay down.

82

He put his hands under his head. "Your mouth, woman."

I lay on the cot and stared at the ceiling of the tent. "Whatever do you mean?"

" 'I haven't met anyone to challenge that belief'? If you weren't worth five hundred dollars, Quinn would've cut your throat for saying it."

"Oh, I think he likes me. Men like sassy women."

Kindle laughed. "No, they don't."

"You do."

"Well, look where it's got me."

I exhaled sharply.

"I didn't mean it that way, Laura. You know I didn't." He reached up for my hand. "Come here." When I didn't move he said, "If I come up there, we'll break the cot. Come here."

I moved next to Kindle and nestled into his side. I inhaled deeply the scent I'd come to know as uniquely Kindle — leather, horse, and sweat — which now held hints of smoky tobacco. My stomach fluttered and a calm came over me as I clutched at his shirt and listened to his heartbeat.

He stroked my hair and said in a low voice, "I wouldn't want to be anywhere else, with anyone else."

"You've given up so much for me."

"I'd been searching for a reason to leave the Army for years. Since Washita in sixty-eight at least. Maybe earlier."

"What happened at Washita?"

Kindle took my injured hand in his and massaged it. "What always happens when men are led by arrogant, vainglorious fools." Kindle sighed. "Our orders were there are no orders. Find the Cheyenne and attack them. Drive them back to the reservation. We went in the winter when they would be in their camp and most vulnerable. Custer drove us relentlessly through the cold and snow until we came upon a village with fifty or so lodges, one with a white flag of truce flying over it. But some braves had gone off and stolen some cattle. They were who the Osage scouts tracked to find the village. It was enough in Custer's mind to justify attacking." I propped myself on my arm so I could see his face. His eyes were narrowed, and he stared into the distance, seeing the past.

"At dawn we attacked. We bore down on the village, firing as we went. I'm not sure how many people I hit, or if I hit anyone. I saw quickly it was a village full of women, children, and old men. I tried to pull my troops back, but they were in the thick of it. No one heard, or if they did, they ignored

84

me. I was absolutely powerless." He swallowed. "I saw these two women hiding in some tall grass, not far from where soldiers were walking back and forth, killing and raping those they could find. I put my finger over my mouth and signed for the women to stay put." Kindle used his free hand and made the sign. "A boy, too young to go on a hunt or war party but old enough to be good with a bow, stood up from where he crouched in the tall grass a ways off and sent an arrow flying at me. It knocked my hat off but my reaction was reflexive. I drew my sidearm and shot him. Right there." Kindle pointed at his covered left eye and finally looked at me. "I'm not sure it was a real arrow. He was a child."

I stroked his beard. "William."

Kindle looked away and swallowed again. When he spoke, his voice was thick. "In the report Custer sent, he said he'd killed one hundred and three warriors. It was more like a dozen. The rest were women, children, and old men. Including the chief, Black Kettle, and his wife. The same chief who I'd helped negotiate peace with in sixty-four in Colorado before fucking Chivington attacked them at Sand Creek." He inhaled. "I was in Denver when Chivington and his men returned. They went through town bragging about it, showing off the mutilated body parts of the Cheyenne. One man made a tobacco pouch out of an Indian's scrotum."

I covered my mouth and grunted in disgust.

Kindle flipped the eye patch up and rubbed his eye with his palm. "I should have left the Army after what happened at Sand Creek. Chivington was state militia, not the Army. That's what I told myself. The Army was all I had left. So I stayed. After Washita, I asked to be transferred under Mackenzie."

"Why Mackenzie?"

"Because I knew he would have control of his men. Wanton killing like Sand Creek and Washita would never happen under Ranald Mackenzie. When this war with the Indians ends, it will be because of him. You mark my words."

"And Custer?"

"Can rot in hell."

I settled my head back on Kindle's chest and listened to the increasing activity outside. Voices raised in merriment. A fiddle being tuned.

"Aren't they worried about an Indian attack?"

"I suppose they think the Indians would rather have their whisky than their scalps."

"Is that wise?"

"Most likely not." A gunshot rang out and I flinched. Kindle kissed my head. "Shh. You're safe. Sounds like they're into the good stuff."

"I meant what I said earlier. About the last honorable man."

"I'm not that honorable, Laura."

I sat up on my elbow. "Were you talking of Washita the other night when you said there was so much I didn't know about you?"

Kindle's hand stilled, and he nodded.

"But, not everything."

"No."

"It doesn't matter." I stroked his beard, leaned forward, and kissed him lightly on the lips. I wrinkled my nose when I pulled back. "I cannot wait to shave your beard."

Kindle played with my hair. "And I cannot wait for your hair to grow back."

I lay my head back on his chest and tried to get closer. "What do you want to do when we get to Independence?"

"I've been thinking we should stay in Saint Louis a spell."

"Won't that be dangerous for you?"

Kindle rubbed my back. "There's a place outside of town where we can live for a while. Until people forget who we are."

"Will that ever happen?"

"Eventually. We'll be safe there. It's remote, peaceful."

"How long will we be there?"

"As long as it takes for you to heal."

I sat up. "Heal? It's not a sanitarium is it?"

Kindle laughed. "No. It's an orphanage. My sister runs it."

"Your sister? You have a sister?"

"I do."

"And she runs an orphanage?"

"For children orphaned by the war. I stayed with her for a while after Washita. We'll be safe there."

"Of course, if you think it's the best place to go." I lay back down.

"Any idea where you might want to go from there?"

I thought back to Maureen and our conversation over tea in a hotel in February. "Heavens, only five months."

"What?"

"Maureen and I arrived in Galveston five months ago. How is that possible? It seems a lifetime." I exhaled. "We ate lunch at the Lafitte Hotel and planned the rest of our journey. We'd decided on San Francisco before I ran into Molly Ebling and thought being on the coast would be too dangerous." I laughed. "What a misjudgment *that* was."

"You want to go to San Francisco?"

"I think so. What do you think?"

"I was hoping to meet Aunt Emily."

"Were you?"

"I thought bringing a handsome man like me to meet her might redeem you in her eyes."

"My God, you're vain. Aunt Emily will love you. Will you wear your uniform?"

"I can probably scrounge one up in Saint Louis."

"England, then."

CHAPTER 7

"What a waste of a good tent."

I pried my dry eyes open and saw Bell silhouetted in the triangular doorway. I nudged Kindle's chest, but realized he was awake when he spoke.

"I imagine we can use it as we please."

"Well, not anymore. Come on." Bell walked away.

Kindle rose and helped me up. He put on his hat, held my hand, and led me from the tent.

The pots had been removed from the fires, which had all been extinguished, save the one in the center of the semicircle of tents and wagons. Men walked by the center pot, ladled a thick stew onto a tin plate or mug, and either found a vacant camp chair to sit on or wandered back to their wagon. My mouth watered as the aroma of the stew wafted over. My stomach growled loud enough to get Kindle's attention. He grinned. "Hungry, Slim?"

"Slim?"

"You're getting a little on the bony side."

"I hate to disappoint you but I've always been on the bony side. How do you think I pulled off dressing like a man?"

He draped his arm over my shoulder and whispered, "I'll fatten you up when we get to Saint Louis."

"Are you saying I will have to wait hundreds of miles for a good meal?"

He jerked his chin in the direction of the pot. "I suppose we'll see."

Kruger and Tuesday leaned against the nearest wagon. I smiled in their direction. Kruger saluted me with his spoon, and Tuesday glared at me. The woman had taken an immediate dislike to me and I couldn't figure out why. Possibly I could; Charlotte *was* rather a prattle mouth. I wouldn't like her, either. I wondered what Tuesday's background was. Was she the daughter of a farmer trying to eke out a living on the frontier? Or had she been abducted from a wagon train crossing the northern plains? I knew from firsthand experience it was possible for Indians to take their captives long distances in a short amount of time. Had she been able to write and communicate her background to Kruger and Bell? Or had she known her entire family was dead and communication was pointless?

Bell handed us each a tin mug. "Beef stew, courtesy of the US Army."

Kindle took his cup and said, "Stolen?"

"Does that offend your cowboy or Army sensibilities?"

"Neither. Just trying to make conversation."

"This poor beeve was lost, roaming the prairie bellowing for its mama. Chilvers is pretty sure it's from the wagon train massacred back in May." Bell watched for my reaction. When he didn't receive one, he turned away with a smirk.

"Tastes good all the same," Kindle said. "Try it, Lottie."

I forced myself to eat the first bite. After, my hunger was too strong to be denied. "I haven't had anything so good since we left Sherman." I batted my eyes at Kindle. "Sorry, darling. Did you make this, Mr. Quinn?"

The midget glanced up from his mug, which I suspected held whisky instead of stew. "No. I just make the whisky."

"I heard a gunshot earlier. Aren't you worried about Indians finding your camp?"

Quinn swirled his mug and studied me, as

if debating whether to answer. Kindle answered for him. "You've got protection on three sides from the wall, so you have guards at the mouth."

"Spoken like a true Army man," Quinn said.

"Don't take an Army man to see it's a natural fortress. With plenty of water."

"The water's the secret to my whisky. I could use any old gyppy water and the redskins wouldn't care, most like. Lots of traders do. But I say if you're gonna do something, do it right."

"Even stealing from Indians?" I said.

"It ain't stealing. Fair trade. Whisky for buffalo robes, hides, meat. Or whatever they want to trade or gamble away." The men within hearing distance laughed.

"Yes, but don't Indians have a weakness for spirits?" I said.

"White men have a weakness for spirits as well. Are you saying they shouldn't be sold whisky at the saloon?" Quinn said.

"You aren't one of those women who preach prohibition, are you?" Bell said with a laugh.

"No. It seems dishonest, somehow, to trade the Indians cut whisky for buffalo robes."

"She's an Indian lover," Bell said.

"I am not." My face burned in anger.

"A Quaker, then?" Quinn said.

"I have no love for Indians. Kill them all, for all I care. But it should be on the field of battle, not going into a camp of drunk Indians and massacring them when they're helpless." Bell chewed his stew slowly and watched me. "That's what you do, isn't it? Quinn sells them the whisky and you and your gang come through and massacre them. Do you abuse the women before you kill them?"

"Lottie," Kindle said, a clear warning.

"Only the pretty ones."

"So not often," Kruger called out to raucous laughter.

Kindle turned so his back was to the group and said in a low voice, "Shut up or you're going to get us killed."

I glanced at Quinn and Bell, who were watching me with marked suspicion. I batted my eyes and laughed. "Good point." I turned my focus on Bell. "I apologize. I'm new to the frontier and can't seem to shake the mores of civilization. I'm quite sure the Indians deserve everything they get," I said, though my stomach churned with disgust at what these men did for sport.

"Are you now?" Bell said. "You'll get the

94

chance to decide for yourself in a couple of days."

Quinn spoke. "We're pulling out tomorrow."

"And we follow a few hours later. Give the redskins time to get nice and drunk."

"Sometimes they do the killing for us," Kruger said. "They get violent when they get drunk, turn against each other."

"Also, give Cuidado time to catch up."

"You're confident he bested our scout," Kindle said. "Wouldn't be so sure about that."

"Want to wager on it?" Bell said.

"What do you have in mind?"

"Your gray."

"And when I win?"

"Your freedom."

"I didn't know we were captives."

"You've got your guns, don't you? Once you're a member of the Bell Gang, there's only one way out."

Kindle ate his stew before answering. "Our freedom. Both of us. Against my gray."

"That's two for one."

Kindle shrugged. "Guess you're not as confident in Cuidado as you say."

Bell walked to Kindle. "If Cuidado doesn't show, you both go on a raid with us, then you're free to go."

Kindle held out his hand, and they shook on it.

"I miss water closets."

I squatted behind a tree about a hundred yards from the camp and heeded nature's call. Kindle stood lookout on the other side. "And paper," I murmured. I pulled my pants up, walked to Kindle, and pulled him away. I didn't want him smelling my mess.

"That wasn't a very good deal you struck, was it?"

Kindle shook his head. "Either way, we go on a raid with him. Where they'll probably kill me and take you to be ransomed."

I looked off toward the camp. A man exited a tent set apart from the others as another man entered.

"So, what's our plan?"

"Leave tonight."

"How? The horses are guarded. And all of our tack is on the edge of the main circle."

"We'll camp over there." He pointed to the tent I'd been watching. "When the watch changes in the night, you and I go tell them Bell told us to take it. We slip out and ride like hell."

So much could go wrong. "It isn't a very good plan."

"Would you rather ride with Bell and massacre drunk, defenseless Indians?"

"No."

"If you can come up with a better plan, I'm willing to hear it."

The man exited the tent, adjusted his pants, and walked off. I sighed. "I have no ideas." I nodded to the tent. "Is that tent a latrine?"

Kindle's expression darkened. "I doubt it. Come on. Let's get our things." I followed Kindle but watched Tuesday duck beneath the flap of the tent.

No one objected when we moved our gear to the edge of camp, between the outlier and the horses. I sat on my bedroll and checked my saddlebag. One side contained Enloe's holster and gun and the medical equipment Harriet had been able to salvage from the ruins of the Indian attack at the Red River: my stethoscope, scalpel, clamp, and tweezers. It wasn't much, but it would serve me in a pinch. I wiggled my fingers. They were a bit more flexible since Kindle had been massaging them.

From the other side of the saddlebag I pulled out my extra shirt, which needed a wash, a hairbrush, a cracked hand mirror, and *The Tenant of Wildfell Hall*. I rubbed my hand over the cover and thought of Harriet Mackenzie with a smile. I wondered what she was doing. Probably sitting in Colonel Mackenzie's parlor needlepointing or reading a book from the fort library. I longed to be there with her, to enjoy Harriet's companionship. My smile slipped. Why was it we appreciated someone fully only when they were lost to us?

Kindle had once told me Harriet and I were more alike than I realized, an assertion borne out when Harriet helped me and Kindle escape from the Army and the Pinkerton in Jacksboro. She'd risked so much, as much as I had risked to save a young girl from the Comanche and Cotter Black. Despite everything that had happened since, I didn't regret it. I hoped Harriet didn't regret helping us.

I pressed the bottom of the now-empty saddlebag. The seams were intact; the bump in the middle confirmation the jewelry sewn inside was safe. I heard a woman's cry and stopped repacking. "Did you hear that?"

"Yes."

There was the telltale sound of a blow being delivered, and then a woman's muffled cry. I jumped up as Kindle said, "Laura," and grabbed at my hand. I pulled it away, went to the tent, and opened the flap. Tuesday knelt on the floor with her back to the door, moving her arm back and forth, as if sawing wood, grunting with every push.

I didn't understand what I saw for a few seconds. Then, the naked legs splayed on either side of Tuesday's kneeling figure jolted me into action. I walked forward, barely hearing Kindle's "Laura!" or feeling his hand grasp at my shoulder. With a roaring in my ears, I grabbed Tuesday's collar and jerked her away and onto her back, revealing the most repulsive sight I had ever seen.

An Indian woman lay spread eagle and naked on the hard, rock-strewn ground, her arms and ankles tied to stakes to keep her from fighting. Her round face was covered in bruises and dried blood. Her pudenda were a raw, bloody mess, thanks in no small part to the thick stick lying on the ground between her legs.

A rage I have never felt in my life, before or since, overtook me. I grabbed the stick, turned, jumped on top of a prone Tuesday, and began savagely beating her. Tuesday was much larger than me, but I had surprise and fury on my side. Her face was soon covered in blood — hers and the Indian's. Kindle grabbed me by the arms and pulled me away from her. Tuesday rose with a quickness belied by her size and punched me in the stomach. I doubled over, and Kindle swung me away from harm, let go of me, and rounded on Tuesday, gun drawn. "Get out of here," Kindle bellowed, "or so help me I will blow your head off."

Tuesday glared at us, spit blood onto the ground, and left.

Slowly, the red left my vision, though my breathing came in short gasps. The Indian woman stared at us through slits where her eyes should have been, the skin around them swollen and dark purple.

"Christ," Kindle said.

"Give me your knife."

"Laura . . ."

"Give me your knife. Now."

He pulled the knife from his boot and handed it to me. He stood between the tent flap and the woman, his body turned sideways, his gun drawn. I knelt down at the woman's feet and signed to her to not move. One nostril was blocked with dried blood, making her breathing wheezy. I gently placed my hand on her foot, which appeared to be one of the few places on her body not injured, and cut the leather strap. The woman's leg didn't move. I picked it up gently and moved it next to the other. The woman winced and whimpered.

"I need my saddlebag, and water."

"This is a mistake."

The flap of the tent jerked back and Quinn and Bell entered. "What do you think you're doing?" Quinn asked.

Kindle held his gun on Quinn and Bell. I straightened, holding the knife. "I could ask you the same thing."

"She was given as payment for whisky," Quinn said. "I own her and I'll do with her as I please."

"Not while I'm here you won't," I said.

Bell pulled his gun and pointed it at me. Kindle cocked his pistol. "Do it and you die."

"He won't do it. I'm worth too much alive, aren't I, Charlie Bell?"

"Your lover isn't." Charlie swung his gun to Kindle.

"You kill him and I'll make sure I don't make it back to town alive. The reward requires I be alive, last I heard." Bell's eye twitched. "Put your gun down. Both of you."

Kruger and Tuesday were in the doorway outside the tent, watching. Bell lowered his gun and Kindle did the same, uncocking his as he did. Quinn jerked the gun out of Kindle's hand.

"How much?" I asked Quinn.

"What?"

"How much for the Indian?"

101

Quinn laughed. "You have nothing to bargain with. We already have you. We'll keep his horse. The clothes on your back are worthless."

"Mr. Kruger, would you get my saddlebag, please?"

"Laura." Kindle grabbed my arm and pulled me back into the darkness of the tent, near the Indian woman's head. "What in God's name are you doing?"

"Helping her."

Kindle rubbed his forehead. "Why? After what was done to you, what do you care?"

I jerked my arm away from him. "I'm helping her *because* of what was done to me," I said in a hoarse, angry whisper. "I fought back, like she did, most like. The Indians held me down like that."

"Stop it."

"What, you don't want to hear the details?"

"Laura, so help me God."

"I don't care who she is, I will never, *ever,* stand by and let that be done to another woman. If I die because of it, so be it."

"You're going to help her and kill us in the process."

"Betray me."

"What?"

102

"Side with them against me. Win their trust."

Kruger returned with the saddlebag. I pushed against Kindle's chest, committing him to the idea whether he liked it or not. "Take their side, I don't care. You've outlasted your usefulness anyway. Mr. Kruger." I walked past Kindle and took the bag from the German's hand. With the knife I cut the stitches at the bottom of the bag, reached in the opening, and removed the last piece of my mother's jewelry, our stake for a new life.

I dangled the sapphire-and-pearl necklace in front of Quinn's face. "This for the Indian."

Quinn reached for the necklace, but I pulled it away. Kindle sidled over to stand next to Bell. "What could you possibly want with that redskin?" Quinn asked.

"To keep you and your men from raping her."

Quinn laughed. "Are you serious?"

When I didn't answer, his smile faded. "You think she's human, but she's not. If the tables were turned, she would be cheering on her warriors as they raped you. Would probably lay a good beating on you as well." Quinn narrowed his eyes. "From what I understand, no one here knows that better than you, except maybe Tuesday. She joins in on the fun and you put a stop to it. Why's that?"

"I'm a doctor. I took an oath to protect life."

Everyone but Kindle laughed.

"Do you want the necklace or not?"

He reached out his hand, but I held on. "I keep my gun."

"No."

"If I'm not much mistaken, Tuesday over there plans to kill me first chance she gets."

Quinn took my gun from my holster and tossed it to Kruger. "Well, you should've thought about that before you beat her with a damn stick." He ripped the necklace out of my hand and walked out. Kindle followed but Bell put a hand on his chest. "Where do you think you're going?"

Kindle glanced at me and back at Bell. "She's on her own." He pushed Bell's hand from his chest and walked out of the tent.

CHAPTER 8

Kindle's parting comment rang in my ears: *She's on her own.* There was too much anger and bitterness in his voice for it to be an act.

A lantern hanging on the center pole of the tent gave feeble light to the scene. Other than the oil lamp, a pile of torn clothes I assumed were the woman's, and the saddlebags at my feet, it was empty. Certainly nothing to help me care for her. I lifted my hand to rub my forehead and realized I held Kindle's knife in one hand, the bloody stick in the other. I could cut her loose, at least.

The woman watched me bend down and cut her other leg free. I moved forward and knelt by her side. When I cut her hands free, would she attack me? Kill me? It was certainly a possibility. I would have tried in her shoes.

I remembered my own ordeal. The Indians had raped me into unconsciousness. I was in no condition to fight back in the end.

"Do you speak English?"

The woman stared wordlessly at me.

I made the sign Kindle taught me for friend. "I am going to help you." I tried to remember the sign for help, and couldn't. "Friend," I repeated while signing. I took a deep breath and cut one hand free, then the other.

The flap of the tent jerked open. Kindle stepped in, threw a buffalo robe on the ground, and left. My gear, including my and Kindle's canteens, spilled out of the robe. The woman's deerskin dress had been cut to shreds and was useless. I retrieved the buffalo robe and canteen and returned to the woman. I helped her sit up and wrapped the robe around her. "There, now. We'll worry about clothes after we get you cleaned up." I opened the canteen and held it up to my lips. "Drink."

She reached out for the canteen with trembling arms. "Shh. I'll help." I held it while she drank. She nodded when she was done, wrapped the robe tighter around herself, and stared at me. I placed my hand on my chest. "Laura. My name is Laura." I pointed to her, then back to me. "Laura."

"Aénóhé'ke."

"Ah-eh-noh-eh-kay?" The woman nodded. I repeated her name, slowly, two or three times, until it didn't feel quite so foreign in my mouth. "Aénóhé'ke."

I mimed brushing my hair with two hooked fingers, then extended them up to my forehead and circled them. "Doctor. Medicine woman. Help."

I opened my saddlebag, pulled out my extra shirt, and stopped. Enloe's holster and gun were at the bottom of the pouch. I shook my head. Kruger obviously hadn't checked my bag before giving it to me. I wondered who the brains in the outfit was, because so far, none of them seemed smart enough to lead a gang of outlaws.

I tore a strip of cloth from the hem of the shirt, doused it with water, and cleaned the woman's face. I cleaned the blood-soaked rag and reached toward her torso but didn't touch her. "Wash?"

The woman opened her robe and allowed me to clean her neck, breasts, and stomach, her penetrating gaze never leaving my face. There were long scars on her arms, as if her skin had been flayed.

I smiled encouragingly at her. "I apologize if it's cold. We have to make do with what we have." I moved on to her legs and feet. Her legs showed old scars, but they were too uniform to be from a beating. Most likely self-inflicted. I knew it was tradition in some tribes to self-mutilate when a loved one died. *I wonder whom Aénóhé'ke lost?* I ran out of water before I reached her ankles, which were bloody and raw from where the ropes had tied her down.

I pulled my stethoscope from my saddle-bag and put it in my ears. "Listen," I said, miming on my body how I would listen to her heart, lungs, and abdomen on hers. I took off the stethoscope and cautiously put them in her ears. She furrowed her brow in confusion, until I placed the end over my heart. Her eyes widened. "Heartbeat." I placed the end of the stethoscope against her breast. The woman smiled and nodded.

I put the ends in my ears and listened. Her heartbeat was strong and slow. Her lungs sounded good as well. With luck, the whisky traders or the Indians who had her before had only beat her face, not her torso. I smiled and nodded. "Good." I hung my stethoscope around my neck. "Lay." I motioned with my hands for her to lie down. With a slight hesitation and a good deal of wariness, she did. I held my hands out, placed them gently on her abdomen, and pressed down. I stared at the bloody stick next to me as I felt for internal injuries. The stick was short and thick, and based on where the blood stopped, not long enough to perforate her uterus, though the nubs on the side of the stick had most likely shredded her birth canal. I shook my head. The depths of human cruelty never ceased to amaze me.

A quick exploration of her ribs confirmed none were broken. I listened to her abdomen with my stethoscope and confirmed there were no internal injuries, a relief since I couldn't help her if there were.

I sat on my knees next to her. I didn't want to take the chance she would misunderstand if I tried to examine and clean her pudenda. I needed more water but didn't want to risk leaving her in the tent by herself. She might run, or Tuesday might be lurking outside to finish her off. I picked up my discarded knife. The Indian woman sat up and flinched away from me.

"No. Friend. Wash. Water." I signed water, and rubbed my arms and chest. "Wash. Outside." I jerked my thumb to the door and held out my free hand. The woman rose on shaky legs. I grasped her elbow with my free hand. "Lean on me." We walked out of the tent.

Kindle, Quinn, Bell, and Kruger were around the central fire, each with a bottle of whisky in their hands. The good stuff, if the group's laughter was any indication. Kindle caught sight of me and his smile dipped before he tilted his head back and took a long pull on his whisky bottle, his gaze never leaving mine. He turned his attention to Bell, and laughed again. I walked off with Aénóhé'ke.

We walked around the picketed horses to the far edge of the pool, away from prying eyes. Aénóhé'ke paused at the water's edge, glanced over her shoulder in the direction of the camp, and then back at me. I motioned to the water and held up my knife, pointed to myself, and signed *Stay*. I touched her robe at the shoulders and waited. When she nodded, I removed the robe and she gingerly stepped into the water. I draped the robe over my arm and kept my eyes half on Aénóhé'ke and half on the camp.

Aénóhé'ke bent down and immersed herself into the water up to the shoulders. She tilted her head back and ran her hands through her hair. I called out to her and mimed for her to wash her sex. Not knowing precisely how injured she was, and doubtful the woman would allow me to examine her, I had to assume there was a great risk for infection. And I had nothing with me to bandage her with, let alone medicine. I doubted Quinn would give me any whisky to use for sterilization.

I glanced back toward the camp and jumped when I saw Tuesday squatting a dozen yards away, watching us. I gripped my knife with a hand slick with nervous sweat. Tuesday would easily be able to overpower me. Aénòhé'ke was motionless in the pool, watching Tuesday as well. We stood there, a frozen tableau, for a full minute.

"Aénòhé'ke. Come," I said and motioned. Keeping her gaze on Tuesday, Aénòhé'ke walked out of the water. I placed the buffalo robe on the woman's shoulders and walked with her back to the tent.

Tuesday didn't move.

When we were alone in the tent I tried not to let my nervousness show. I gave Aénòhé'ke my extra clothes to dress in and motioned for her to lie down and sleep. She lay on her side, pulled her knees up to her chest, and tightened the buffalo robe around her. I sat down nearby, cross-legged, with the knife in my hand. Facing the tent opening, I prayed I would be able to stay awake the entire night.

After midnight, Kindle stumbled into the tent, reeking of whisky. I jerked upright, and shook my head. I'd fallen asleep. A great guard I'd made.

Kindle swayed on his feet and looked around the dark tent. When his eyes finally landed on me, he nodded, said, "There you are," and plopped down next to me.

"William, what are you doing?"

He lay on his side, propped onto one elbow. His head wobbled loosely on his neck until he finally got control and looked up at me. "I did what you wanted. I won them over."

"All the more reason you shouldn't be in here."

He waved his hand roughly toward the door. "They're all passed out. Drunk as skunks. Quinn's good stuff is good."

I covered my nose. Kindle's breath was atrocious. He put his arm across my lap. "Come here."

"William, you're drunk."

"I am."

"You don't want to do this."

"Do what?"

"Try to seduce me."

"Seduce you? I did that back at Fort Richardson. We're way past seducing."

"Oh, is that what you did?"

"Yep. Took more effort than I thought it would, but damn, was it worth it."

"William, you need to leave before you

say something you cannot take back."

He narrowed his eyes and pursed his lips. "You're right." He played with my shirt cuff. "So let's not talk." His hand moved to my hip and he pulled me toward him. "Lay down with me. Like this afternoon. I want to feel you next to me."

When I hesitated, he continued. "I did what you asked, though I think this is all a damn fool idea. The least you can do is this."

I sighed and lay down on my back next to Kindle.

"Put the knife down, woman." He gently took it from my hand and placed it behind his body.

"What if Tuesday comes in?"

Kindle's hand rested on my waist. "Don't worry about her; she's letting Kruger throw a leg over her."

"I thought you said they were all asleep."

"Or otherwise occupied. Shh. No talking."

I clasped my hands together over my chest and stared at the ceiling. Kindle's hand rubbed my stomach. "Laura," he whispered. "Is that what they did to you?"

He didn't need to elaborate. I closed my eyes and saw the stick between Aénóhé'ke's legs. "I don't know," I lied. "I was unconscious for a portion of it."

"Did my brother have you?"

113

I met Kindle's gaze. "No."

Kindle closed his eyes and exhaled, relief clear on his face. "Was Bell right?"

"About what?"

"At the spring. Why did you invite me in if you didn't want me to touch you?"

My voice was low and hoarse when I spoke. "I needed to know if you wanted me."

"I do," Kindle said. His voice was hoarse with desire. He placed my hand on the front of his pants. His throbbing erection took me back to the first night we made love in the fort library. The desire and wonder when I touched him for the first time. My breath caught.

He unbuttoned his pants and freed himself. His hand covered my own, but he let me set the pace. He was close to climax when he stopped my hand and closed his eyes. "Not yet." I didn't stop, too full of the power I had over him, remembering how glorious it felt when he wanted me. Wishing I could want him in return.

He opened his eyes, leaned forward, and kissed me gently. I forced myself to not recoil from the taste of whisky on his tongue. He pulled back, pressed his forehead against mine, and cried out in release.

I wiped my wet hand clean on the hem of

his shirt as he caught his breath. He collapsed onto his back with a smile as I buttoned his pants. He lifted up and removed the knife from beneath him and handed it to me. His eyes flicked to the other side of the tent and his smile evaporated. "What are you looking at?"

Over my shoulder, I saw Aénóhé'ke watching us.

"Turn away, goddammit," Kindle growled.

I sat up, blocking Aénóhé'ke from his view. "William!"

"She doesn't need to be watching us."

"Her eyes are almost swollen shut. And, maybe we don't need to be doing this in front of her."

"She's no innocent."

He tried to pull me down to lay with him, but I pushed him away. He didn't seem to notice, just closed his eyes and clasped his hands over his chest, a picture of drunken contentment.

I shoved his shoulder. "Get up. You have to leave."

"Why?"

"Because if they catch you in here they'll kill us. If you weren't stinking drunk you'd know that." I kept pushing against his shoulder until he waved his arm as if to swat me away and sat up.

"Fine. I'll go." His eyes were rheumy and hooded from drink. "Kiss me good-bye."

"Really, William."

"I'm not leaving until you do."

I pecked him on the cheek. "Now get out of —" He pulled me to him and kissed me roughly. I pushed against his chest, but his arms held me tight, pinned me to him. When he pulled away he was grinning.

I slapped him before he opened his eyes.

I scrambled to my feet and pointed to the door with a shaking arm. "Get out."

Kindle rose and stood before me, rubbing his jaw. I held his gaze, chest heaving, pushing down an emotion I never expected to feel in Kindle's presence: fear.

Kindle's countenance transformed from anger into something like horror before my eyes. He dropped his hand and reached out to me, his voice strangled. "Laura."

I stepped back. "Please leave."

He turned and was at the door in two steps. He stopped, turned his head to the side, and said, in a barely audible whisper, "Forgive me," before walking out of the tent.

I lowered my unsteady arm and hugged myself to stop my shaking. I picked up the knife and turned to take up my post again, ignoring Aénòhé'ke's steady gaze.

CHAPTER 9

Cuidado returned with Little Stick's yellow calico braid dangling from his saddle horn and a summer storm dogging his heels. He found us readying to leave Red Rock. Quinn and his traders dispersed early in the morning in four directions, each with a teamster and two guards armed with Spencer repeating rifles. We would follow Quinn's wagon, headed for the northern portion of Indian Territory. Welcome news since it would get us closer to our ultimate destination, though with the return of Cuidado, Kindle had lost his bet and his gray. We were now officially Bell's prisoners.

Dressed in my spare clothes and wearing a piece of her torn deerskin dress like a shawl, Aénóhé'ke helped me saddle our horse. She lifted the saddle onto the palomino's back and winced in pain. I tried to take over the task but she pushed me away. I stood back and glanced around the abandoned trader camp.

Bell, Kruger, Tuesday, and Cuidado were in a group a little ways off, talking and looking in my direction too often for comfort. Kindle saddled his horse alone, neither with Bell's group nor with me, an island unto himself, accompanied only by a raging hangover, if his countenance was any indication.

I mounted my horse and held my hand out for Aénóhé'ke. She took it and leapt up behind me. She grunted in pain as she settled on the back of the horse. Knowing the agony she was in, I placed my hand on her leg and squeezed it in encouragement. We rode to Kindle, who was adjusting his saddle to Bell's blaze-faced sorrel. His rifle scabbard was empty as were his holsters. I said his name softly, and he ignored me. "William," I said, firmly. He looked over his shoulder. His hat was pulled low, shadowing his eye, but I could see the frown beneath his beard. My horse shielded him from the gang's prying eyes. I handed him the knife he had given me the night before. He knelt down and put it in the scabbard inside his boot and returned to tending his horse.

My chest constricted. I had spent a long, sleepless night wondering if either of us were the same people who fell in love at Fort Richardson. I was changed, maybe irrevocably. I saw threats everywhere, even in a kiss from the man I loved, a kiss similar to ones we shared the night before we separated on the Red River. Of course, he would think of it as passionate, whereas this version of me felt nothing but terror as he held me. How could I explain to him the alarm that flooded my chest at being pinned, motionless, by strong arms? How would I ever be able to let Kindle lay on top of me without panicking?

As darkness gave way to twilight, so too did my anxiety about what I might never regain change to fury at what I'd lost. I'd never realized what had been missing from my life, how my happy, satisfying existence could be made better, complete by the hands of another. It wasn't as simple as loving and being loved; I'd known platonic, familial, and romantic love before. Never, though, had I known lust and passion and the primal connection these emotions brought with them. The breathless physicality of stripping away all guile and baring myself to another and the yearning and acceptance offered in return.

The loss of that desire, that hunger, was keener than I expected. I loved Kindle, would always love him, as he would me. But, without that component of our relationship — with the memory of it taunting me — I would never truly be happy. Our life would be half-full.

I refused to let that happen. I refused to let Cotter Black win.

Bell rode up. "We have to get riding if we're gonna beat this storm."

Kindle mounted the sorrel. "Stay or go, we won't beat this storm. But you're the leader. Lead on."

Bell stared at me under furrowed brows. "What's got your dander up?"

I unclenched my jaw. "If I had a gun right now, I'd blow your head off."

Bell's eyes widened and Kindle looked slowly up from the reins in his hands. "Because of that whore?" Bell motioned to Aénóhé'ke. "I didn't even fuck her, no thanks to you." He kicked his horse and trotted off. Kindle reined his horse around to follow.

"William, wait."

He pulled up and we stopped beside him.

"About the kiss . . ."

"Laura . . ."

"No, listen," I snapped. I wasn't going to wait to clear the air, to ride on without him knowing where we stood. I met his eyes. "I cannot be pinned like that." He opened his mouth but I didn't let him speak. "I know you didn't mean to, but . . . I just cannot be held like that. Not yet. Maybe not ever." I paused. "Do you understand?"

Cuidado rode up, and stopped next to us. He looked between the two of us, suspicion clear in his expression. *"Vamos,"* he said.

Kindle kicked his horse into a trot to follow Bell. Cuidado glared at me for a moment more and nudged his brown-and-white paint mare to follow the others.

We fell in line behind and rode away from the shelter of Red Rock. Aénòhé'ke shifted behind me. I glanced over my shoulder and saw her watching the formation recede. She faced forward with a determined thousand-yard stare. Her eyes focused on me, and after a brief flicker of a smile, she returned her focus to somewhere, or something, in the distance.

Behind us, Tuesday's horse snorted.

We blew my horse trying to outrun the storm.

Ahead of us the sun rose in the bluebird sky, beckoning us forward, away from the storm howling at our backs. Wind pushed us across the plain, swirled around us, and changed direction to push us back, our only

121

respite coming when we dipped down between the rolling hills.

Aénòhé'ke and I fell behind, Piper laboring under our double weight, losing sight of the others for increasingly long stretches. It was little comfort Tuesday stayed behind with us. If she decided to take revenge for the night before, we were defenseless; I'd given Kindle the knife and Enloe's gun was wrapped in the buffalo hide tied to the back of my saddle.

We crested a hill and saw the four men cresting the next. Kindle pulled up and turned to find us, his horse throwing his head and prancing. He kicked his horse into a run toward us, motioning for us to come toward him. His panic carried across the expanse and I turned to look behind me.

Fingers of lightning reached out from a dark boiling sky and touched the glowing orange horizon. The clouds rolled and swirled into a column, as if being shaped by an unseen hand. Lightning flickered, and a boom of thunder shook the world. Fat pellets of rain fell as I tried to make sense of a sunset in the middle of the day. Kindle's voice was indistinct, dispersed on the wind circling us.

"Ho'éstave."

I looked at Aénòhé'ke. "What?"

Tuesday grabbed the reins of my horse and pulled us down the hill. The mare pulled against her, deciding this was as far as she would go. The horse dropped to her knees. With more presence of mind than I, Aénóhé'ke grabbed the back of my shirt and jumped from the horse, pulling me free with her as the animal collapsed on its side.

At a full gallop, Kindle rode toward us, arm out. Aénóhé'ke took his arm and swung herself up behind him. Tuesday held her arm out. I pulled myself behind her with the awkward difficulty of a woman raised in the city. She kicked her horse into a run and I almost fell off the back, but grabbed the edge of her saddle in time. I bounced around, trying to find purchase, and finally wrapped my arms around Tuesday's ample torso and clung to her for dear life.

Inexorably, the storm bore down, hammering us with rocks, sticks, and large balls of ice. The wind ripped our hats off and pulled at our shirts. Lightning and thunder like the boom of battlefield cannons cracked the sky wide open. Fire leapt from the ground in front of us and, fed by the wind, raced across the ground. Over my shoulder, the golden horizon raced forward.

Kindle and Aénóhé'ke ran through the wall of flames, never breaking stride. "No!"

My scream was lost in the roar surrounding us. Tuesday reached her arm back and held me close to her, kicked her horse, and we followed Kindle into hell.

Inside the walls of fire, the scene was strangely calm. Acrid smoke surrounded us, muting the sound and the violence of the storm raging outside. The horse's hooves pounded on the hard ground and it snorted as it tried to breathe in the smoke. Clumps of fire burned here and there, forcing the horse to change direction until soon we lost our bearings. The horse stopped and twirled in a circle, unsure where to go. Tuesday used both hands to pull at the reins, trying to move him in the right direction, and with a grunt of anger, kicked the horse violently. The horse snorted, shook its head, and bolted forward with a jolt.

I flew off the back of the horse. The last thing I saw was the pale yellow sun in the smoke-filled sky.

As I got closer, I heard the tune she sang and recognized the voice instantly.

"Maureen?"

Maureen O'Reilly, the closest person to a mother I ever had, turned to me. Her hands were covered with flour, and there was a disapproving smile on her face. The smile she gave me when she wanted to be severe but couldn't hide her pride in me for all that.

"Katie Girl, what kind of mess have you gotten yourself in now?"

"I'm lost."

"Are you now?"

The land around us was barren. "I think I'm going to die here."

Maureen wiped her hands on her apron. "It's not like you to give up."

I exhaled. "I'm so tired, Maureen."

She reached out and stroked my short hair. "I know, Katie Girl."

Tears choked my throat. "I miss you. I'm sorry I brought you out here."

She smiled and patted my cheek. "What's done is done. You have to move forward."

"I can't."

"You don't want to."

"I do. But I can't forget."

"Look forward." I gaped at her with incomprehension. She smiled and shook her head. "You always were too busy being right to see what was in front of you. Get up. Move forward."

I pushed myself up, and walked on until the world fell away beneath me. I tumbled down the hill, head over feet, and slid to a stop next to a large, warm wall. Every muscle in my body hurt. My eyes were dry and I struggled for breath. I reached out for the wall and touched hair. Warm breath snuffled on my neck and cheek, followed by a low nicker of recognition.

"Piper," I said, patting the palomino's side. I sat up and leaned my back against the horse. The small dip had miraculously been saved from the fire. Smoke drifted along the tops of the hills above us. I found my canteen, uncorked it, and drank deeply, the lukewarm water a panacea on my parched throat. I sighed and twisted my neck from side to side. The back of it felt as if it was being beaten by a hammer. I reached back to massage it, felt a bump the size of a walnut, and knew I was concussed.

I shook the canteen. Half-full, at most. I corked it to save the water and dug into the saddlebag for hardtack or a piece of jerky. I ate and contemplated what to do next. I had a gun with four rounds, little water and food, was injured and on foot in the middle of Indian Territory. I didn't even have my hat.

"A bad predicament any way you look at it, Piper. What do you suggest we do?" The horse gazed at me with one big, brown eye and shook her head. "Lot of help you are."

I chawed off a bit of hardtack. "Surely Kindle will come back for me. I'll wait here for him."

The horse snorted and turned her head away. "You're right, it's a horrible idea. The Lord helps those who help themselves. Or something like that." I leaned forward and whispered to the horse. "I haven't been much for church these last eight years."

The boom of cannons shook the ground. The storm clouds above me roiled and growled as the thunder receded. Fingers of lightning touched the horizon. Rain, warm and gloriously wet, flushed from the sky. I lifted my face to the rain, and let it wash away the grime, fear and indecision covering me like a second skin.

I kissed Piper's forelock, thanked her for carrying me so far, and shot the palomino in the head with my gun. Three rounds left. I hoped I wouldn't regret using one to put the foundered horse out of her misery.

I walked away, carrying my saddle on my

right shoulder and my saddlebags around my neck. My head throbbed, my left forearm felt like a knife was repeatedly slicing into it, and my right hand, burned and weak from being broken by the Comanche, struggled to steady the saddle on my shoulder. I wanted to walk in the low areas between the hills but knew there would be little chance of anyone seeing me if I did. The small hill in front of me was as imposing as the Dover cliffs.

I put my head down and climbed.

I dropped my gear when I reached the top, exhausted and afraid my head was going to explode. When I caught my breath, I surveyed my surroundings. As far as I could see, small hills rose and dipped. "Where's a goddamn plain when you need it?"

I evaluated my gear for what to jettison. The saddlebags stayed with me. They held the last of my medical tools and my gun. I would walk over coals to keep them. I could leave the saddle; there wasn't a horse to put it on when I caught up with the group anyway. But, I would have to buy another one down the road and money was scarce. I would carry it as long as humanly possible. I would need the buffalo skin at night when the temperature dipped. I inhaled, picked up my gear, and walked on.

On hill five I saw a familiar-looking cactus with a piece of my shirt impaled on a long needle. On the eighth hill, the scorched ground stopped suddenly and was replaced with waist-high buffalo grass. On the tenth hill, I stopped counting.

As I walked, I watched the storm in front of me recede into the distance, replaced by a cloudless royal blue sky. Slowly, the sky turned the deep blue of a Union officer's coat and the sun behind me fell to the earth. It would be night soon. I crested the final hill and saw a rider in the distance, loping toward me. I dropped my gear and put my hands on my hips, trying to catch my breath. Exhausted as I was, I couldn't help grinning as Kindle rode his towering gray toward me with Aénóhé'ke at his back. He pulled up and took in my bandaged arm, the saddle at my feet, and saddlebags around my neck.

"Took you long enough," I said.

He shook his head and a slow grin of admiration spread across his face. "Sometimes I wonder if you need me at all."

CHAPTER 11

The three of us celebrated my survival by camping in the valley of two hills and with a buffalo-chip fire. Kindle hobbled his gray and made coffee. Aénòhé'ke had wandered off, I guessed to relieve herself. She may have decided now was the time to leave and was making for her tribe. Frankly, I was too exhausted to care.

Kindle handed me a tin mug of coffee and sat down next to me.

I sipped the chicory coffee and smiled, almost laughed.

"What?"

"I was thinking of the first bad cup of coffee I had at Richardson. Waterman told me to get used to it, and indeed I have."

"Here I come back for you and you immediately set in on my coffee. No gratitude, I swear."

"And I swear you hear only what you want to hear. I said I liked it."

"Not in so many words."

I bent down and looked Kindle in the eyes. "I love your coffee. It's the best coffee I've ever had."

"That's more like it."

Smiling, we held each other's gaze, falling into the familiar flirty banter that had been a hallmark of our relationship from almost the beginning. For a brief moment, the dream I'd had of our future together was clear; the two of us in a drawing room, discussing current events, household matters, my patients, or our children. A life I'd never imagined or wanted until Kindle, a life that didn't compute with the two people from the whisky camp. My smile slipped and the events of the night before seeped between us.

I glanced away. "How did you get your gray back?"

In the brief silence, I wondered if Kindle would confront me about my demand earlier, but he didn't. "I yanked Bell from the saddle."

"I would have liked to see that."

"It felt good. But, not as good as what I did to Tuesday."

"Dare I ask?"

"She'll have a shiner for a few days."

I grimaced, knowing all too well what it

was like, and thinking how it was one more battle scar for a woman who'd been damaged and bruised enough by men.

Kindle saw my reaction. "You don't feel sorry for her, do you?"

Aénóhé'ke returned holding a thistle, and I remembered my rage at the abuse Tuesday had inflicted on the young Indian. I suspected she learned it from personal experience. Under different circumstances, I would have been defending Tuesday from the same. I turned to Kindle and shrugged a shoulder. "No."

"She's lucky I didn't kill her. When I saw her ride up without you." Kindle threw a rock into the fire. Aénóhé'ke picked up my saddlebag and searched through it. She paused and stared in one side. Her expression was inscrutable. She went for Kindle's saddlebag.

"What's she doing?" Kindle said.

"How would I know?"

Aénóhé'ke tossed Kindle's saddlebag down and stared at us. She sighed and pointed to her forearm, then the thistle, then mimed drinking.

"I think she wants to make a thistle tea to help my burn," I said.

I drank my coffee in three gulps, threw the dregs into the fire, and handed the cup

134

to her. She nodded and set to work. She poured water into the mug, sat it in the middle of the fire, and stripped leaves from the thistle.

"I'm surprised they let you leave to find me. How do they know we'll return?"

"They have our guns."

"Except one." I pulled Enloe's holster from my saddlebag. "This morning I hid it in the buffalo skin, in case they wised up. They didn't. Honestly, they aren't very good bandits."

"Oscar Enloe keeps saving our bacon," Kindle said. "How many rounds do you have left?"

"Three. I used one on Piper." I dropped down next to Kindle and handed him the holster.

Kindle leaned forward and cupped the back of my head. I flinched. "Ow."

He gently probed the knot. "Christ, Laura. What happened?"

"When I fell off the horse I hit my head."

"What can I do?"

"Were you about to kiss me?"

"Yes."

"Let's start there."

He leaned forward and paused. "I'm sorry for last night. The whisky got the better of me. It won't happen again."

"The drunkenness or the roughness?"

The corner of his visible eye twitched. "Either."

I cupped his face and kissed him gently.

Aénóhé'ke knelt beside me, interrupting the next kiss before it happened. With gentle hands she unwrapped the bandage on my forearm. I hissed and turned my head away as she peeled the bandage from the burn. "Oh my God," Kindle said.

I kept my head averted and said, "It's bad, isn't it?"

Kindle nodded. "Shouldn't you look at it?"

I grimaced. "The one injury I cannot stomach is burns. On others, I can handle myself tolerably well. But . . ." I swallowed the bile in my throat. "I was never good at them before, but after the massacre . . ."

Kindle rubbed my healthy arm. He knew the story of how I'd watched the Kiowa burn a man alive, had smelled the burning flesh and heard the crackle of fat popping in the heat. I kept my eyes on him and asked, "What is she doing?"

"Soaking your bandage in the mug. With the thistle."

"Is she? Interesting. I need to sketch and chronicle that, for future reference."

Kindle grinned at me. "You are one remarkable woman, Laura Elliston."

I shrugged, but couldn't keep at bay the flush of pleasure at his compliment. "I try."

"I can't believe you carried your saddle for hours. Why didn't you leave it?"

"I thought to, but since I gave away the last of my mother's jewelry, I knew we'd be ill able to afford a new one."

"Is that so?"

"What? You don't believe me?"

"I think you carried it to prove you could do it. And to impress me."

"It might have been part of my motivation. Did it work?" He nodded and watched Aénȯhé'ke. "Are you angry with me for buying her?" I asked.

Kindle sighed. "I wasn't angry you bought her, I was angry at the price." He turned his attention to me. "We're broke, as you carrying your saddle halfway across Indian Territory proves."

"Yes, I know, and I'm sorry. But, I couldn't stand by and let them abuse her." I covered my eyes, hoping to banish the visual of Tuesday raping Aénȯhé'ke with a stick. Kindle touched my knee.

"Of course not." What was unsaid between us, but understood, was I would have killed Tuesday with my bare hands if Kindle hadn't pulled me off. "We don't have any money, and only one gun."

"And one horse. I've got to stop naming my animals *Piper*. They never come to a good end."

We watched Aénóhé'ke pull the mug from the fire with the denuded thistle stalk.

"What are we going to do with her?" Kindle asked.

"I didn't think that far ahead. Do you have any ideas?"

He sighed. "Once we get clear of Bell, I thought we'd take her to the Quakers."

"Will they be able to determine what tribe she's part of?"

"She's Cheyenne."

"How do you know?"

"Bell told me. She was a Kiowa slave."

"And they traded her for whisky."

"Yes."

I clenched my jaw and my face went hot with anger at how women were treated as little more than men's possessions.

"I wonder how she got to be a slave," Kindle mused.

"Why?"

"The Cheyenne made peace with the Kiowa and Comanche thirty years ago. I suppose there could've been a dust up between them, but it would be more like they'd band together against the settlers than fight each other."

Aénóhé'ke returned and knelt next to me. She lifted the wet, steaming strip of cloth from the mug. She shook the cloth slightly, until the steam coming from it dissipated. She took my right arm and slowly lowered the cloth onto the burn.

"Does it hurt?" Kindle said.

I nodded and breathed through the excruciating pain. Aénóhé'ke took my right hand in hers, dabbed the wet cloth on the burn, and dipped the cloth in the thistle tea again. This time she cooled it, squeezed it out, and wrapped it around my arm. The initial pain was eventually replaced by a pleasant cool sensation. Aénóhé'ke tied the bandage and rose.

"Thank you," I said.

She smiled and nodded and sat across the fire from us.

"You said once we get clear of Bell. How are we going to do that?"

"We need our guns and there's only one way to get them back."

I was afraid I knew the answer, but I asked the question anyway. "How?"

"We're going to have to kill who needs killing."

With three people and one horse, we made

poor progress. Charlie Bell and his minions caught up with us midday.

"Pay up, Kruger," Bell said. He held out his hand to the German. "He bet me you ran."

"I'm a man of my word," Kindle said.

Kruger pulled a crumpled sawbuck from his vest pocket and handed it to Bell. Bell pocketed the money and narrowed his eyes at Kindle. "You keep saying. Give me my horse back." He got off the blazed-faced sorrel, gave Kindle his reins, and took Kindle's from him. Bell mounted the gray and held his hand out for me. "I'll make sure you don't fall off."

I threw my saddlebags over the back of Bell's horse and mounted. Kindle and Aénóhé'ke mounted his and we set off.

Cuidado rode ahead to scout. Bell kicked the gray into a trot and Kruger, Kindle, and Tuesday fell in behind us.

"Where are we going?" I asked.

"Quinn was heading to the Caddos, then the Wichitas before they head to the agency to get their allotment. We're following."

"And, then what? Six people raid an Indian village of hundreds? I know you are a gambler, but I do not like those odds."

"Best we can hope for with the Caddos is they have a small village. They aren't buffalo

140

hunters like the plains Indians. The Wichitas are. Their warriors are off the rez hunting buffalo. Which means it's old men and
women and children left. Drunk old men
and women and children we can handle."

"Sounds cowardly, if you ask me."

He turned in his saddle. "Why in hell
you'd care what happens to a bunch of
savages, I don't understand. Tuesday, I get.
She's out to make every Indian she meets
pay. *You* buy one and take care of her. She'll
turn on you first chance, mark my words."

"I don't expect you to *get* me. You're a
man and can't possibly understand. So your
plan is to drag us around Indian Territory
raiding defenseless villages? What is our
destination? Where will you turn me in?"

"When I get tired of you. What should I
call you? You've never actually said."

"Laura is fine."

"But, it ain't your real name."

"Is Charlie Bell your real name?"

"Good point." Our horse walked around a
five-foot-tall, vicious-looking plant. "That's
there's a bull nettle. Fall into that and you'll
die a painful death."

"I'll keep it in mind."

"We got a ways to go, why don't you tell
me a story?"

"About what?"

141

"Oh, I don't know. What happened to your voice? Or have you always sounded like a man?"

I bristled. I knew I had no right to be vain. I'd lost weight, cut my hair, hadn't had a true bath in almost a month, and almost every area of my body had been bruised, injured, or scarred. But, when I bothered to imagine the image I presented to people, it was of a confident woman, plainly but smartly dressed, head held high, with shining golden hair and an alto voice that intrigued rather than repulsed.

"A man took exception to what I said and punched me in the throat."

"How long ago?"

How long had it been? Four weeks? Six? I'd lost track of time. "About six weeks, I suppose. Where are you from, Mr. Bell?"

Kruger laughed. "Mr. Bell," he said, in a heavily accented parody of a refined voice.

"The greatest place on earth."

"He means Texas," Kruger said.

"Excuse me if I don't share your enthusiasm," I said.

"You had a hard ride of it in Texas, didnja?"

"That's one way to put it."

"Well, the Indians' days are numbered, mark my words. No thanks to the Army. No offense, Major," Bell said.

"I was a captain," Kindle said.

"I suppose the Captain and the Murderess doesn't have the same ring to it. Guess Henry Pope took some liberties."

"Henry Pope came up with the name?" I asked.

"He did." Bell spat on the ground. "He's one tough motherfucker. Should have died after the beating he got."

"You were in Jacksboro at the time?"

"Best place to hide out from the Army is right under their nose," Kruger said.

"Don't tell the Army man all our secrets," Bell chastised. "Though, I guess it don't matter now. They catch you, Captain, and they'll put you in front of a firing squad."

A firing squad? I turned to Kindle. "Is that true?" When Kindle didn't answer, I knew it was. My breath caught, and I turned around to stare at the back of Bell's neck. Why would Harriet help Kindle escape if she knew the consequences? Did she think her forged letter from her brother, the colonel, would save Kindle?

Bell turned his head and said in a low voice only I could hear, "You didn't know that? I can see why he would risk it all for you. You're a handsome woman. At least, you were. You could be again."

143

"What do you mean, I was?"

"You don't remember me from the road to Jacksboro?"

My brows furrowed, then cleared. Kindle and I had met two men on the road to Jacksboro not long before I was abducted but hadn't paid either too much attention. We were in the middle of a disagreement about the kiss we'd shared. Our first. I realized later Cotter Black had been one of the men. "You were with Black that day?" I whispered.

"Look!" Kruger said. "Cuidado."

We all kicked our horses into a gallop to meet Cuidado. The horses shook their heads and danced around when we pulled up. Cuidado's horse went around in a circle.

"What is it?"

"Quinn's train was attacked about two miles back."

"They dead?"

Cuidado nodded. "Took the wagon. Tracks went off to the northeast."

"How many?"

"Five."

Bell grinned. "Excellent."

"Whoever is going to incapacitate your Indians for easy killing now that Quinn's dead?" I asked.

"We'll worry about that later. Right now,

there's Indians that need killing."

I caught Kindle's eye before Bell urged our horse into a determined trot. Kindle's nod was almost imperceptible. We headed northeast in silence.

there's Indians that need killing."

CHAPTER 12

The Indians were camped haphazardly on the south bank of a river, amid a grove of cottonwood trees.

Kindle watched them through his brother's spyglass. "Arapaho." He handed the spyglass to Bell, who inspected it suspiciously, before gazing through it.

Though we were five hundred yards away and behind the crest of a hill, the glow of the Indians' fire lit up the night and their celebration carried across the landscape. I fought against my memories and focused on my throbbing forearm.

"Give 'em a couple more hours," Bell said. "They'll be less likely to shoot straight."

Kruger took the spyglass. "You see Quinn's scalp?"

"I did. That fucker is mine."

We retreated down the hill and made cold camp. I held Kindle back so he, Aénóhé'ke,

146

and I walked behind. I told him about Bell and Black and the road to Jacksboro. Kindle narrowed his eye at Bell and nodded. "I winked at you," he whispered. "Behind the eyepatch."

"I hardly think this is the time to be flirting with me."

"It's always the right time to flirt with you, Slim," he said, and walked off to join the men and Tuesday.

"I don't like that name," I said. Aénóhé'ke's expression was blank. I shook my head and we joined the group.

"Major, you get to lead us down," Bell said.

"What?" I said.

"He's a cavalry man, right? Good at leading charges. You pick off the first Indian, and we'll take care of the rest."

"That's your plan? To charge down there guns blazing?" Kindle said.

"That's the plan."

Kindle shrugged, but smiled as if humoring a child. "You're the leader."

Bell bristled. "You're goddamn right I'm the leader."

"How'd that happen?" Kindle said. "I'm curious. I mean, of the four of you, you seem the least likely leader. Besides Tuesday. Can't hardly lead if you can't talk."

147

Tuesday glared at Kindle, but he continued, seemingly oblivious. "And, she's a woman. What self-respecting man would be ordered around by a woman?"

"Think you should look in the mirror, Major," Kruger said.

Kindle chuckled. "Fair point, Herr Kruger. Cuidado, why do you follow this boy?"

"Boy?"

"How old are you, Bell? Eighteen? Twenty? How many raids have you done since Black left? You were part of Cotter Black's gang, right? No way he handpicked you to be his successor."

Kruger and Cuidado glanced at each other. Bell's fists were balled. "Stand up."

"Keep it down," Cuidado said. He motioned in the direction of the Indian camp.

"Don't tell me what to do," Bell said, though his voice was noticeably softer.

Kindle met Bell face to face. He towered over the smaller man. With the slightest shift in Kindle's demeanor he took on the bearing and countenance of his dead brother, John. Bell tried not to quake beneath Kindle's harsh gaze when he saw it.

"Now you see the resemblance. You rode with my brother, didn't you?" Kindle said, voice soft. "You all did."

"When I found out he planned to sell guns

to Indians, I killed him," Bell said.

I laughed.

"What?" Bell snapped.

"You did not kill Cotter Black," I said.

"I did. Up in Palo Duro Canyon not six weeks ago."

I looked at Kruger, Cuidado, and Tuesday. "Is that what he told you?"

"What happened to the guns?" Kindle said.

"What?"

"If you kept him from selling guns, where are they?"

"They were useless. No firing pin."

"So you killed him for nothing," Cuidado said.

"He was arming Indians!"

"With useless guns," Kruger said.

"Think Cotter Black would go into this raid like a cavalry charge?" Kindle said.

When no one spoke, Kindle continued. "The plan is this: Laura and Aénóhé'ke will take care of the Indian's horses. The five of us will come at them from three sides. They're backed up to a river and drunk. It'll be a shooting gallery. It shouldn't take more than five minutes."

"I like the Major's plan better," Kruger said.

"When it's over, you take the whisky

149

wagon and two of the horses. We take the other horses and you give us back our guns."

Bell laughed. "Why would I do that? I'm taking her to Darlington and turning her in."

"I guess you didn't notice what the Indian brandishing Quinn's scalp wore around his neck." Bell's expression was blank. "Laura's jewelry. With the horses and whisky, it's all worth more than Laura's reward. You get your bloodlust sated, whisky to sell, two Indian ponies you can trade at Darlington, and six hundred dollars for the necklace in Saint Louis. Think of all the riverboats floating on the Mississippi waiting for you to cheat a bunch of Eastern farmers out of their money."

"I like that plan better," Kruger said. "Never been to Saint Louis."

"Shut up, Kruger."

Kruger rose and walked to Bell. Kindle stepped back slightly to give him room. "What did you say?"

You could almost smell Bell's panic. "Kruger, listen to me. Why would we do what he wants? We can have everything, including the reward for the woman and the reward for turning him in."

"Did he say *we*?" I asked Kruger. "You shouldn't trust him. The only way he could

150

get you to follow him was by lying about killing Black. How do you know he's not lying to you now?"

"I'm not lying! I'll share it all with you three. It's what we've always done."

Kruger turned to me. "How do you know he's lying about Black?"

"Because I killed him," I said.

"Bullshit," Bell said.

"Black had the Comanche attack the patrol taking me to Sill. On the Red River. They took me to an Indian named Quanah, but not before they all took turns on me. When I got the chance, I put a gun to the back of Cotter Black's head and pulled the trigger."

Kruger, Cuidado, and Tuesday stared at me in astonishment. "She did. I was there." Kindle addressed Bell. "How do you think I got his horse? His spyglass?"

"I don't remember seeing you there, Charlie Bell," I said.

"Enough talk," Cuidado said. "We go with the Major's plan. At midnight."

The Indian tasked with guarding the horses was so drunk he didn't move when Aénòhé'ke and I stole them out from under him. I motioned for Aénòhé'ke to take the horses back behind the hill to our cold

151

camp. She shook her head and pointed back and forth between us.

I sighed and looked in the direction of the sleeping Indians. I didn't want to leave Kindle unprotected. When the five left to take their positions, I'd donned Enloe's holster and checked my gun. Three bullets. It was the one thing Bell and his men didn't expect. I didn't want to use the bullets on another human, but if Bell targeted Kindle, which I suspected was precisely his plan, then I would.

I hadn't counted on Aénòhé'ke wanting to stay by my side.

When I turned back to Aénòhé'ke I saw the sleeping guard was no longer asleep, but sitting up, looking around as if confused by where he was. His gaze landed on me, Aénòhé'ke, and his string of horses. I pulled my gun and shot him before he could sound a cry of alarm.

Unfortunately, my gunshot did, and all hell broke loose.

The horses Aénòhé'ke held whinnied, reared, and tried to bolt. She held on to the rope and leaned back into it, forcing them down. She jumped on the nearest one and with the hand not holding the lead rope of the string of horses motioned for me to get up behind her. I heard the Indians wake and yell at one another in confusion. Then I heard the pounding of horses' hooves.

Thinking only of Kindle, I ran toward the noise.

A small Indian with a rifle in his hand stopped dead in his tracks when he saw me. His astonishment saved me — and doomed him. I raised my gun and shot him in the eye, picked up his rifle, and ran on.

Though no more than eight people could have been fighting, the scene was chaotic. Cuidado jerked, fell from his horse, and was immediately set on by an Indian. Kruger's head exploded and he fell back onto his horse, but not off. His horse ran through the fire, out into the darkness, and was gone.

Bell dropped the Indian wearing my necklace. I watched Kindle take aim at Bell, but before he took the shot, someone tackled me from behind. I fell hard on my chest, the wind knocked out of me. Someone grabbed my hair, lifted my head, and banged it against the ground again and again.

She'll turn on you first chance, mark my words.

Aénóhé'ke.

My arms were pinned beneath me and I couldn't move from the weight of my attacker. My vision swam with red and black dots and I went limp. She lifted my head

153

and pulled it back as far as it would go. Above me the dark sky was sprinkled with stars, like grains of sugar spilt on a cast-iron skillet. The stars were blocked by my attacker's bruised and deformed face. She opened her mouth, and with a bloodcurdling scream, revealed a toothless maw with a nub far in her throat where her tongue should be.

Blood and gore flew from her mouth at the same time I heard the gunshot. With her hand grasping my hair, Tuesday fell on top of me, dead. I tried to push myself up, but couldn't move, or breathe. The weight was lifted and gentle hands turned me over.

Aénòhé'ke knelt beside me, my smoking gun in her right hand. For a split second, I thought she was going to kill me. If I hadn't felt so horrid, I might have cared. Instead, she helped me sit up and grabbed me when I swayed and almost fell over.

Kindle jumped from his horse and came to me. With his strong arms he lifted me from the ground, carried me to the whisky wagon, and lay me down on a buffalo robe in the back. He left and returned with a mug of whisky.

I drank it and coughed. "Rotgut," I said, and took another drink. "It's growing on me." I lay back. My head throbbed, front and back. "Is everyone dead?"

Kindle took my hand. "Yes."

I threw my forearm over my face. "I am the angel of death," I said.

"Shh," Kindle said. "No, you're not."

"I'm not going to live to see England again."

"Yes, you are."

I shook my head, and with a certainty I hadn't felt in months, knew it to be true. I wouldn't make it, but I would die to make sure Kindle did.

Aénóhé'ke walked up to the wagon and held out my mother's necklace. I took it, stared at the square sapphire pendant, and tried to remember the life I had before, to remember the woman I had been. My life back East was like a book read long ago, fondly but vaguely remembered. Instead, I saw clearly a parade of dead people — Maureen, Amos, Cornelius, Cotter Black, Oscar Enloe and the other nameless bounty hunters, the two Indians I had killed, and the dead surrounding me. After Palo Duro Canyon, I told Kindle to call me Laura because I believed Catherine Bennett to be another person. Now, staring at my mother's sapphire-and-pearl necklace, I knew the truth of it.

Catherine Bennett was dead.

PART TWO:
SWEET MEDICINE

Part Two:
Sweet Medicine

CHAPTER 13

I was unconscious when the Indians arrived
the next morning. Raised angry voices
broke through the dark curtain covering my
mind. My eyes fluttered open to see Kindle
and Aénòhé'ke arguing with four Indians
dressed as white men.

Aénòhé'ke was between the four Indians
and Kindle, her arms out as if to separate
them, speaking as animatedly and quickly
as the men. Kindle raised his hand to show
them he wasn't armed and glanced over his
shoulder at me. He saw I was awake and
came over.

"Laura. How do you feel?"

I sat up and swayed. He put his arm
around my shoulders to steady me. "Dizzy.
Queasy. Hungover."

"And how do you know what a hangover
feels like, Slim?" How he could tease me
when four angry Indians were ten feet away,
I didn't know.

"I'll tell you later. Who are they?"

"Their friends." He pointed to the dead Arapaho on the ground.

"I suppose if they wanted us dead, we would be already."

"Let's hope you're right. Are you okay?"

"Yes. Go."

I swung my legs off the back of the wagon, steadied myself against the side, and watched. Aénóhé'ke apparently told an enthralling story. The men were quiet and looking back and forth between her and me. The Indian at the front of the group stared at me with a steady, inscrutable expression. He was tall and handsome and held himself regally. He reminded me of Quanah, the Comanche chief who sold me to Cotter Black for guns. Whereas Quanah was fierce, this man seemed calculating. He held up his hand and Aénóhé'ke stopped talking. He turned his attention to Kindle.

"I am Bob Johnson."

Luckily, nausea kept me from laughing. "You're joking."

Kindle shot me a warning glance.

"Aénóhé'ke tells us your woman saved her," Bob Johnson said.

"Yes."

"She also says she killed two of our brothers last night."

160

Kindle's head moved slightly in my direction. I had been too dizzy to give a description of what happened the night before. "If she did, it was in self-defense. Your brothers killed the whisky traders whose wagon this was and stole the whisky. The men we were with were out for blood."

"And you assisted."

"We did what needed to be done to escape the men. We were their prisoners."

Bob Johnson glanced around the site, his eyes settling on the ten horses and two oxen picketed beneath a cottonwood.

"We will give you five of the horses and the whisky," Kindle said.

Bob Johnson turned his gaze back to Kindle. "We want the white men's guns."

"You can take the Indians' weapons. We keep the white men's. You can comb through the dead's possessions and take what you want."

They wouldn't find much. The night before while I watched woozily, Kindle and Aénòhé'ke had gone through everyone's pockets and saddlebags and taken the money and what valuables would help us on our journey. Bob Johnson's companions moved toward the dead bodies. Apparently, they all understood English.

"We want the wagon."

161

"We need the wagon to travel to Independence. My wife is not well, as you can see."
I didn't need to try too hard to look sick.

"The Indian woman goes with us," Bob Johnson said.

"No." I stood on wobbly legs. Aénòhé'ke came to me and held me up. "She has been sold and traded enough. We are taking her to Darlington Agency so we can find her tribe and reunite her with her people."

Bob Johnson spoke to Aénòhé'ke. The Indian woman paused before answering firmly.

"She isn't part of the deal," Kindle said. "We do not trade humans like horses or cattle."

Bob Johnson leveled his gaze at Kindle. "Your woman bought her."

"To save her, not to abuse her."

"We will take her to her people."

"You're welcome to ride to Darlington with us, to make sure we keep our word." Kindle rested his hand on the gun at his hip. "We will not hand her over unless it is what she wants."

Though Bob Johnson's eyes didn't move, I could tell he noted Kindle's movement to his gun. He spoke to Aénòhé'ke at length, and she replied in kind with hand signals so quick, I wouldn't have been able to under-

162

stand her even if I knew more than *friend* and *thank you*.

"We will travel with you," Bob Johnson said. "Five horses, the whisky, and the guns."

"Your brothers' weapons, five horses, the whisky and found."

"You have already picked over the bodies, there will be little found to be had. I want the Mexican's bandolier."

"Without the bullets. They will do your guns no good."

One side of Bob Johnson's mouth curled into a smile. He stuck out his hand and Kindle took it. "Now, let's talk horses."

Kindle and Bob Johnson walked to the string of horses and divided them up. The Indian wanted Kindle's gray, but he refused to part with it. When they finished, the Indian spoke extensively. Kindle stared at the ground in contemplation and glanced in our direction. He nodded and walked away.

Kindle came to us and took me from Aénóhé'ke. He motioned *Thank you* to the woman and helped me walk to the front of the wagon.

"Should we have given them so much?" The night before, we'd talked about how trading or selling the horses and guns would allow us to hold off selling Mother's necklace a while longer.

"Trading with them bought goodwill. You never know when we will need it."

"What did he tell you?"

"Aénóhé'ke is Cherokee. She was a child when she was taken by the Cheyenne. She was adopted and raised Cheyenne, married a warrior."

"How did she get traded for whisky by a band of Kiowa?"

"Her husband lost her in a game of dice with the Kiowa."

My jaw dropped. "My God. That's reprehensible."

Kindle's expression turned stern. "Indians aren't the only men who gamble with flesh. I've seen white men do the same with children, slaves, and yes, wives. The Cheyenne are one of the few plains tribes that don't treat their women like chattel. My guess is the warrior has been shunned for his bad judgment."

"I should hope so." Aénóhé'ke's attention alternated between us and Bob Johnson and his companions, as if trying to decide where her loyalty lay. "How far is Darlington?"

"Less than a day's ride, I expect."

"Will the Army be there?"

"They bring the allotment."

"Then it's not safe for us. Should we let

Bob Johnson take her and ride on for Independence?"

Kindle's gaze moved to my forehead. "Yes, but you're not fit to travel."

"I'll be fine."

"Your eyes are glassy and you're swaying on your feet."

"Am I?"

"Yes. You need a bed, and good food. We go to Darlington, for a day at least. It will be crawling with Cheyenne and Arapaho and Army men. Let's hope none of them recognize me."

Midday we rolled out of the cottonwood grove and north toward the Darlington Agency. Along with the extra saddles and gear we hoped to sell to the livery, the bodies of the four members of the Bell gang were in the back of the wagon, covered with a buffalo robe. Kindle said there was an even chance there was a bounty on their heads and we could use all the money we could get.

I drove the wagon and Aénóhé'ke sat shoulder to shoulder with me, effectively holding me up. The midday sun beat down on us from a cloudless sky. Grasshoppers swarmed and chirped with each step the livestock took across the parched landscape.

165

Any evidence of the storm the day before had evaporated, leaving only the dusty scent of sun-baked grass. Occasionally, we would roll across wild sage and the aroma of anise and lemongrass would tease me, relax me briefly, before dissipating into the enormous sky.

My vision swam and tiny pinpricks of light flashed in my peripheral vision. I wanted to lie down and sleep forever, but could not. Kindle rode next to us and watched me. When I tipped forward Aénȯhé'ke caught me, took the reins from my hands, and with one hand around my shoulder, drove the two oxen with the other.

"Stop," Kindle ordered. Aénȯhé'ke understood that word in English, at least. He edged his horse next to the wagon and motioned to Aénȯhé'ke. She pushed me to my feet and helped me climb on in front of Kindle. He wrapped one arm firmly around me, said, "Lay your head back." I did as I was told, and turned my face into his neck. The brim of his hat shielded me from the sun. He smelled of sweat, leather, and horses. I smiled and closed my eyes.

I don't remember the rest of the trip.

CHAPTER 14

Voices floated around me like vapors, briefly distinct, then dispersing into the ether before I could comprehend what was being said and by whom.

"Severely concussed . . ."

"I would ask where you're going but know you shouldn't tell me."

"Oh, Catherine, for someone so intelligent you're so naive."

"You do remember, don't you?"

"You cannot be here!"

"Never seen the like before . . ."

"Everyone has secrets . . ."

"He'll never want you."

My eyes opened. The room smelled of newly cut lumber and sage. Sunlight streamed through the opened windows. A breeze wafted the sheer curtains, bringing fresh air and the sounds of the town in to greet me.

Was I back in Jacksboro?

Had I ever left?

The room was simple: a bed covered in fresh linens, side table with an oil lamp, a chest of drawers, and a straight-backed chair in the corner, on which sat an Indian woman. She gazed out the window, a boldly striped blanket wrapped around her shoulders and her hands folded serenely in her lap.

"Aénòhé'ke."

The woman turned her gaze to me and smiled. "Laura." Her expression was troubled. Then she said, with more difficulty, "Charlotte."

I nodded and was happy to note my head did not hurt, due in no small part to the bitter aftertaste of laudanum on my tongue.

Aénòhé'ke stood, raised her finger as if telling me to wait, and left the room, giving me time to take stock of myself.

I pulled the sheets back and sat on the edge of the bed. "I cannot wait for the day I am not constantly assessing my injuries or my surroundings."

I wore a clean nightdress and nothing else. For the first time since we left Jacksboro I did not feel gritty or grimy, which only could mean someone had taken the time to bathe me. Next to the oil lamp was a small amber snuff bottle filled with sprigs of sage.

I picked up the bottle and inhaled the soothing scent. Energized, I went to the window, taking the sage with me.

In the near distance, tipis were set up as far as I could see. Indian men wearing a mixture of traditional Indian attire and white men's clothes lounged around while the women and girls bustled about with their chores. Boys ran in and around the tipis, playing what looked like chase, but Kindle had told me its real purpose was to teach the boys about the buffalo hunt. And war. None of these Indians looked like warriors.

"Mrs. Martin! You shouldn't be out of bed."

The agency doctor stood in the doorway. I could not take my eyes from the medical bag he held. What was inside? How well did he keep his instruments? Did he have a small bottle of whisky in there for himself? His golden hair was brushed back from his tall forehead and hung in ribbons almost to his shoulders. His coarse and curly beard covered his cheeks and upper lip, leaving his cleft chin bare, like a masterpiece in a gilded frame. His appearance didn't engender much faith in his abilities.

"How long have I been in bed?"

"One day only. I recommend a week of

bed rest, at a minimum. You were severely concussed. Come, lie down." He waved me over and I obeyed. I held my bottle of sage to my chest like a child holding her dolly.

"May I sit?" I said.

"Of course."

The doctor placed his bag next to me, bent down, and looked into my eyes. His were an indistinguishable green, more moss than emerald, but kind, and much to my relief, sober. His clothes were unsoiled, merely wrinkled, and his hands were much cleaner than I would have expected.

"Follow my finger."

I did so without comment. He nodded, opened his bag, and removed a stethoscope. While he listened to my lungs and heart, I peeked into his bag and was assaulted with an overwhelming pang of anguish and longing. His instruments, though old, were well cared for and pristine. Small bottles of whisky and laudanum were tucked into a corner.

"What is your name, sir?"

"Hugh Cairns." He placed his stethoscope into his bag and buckled it. Dr. Cairns folded his hands in front of him and studied me. "Mr. Oscar tells quite a story."

Since Cairns called me *Martin,* I had to assume Kindle had told them a version of the story I spun for Bell. I didn't want to take the chance of contradicting him.

I covered my mouth and said in a shaky voice, "Did he turn the bodies of those odious men in?"

Cairns nodded. "And said you and he, along with the Indian, managed to kill them all."

"It was all so chaotic. I remember little of it, except I was terrified. But I trusted Mr. Oscar to get us through it, and he did."

Cairns pursed his lips and scrutinized me with those green eyes of his. He was used to being lied to regularly, I suspected. "You have an impressive assortment of injuries. Old and new."

I touched Cairns's arm lightly. "I feel much better now due to your care. Thank you." I stood and tried to mask my dizziness. "I would like to find Mr. Oscar."

Cairns missed nothing. He grasped my arm. "You should be in bed."

Kindle strode into the room, followed by Aénóhé'ke. I wanted to fall into his arms, and reached out to do so, but caught myself. I had no idea what story he'd told. Instead, I placed my hand on my chest and said, "Is it well and truly over?"

"Yes. It is."

I covered my mouth and turned away,

171

pretending to be overcome with emotion.

"Dr. Cairns, would you excuse us?" Kindle said.

"Of course." Cairns picked up his medical bag and walked to the door, where he turned. He motioned to Aénòhé'ke, "You, too. Out."

Aénòhé'ke glanced between us. Kindle said, "She can stay."

When the door closed, Kindle came to me and took me in his arms. "How do you feel?"

"I am getting used to being battered and bruised. What did you tell them when you turned in the bodies?"

"Agent Darlington was so thrilled to have those four in hand he didn't scrutinize my story too much. I told them what you told Bell, about your abusive husband. I'm a Good Samaritan helping you get across Indian Territory and to your family back East."

"Very clever." I decided it best not to tell Kindle he'd muddied the surnames up. Now I was Charlotte Martin. I looked forward to the day I could have an alias for longer than a day or two. "How much was the reward?"

"Cuidado was the only one with a price on his head, and only fifty dollars. The US marshal has to authorize the bounty, and he's out searching for Bell and Quinn. They don't know when he'll be back."

"We can't wait, can we?"

Kindle shook his head. "Darlington has five hundred Indians camped around his agency. He couldn't care less about us. The marshal on the other hand . . . We'll rest for a couple of days, stock up on supplies, and leave."

"What about Aénóhé'ke?"

Kindle lowered his voice. "She's part of Stone Calf's band."

"Are they here?" I whispered.

"Yes." Kindle tried to look unconcerned and failed.

"Which means what?"

"His band was with Black Kettle at Washita."

"Will they recognize you?"

"We didn't attack their camp. They were farther down the river. We should be safe."

I walked to the bed and leaned against it, my head swimming. "Why don't you rest, Laura?"

"Where am I? Whose room?"

"You're in the single men's residence. It doubles as a hotel. I have the room next door."

"Cairns is suspicious." I rubbed my forehead. "I am not sharp enough to tell effective lies."

"I'll keep him away so you can rest." Kindle rubbed my arms and kissed my forehead. "Are you hungry?"

I realized I was. "Famished."

"I'll have supper sent down."

"What time is it?"

"Almost seven."

"Good heavens. Where are you going?"

"I am going to see if the Darlington residents are talking about the Murderess and the Major." Kindle's mouth quirked up. "I'm half tempted to hunt down Henry Pope and show him how much I appreciate the name."

I looked down and away. "He got half of the title right."

Kindle lifted my chin. "Anything you've done was to survive. There's a difference. You'll feel better after you eat."

I smiled weakly. "If you say so." I climbed into bed and curled into a ball facing the window.

The dead haunted me. As a doctor sworn to help people, to preserve life, I should have felt something for these men, for my responsibility for their deaths. Instead, I felt nothing. No guilt. No remorse. If confronted with the same situations, I would do the same thing. Somewhere along the way, my instinct for survival had outstripped my instinct to heal. Even if, by some miracle, Kindle and I made it to England, I wasn't sure I would be able to take the caduceus back up, to reclaim the title of doctor when so many of my actions had flown in direct contradiction to my oath.

The sun coming through the window was muted when Aénòhé'ke returned with my supper. I sat up and she placed the tray on my lap. I stared at the plate of beans and biscuits and laughed.

Within seconds, my laughter turned to sobs.

Kindle stumbled into the room after midnight and tripped on Aénòhé'ke.

"Excuse me," Kindle said in a hoarse whisper. "What are you doing here anyway? Why aren't you with your people?"

"William." My voice was cold, angry.

"You're awake."

"I've been waiting on you."

"You shouldn't have."

"Why, so I wouldn't see how drunk you are?"

"No, because you need to rest. I'm not drunk."

"I can smell the whisky from here, William."

I could see Kindle through the gloom. He swayed on his feet as he removed his waistcoat and shirt. "Someone spilled whisky down my shirt."

"I thought Quakers were teetotalers."

"Not everyone here is a Quaker. Thank God." He draped his gun belt over the bedpost, removed his boots and trousers, and left them where they lay. He climbed into bed next to me.

"Shouldn't you be in your own room?"

"I'll leave before anyone is awake." He lay on his back, staring at the ceiling.

I moved over to make room for him.

"Don't worry. I won't touch you."

"That isn't why I moved over."

"If you say so."

My determination to reach out to Kindle and reclaim our physical connection was crushed beneath the smell of whisky on his breath and his harsh words. Instead, we each lay on our backs, hands clutched over our stomachs, staring at the ceiling. I wondered if he realized this was the first time we'd shared a real bed. Before the Red River attack, when I'd imagined this event, it wasn't in a frontier hostel with Kindle reeking of whisky and afraid to touch me —

and me not wanting him to.

"What did you find out?"

"We aren't as interesting as we think we are."

"What do you mean?"

Kindle's eyes were closed. "Everyone's talking about the governor sending Big Tree and Satanta to Huntsville instead of hanging them. I don't think anyone's connected John Oscar and Charlotte Martin to the Murderess and the Major." He smiled. "The eye patch and the beard help."

"You're going by John?"

"Yes. It was all I could think of."

Our eyes met, but neither mentioned what we were both thinking: he'd taken his brother's Christian name as an alias. "I think we should leave as soon as possible," I said.

"Day after tomorrow. We've been invited to dinner with Darlington and his family."

"You didn't say yes, did you?"

"Of course I said yes. Declining would've raised suspicions." He touched my face. "I bought you some new clothes with the money from the horses. They're in the chest. A dress and men's clothes as well. We will leave first thing, day after tomorrow."

"If you think it's safe."

He closed his eyes and settled back into

his former position. He nodded. "No one knows us here, or suspects. We will be fine for one more day."

CHAPTER 15

Before the sun rose, Aénóhé'ke and I snuck out of the bachelors' quarters and went for a walk. True to his word, Kindle woke early and stumbled to his room, pale, bleary eyed, and reeking of alcohol. It was the second night in less than a week he'd drank to excess. If I was honest with myself, I didn't like the Kindle who came to my bed when he had been drinking. He'd been on his best behavior last night, but he felt like a different man from the one I fell in love with at Fort Richardson.

If pushed to describe the Darlington Agency, I would say it was the US Army's idea of a town. Plain buildings laid out on a grid, with a wide thoroughfare leading to nowhere. The single men's quarters were at the end of the thoroughfare, with the few erected buildings spread out across a plain so flat and vast I thought I was back on the Llano Estacado.

Aénóhé'ke tugged at my sleeve and nodded in the direction of the tipis by the river. I paused, the idea of walking voluntarily into an Indian camp too terrifying to consider. Aénóhé'ke patted her chest, then pointed at me, and I knew she promised my safety. I thought again of Bell's admonishment about Aénóhé'ke. I'd always prided myself on being able to read people, especially other women. In the last few months, I'd had that particular bit of hubris thrown back in my face more than once.

"Come," she said. "Safe."

I let her lead me on.

The Indians were camped on the bank of a river that was indistinguishable from every other river I'd crossed since leaving Austin four months earlier: muddy and shallow, with cottonwood and hackberry trees clinging to its banks. Down the river a ways the banks were denuded, and I knew as the number of agency buildings increased, the number of cottonwoods and hackberries would decrease. I wondered if Cairns was cognizant of the threat of dysentery with this many people sharing the same water source. I paused and turned, instinctively wanting to discuss the situation at Fort Richardson with him. I stopped and grasped my stomach, again afflicted with the sense of longing and anguish at the loss of my profession. Aénohé'ke, ignorant of my past and what I'd lost, looked puzzled. I smiled weakly, turned from the agency, and walked toward the tipis.

The tipis were arranged by band in half circles on the bank of the river, with a large area in the center for communal gatherings for the entire tribe. Farther downstream I saw a herd of picketed horses being tended to by young braves. Women and girls were laughing and talking as they hauled water from the river. Children too young to work ran around the camps. Old men, their faces maps of wrinkles, walked toward the river.

I counted six half circles as I followed Aénohé'ke to a cluster in a place of honor next to the main area. Two dogs darted in front of me, licking their snouts and looking guilty. A woman brandishing a metal ladle pursued them, yelling admonishments in Cheyenne. She stopped when she saw us, and her irritated mien changed immediately into one of joy.

"Aénohé'ke!" Even if I had been able to understand Cheyenne, the rest of what the woman said was lost in a jumble of joyous female voices as they descended upon Aénohé'ke from seemingly nowhere. The women surrounded the young woman, touching her, all speaking at once. Aénòhé'ke's happiness at being reunited with her tribe animated her usually plain features into a thing of beauty. She spoke as loudly and rapidly as the women surrounding her who touched her injured face and gestured wildly as questions were asked and answered. How they could understand anything in the cacophony, I had no idea. I was forgotten, or unnoticed, pushed back by the crowd of women until I found myself surrounded by a gaggle of curious children talking as rapidly as their mothers and grandmothers.

Little hands touched and patted me as if making sure I was real. One little girl turned my injured palm up, touched the bandage, and raised her eyebrows, as if knowing instinctively I didn't understand a word of what they said. Her eyes were so large, brown, and innocent I couldn't help but smile and answer, "I burned my hand." I mimed touching my hand and pulling it back quickly, and said, "Ouch."

The children went silent and all stared at me in astonishment. "Burn," I said. One little boy said something, and the chatter resumed, but now it had the tenor of an argument. The little boy tried to lift my skirt. I quickly removed his hand and said,

182

"No." The little girl who asked about my hand stepped in front of me and appeared to be my defender. She turned, poked my breast with her finger, and returned to arguing with the little boy. I kept hearing the same phrase over and over, from all the children now. I was perplexed and searched for Aénôhé'ke, but she was nowhere to be found. Instead, Bob Johnson walked up. "They are debating if you are a man or woman."

"Heavens. And have they decided?"

He spoke to the children, who had quieted on his arrival. They continued their fierce debate until he held up his hand. He said one word and my little defender raised her nose in the air, crossed her arms, and nodded. The little boy waved the girl away and walked off, disgusted at being bested by a girl, most like.

The little girl looked up at me and said the phrase they had been repeating.

"She's given you a name," Bob Johnson said.

I knew Indian names were given based on any number of signs, events, or characteristics of the baby, even when they weren't necessarily complimentary. I thought of Little Stick and his unfortunate name. "I'm afraid to ask."

Bob Johnson smiled. "Talks Like a Man Woman."

"Oh." I glanced down at the little girl who was obviously proud of naming me. "Thank you," I said. I touched my fingers to my chin and brought them forward. "I suppose it could be worse," I said to Bob Johnson. Today he wore a breastplate adorned with bone beads over a Union soldier's coat with golden epaulets on the shoulders. His hair was braided on either side of his head, on top of which sat a tall hat with a turkey feather stuck in the headband. "You look nice this morning. What is the occasion?"

He nodded upstream. "There is a photographer from the East here taking pictures."

"Indeed?" One more person to avoid. "Have you had your picture taken before?"

"No. Have you?"

"Once. I wish I had smiled. No one ever smiles. We will be viewed by people in the future as a dour, unhappy lot with our serious expressions."

"I should smile?"

I chuckled. "Probably not. The photographer will tell you to look serious and will think the smile ruined the picture."

"How do you feel this morning?"

"Woozy, but better. Thank you."

"Where is John Oscar?"

"Asleep, I think."

"Tell him if he has questions he should come to me."

I furrowed my brow. "Why?"

"He is not . . ." Bob Johnson eyes searched the sky as if it would provide the word he needed. "Unobvious."

"Subtle?"

He pointed. "Yes. Subtle."

I thought of Kindle stumbling drunk. If people weren't suspecting us before, they probably were now. Bob Johnson watched me and I wondered if he'd put two and two together.

"Your English is good. Where did you learn it?"

"My father was a white man. Had a trading post up on the Arkansas River. My mother was Cheyenne. When she died, my father sent me to school in Saint Louis, married my mother's sister, and had four more children. The Cheyenne culture is matrilineal. When I returned, my mother's clan took me in."

"Those men who were killed, they were your father's sons?"

A hint of a smile crossed Bob Johnson's face. "They were Arapaho. We are allies, the Cheyenne and Arapaho."

"You cheated us."

185

"I learned my negotiating tactics at the foot of my white father, and more recently, the American Army."

"You work for the Army?" I stared at the officer's coat he wore.

Bob Johnson nodded. "I have not always been on their side but now I am a tracker and interpreter."

The little girl took my hand and tugged me toward a tipi and said the one Cheyenne word I recognized: "Aénȯhé'ke."

"I'm being summoned. Excuse me."

I let the girl lead me away and I thought of Bob Johnson. He was shrewd and I suspected his loyalties shifted based on what would benefit him in the moment. I would need to talk to Kindle about him.

We stopped outside the largest tipi in the semicircle. The top was blackened from years of smoke. A stick figure representing a woman was painted above the door. In one hand she held a spray of flowers and leaves, in the other she held a stick of fire. Above her head were dots with tails trailing up toward the moon. The girl was halfway in the tipi and tugged on my hand again. I pulled my hand from hers and stepped back.

I pressed my hands against my throbbing temples as images of a similar tipi I entered as a battered and abused captive flooded my mind. Yahuea Muea beating me with a stick. Anna helping me bandage my hands on the bank of a creek. Cotter Black sitting across the fire from me. A horse neighed in the distance. Someone touched my shoulder. I yelped and jumped away.

Aénòhé'ke stood next to me, hand outstretched, a contemplative expression on her face. Aénòhé'ke waited while I calmed my rapid breathing. "I should go back," I said, pointing in the direction from which we came. "You have found your family, and I am glad. You are safe now."

Of course, I knew it to be a lie. She would be bombarded with memories of being raped in the weeks and months to come. Possibly for her entire life. The idea I might never be free of what happened revolted me. Would the sound of water splashing and horses neighing always bring the Canadian River into my mind? Would Kindle ever be able to touch me without me flinching, without me thinking of warriors standing over me, waiting their turns?

Aénòhé'ke moved to stand mere inches from me. She took my right hand and ran her thumb over my knotty fingers, fingers that had been broken by the Comanche, fingers that Kindle massaged daily, almost absently, fingers that were becoming more limber and aching less as a result. Her dark eyes bored into mine and she placed her left hand on my shoulder. "Laura, *you* are safe."

My skin hummed and tingled where Aénóhé'ke touched me. A feeling of contentment and well-being washed over me. I wanted to bottle this feeling and carry it with me so whenever memories intruded I could unstopper it and be soothed with a sip. I believed happiness was possible and a surge of affection for Aénóhé'ke flowed from me like a river. She returned my smile and pulled me toward the tipi. I followed, as trusting as a child. I walked into the tipi, and as my eyes adjusted to the darkness, the realization of what she'd said hit me.

Aénóhé'ke knelt down to the right of the woman who sat in the place of honor. All of the Cheyenne women who had crowded Aénóhé'ke outside sat on their knees around the fire and watched me expectantly.

"Aénóhé'ke?" I said.

"Yes?"

"You speak English."

"Please, sit."

The woman in the center was younger than I would have expected the leader to be. She motioned to the vacant place next to her. When I moved to the right, a woman shooed me to the left and motioned for me to walk on the outside of the circle. I did, and sat to the left of the woman whose tent I suspected I was in. I sat on my knees as the other women did.

My young defender walked to the woman in the center and gave her a small tin cup. The woman smiled her thanks and turned toward me with the cup cradled in her hands. She drank from the cup and offered it to me and I repeated her actions. She then passed the cup to Aénóhé'ke who sent it around the circle. After everyone had drank, the woman spoke.

"Thank you for bringing my daughter back to me."

I dipped my head in acknowledgment.

"You saved Aénóhé'ke from savage men. She is in your debt."

"There is no debt."

"You paid for her."

"I did, but to free her, not to own her. She has found her family and is happy. It is payment enough."

"A white woman who doesn't expect something from an Indian. You are a rare person indeed, Talks Like a Man Woman."

"You know my name, but I do not know yours."

189

"My name is too difficult for white men to say. They call me Falling Stars Woman. Running Brook named you Talks Like a Man Woman, but Aénòhé'ke says your name is Charlotte." The English name fell from her tongue with difficulty.

Kindle and I had talked around Aénòhé'ke, thinking she did not understand what we said. Was she now one more person whom I couldn't trust? "Yes. And you can speak English."

"Yes. I learned from one of our captives when I was a child," Aénòhé'ke said.

"Weren't you a captive?"

"I adopted her," Falling Stars Woman said. "I had lost my daughter to a raid and Stone Calf brought her to me to replace her."

"So you stole another woman's child to assuage your grief?"

"I do not know that word."

"Did you ever give a thought to the other woman's feelings about losing Aénòhé'ke?"

Falling Stars Woman shrugged. "It has always been done this way. Though our way of life is coming to an end. The white man wants to turn us into children who rely on him for handouts, to plant us in the ground like corn, instead of letting us roam our land as our ancestors did for hundreds of winters."

I thought of my abduction and abuse at the hands of Comanche warriors, of the Salt Creek attack, of Aénóhé'ke being stolen from her true family with the possibility of never seeing them again. "It is not a way of life I would mourn. The violence, the uncertainty. At least with our way you will not live in fear of being attacked and killed, of your children being taken away. Freedom from fear is a better life than violence begot by a freedom to roam."

A man's voice carried through the tipi. Falling Stars Woman called out and the flap of the tipi flew open as he entered and walked to the right, talking loudly in Cheyenne. The women around the circle who had been silent until then rose and left with knowing smiles on their faces. Falling Stars Woman stood and spoke as loudly and as quickly as the man. They talked over each other until the man stopped suddenly. He stared at me, then at Aénóhé'ke as Falling Stars Woman continued to speak, gesturing between the two of us. The old man smiled and patted Aénóhé'ke on the head before planting a kiss there. Aénóhé'ke grasped his hand, kissed it, and said something to him. He patted her shoulder, then turned back to Falling Stars Woman and continued his harangue, this time with gestures. Aénóhé'ke rose and motioned for me to follow her out of the tipi. The man ignored me completely.

Once out in the bright sunlight, Aénóhé'ke said, "He is searching for the medal the Great Father gave him when he visited Washington in forty-six. He thinks Falling Stars Woman put it somewhere wrong when she was cleaning."

I smiled and thought of the same argument Maureen used to have with my father who would invariably find the missing item precisely where it should have been.

"Why didn't you tell me you could speak English?"

"It was the only defense I had. Listening to the men who raped me, knowing about their plans, was the only chance I would have to escape. I wanted to know why you helped me."

My throat constricted. "And do you?"

"No."

"Wouldn't you help a woman being violated as you were?"

"If she was the enemy of my people, no."

"Even now, with what you went through, you would stand by and let it happen?"

"We understand it is what happens when we are taken. It is why our men fight so

192

when we are attacked by our enemies, to allow their women and children to escape."

"If your warriors return today with a female captive and violate her, you will stand by and watch it happen? Knowing what *your enemy* is going through?" When Aénòhé'ke didn't answer I said, "I do not hate anyone so much I would allow them to suffer that." My throat closed up and I turned away and thought of how a Comanche woman had hated me on sight, had relished beating me. That the Comanche considered me her enemy I fully believed. Aénòhé'ke and Falling Stars Woman, on the other hand, had taken me in and treated me as an honored guest.

"I would never let it happen to you," Aénòhé'ke said in a quiet voice. "I owe you a debt."

"You owe me nothing."

"You have been through what I have. It is why you helped me."

I nodded once.

"White men or Indian?"

"Comanche." Aénòhé'ke inhaled. "Somewhere on the Canadian, I was told. We'd ridden through the night. I had no idea where we were, don't remember anything about the place other than the sound of water, laughing men, and their grunting." I

193

turned my head away and tears leaked from my eyes. I remembered more; I remembered everything. But I did not need to explain my experience to Aénóhé'ke. "I have no love for your kind, but when I found Tuesday in the tent with you, I didn't see an Indian being violated. I saw a helpless woman." I sniffed and wiped my eyes. "I would do it again. For anyone. I only wish I'd killed Tuesday with my bare hands."

I lifted my hand to shield my eyes from the sun. A sharp pain pierced my temple. "What is wrong?" Aénóhé'ke asked.

"Nothing." Maybe Dr. Cairns would have laudanum. The thought of floating away from everything was enticing. The old man walked past wearing a large silver medal. "Who is he?"

"Falling Stars Woman's father, Tall Buffalo. He is the medicine man of Stone Calf's tribe."

"Is he how you learned of the thistle tea?" My burned arm was now bandaged with one Dr. Cairns had applied, but Aénóhé'ke's crude bandage had been more soothing.

"Yes, and Falling Stars Woman. Her medicine is better than her father's, but no one in the tribe will say so."

"Sounds familiar," I murmured.

Tall Buffalo and other men, all dressed

carefully, formed a loose cluster and walked upriver, each inspecting the others' choices of attire. At least I assumed it was the subject, based on their gestures and laughter. Falling Stars Woman returned carrying two long sticks sharpened at one end and padded with hide at the other. She shook her head with a smile and spoke in Cheyenne to Aénóhé'ke, who laughed.

Falling Stars Woman interpreted for me. "If it would've been a snake, it would have bit him."

"Thank you for your hospitality," I said. "I must get back."

"Come tonight. We will be celebrating Aénóhé'ke's return."

"Thank you, but we are to have dinner with Mr. Darlington, I believe."

"You will be finished before the sun sets," said Aénóhé'ke. "We celebrate under the stars."

"Bring your husband," Falling Stars Woman said.

"Mr. Oscar isn't my husband," I said.

"Aénóhé'ke said he was."

I remembered Aénóhé'ke witnessing me satiating Kindle at the whisky camp. "Oh. I'll bring him," I said.

Falling Stars Woman waved and returned to her work, Aénóhé'ke following, laughing and talking with the other women. I searched my memory for a time when I'd had such camaraderie with a group of women and came up blank. I seemed to form attachments with individuals easier than groups, as evidenced by my relationships with my cousin Charlotte, Maureen, Camille, Harriet in the end, and now Aénóhé'ke. I had always striven to break into the men's world instead of being content to live with the women. Nothing about the female situation appealed to me, even now, but as I watched the women go about their work together, I wondered at what I'd lost.

CHAPTER 16

I returned to the room to find Kindle looking rumpled and sewing the bottom of my saddlebag.

"Where have you been?" His voice sounded like sandpaper on wood, giving further lie to his assertion of sobriety the night before. I walked to the chest and poured a glass of water.

"I walked with Aénóhé'ke to her tribe, drank some rather delicious tea — at least I think it was tea — and returned. How do you feel?"

"Fine. Why do you ask?"

He obviously hadn't looked in a mirror and didn't seem in the mood to admit his intoxication from the night before. "No reason." I sat on the bed next to him and handed him the water. He drank, watching me.

"Thank you." He went back to his work.

"You're welcome." I held the glass and

watched him sew. He used a piece of leather to push the thick needle through the small holes. "Why are you sewing my saddlebag?"

"I've put half our money as well as your necklace inside." He lifted the saddlebag to look at the bottom. It was slightly bulky, but it wasn't too noticeable.

"Excellent job."

"Would you like to take over, considering your advanced needlepoint skills?" His mouth quirked up into a half smile.

"No, I will do my best Aunt Emily impression and sit here and point out your deficiencies."

"I cannot wait to meet Aunt Emily."

"I hope we live long enough to meet her."

"Of course we will."

"Hmm. It is easier with such a large needle if you push up." I sipped the remaining water and put the glass on the side table. "She has a weakness for men in uniform. She would never admit a weakness for anything, but Charlotte and I used to watch and laugh at how her eyes lit up when officers would attend the balls."

"Charlotte is your cousin?"

"Yes."

"And the inspiration for your name?"

"Yes." I pointed to his work. "If you use the same hole it would be much easier."

When he didn't continue my eyes met his. "Are you sure you don't want to do this?" he said.

"Quite." I held up my hands. The fingers on my right could have been the fingers of an octogenarian with severe arthritis, and the left was burned.

"Of course." He put his work down and lightly grasped my hands. He caressed my knobby right hand. "Can you?" Kindle made a fist.

I tried and succeeded in forming a claw. "It's better since you've been massaging it. I can shoot a gun, but I couldn't save the life of the victim. Which I suppose out here is more important."

He massaged my hand. "Does this hurt or feel good?"

"A little of both. But do not stop."

I watched his long, slender fingers rub my hand before moving to each individual finger. I switched my gaze to his face and saw his brows furrowed in concentration. "One of the first things I noticed about you was your hands," I said, voice low. "They look like the hands of an artist, not a cavalry officer."

His eyes met mine, but his massaging didn't stop. "I was a pianist, not an artist."

My head jerked back in surprise. "Were you?"

Kindle nodded and focused again on my hands. "My mother taught me. My father thought it was a sissy thing for a boy to do, so of course John thought so as well. My father forbid it, so my mother could teach me only when my father and John weren't around. The slaves hated my father and adored my mother so they kept our secret. They kept a watch out for whenever my father or John would return. My mother would slide to the middle of the bench and I would retire to a chair where I read something appropriately masculine." His hands stopped and he gazed into the middle distance. "God, she played beautifully. She was partial to Bach, but could also play a reel for the slaves to dance to." He took my index finger and bent it up and down, slowly. "After I tried to help the slave, Cotter, escape, we stopped."

"Why?"

He silently flexed my finger for a minute, and moved to the middle finger. "My father questioned all the slaves. There was no way a child and a slave could have planned an escape without anyone else knowing, he said. We weren't stupid enough to tell the other slaves." He moved to my ring finger.

"You told your mother, didn't you?"

He nodded. "My father found out and broke her hand as punishment." I inhaled sharply as he moved to my pinky finger. "The doctor'd treated my mother enough to know what went on. My mother didn't leave her room for six weeks. When the doc returned to remove her cast, I heard him tell my mother's slave to massage her hand daily, multiple times, to help her get her mobility back. When I visited Mother for the first time I didn't recognize her. She'd aged ten years in six weeks. I came in every day after breakfast and massaged her hand. She never said a word. She never left her room again."

"William."

"Flex your fingers like this." He waved his fingers into a fist. I did, and was surprised at how they felt slightly more limber. "Better?"

"Yes."

He lifted my hand and kissed my fingers, lingering there. He looked me in the eye. "Every day. After breakfast."

"Yes, sir."

He cocked an eyebrow. "Yes, sir? I like the sound of that."

I nudged my shoulder against his. "Get back to work." He took up his needle and sewed. I put my hand on his back and rubbed it in circles. "Will you play for me someday?"

He nodded. "Do you play?"

"Heavens, no. Nor do I sing. I tell you my only talent was needlepoint. It is nigh on impossible to land a suitable husband when all you can offer is a beautifully stitched pillow or a screen. Though I never had the patience to finish a screen."

"I appreciate your stitching skills."

"I hope I never have to use them on you again. How are your shoulder and thigh by the way? I have been so focused on my own injuries, I have forgotten to check on yours."

"I am fine."

"I will check when you finish."

"Laura, I am fine."

"Would you please let me do something for you?"

"I wish you could finish this saddlebag."

"You're persistent." I walked to the small mirror hanging over the chest. When I'd dressed earlier the room had been too dim to see well. I wished for the dimness now as I saw myself for the first time in two weeks.

My honey blond hair had faded to almost white and was the texture of straw. My skin was tanned and small lines that hadn't been there before radiated from the corners of my eyes. My lips were cracked and my forehead was bruised from where Tuesday had banged my head into the ground. I turned away, covered my face with my hands, and burst into tears.

Kindle was across the room and holding me in his arms in a trice. He didn't speak or shush me, but allowed me to vent my feelings, soggily, into his shoulder.

"I cannot do this," I said, in between sobs. "I don't recognize myself. I mistrust everyone and I am exhausted. Oh, how exhausted I am. I want to sleep for days."

He led me to the bed and I lay down. He lay down next to me and pulled me onto my side, facing him. He held my hands gently, pushed a stray piece of hair behind my ear, and waited for my sobs to subside. I reached up and covered his eyes. "Don't look at me."

"Why?"

"William, you know why."

"I thought I was the dandy between the two of us."

"Two weeks on the trail made you look rugged and handsomer. I, on the other hand, look like my aunt's charwoman."

He pulled my hand away. "Laura, you're being ridiculous."

I turned over and away from him but

pulled his arm close to my chest and nestled back against him. "I've always been vainer than I care to admit. One of the most difficult parts of being a doctor was diminishing my looks. No one takes a handsome woman seriously about anything but marriage, family, and housekeeping. Possibly charity, which is the one allowed outside interest." I sighed. "I love beautiful clothes, wearing them, shopping for them. It was the one thing Aunt Emily and I had in common. And, my hair was beautiful."

"It will be again."

I knew Kindle was trying to make me feel better, but his subtle admission about the state of my hair stung.

"I was given a name by one of the Cheyenne girls."

"Were you?"

I nodded.

"Are you going to make me guess?"

I sighed, wondering why I had brought it up. "Talks Like a Man Woman."

When Kindle remained silent I turned slightly and looked over my shoulder at him. He was smiling. "It isn't funny."

"It's perfect for you, and not because your voice sounds like a man."

I turned away from him again. "You think it does. I knew it."

"No, Laura." He moved my hair away from my neck and kissed it, sending shivers down my spine, awakening a memory of a disheveled desk, a broken lantern, and the soft patter of rain on a window. "You've always had a husky voice, and I love it. No, it's perfect because you speak your mind like a man."

"Hmm."

Kindle pulled my collar away and kissed the top of my shoulder. "You are as beautiful to me today as the day I met you."

"Would that be dressed as a man and covered in blood at Antietam, or dressed like a woman and covered in blood in Texas?"

"I was thinking of the woman I was with in the fort library the last night at Fort Richardson. She was the real you. She's who I see when I look at you."

I blushed remembering how eager I was, how much I enjoyed laying with Kindle. How his touch woke something in me, even now, though my mind struggled with visions of other men.

He pulled me closer and tucked his knees into mine. "We fit together nicely."

"We do."

"This isn't the worst bed I've slept in on the frontier, but it's nothing compared to what waits for us in Saint Louis."

"At the orphanage?"

"Yes."

"Tell me."

"It's a feather bed, left over from the plantation days. It's like what I imagine sleeping on a cloud would be like. You will sleep like a baby."

"Not with the way you snore."

"I don't snore."

I looked over my shoulder. "Yes, you do."

"I don't believe you. But" — he kissed me on the cheek — "to be safe I will leave so you can get some rest."

I put my hand out to stop him from rising. "Don't leave. We so rarely get to be truly alone."

He settled back into the bed, one arm protectively across my waist, the other beneath my head.

I breathed deeply, listening to the distant sounds of the daily activities of the agency. Animals tramping down the street, the ringing of an anvil, the creak and jingle of wagons pulled by mules. Kindle's chest rose and fell against my back in a steady, comforting rhythm, his arm heavy and secure around me, his legs molded to mine. I was safe. Protected. Loved.

My stomach flipped with nervousness and

fear. I moved Kindle's hand to my breast. His breath caught.

"Are you sure?"

I swallowed and willed my voice to be steady. "Yes. I'm sure."

Kindle rolled off the bed, went to the door, and wedged a chair beneath the doorknob. I sat on the edge of the bed and watched him check the curtain was closed across the lone window. When he approached the bed, I stood to meet him. With my knees shaking beneath my skirt, I unbuttoned my bodice, and steeled myself to reclaim what had been taken from me.

"Where are you taking me?"

I'd been asleep for hours when Kindle woke me with a kiss on my cheek. I had been trying to wake for a while, dreaming my eyes would not open, even when I tried to pry them open with my fingers. Panic was setting in when Kindle's soft whiskers and warm breath tickled my cheek. "I have a surprise for you."

Outside, the late-afternoon sun was low in the sky and a herd of cattle lowed in dismay as they were herded down the middle of the street. Soldiers waved their hands, whistled, and slapped lassos against their legs to keep the stupid beasts moving. Many of the animals, frightened or possibly plain mean, defecated puddles of shit onto the muddy street.

"The allotment arrived," Kindle said over the noise. He pointed down the street to a long line of wagons waiting to be checked over by an older gentleman with long gray hair flowing from a flat-billed hat. "Brinton Darlington," Kindle said.

"If you tell me my surprise is lowing cattle, I might hit you."

His mouth quirked up on one side and his eyes twinkled. My heart flopped around in my chest like a fish on dry land. Kindle looked happier than he'd been since Fort Richardson. Surely, it wasn't due to the uncomfortable bout of love making from a few hours earlier?

After, when Kindle had left me to rest alone, I lay in bed staring at the ceiling as his seed trickled out of me, and waited for the pain between my legs to subside. Despite Kindle's gentleness, it was like he'd taken a scalpel to me. I'd pulled my skirt up, found I wasn't bleeding — thank the Lord — and decided the time had come to assess my injuries as a doctor would. I reset the chair beneath the door handle, removed the mirror from the wall, and steeled myself for the worst.

Dr. Ezra Kline had treated me when Kindle brought me back to Jacksboro after the events on the Canadian and in Palo Duro Canyon. Ezra and my father had been friends since medical school, and since my father's death, Ezra had been like a father to me. His son James had been a lifelong friend — briefly my lover — and helped me escape New York when the Langtons leveled the murder accusation against me. I am sure Ezra never imagined he would one day have to tend to me the way he did. What would have been going through his mind as he sewed me up and terminated my pregnancy, I have no idea. But, he had done a superb job. Outwardly, I was healed. I wouldn't know the extent of the internal damage until my menses did or did not come.

Even staring at Kindle during the act didn't banish the images from the Canadian. Knowing he wanted me despite what had happened didn't make me want him. There had been no physical connection, no reclamation of the passion I remembered. I'd wanted only for it to be over and for him to leave so I could cry in peace.

Now, though, standing on the porch of the house and seeing the man I fell in love with for the first time in weeks, knowing I could make him happy with little effort, I knew I would give myself to him when he asked and hope over time it would get easier, and more pleasurable.

I touched his cheek. "I am beginning to like your beard."

"Are you? Because I'm looking forward to the day you shave it off. Come on." He picked me up off the ground and cradled me in his arms. I squealed in surprise and he marched across the muddy road.

"What are you doing?"

"I am being chivalrous and carrying you across the road."

"You are going to throw your back out."

"You'll have to fatten up considerably for me to throw my back out carrying you, Slim."

"We're across the road. You can put me down now."

"Now I'm proving a point."

"You're incorrigible."

"Which is one of the reasons you love me. Admit it."

"Fine, I admit it. Tell me where you are taking me."

"And ruin the surprise?"

I sighed dramatically and laid my head on his shoulder.

"And you, my dear, have a penchant for

210

the dramatic."

"I do not," I said.

"You do. You dramatize the trivial and downplay the significant."

"Would you like for me to be dramatic all the time?"

"No. You have the perfect balance. Though I would like it if you would lean on me a bit more."

"I cannot lean on you any more than I am currently."

He stopped at the front door of a house and set me down. "You know what I mean, Laura. You aren't alone anymore. Let me take care of you. Protect you."

"William, you have been protecting me."

He looked away and pressed his lips together. "Not well enough."

I touched his chin and forced him to face me. "So many have died in your efforts to protect me."

His eyes narrowed and his voice was harsh. "I don't care about the fucking bounty hunters, Laura. Or Bell's gang."

I dropped my hand and looked away. Grime-covered soldiers and cowboys walked down the wide thoroughfare searching for a bath and a shave most like. They seemed harmless enough, but I wondered if faced with a situation such as Washita or Sand

Creek or the whisky traders' camp, would they take advantage of a weaker, helpless woman? Would I ever be able to look at a man without fear that if given the chance they would do me harm?

"What happened to me," I said, voice thick, "wasn't your fault." I forced myself to meet Kindle's eyes and to give strength to my statement, one I almost believed.

Kindle grabbed my upper arms. "Do not absolve me. You begged me to stay with you and I refused. I will never forgive myself."

"If you would have stayed, you would have been killed like all the other men. And I would be God knows where at the mercy of your brother."

"I've been a weak man for a long time. No more. I will do whatever I need to do to protect you. If that means killing a hundred more bounty hunters, then so be it." He knocked on the door.

I pulled back, horrified. "I don't want you to kill a hundred men for me."

The door opened and a petite old woman dressed in the plain attire of a Quaker opened the door. Her hair was wet at the temples and her sleeves were rolled up to her elbows.

"John Oscar, I was beginning to wonder if you were coming. And this must be Charlotte. I'm Isabel Darlington. Come in, come in."

Kindle motioned for me to enter and followed.

The house was simply built, with a center hall running the length of the building to a kitchen, and two rooms off each side of the hall. The front left room was an office, the right front a parlor, and the two rear rooms were bedrooms. Each room was sparsely decorated in the Quaker way. Small bottles of wildflowers set about on tables were the only nod to extravagance.

The old woman motioned for us to follow her to one of the bedrooms. "This way, this way. Now, I have one more pail of water to bring."

"Mrs. Darlington, I asked you to not do that. I don't want you to hurt yourself."

"Mr. Oscar, you are so kind, but I have been hauling water my entire life."

"You will not haul water today. Allow me." Kindle rolled his sleeves up as he went into the kitchen.

Mrs. Darlington pursed her lips, but there was a twinkle in her eyes. "That is a fine young man. Come on, then. Let me show you what he has arranged."

I walked into the bedroom behind Mrs. Darlington, dazed, and gasped when I saw steam wafting up from a large metal tub.

"Now, you are probably wondering what a Friend is doing with an extravagance like a sit-down tub, and it's a fair question. The answer is this: I love a soak now and then. Brinton allows it for medicinal purposes, old bones and all. And between us, he's known to soak in it every now and then himself. Ah, here he is."

Kindle held two buckets of water in his hands. He poured one, then the other into the tub, straightened, and smiled. "We've been on the road too long. You deserve a real bath."

"I have soap and a washcloth for you, and an egg, honey, and oil mixture for your hair. Mr. Oscar said your hair is a lamentation to you. This will make it feel fine, trust me. Now we will leave you to it. There are clothes for you on the bed. When you're done, dinner'll be ready." She shooed Kindle out in front of her and I was left alone with the bath of steaming water. After staring at the bath in astonishment for a minute, I undressed quickly, leaving my clothes in a pile on the floor, and settled into the tub with a contented sigh.

I leaned my head back against the edge of the tub, and let the water envelop me in its warm embrace. The only sound was the slap of water against metal, and eventually, that too stopped. I estimated I had ten minutes before the water began cooling and had intended to think of nothing at all and would have if the door hadn't opened.

I expected Mrs. Darlington, but instead saw Kindle sneaking in and closing the door softly.

"Mr. Oscar, whatever would our Friend think?"

"She's across the way at her daughter's house." He leaned against the door. "How is your bath?"

"Exquisite. Thank you. What is the matter? It looks as if the door is holding you up."

"It may be."

"Why? Are you sick? I never checked your shoulder and thigh."

"No, I am fine. I . . ." He sighed, and stepped forward. "We will be in Saint Louis in a week. There is a church there. I know a man who will marry us under our real names. We can be whoever we want after, but our pasts are as bound together as our future."

"Did you come in here to ask me to marry you?"

Kindle chuckled. "No. I came because the thought of you feet away in a warm tub was

215

too enticing to pass up." His eyes settled on the water covering me. "I told you I was a weak man."

"What you consider weak, I consider honorable."

Kindle laughed. "Honorable?"

"A weak man wouldn't be standing by the door."

"My view is better than you think." Kindle moved forward, his eyes resolutely on mine. "Laura, will you marry me when we arrive in Saint Louis?"

"I would marry you tonight if everyone didn't already think I was married."

Kindle grinned and stepped back toward the door. "Better hurry. The concoction Mrs. Darlington gave you should sit on your hair for a few minutes. Don't want to rinse it in cold water, do you?" He winked at me, opened the door, and left.

I dunked under the water. Despite all I'd been through Kindle loved me, wanted to marry me. His bastard of a brother had been wrong about everything. I grinned and sat up, water sloshing over the side of the tub. Happiness bubbled up within me and burst forth in a peal of laughter. I reached for the soap and shampooed my hair, wondering what our wedding would be like, thinking about our wedding bed — our real wedding bed — and was determined to do whatever I could to enjoy it. I supposed I needed to filch some vegetable oil from Mrs. Darlington.

I rinsed my hair and put the honey-and-egg mixture on, the question of how Kindle knew so much about a woman's hair treatment flitting through my mind and back out, chased away by images of a happy future.

CHAPTER 17

A new woman left the Darlingtons' bedroom. Refreshed, relaxed, and looking forward instead of back, I wondered what Kindle would think about my transformation. Did my appearance match my inner happiness? A quick glance in the small mirror on the wall said it did. Quite possibly, it was the improvement in my hair. It would take months for it to grow long, but for the moment, it was downy soft and framed my face rather fetchingly, though nothing could keep me from looking like a Quaker in the plain gray dress I wore.

The kitchen was chaotic with women working. But it became quickly apparent Isabel Darlington was fully in command. She directed her charges with a smile and a please and thank-you and the women responded quickly, efficiently, and without rancor. Mrs. Darlington caught sight of me in the doorway and her face bloomed with joy.

"Why, Mrs. Martin, I wouldn't have known you!"

The younger women stopped what they were doing in unison and stared at me. To a one, they wore plain gray dresses with white collars. Their hair was pulled back severely from their faces into buns at the napes of their respective necks. I wondered how Mrs. Darlington could tell them apart.

"I cannot thank you enough for the bath."

The women went back to work. "Well, it did a wonder on you, and that's a fact. Mr. Oscar is outside talking to a new arrival. Can't remember his name. He keeps looking toward the house, waiting for you to emerge."

"The new man?"

Mrs. Darlington laughed. "No, you silly goose. Mr. Oscar. I think he's harboring stronger feelings than a mere Good Samaritan." She raised an eyebrow and flapped her hands at me. "Go on, put the poor man out of his misery."

"Are you sure I cannot help?"

"What a sweet offer, but you'll just gum up the works."

She didn't realize how right she was. Maureen had shooed me out of the kitchen more times than I could count. I suspected I wasn't as incapable as Maureen said, but she had preferred to be in control of everything around her. Maureen and Mrs. Darlington would have gotten along like a house on fire.

Two long tables with benches were set up behind the house. Uncut by trees, the plains stretched out to the west, where the sun sat low and bloodred on the horizon. I shielded my eyes against it and searched for Kindle. He saw me, peeled off from a clump of men, and strode over. I grinned. Despite being clean and put together, his eye patch, beard, and longish black hair made him look like a pirate. A teasing comment tickled the tip of my tongue, until Kindle got closer and I saw his expression.

"Pope's here."

"The pope?"

Kindle chuckled. "Yes. The Holy See is touring Indian Country." He shook his head. "Henry Pope, the bastard who gave us the Murderess and the Major moniker."

I leaned to the right and peeked around Kindle's shoulder. Sure enough, there was Henry Pope, watching us, his thumbs hooked in the armholes of his vest. He saw me, touched a finger to his derby, and grinned.

"Good Lord, can't anything ever be easy?"

"The good news is he seems to be playing along. Didn't flinch when he met me, though he did snigger at my eye patch. I don't blame him. I look ridiculous."

"He's jealous. He could never pull an eye patch off like you do."

Kindle raised his eyebrows. "You like it."

"More than I should. Enough about the eye patch. We can flirt with each other later. What are we going to do about Henry Pope? What is he doing here anyway?"

"He's touring Indian Territory to write a story about them. He heard about Soule at Sill and decided to follow him. Maybe pool their resources."

"Who's Soule?"

"The photographer set up by the river." Kindle lifted my hand and pressed his lips to my fingers. "You look beautiful, by the way."

I tilted my head to the side. "Thank you for my bath."

He touched my hair. "I miss your long hair."

"Mrs. Martin!" Henry Pope walked up, and Kindle's face turned to granite. We met Pope together. Mrs. Darlington and her helpers went past carrying food-laden dishes. "How nice to meet you!"

I smiled. "You must be the newspaperman Mr. Oscar told me about."

Henry Pope turned slightly to watch the women walk out of earshot and turned back. "Miss Bennett."

I kept my sweet smile. "I don't know who you are referring to. Do you, Mr. Oscar?"

"Nope."

"Mrs. Martin. Charlotte?" Henry Pope said.

I inclined my head. "Mr. Pope." I stepped forward and turned serious. "How are you feeling? Have you recovered from your injuries?"

Henry Pope's head jerked back slightly, as if astonished. "I'm better, thank you."

"I wanted to visit you, but I wasn't allowed to leave my room, for obvious reasons. I'm so sorry for what you went through, and any part I might have played in it, though unintentional."

Pope studied me. "Cotter Black was insane."

"Yes, he was."

"Are you going to turn us in?" Kindle said, dispensing with any pretense of civility.

Henry Pope switched his gaze to Kindle. "I should. I took a beating from your brother, because of you." Pope pulled his mouth open to show a row of broken back teeth. I stepped forward and inspected them.

"Are you in much pain?"

Pope patted his coat pocket. "Nothing my flask can't help."

"Even if I had a full complement of my medical tools, I don't think there's anything I could do to help you." I pursed my lips in thought. "I know an excellent dentist in New York City, if you're going that way."

"I'm not sure where I'm going."

"I'll write the name down for you, just in case. Obviously, I'd rather you not mention who referred you."

Pope stared at me beneath furrowed brows.

"I can see you're still unsure about turning me in. If you could just wait until we eat a good meal?" I said with a smile. "I would like to have one night with a semblance of normalcy."

"No need to ruin a good meal with retribution and revenge," Pope said.

Pope turned and walked toward the tables, which were now set with food. I put my arm through Kindle's and said, "William, let me deal with Henry Pope."

"Do you think you can manipulate him into letting us go?"

I grimaced. "*Manipulate* is such a harsh

word. I prefer *sway*. Don't get jealous if I flirt shamelessly with him."

Kindle's mouth quirked up. "Poor Henry. He doesn't stand a chance."

I winked at Kindle and was stepping over the bench to sit next to Henry Pope so I could bombard him with charm when Mrs. Darlington stopped me. "This is the men's table. The women sit over there. After the men are served."

Kindle squeezed my hand in warning. He knew being relegated to the females' table would chafe Catherine Bennett or Laura Elliston, and it did. Charlotte Martin, however, wouldn't care in the least. I smiled my most vacuous, charming smile and said, "Well, of course we do." I stepped away from the table and released Kindle's hand. "Are you sure I can't help you serve?"

"Not at all. You're our guest. You go make yourself comfortable."

I cut my eyes to Kindle, who was trying not to laugh, and went to the women's table with a forced smile.

I sat facing the west and watched the sun set. The one redeeming feature of the vastness of the plains was the stunning display of color Mother Nature put on every night at sunset. A breeze fluttered the simple tablecloth and I reached out to keep it from flying. Two young men whom I hadn't noticed lunged to help.

"Thank you," I said. "It almost got away from me." I stood at the end of the table and straightened the cloth while one of the men did the same on the other side.

The tall man, who was slightly older than the other, spoke. "Are you not eating?" His eyes drifted to the table of men.

"Yes. After the men are served."

The young man walked forward, hand extended. He smelled of chemicals. "William Soule, and this is my assistant, Joshua Bain."

"A pleasure to meet you. I'm Charlotte Martin."

Soule's eyes lit up. "The woman who took down the Bell Gang?"

"Along with Mr. Oscar and a Cheyenne woman."

"I would love to photograph the three of you."

"Oh." My stomach dropped. "How kind of you, but I don't want to immortalize my injuries."

Souls gaze drifted to my forehead. "I have powder to cover, if you like. It would be a fantastic photograph." His brow furrowed and though his gaze never left my face, I knew he was lost in his vision of staging the photo. He jolted himself out of his musings and said, "I'll talk to your husband about it," and walked off.

One of the women clapped and the children who'd been running around playing turned serious and made their way to my table. I sat at the far end, hoping it would discourage their curiosity, but it only made them more determined. A boy about twelve walked up to me. "You the woman who killed the Injuns?"

I exhaled and furrowed my brow. "I suppose."

"It's a sin to kill."

"I know."

"You're going to hell."

"I may very well be."

His eyes widened. "Burning in eternal flame doesn't scare you?"

"Of course it does, but I would rather live another day to worry about it than have it arrive."

"What's wrong with your voice?"

"A bad man crushed my vocal cords."

"What happened to him?"

"He died."

"Did you kill him?"

"My, aren't you full of questions? What's your name?"

226

"Elijah Darlington."

"Elijah! Leave Mrs. Martin alone!" Isabel Darlington bustled forward and shooed Elijah away, much in the same way she had me earlier. Elijah went to the end of the table and Mrs. Darlington shook her head as she set a plate of biscuits down. "That boy is too curious for his own good."

Everyone was seated, and Mrs. Darlington bowed her head. "Dear Lord, bless this food to the nourishment of our body and our body to thy service. Amen."

My head was barely level when the woman across from me said, "Is what they say about you true?"

Mrs. Darlington served herself a spoonful of mashed potatoes and passed the bowl to me. "This is Elijah's mother, Meg, as if you couldn't tell. Let the poor woman get some food in her before you bombard her with questions."

The mashed potatoes were creamy white and topped with puddles of melted butter. My mouth watered. "What is it they're saying about me?" I asked Meg.

"That you ran away from your husband?"

The clicking of serving ware stopped and everyone's attention turned to me. Mrs. Darlington didn't interject, apparently as interested as her daughters. "Yes. Mr. Oscar

227

saved me from a life of cruelty. Something I hope none of you know anything about. He's taking me to the railroad in Independence so I can return to my family in the East." I hurried on, hoping to keep them from asking about the men I'd killed. I wasn't sure Mrs. Darlington's opinion would survive that bit of truth telling. I smiled thinly and passed the potatoes. "Tell me about yourselves and how you came to be here."

"Brinton — Mr. Darlington — and Lawrie Tatum were two of the first agents chosen under President Grant's new peace policy. Mr. Tatum is the agent at Sill," Isabel said.

"How long have you been here?"

"A little over a year. Meg's husband is the blacksmith. Deborah's husband is the carpenter. Sarah's husband is a bit of a jack-of-all trades. Lately, he's been helping with carpentry. Eventually, he will be the agent teaching the Indians how to farm."

The mashed potatoes melted in my mouth. "What are your jobs?"

"I am teaching the women and children English," Sarah said. "The challenge is getting them to come regularly."

Isabel nodded. "They say they want to adapt but when it comes down to it, they don't understand the need to change their ways. They'll try for a while, get bored, and leave as soon as the allotment comes in and return to their traditions."

"Mr. Oscar said the allotment arrived?"

"Such as it is," Sarah said.

"What do you mean?"

"There's never enough, which angers the Indians."

"And leads to them leaving the territory to hunt buffalo, which leads to raids on the settlements," Meg said.

"Why?"

"Because the settlers are displacing the buffalo," Sarah said.

"It will take time, patience, and God's grace to civilize the Indians," Isabel said. "But it can be done. Look at the Cherokee in Tahlequah. A wonderful example of what acclimation can do. As I said, we've been here a little over a year. What you see here, the few buildings we have, will grow quickly."

Everyone was served and the conversation lulled while we tucked into fried steak, mashed potatoes, boiled carrots, and of course, biscuits. I held the biscuit in my hand and was thankful the bath had resolved my equilibrium so I didn't burst into tears at the sight of it. I understood biscuits were easy to make with limited means on the frontier, but it didn't mean I wanted to eat them at every civilized meal. I put it down, but Meg noticed my expression. "Don't like biscuits, Mrs. Martin?"

"Please, call me Charlotte. And, no, I've had one too many since I've been in Texas, is all. At least you aren't serving beans."

"Wait until you taste Deborah's cobbler," Sarah said. Deborah, who'd been silent for the entire meal, but had kept looking over at the men's table, turned her attention to us.

"They aren't talking about anything worth hearing, Deb. I guarantee you," Meg said.

Deborah's upright comportment stiffened further at the rebuke. "There is no reason why men and women cannot sit together while eating. This tradition we have —"

"Thank you, Deborah. We know what you think of this tradition," Isabel said.

"Since the slaves are freed, Deborah's decided next it's women's turn to be freed," Meg said.

"I want women to have the right to vote," Deborah said. "It is not a scandalous or original cause. Women Friends have been speaking of it for thirty years. We can hardly expect men to take us seriously if we are not allowed a place at the table."

Meg raised an eyebrow at me and rolled her eyes, apparently thinking she had an ally. I was not sure I wanted to be allied with her.

I addressed Deborah. "I, for one, cannot wait to return to civilization, where I will fight alongside you for women's right to vote, for women to get a place at the table." Deborah flushed with pleasure, but it was Meg's turn to bristle.

"On the other hand, I have forced myself into enough male conversations to know Meg is also right. I suspect the reason they do not want us at the table is because they know they will have to broaden their base of knowledge from politics, gambling, and business to carry on intelligent conversations with us."

"Hear, hear." Sarah lifted her glass of water in toast to me. Everyone but Isabel raised her glass. When we set them down, Sarah changed the subject. "Did you see the Indians lined up and waiting to have their pictures taken? The beadwork on their clothes is stunning."

Isabel leaned over to me. "Sarah is also our seamstress."

"I can sew," Meg said.

"We all can, but Sarah is the best. As Deborah is the best cook, and you are the best nurse. God gave us all different gifts to use to His glory. Who's ready for cobbler?" Deborah rose and went into the kitchen.

"Me!" Elijah said from down the table.

"After the adults have been served," Isabel said.

Elijah crossed his arms and pouted. "That's a custom I'd like changed," he said, and all the women laughed.

"What is your strength, Isabel?"

"Leading." She gave me a quick wink as Deborah placed the cobbler in front of her. She spooned a heaping serving into a bowl and handed it to me.

"Oh, Isabel, it is too much. I will never eat all of it."

"You haven't tasted it yet," Deborah said. "Here's some cream, fresh from the cow."

The glass bottle was warm beneath my hand. I poured a tiny amount of cream on the top and passed it to Sarah.

"There's plenty," she said, and splashed more of the thick cream over my cobbler. "It cuts the sweetness," she explained.

While everyone watched me with anticipation, I dipped my spoon into the cream-covered cobbler and took a bite. My mouth exploded with flavors it hadn't tasted in months. A hint of cinnamon and sugar contrasted perfectly with the tart apples.

The buttery crust melted on my tongue. And the cream. Heavens above, the cream. I'd never eaten cream this delicious in my entire life.

I swallowed and dipped my spoon in the cobbler for the second bite, all nausea forgotten. "It's sinful how good it is."

The women all laughed. "Indeed it is," Isabel said.

"Elijah better keep a watchful eye on his cow. I'm tempted to steal it tomorrow."

"I heard that," Elijah said from down the table.

"Tomorrow? Are you leaving so soon?" Isabel asked.

I pulled the spoon slowly out of my mouth, chewed, and swallowed while the women watched me. "I believe so."

"Dr. Cairns will not be pleased," Meg said. "He thinks you should rest for a few more days. I agree. You took quite a hit on your head."

"I slept for most of the day, and I feel much better."

"Which will only prove Dr. Cairns's point. Imagine how much better you will feel after another day of rest."

Isabel placed her cool, dry hand over mine. "Let us take care of you, Charlotte."

"Once your bruise heals sufficiently, you

can have your photo taken with Mr. Oscar and the Indian girl you saved," Meg said. "I overheard Mr. Soule mention it to you."

"Are you going to have your photographs taken?" I asked to turn the conversation.

"If poor Mr. Soule has any glass left to photograph us," Sarah said. "His first priority is chronicling the Indians in their native dress, he says, before they are civilized."

"And Mr. Pope is here to write about them and the agencies," Isabel said. "Our job is to make sure everything runs well and Mr. Pope's story about Darlington is favorable. We're here to treat the natives as God's children and to teach them how to survive in a white man's world. If we fail, the men in Washington who favor extermination will win."

"I thought the extermination policy was regarding the buffalo?" I said.

"It is, though since Sherman had his near miss down in Texas, he's told his officers to drive the Indians to the reservation by any means necessary. Hopefully, the loss of the buffalo will drive the natives onto the reservation, where they will be taught to acclimate."

"The adults are almost hopeless," Sarah said. "They will receive their allotment and return to their camps down the Canadian.

All the good we've accomplished while they're here will be lost."

Sweat prickled my upper lip. "Did you say the Canadian?"

"Yes. We were closer to the fort but decided to move farther downriver to keep the Cheyenne and Arapaho away from the Kiowa and Comanche. Most Cheyenne and Arapaho want peace with us, but there are a few bands who can be cajoled by the Comanche to go on the warpath."

"Who can blame them after Sand Creek and Washita?" Deborah said.

The table in front of me tilted. My voice sounded far away. "This is the Canadian River?"

"Yes, dear. Why?"

I shook my head, trying to dislodge the memories flitting through my mind. "Nothing."

A sharp pain shot through my abdomen and down between my legs. I shifted in my seat. This wasn't real. I was healed. I had checked myself today.

The men at the table behind me laughed. I jerked my head around, expecting to see the next Indian striding toward me, naked, laughing.

"Charlotte?" The voice was far away, deep

beneath the mocking laughter ringing in my ears.

I saw Tuesday hunched over Aénóhé'ke. Me straddling Tuesday, bludgeoning her with a bloody stick. The hole in the back of Cotter Black's head as he fell forward onto the red-rock floor of Palo Duro Canyon.

"Charlotte?"

I turned to the left and saw Maureen sitting there, concern all over her face. "You're gonna wander off one day and be taken by them savages and I'm gonna have to live with the images my whole life."

"Maureen?"

"No, dear. It's Isabel."

I swayed toward the woman and fell off the end of the bench, unconscious.

CHAPTER 18

"Charlotte? Charlotte, can you hear me?"

Dr. Cairns's face hovering over me. "Who's Charlotte?"

"Here, give her some water," a woman's voice said.

"Don't you have anything stronger?" Kindle said.

"We're Friends, Mr. Oscar," came an authoritative but kind male voice.

"Here." A stocky man wearing a derby stepped forward and held out a flask. "Newspapermen always have whisky."

Cairns tipped the flask to my lips. I sipped and sputtered. "Rotgut, Mr. Pope."

Pope smiled. "Newspapermen can't afford the good stuff."

Cairns tried to tip more into my mouth but I pushed the flask away. "No, I'm fine." He helped me sit up. "What happened?"

"You fainted, dear," Mrs. Darlington said.

"Did I?" I thought back to what had

237

preceded the swoon. "Maybe I will have another sip of your whisky, Mr. Pope. If you'd be so kind."

The flask was presented and I sipped. "Thank you."

"You should be in bed," Dr. Cairns chided. "Sitting out here in the sun is too much for a woman in your condition."

"I am fine," I said. Cairns and Kindle helped me stand. Kindle held me close while I steadied myself on my feet.

"What brought it on?" Pope asked.

"We were talking of the agency's move down the Canadian," Deborah said.

Kindle's grip tightened. "Would you like to return to your room?"

"Yes, I think you should," Cairns said.

"No. I suppose the bump on my head and the warm bath caused my swoon. I am so sorry, Mrs. Darlington. The cobbler is getting cold."

"Nonsense. Everyone knows cobbler is as good cold," Mrs. Darlington said.

I smiled, appreciating her levity.

Pope returned his flask to his inner pocket and watched Kindle help me back to the bench.

"I am fine. Go back to the men." I squeezed his hand and smiled. Worry creased his brow. He knew the significance of the Canadian. Cairns bent down and looked me in the eyes. I tried to keep my own as steady as possible. He wasn't buying it. He straightened. "I advise you to go back to your room and rest."

"Let me rest here for a bit first, and I will. I promise."

"Come on, Oscar. I want to hear more about these whisky traders. You do have some adventures, don't you?" Pope winked at me and ushered Kindle back to the men's table.

The women chattered about their day for a while, letting me reacclimatize in peace. The tranquility and happiness from earlier vanished. I tried to separate the visual of Kindle loving me and the Comanche violating me. I felt Isabel Darlington's hand on my arm. "Charlotte," she said quietly. "Walk into the kitchen with me to get more cream." I nodded, rose, and followed her.

When we were alone in the kitchen she ordered me to sit. She sat down and grasped my hand. "Focus on your breathing." With a soft smile she nodded to me and closed her eyes. I did the same.

Her hand was steady on mine. Cool and dry. The distant murmur of conversation from the diners outside faded away until all I heard was Isabel's and my gentle breath-

239

ing. Sitting there, silently, I felt faintly ridiculous. I knew this was the Quaker way, sitting in silence and awaiting the voice of God. God hadn't been too terribly concerned with my well-being for the last few months. I had serious doubts he would deliver a thunderbolt of clarity in the middle of a frontier kitchen. I should be up, doing something, speaking to someone, reading the latest medical journal, practicing my stitches, visiting patients.

You have none of those responsibilities now.

I opened my eyes. Only Isabel was with me, sitting silently, her eyes closed, an expression of complete tranquility on her face. I furrowed my brows and closed my eyes again. If stating the obvious was the best God could do, I was doomed.

I sat back and pulled my hands from Isabel's. She opened her eyes.

"I apologize. I understand what you are doing," I said. "But I do not believe as you do."

Isabel smiled contentedly. "I know. I rarely hear God's voice, even in meeting, but I always feel his presence and it calms me. At least once a day I sit in silence with God. It washes all of my worries, frustrations, and anger clean away."

"Anger? You?" She was the most serene

woman I'd ever met. Sitting with her I did feel calmer and could almost forget what had brought on my swoon.

"I had quite the temper growing up. This gray hair was once red. Brinton always says if God can tame me, taming the Indians will be a cinch."

We turned toward a knock at the door. "I saw you come in," Kindle said.

Isabel rose. "Time to clean up, I suppose."

"Let me help."

Isabel put a hand on my shoulder. "I won't hear of it. Let Mr. Oscar take you back to your room. I hope you consider staying on for a few days to recuperate. I believe recent events confirm the necessity."

I smiled wanly, but didn't want to commit. "Thank you for your kindness."

She left and Kindle took her place. "What happened?"

I rubbed my forehead and felt the painful bump in the center. I grimaced. "Nothing. I'm fine."

"Stop it, Laura." My head jerked up at his rough voice. "Don't tell me you're fine. You look like death."

I dropped my hand onto the table. "Please forgive me. Does it bother you to see the result of everything I've gone through for the past few months? I'll try to do a better

241

job of shielding you from it. How thoughtless of me."

I walked to the other side of the room and stared out the window. Everyone was finished with dinner but no one was moving to rise from the tables, enjoying a respite from the work of the day, and quite possibly, the setting sun.

"That isn't what I meant," Kindle said.

I crossed my arms. "I don't know if it was the Canadian. Your brother said it was but he told so many lies . . . . It isn't only the name of the river. Sounds, smells bring it all back." I exhaled a sharp, disbelieving laugh. "Splashing water. Croaking frogs."

"I want to help you."

I looked over my shoulder but didn't turn. "How?" He remained silent, as I knew he would. "Besides turning back time and killing your brother at Antietam, what could you do, exactly?" I gazed out the window. "I can forget about it for a while, be happy, even, like this afternoon. But, it always returns." I pressed my fist into my stomach. "What happened is deep inside me, a part of me." My voice broke. "And I don't know how to eradicate it."

Kindle didn't speak or move. The sun settled completely beneath the horizon, the signal for everyone to rise and clean up.

They would be coming into the kitchen soon.

"We leave in the morning. The sooner we get you out of this country the better. We can ride hard and be in Independence in a week," Kindle said.

"No."

"What?"

I turned. "I'm tired of running."

"Pope is itching to betray us, I can tell."

"He won't."

"How do you know?"

"If he wanted the money he would have done it immediately. He wants something else."

"What?"

"A story, probably."

"Christ." Kindle ran his hand through his hair and paced the kitchen. He stopped. "You want to give it to him?"

"No, Kindle. I want to rest like Cairns says. It is the exact advice I would give to myself as a doctor. I should heed it."

Kindle stepped to me and rubbed his hands up and down my arms. "We'll leave after the allotment." He held out his arm. "Let's go back to your room. And rest."

We thanked our hosts and walked down the wide thoroughfare back to the residence, where we found the young Cheyenne girl,

243

Running Brook, waiting for us on the porch steps.

"Aénòhé'ke sent me," the girl said.

"For what?" Kindle said.

I put my hand to my temple. "I forgot. Aénòhé'ke invited me to a celebration tonight. Her homecoming."

"I thought you were going to rest?"

"I promised I would go. Please come with me. I don't think I can face them all on my own."

Kindle studied me with his one uncovered eye and rubbed his beard. He nodded. Henry Pope walked up. "Hello. And who's this?"

"Running Brook," I said. I took Henry Pope's arm and pulled him down the street. "Come on, Henry. I'm going to help you get your Indian story."

"You are?"

"Yes. We're going to an Indian welcome-home party. Do you have your pencil and paper?"

He patted his coat pocket.

"I thought that was your flask."

He pressed his hand on one pocket, then the other. "Yes, there it is. Safe as houses."

Kindle fell in beside us. In the distance, the drums started beating.

CHAPTER 19

The four of us could have been invisible for all the attention the Cheyenne paid us as we walked into the village. Children ran in and around the tipis playing chase. Dogs yapped and nipped at their heels before rushing off to scrounge for food. The bottom half of the buffalo hides covering the tipis were folded up to take advantage of the evening breeze. In one men sat around a fire passing a long pipe. In another, women talked and laughed. A young brave talked to a young woman who demurely looked at anything but him. Nearby, a young man played a wooden flute quite beautifully while a girl was teased and encouraged by her friends between her quick glances at the brave, to make sure he played for her.

The drums we'd heard earlier accompanied a group of men and women playing various instruments — rattles, hand drums,

flutes, and something like a small guitar —
while men and women of all ages danced.
We stopped and watched them. Running
Brook stopped next to us and watched.

I chuckled. "It looks like they're dancing a
reel."

"Doesn't look like the penny dreadfuls
describe, does it?" Henry Pope said.

The dancing fire flickered shadows on
Pope's face. "I've never read one."

"Very entertaining. I suppose you were
too busy with medical journals to read for
pleasure."

I thought of all the nights I'd spent in the
basement room with a resurrection man,
dissecting cadavers to improve my surgical
skills. I flexed my injured hand. "Something
of the sort."

"I've read them," Kindle said. "They're
all a load of shit written by men who've
never stepped foot past the Mississippi. Possibly the Potomac."

"You read?" Pope said.

Kindle growled, though with the commotion around us, I don't think Pope heard
him. But Pope saw Kindle's expression and
grinned. "I figured there were other enter-
tainments you enjoyed more."

Standing between the men it was difficult
to know where to look, or to be sure the

expression I saw was the true reaction to whatever barb they were throwing at each other. I realized they knew each other better than I'd assumed, or than Kindle had ever implied.

"Henry," I said, "we heard there was a Pinkerton in Jacksboro looking for me. What can you tell us about him?"

"He's a big mick who's more shrewd than intelligent. He was in town the night you escaped, but he decided to go sporting instead of doing his job."

"We know that much. Did he go back to New York or is he on our trail?" Kindle said. Kindle spoke to us, but his eyes roamed over the Indians surrounding us, as if searching for someone. Or was he on edge, watching to make sure we wouldn't be attacked? I glanced around. Impossible. These people were socializing as if it was market day in town, or a Sunday-afternoon church potluck. Violence was the last thing on their minds.

"He was heading to Fort Worth, but I doubt he was heading back East. You made him look a fool by escaping under his nose."

Kindle lost interest in Pope's story and was staring at Tall Buffalo watching us from the other side of the dancers. He leaned to his left and spoke to Bob Johnson, who stood and walked around the dancers to the three of us.

"Tall Buffalo wants to welcome you."

We moved forward. Bob Johnson held his hand out to me. "Only the men."

"Am I to stand here by myself?"

Bob Johnson smiled condescendingly at me. "Aénóhé'ke is in Falling Stars Woman's tent. Through there." He pointed at the semicircle of tents downriver. "Running Brook will take you."

Kindle pulled me away from Bob Johnson and said, "It's fine."

"What if he recognizes you?"

Pope came nearer, his broad back shielding me and Kindle from Bob Johnson, giving us a little more privacy, though we continued to talk low.

"Why would he recognize you?" Pope said.

Kindle rubbed his beard. "He won't. I can play a part as well as you can, Laura. Go find Aénóhé'ke."

"How can you tell her to go off by herself with a bunch of Indians, after what she went through?" Pope said, stepping toward Kindle.

Kindle straightened and narrowed his visible eye. "She saved Aénóhé'ke's life. There's a debt there that will keep Laura safe."

"Are you okay with this, Laura? Do you

want me to stay with you?"

I wasn't sure if Pope had completely forgiven me for Cotter Black's attack, but if he was brave enough to challenge Kindle about my safety I couldn't see him handing me over to the Pinkertons and a date with a noose. I put my hand on Pope's arm and smiled. "You're so generous to offer, Henry. You go get your story. Aénóhé'ke won't hurt me."

Reluctantly, Pope left me and walked to the circle of elders with Kindle and Bob Johnson.

Running Brook pulled on my hand. "One minute." Tall Buffalo spoke for a few moments, lifted the pipe he held above his head, tapped the bowl on the ground, then moved it to the left, then the right before smoking. He passed it and the man to his left did the same, all the way around the circle to Kindle, who mimicked their actions. I relaxed, slightly. Somewhere in my memory was the knowledge smoking a pipe together was a sign of friendship. Where I knew it from, I had no idea.

I let Running Brook pull me along to Falling Stars Woman's tent. The bottom half was folded up and the women inside played a heated game involving sticks and flat dice made of what looked like bone. The sticks were laid on the ground in a pile, obviously their ante, and a woman shook a basket and tossed the dice into the air, catching them in the basket. The women leaned forward to count the faces. Half of the group groaned and half cheered. I smiled. The details of the game were different, but the highs and lows of gambling were the same the world over, it seemed.

Aénòhé'ke glanced up from the game and noticed me. She rose to the objections of her opponents, who saw me for the first time as well. Aénòhé'ke's eyes were still slightly swollen from her time with the whisky traders, but they were sparkling with good humor and happiness. I marveled at how she seemed to have put her ordeal completely behind her in less than a week.

"I wondered if you were coming," Aénòhé'ke said.

"We were watching the dancers." I turned in the direction from which I had come.

"Where is your husband?"

"With Tall Buffalo. Did you see the allotment arrive?"

Falling Stars Woman nodded. "Mr. Darlington sent a message it will be distributed tomorrow afternoon. We will leave the next morning for our winter camp."

"Winter? It's hard to think of winter when

it is so hot."

"Come," Falling Stars Woman said. "Eat."

Though I wasn't hungry I followed them into the tent. The gambling sticks were picked up and I was led to the same spot I'd sat in earlier in the day. The other women worked together until everyone was seated around the fire, the pot of meat in front of Falling Stars Woman. She removed a chunk of meat, cut it into five pieces, and lifted them to the sky, lowered them toward the ground, then pointed them east and west. Aénóhé'ke sat next to me and explained. "She is honoring the spirits."

Falling Stars Woman ladled stewed meat onto a tin plate and handed it to me. I picked up the meat with my fingers and ate it, wondering all the while what type of meat it was but too afraid of offending to ask. It was slightly gristly, but the flavor was surprisingly good. It was better than rattlesnake, at any rate.

I smiled and nodded. "Very good, thank you."

Falling Stars Woman served the other women and we ate in silence for a few minutes. I never did well with silence so I asked the question that had been lingering in the back of my mind for a few days.

"When I burned my arm," I said, lifting

251

the bandaged limb for everyone to see, "Aénóhé'ke boiled a thistle tea to doctor it. How did you learn of its healing powers?"

The women around the circle seemed to relax, as if settling down to hear a long, well-loved story. The children inched closer to the tipi, but did not enter. When the rustling had quieted, Falling Stars Woman began.

"Many years ago, a baby was found by an old woman, in a wickiup amid the sweet roots that make mother's milk flow. She named him Sweet Medicine and took him in and raised him as her own, for she didn't have children. He grew faster and learned quicker than the other children. When he was young there was a drought and the People were starving. He told his grandmother to find an old buffalo robe, the dirtiest, rattiest one she could find, and bring it to him. She did, and he instructed her to wash it in the river and scrape it clean. When she returned, Sweet Medicine cut the hide into one long strip, fashioned a hoop, and wove the hide in and out of the circle, making a net. He took four sticks, whittled them into points, and hardened them in the fire. Then he told his grandmother to follow him outside to play the hoop-and-stick game."

There was something soothing, mesmerizing, about Falling Stars Woman's voice. It was as if I were in a trance, as if I could see the events she recited happening before me, like a play on a stage. The hoop and sticks she mentioned were suddenly in her hand, and she brandished them to the crowd, but without the showmanship of a carnival barker. Instead, with a reverence usually reserved for a religious ceremony.

"Sweet Medicine ordered his grandmother to roll the hoop while he threw the pointed sticks into the center, hitting the same spot every time. Then he said, 'Let me hit it one more time and turn it into a buffalo calf.' Sweet Medicine threw the stick and a calf appeared, collapsed on its side, the stick in its heart. Sweet Medicine gave the calf to the People, telling them to eat, and no matter how much meat they cut from the calf, they did not pick it clean.

"On Sweet Medicine's first buffalo hunt, he killed a yellow buffalo calf. Since he had no father or grandfather to celebrate the event, he cleaned the calf himself. A chief who wanted the hide demanded Sweet Medicine give it to him. Sweet Medicine offered the man half of the calf's meat because he revered his elders, but did not want to part with the skin. The chief was angry and tried to take the skin. Sweet Medicine took a leg bone and hit the chief over the head, killing him, and angering the rest of the tribe. Sweet Medicine fled for his life.

"The tribe searched and searched for Sweet Medicine and every time they saw him, and thought they were near to catching him, he was always just out of their reach. Finally, exhausted, the People gave up searching for him.

"Sweet Medicine wandered for years, until he came upon a mountain shaped like a tipi. He entered into a cave and found what looked like men and women, but were really spirits. They welcomed him and told him they'd been waiting for him."

Falling Stars Woman held up four arrows. "The spirits gave him four arrows; two for war, two for hunting, and explained to him the great powers they contained and the rules by which the People ought to live."

I leaned over to Aénóhé'ke and whispered, "Are those the arrows?"

"No. The arrows are protected by a special chief."

"The spirits taught Sweet Medicine how to renew the arrows, the wise laws of the forty-four chiefs, how women should be honored, and many things so the People could survive and prosper." Falling Stars Woman looked at me. "Including how to use plants, berries, and roots, and how to pray to the spirits to cure sickness.

"When Sweet Medicine returned to the People he found four boys playing with buffalo figures outside the village. Their ribs were sticking out, for they were starving. He turned the stick figures into buffalo meat and told the boys to fill their bellies, and there would be enough for their parents and grandparents as well. He ordered them to have two hunters come to him the next morning. The hunters went to find Sweet Medicine three mornings in a row and did not find him. On the fourth morning, Sweet Medicine stood on top of a hill and told the warriors to have the People build a great lodge and to cover the floor with sage and sweetgrass. Everyone must wait for him in the lodge; no one must see him approaching.

"They did as they were told and Sweet Medicine approached the lodge, calling out four times, *People of the Cheyenne, with a great power I am approaching. Be joyful. The sacred arrows I am bringing.* All night long, Sweet Medicine smoked a deer-bone pipe and taught the People what the spirits had taught him. When they emerged from the tents the next morning, the plains were filled with buffalo.

"Four lives the spirits gave Sweet Medicine, but he was no immortal. Before he died, he told the People of a vision of light-skinned bearded men with sticks that spit fire who will invade our land and drive us before them. These men will kill the animals we rely on for food, clothing, and lodging. Strange animals will accompany them, one to ride, another to eat. They will introduce evil and strange sicknesses and try to have us forget Maheo, the creator, and the things Sweet Medicine taught us. He said we must be strong, especially the women, because we are the creators of life and if we weaken, the Cheyenne will cease to exist."

Falling Stars Woman went silent, letting Sweet Medicine's final admonition sink into the women around the fire. In the distance, the men and children celebrated, but the women were subdued, knowing and living the truth of Sweet Medicine's long-ago vision.

I opened my mouth to thank Falling Stars Woman for the story and to ask more about the medicines they used when the tenor of the outside celebrations changed. The sounds of horses' hooves and whooping made everyone around the fire stand and exit the tent.

We joined a stream of people heading

toward the commotion. People around me began to whoop and clap and talk loudly. I could see only bits and pieces of the activity in the center circle through the tipis and the people in front of me. I coughed as dust from the running horses swirled in the air and combined with the smoke from dozens of fires. On the edge of the main semicircle Aénóhé'ke stopped, while the rest of her tribe streamed ahead, whooping at the warriors making a spectacle around the large center fire. I stopped next to her and saw Kindle across the way, watching the warriors with a narrowed eye. Pope was next to him, taking notes.

My eyes were drawn to the poles the warriors held aloft. At the top of each was a circle much like the one Falling Stars Woman had used as a prop in her story. Only one side of these hoops was covered with hair, some of it short, some of it long. One had a long blond braid. My blood ran cold when I realized what they were.

Aénóhé'ke stared at the spectacle, her arms crossed over her chest. Her eyes seemed to follow one warrior in particular: a warrior on a white horse painted with red stripes on its withers. The man holding the blond pigtail aloft.

"Who is he?" I asked.

257

Aénóhé'ke's eyes never left the man. "My husband."

Kindle was beside me. He grasped my elbow. "Let's go," he said in my ear. He propelled me away, leaving Aénóhé'ke staring daggers at her husband.

"Where's Pope?"

"He'll be fine," Kindle said.

We were halfway down the thoroughfare through the agency when the din of celebration faded to a murmur. We walked up the steps into the single men's quarters, down the hall, and to my room. When the door was closed behind us I said, "What's wrong?"

"I didn't want to risk being recognized by a warrior in high spirits after a raid."

"If someone recognizes you, you think they will kill you?"

Kindle shrugged. "At Washita Custer used Cheyenne women and children as shields so we could escape. And, took those women and children captive. He took one woman as a wife and got her pregnant, I hear." Kindle practically spat the words out.

"You truly hate that man."

"You have no idea."

"So on one side of the Agency we have the Army camped, where you might be recognized, and on the other side you have

258

the Indians who might recognize you."

Kindle nodded. "And, in the middle we have Henry Pope, who wants our story."

"I knew it!"

"And Soule, who wants our photograph."

"We should leave."

Kindle studied me. "No. You're not strong enough yet."

"I can manage."

"We don't have a scout."

"What about Bob Johnson?"

"How would we pay him? Your necklace it too valuable. We need the reward money."

"And we don't know how long until the marshal arrives."

Kindle shook his head.

"Good heavens. What are we going to do?"

Kindle tossed his hat onto the dresser and ripped off the eye patch. He rubbed his eye, and then raked his hands through his hair. The skin around his eye was red and irritated from the leather, making him look like he'd taken a punch to the face.

"Hell if I know."

CHAPTER 20

The nightmare always started the same.

I sat at the kitchen table in my New York home. Dust covered the surfaces of the room, but a pot of Irish stew bubbled on the stove, a wooden spoon sticking out of the pot as if just used. I walked down the hall, calling for Maureen. Not finding her, I walked out the front door and onto the Texas plains. The wind whipped around me, releasing my hair from its untidy bun, and blowing the petals from the carpet of wild-flowers. The petals swirled around me, obscuring the landscape, but Maureen's voice rang out clear.

I turned. Through the smoke I saw flames consuming our schooner. I ran forward, toward the sound of Maureen screaming my name. "Katie!" Horses surrounded me, running in a circle, ridden by unseen men. I tried to escape but fell to the churned, bloody ground. I crawled toward a rushing river but made no progress. My hands and legs were mired in the mud. Someone grabbed my ankle, pulled me back, and turned me over. Cotter Black stood over me, holding a knife and smirking. He lifted the knife and cut his face from temple to jaw, his blood flooding down onto my face and dress. I turned my head to the side to avoid the blood and he fell on me, pinning me to the ground. I struggled to break free, but someone held my legs. Aénohé'ke sat on my chest, holding a knife and pinning my arms to my sides with her legs. She lifted the knife over her head and screamed. Where her mouth should be was a black, vacant maw, out of which flew a blood-covered hawk. It landed on my face and stabbed me in the eye with its beak.

I screamed and thrashed and tried to get away from Aénohé'ke and the hawk, but my feet were tangled in sheets and my shoulders were being pressed into the mattress. Above me a bearded man hovered, saying a name over and over.

"No! Please, no! Let me go!" I screamed and thrashed and finally I was free. I jumped from the bed and landed on my knees. I crawled away as fast as possible across freshly hewn boards. I nestled in the corner and pulled my legs to my chest. I watched the man in the bed while my chest exploded with pain as I tried to catch my breath. He stood, walked to the dresser, and poured a glass of water. He held it out to me.

William.

I took the glass with a trembling hand and spilled more on my nightdress than I drank. I clutched it to me.

"Dreaming of Antietam?"

There had been few nights on the trail when I hadn't woken, screaming, from a variation of the same dream. The Antietam lie had slipped out on the first night, and Kindle might have even believed it. He was long past believing it, and I was long past lying about it.

I shook my head and tried to drink again. My hand was steady and I gulped the water as if dying of thirst. I handed the glass to Kindle, who put it down and extended his hand to help me up. Though the dream wasn't about him, had never been about him, I couldn't meet his eyes.

He led me to the bed, tucked me under the blankets, and then went to the other side and crawled in beside me. We stared at the ceiling, not touching, a replay of the night before, though it seemed like an eternity ago. I knew sleep would not come for me, but thought Kindle had dozed off and was surprised when his voice broke through the silence.

"Is it always the same?"

"No."

Aénóhé'ke was new, and the rest went along in the same vein with different actors. Some nights the Comanche were predominant, some nights Cotter Black. One night I murdered all five bounty hunters with a bullet to the backs of their heads. But, the one aspect that never changed was Kindle's absence, not only from the events of the dream, but also from my thoughts. It was as if in my dream world he didn't exist. He never saved me, nor did I ever think he would.

"You know it's the best of our bad choices."

"I know," I lied.

Before bed we'd talked for hours, hashing out how best to ride through the gauntlet of enemies surrounding us to get to Independence, Missouri. Asking the Army for protection was never considered. The Army wasn't so big Kindle wouldn't be recognized, as evidenced by the sergeant a few days back. It was too dangerous to wait for the US marshal to receive our reward for Bell and his friends. As such, we didn't have enough money to hire Bob Johnson to scout for us and striking out with just the two of us was risky because of me. I was little more than dead weight, with few survival skills, though I was learning. Which left us with one option: traveling with the Cheyenne.

"Tall Buffalo knows — everyone knows — the allotment will fall short. It always has," Kindle had said, pleading his case. "They will have to go on a hunt, which means north, which means out of Indian Territory and closer to Independence."

I'd walked to the window and stared out in the night. I began to shake.

"Tall Buffalo offered to send a scout with us the rest of the way."

I turned sharply. "You've already made the arrangements, haven't you?"

"I have."

"So this discussion was to humor me? To make me believe I had some sort of say, though I do not?"

"Laura, though this is going to chap you something fierce, there are times when you're going to have to sit back, shut up, and let me make the decisions. I have lived in the West for years. I know these people, how they think. Whom we can and can't trust. I trust Tall Buffalo a helluva lot more than I do Darlington."

"What? Why?"

"Because Darlington is a good man who believes in law and order. He would turn us in, not out of spite but because it's the right thing to do."

"You saw what those warriors were brandishing tonight."

"I did."

"And, you want to travel hundreds of miles with them? It makes no sense."

"The Cheyenne are no different from the US Army."

"Oh, this should be rich."

Kindle shook his head in frustration. "There are men who want peace, who want a resolution to the problem with as little bloodshed as possible, like Mackenzie, Tall Buffalo, Darlington, and Tatum. Then there are men like Custer who see the Indian problem as a way to be covered in glory, or men like Chivington who think it's God's divine will we eradicate the Indians. These warriors are no different. They think the way to be revered is to raid and count coup."

"Where do you fall?"

"Right now, my only purpose is to get us out of Indian Territory alive. I'll kill whom I need to make sure it happens. Indian or white man, doesn't matter."

I covered my face with my hands. "What have we become? If I'd had any idea of what we would have to do I would have gladly let my hands be bound in chains and returned to New York."

"We've been over this. It's too late for that. We've committed to a path and we have to see it through."

"Is it true you would be shot for desertion?"

"With my record, most likely."

"What does that mean? Sherman and Mackenzie seemed to think highly of you. Harriet was half in love with you."

Kindle sat on the bed and removed his boots. "I have mistakes in my past I'd rather leave there. We're going with the Cheyenne. End of discussion." He took his clothes off and laid them over the footboard. He'd pulled the blankets back to get in bed when I told him to wait.

"Let me check your wounds."

He straightened and let me unbutton the top of his union suit and pull his left arm out. The scar from the surgery I had performed at Fort Richardson three months earlier was straight and had healed nicely. Kindle released his right arm and I pulled the bottom down past the scar on his thigh where I'd removed an arrow. This scar wouldn't have made a textbook as a great example of stitching, but the sky had been darkening and a storm was bearing down on me when I did it. But, it was as healthy as the one on his shoulder. I stepped back, trying to ignore his growing erection. I supposed ordering me around like a traditional wife excited him. Even if I had wanted him to touch me before, I didn't then.

You're a fool.

Camille King's voice was clear in my mind. The most successful madam on New York City's Twenty-Seventh Street didn't suffer fools. I learned the hard way when I'd asked her how she could submit to men like she did. She laughed for a good minute before replying.

I don't submit to men. I give myself to them.

That's worse.

It's when the men think they have the most power that you do. Men only have power when women give it to them.

"Laura?"

I banished the memory from my mind. Kindle watched me from under furrowed brows. Would I change his mind about traveling with the Cheyenne if I gave myself to him? I shook the idea from my head. I didn't want to be the type of woman who would manipulate her husband to get what she wanted, nor did I want to know if Kindle would be so easily conned.

"Is there any pain?"

He threaded his arms through the union suit and buttoned it. "Occasionally I'll feel a sharp twinge, but nothing debilitating."

"I've noticed your limp is almost gone. Except when you get off a horse."

"The leg stiffens up when I ride, but it's manageable."

Kindle got into bed and pulled the blankets over him. He tried to fluff the flat pillow and instead turned onto his side and pushed his arm beneath to add lift. "We leave with Tall Buffalo's band after the allotment, probably tomorrow afternoon. If you're thinking turning yourself in is the answer, get it out of your mind. It's a death sentence for us."

Now, hours later, we lay in the bed, the sky lightening outside the window. The terror of my nightmare was dissipating, but my daytime fear of Indians, of warriors, was thickening and hardening around me.

"What can I do to help you?" Kindle said.

"I don't know."

He lifted his arm and I put my head on his chest. He pulled me close, running his hand up and down my arm. "I had nightmares about Antietam, too."

"They aren't about Antietam."

One side of his mouth crooked up. "Mine

268

weren't, either. I kept reliving the fight with my brother, killing my father. Cotter Black, the slave."

"How did you get rid of them?"

"Whisky. Lots of whisky."

I settled my head back on his chest. "Laudanum helped at Richardson."

Kindle's head moved. "You had the dreams at Richardson?"

I nodded.

Kindle pulled me closer. "You don't have to be afraid of the Cheyenne. I'll be right by your side. Every day. And Aénóhé'ke will be there. Your saving her protects you much more than I can. No one will hurt you. I promise."

"You can trust them. I'll trust you."

Kindle chuckled and kissed the top of my head. We fell into a doze. The morning sun streamed into our room.

"She's recovering from grievous injuries."

I propped myself on my elbow. By the brightness and the sounds of activity outside I guessed it was midmorning or later. I heard Kindle talking in the hallway.

I rose from bed and went to the door to better eavesdrop on the conversation.

"I have spoken with the Indian woman and she is amendable to the idea. She's never been photographed," Soule said.

"Photograph her alone, then."

"But, it would be a better photo with the three of you. With your eye patch and that scowl of yours . . ." Soule cleared his throat. "It will show that white men and Indians can get along, can combine for a common good."

"Oh, you're out here for the common good, and not to line your pockets with gold when you return East?"

"There's no reason I can't do both. You've already agreed to give Pope your story —"

"We have, have we?" Kindle said.

Someone stepped forward in the hall. "I understand your hesitation, but I promise not to use your real names," Pope said. I imagined Pope's mouth turning up into a smirk. Lord only knew the kind of names Pope would saddle us with.

"She has been through an ordeal and is sensitive it shows in her looks."

"I told her last night I had powder —"

"And I wouldn't want a photograph out there she wouldn't be happy with. She's a vain woman, and won't want the picture. And if we don't want a copy, what's in it for us?"

"I'm not sure what —"

"Oscar wants you to pay him, you idiot,"

Pope said.

"Pay you? People pay me!"

"So be it." Kindle knocked on my door.

"Wait," Soule said. "How much?"

"You give us the reward for the killers we brought in and I'll write it over to you. It'll cost you nothing, in the end."

"How much?"

"Hundred twenty-five."

"Dollars?"

"Twenty-five each for the woman, German, and Bell, and fifty for the Mexican."

"I don't have that much money."

"Then you won't get our photo."

"Thirty is the best I can do."

"I see you've got a line of at least twenty-five men out there, at a dollar a pop? Not including all the buffalo robes you got yesterday from the Cheyenne. And, you were at Sill before this, weren't you?"

"Fifty."

"A hundred."

"Seventy-five."

"Seventy-five and three buffalo robes."

"Done." After a moment, which most like included a handshake, Soule said, "Gather up the Indian and come to my wagon."

His footsteps echoed through the hall walls and he was gone.

"You disappeared last night," Pope said.

271

"We'd seen enough," Kindle said.

"You missed the best part. Your Indian girl was not pleased to see her husband. Turns out, he lost her in a bet with a Kiowa."

Behind the door, I grunted in disgust.

"The warrior and his friends are part of the Hima . . . Hima . . . Oh, I can't say it. A soldier band."

"The Dog Soldiers?" Kindle promoted.

"No, Wolf or Bow and Arrow or something."

"The Bowstring Men."

"That's it. They were out hunting for buffalo and raiding with the Kiowa and Comanche. Tall Buffalo sent them away, downriver to their permanent camp. He's afraid Old Man Darlington will get wind of the blond pigtail they were brandishing and refuse to disburse, as well as send the Army after them."

"Tall Buffalo told you all of this?" Kindle asked.

"No, Bob Johnson. What the hell kind of name is that for an Indian?"

"His father was a white man," Kindle said.

"Even so. Sounds like a clerk's name. Well, I'll leave you two to . . . whatever it is you do."

Kindle opened the door and I stepped

back. He paused when he saw I wasn't in the bed. I pushed the door closed.

"You were masterful," I said.

Kindle's expression turned smug. "Thank you."

"The reward for the lot of them was only fifty dollars."

"Soule doesn't know that."

I stepped forward and put my arms around Kindle's neck. "Have I told you lately how much I love you?"

He stared up at the ceiling as if considering and back at me. "I don't think so."

"I do. Very much."

He placed his hand on my hips and pulled me gently forward. "You like it when I drive a hard bargain?" His mouth quirked up into a half smile.

I rolled my eyes. "You are an inveterate flirt." His hands moved to my face, gently caressing it, while his lips almost touched mine. "Kiss me like you did on the road to Jacksboro," I whispered.

I lifted my lips but he moved his mouth away, skimming his lips across my cheek. My mouth followed his but he kept his lips out of reach.

"Why are you teasing me?"

"I want you to work for it," he whispered, his lips almost touching mine, but pulling away when I tried to capture his mouth. I gave up and kissed his neck below his beard. He lifted his chin and I kissed his Adam's apple and moved down to the hollow of his throat.

I pulled his head down and kissed his ear. "How do you know I'll keep trying?" I whispered.

Kindle stilled, and I realized his hands had been roaming over my body. I had leaned into him, and for the first time since the Canadian, I felt a pull of desire for him, deep in my stomach.

"Because you love me."

I took off his ridiculous eye patch and threw it on the floor. "I do."

I pulled him to me and kissed him, softly at first, remembering his lips the first time we kissed, how days later I would lightly pull down my bottom lip to try to mimic how he'd gently bit it, tugged on it. Now, he let me take my time. His body tensed in the effort to hold back. My fingers raked down his bearded cheeks and I deepened the kiss. Kindle pressed me against him as if wanting to fuse us together. His erection was hard against me. I expected him to take charge of the kiss and where it would lead. Instead, he broke away and put his forehead against mine.

His voice was husky when he said my name. "Soule is waiting."

"Let him wait." I lifted my mouth to kiss him but he pushed me gently away. "What is it? I thought you wanted . . ."

Kindle shook his head, and wouldn't look at me. "I know it wasn't comfortable for you yesterday."

"It might be better this time."

"I'll not lay with you again until you'll enjoy it. Until it'll be only you and me in the bed."

I stepped back and hugged myself. "I don't know when that'll be."

"I know."

I choked back a sob.

Kindle stepped forward and lifted my chin so I had to look at him. "I'm not going anywhere."

"Promise?"

"Laura." He kissed my forehead and enveloped me in his arms. "I'm not with you out of any sense of obligation or honor. I hope you agree there's more to us than making love."

I nodded.

"Though I'll not lie and say I don't want what we had at Richardson. I do."

"So do I."

"But, I don't want you to flinch every time

275

I touch you. I can hold you, and kiss you, without it leading anywhere you don't want. It'll be a trial, but I can do it." He moved away. "Now, we need to stop talking about it or I won't be fit to go outside for a while." He sat on the bed and pulled the blankets over his lap. "Go on and get dressed so we can get our reward."

I sniffed and wiped my cheeks and pulled the men's clothes out of the chest. "No need to dress like a man," Kindle said. "Unless you want to."

I paused, and despite my best efforts, my vanity was bruised. "Because I look so little like Catherine Bennett?"

"No. Because I have no intention of letting Soule's glass negative make it back East in one piece."

Soule moved his rolling photography studio from near the Indian camp to the edge of town where the allotment would be distributed. A line of cowboys and soldiers waited patiently for their turns: hair slicked down, collars buttoned, wiping the dust off their boots on the backs of the opposite leg, pushing and teasing their friends about deficiencies, nervously petting their mustaches, practicing their quick draws, twirling their guns and shoving them back in their holsters. Noticeably absent from the line were the Cheyenne and Arapaho and the women. Which made Aénòhé'ke and I stand out like sore thumbs.

Kindle and I exchanged a silent look, and tried to turn away from the staring eyes without it seeming too obvious. Aénòhé'ke faced forward, as if daring the strange men to insult her or approach her.

Soule's assistant hurried down the line to us. "Come to the front. Mr. Soule wants to shoot you before the light changes."

"Shoot?" Aénòhé'ke said.

"It's a euphemism."

"He means take your picture," Kindle clarified. "He isn't going to shoot us."

Aénòhé'ke nodded and we walked past all of the cowboys and soldiers, drawing the attention we'd tried to avoid. Kindle and I kept our heads down and turned away.

The assistant bounced on the balls of his feet while he waited for Soule to appear from beneath the camera's black cloth. A tableau of four men, two sitting, two standing, was arranged in front of a makeshift backdrop on the other side of the wagon. Soule straightened and said, "Steady." The four men were stock-still, knowing any movement at all would blur the picture. One man's eyebrows were lifted to the brim of his hat. Suddenly his head jerked forward and he sneezed.

"Done." Soule removed the wooden case holding the glass negative and gave it to his impatient assistant, who ran into the wagon.

"Take another," the sneezer said. "I moved."

"Why take two when one will do?"

"I'll pay."

"I apologize, sir, but I have a firm policy on one photo, especially out here where my supplies are limited. What if I ran out of glass with one group left? It wouldn't be fair to them, would it?"

The men in front of the camera went to Soule and handed him a silver dollar each. The sneezer glared at him, but Soule was unfazed. "I will develop your picture to-night."

"Each one of us gets a copy," the sneezer said.

"Of course."

Soule turned and saw us. "Finally, my bandits!"

"We aren't bandits," Kindle said.

"Thank you for agreeing to come."

I bent my head in acknowledgment. Kindle held his hand out to Soule.

"Now?"

"We aren't sitting until we have the

money."

"But, I don't . . ."

Kindle grasped me gently by the arm and we turned to leave.

"Stop." Soule went into the wagon and returned. He gave Kindle a small bag of coins, which Kindle opened. He glared at Soule and counted the money.

"Pick any three buffalo robes you want." He motioned to a pile on a separate uncovered wagon.

"Aénóhé'ke, choose three buffalo robes for yourself," Kindle said.

The Indian furrowed her brows but did as told.

"Each of us gets a copy?" I said.

Soule's smile was thin. "Two. One for the Indian, and one for the couple."

"Fine," Kindle said.

"Have you ever had your picture taken?" the photographer asked us all.

Kindle and I nodded. Aénóhé'ke said, "No."

"You speak English! Excellent! Oh, and here's Mr. Pope!"

Henry Pope walked around the wagon with a huge smile on his face and his derby sitting crooked on his head. He caught sight of me and stopped dead in his tracks. "Don't you look lovely." As soon as he said it, his face flushed with embarrassment. I glanced at Kindle, who was watching Pope with raised eyebrows and an amused expression.

"You have a line full of unhappy men, armed to the teeth, I might add," Pope said, hurrying to change the subject.

Soule waved the danger away. "They won't get their photo taken if they kill me."

"What about your assistant?"

"He's an apprentice."

"Which means you're working him to death and paying him little," Pope said.

"Which means he hasn't learned the camera yet. He's developing the negatives. What is taking him so long?"

"May I go check on him?" I asked. "I would love to see the inside of your studio."

"Yes, thank you. I'll get your husband and the Indian set. Knock first."

"Her name is Aénóhé'ke," I said. Soule opened his mouth to speak but I interrupted him. "And, before you say whatever's about to come out of your mouth, remember she understands you."

I went up the wagon steps, knocked on the door, and was told to enter. The assistant blinked at the light streaming through the open door. "He sent you, didn't he? That man."

280

"May I come in?"

"Yes."

I closed the door and we were thrown into complete darkness. "Do not move," he ordered.

I heard the young man moving assuredly about the small space. The smell of chemicals was overpowering. I couldn't believe how completely dark it was. I was caught wiggling my fingers in front of my face when he turned up the wick of a lamp. He laughed. "You get used to it."

"I'm sorry, I've forgotten your name."

"Joshua Bain."

"Nice to meet you. This is so fascinating," I said, motioning to the pans of chemicals. "It's so organized."

"You have to be in such a small space."

"I can imagine. How in the world do you keep the glass from breaking?"

"It's not easy," Bain said. "After they're developed and printed, we wrap each one in cloth and put it in here." He pulled out a drawer and inside were dozens of cloth-wrapped squares. "Before we leave, we will fill it with sawdust, to give it extra protection. But, we lose a fair few. It's why he takes so many. It's also why we print copies on paper before we leave. At least we will have that. If he thinks it's going to be a big seller, he'll print a dozen or more."

"Indeed?"

A knock sounded on the door. "We better get out there. He thinks your photo is going to make his business."

Soule positioned us as I knew he would; Kindle sitting on a chair, with me and Aénòhé'ke standing on either side, our hands on Kindle's shoulders. Bain brought him the chemically treated piece of glass and the photographer slid it into place in his large camera. "Look at the camera and don't move." Soule ducked his head beneath the black cloth, then reappeared, glaring at me. "Why are you smiling?"

I shrugged. "Why not?"

"You killed a gang of outlaws and you look like someone told you a joke."

I repositioned my holster, which was partially hidden by Kindle's chair. "Can you see my gun? I want to make sure everyone sees my gun."

Soule looked horrified. "What kind of woman smiles and makes jokes about killing?"

I rearranged my expression to suit Soule's idea of propriety. Just before he said, "Steady," I turned my head to look at Aénòhé'ke and smiled.

CHAPTER 21

"Why did he give us buffalo hides?" Aénóhé'ke asked as we walked away from the photography wagon.

"He wanted our photo more than we wanted to give it to him," I said. Aénóhé'ke scowled at the hides she carried against her chest. "Do you not want the hides?"

"I would rather have a horse." She addressed Kindle. "Your horse."

"Everyone wants my horse," Kindle muttered. "He's too big for an Indian pony. And, he's worth a lot more than three hides."

Aénóhé'ke stopped and faced us. "Tall Buffalo tells me you're traveling with us from Darlington."

"Yes."

"And, you want to go to the river."

"Yes."

"I will take you there. In exchange for your horse. Both of your horses."

283

I deferred to Kindle, not having any idea if this was a good deal or bad.

"I would prefer a man scout for us."

"I'm as good a scout as Bob Johnson, probably better."

"Oh, you are?"

Aénòhé'ke nodded. "You hunt, I cook at night, scout during the day, take equal watch."

"What do I do?" I asked.

Aénòhé'ke smiled. "Heal."

My head jerked back and I felt my face flush. "What do you mean?"

"Falling Stars Woman saw your fear, your pain. I felt it when I touched you yesterday. I saw it when you set me free."

Emotion clogged my throat. Kindle touched the small of my back, for comfort or support, I wasn't sure.

"We can help you cleanse your spirit," Aénòhé'ke said.

"How?"

She smiled again. "Soon. First we must get our scraps from the government and go on a buffalo hunt." She walked off carrying the hides.

"Do you have any idea what she's talking about?" I asked.

He nodded slowly.

"Should I be worried?"

"No." He smiled down at me with his crooked, playful smile. "Praying with Isabel Darlington didn't help. A cleansing ceremony might."

"Am I going to have to dance naked under a full moon?"

"Is it wrong of me to hope so?"

"Yes, very." I laughed, though tears had pooled in my eyes. "Thank you."

"For wanting to see you dance naked in the moonlight?"

"No, for making me laugh."

He put his arm around my shoulder and kissed my temple. "At your service. Now, tell me about the inside of the wagon."

We walked to our room while I told Kindle where the glass negatives were kept. "Do you have a plan?"

"I hoped you did."

"Besides flirting with Joshua Bain while you nick the negative, no."

"We shouldn't have to get that desperate."

Henry Pope squeezed between us and put his arms over our shoulders. "You two look like you're plotting something."

"Do we? I would think we look like a couple walking down the street," I said.

"I don't think the two of you will ever merely look like a couple walking down the street." Pope's breath smelled faintly of whisky.

"Have you been drinking already, Henry?"

"Maybe a little nip in my coffee. My teeth, you see. You two aren't plotting how to shake ole Henry Pope, were you?"

"We would never try to shake you, Henry."

"Good to hear."

"You always have the whisky," Kindle said.

"And we always seem to need it," I added.

Pope's voice deepened, as if performing onstage. " 'As we talked over the many miles of trails we traveled, I marveled at how in sync the couple was, even finishing each other's sentences.' " He smiled and said in his normal voice, "See? I will write a glowing feature on you. It will make you famous and land me a secure job."

We stopped and disentangled ourselves from Pope. "We are giving you security and giving Soule riches," I said. "We're becoming infamous, which we don't want to be."

"And, what is it you want, Dr. Bennett?"

My breath caught at hearing my professional name. I realized how much I missed it. As Kindle had said days earlier, we were way past that now. "I want to live in peace, with Kindle. Preferably in a cabin in the woods."

Kindle raised an eyebrow. "A cabin in the

woods?"

"On a stream." The men stared at me with good humor. "What? You asked what I wanted, and that's it."

"I thought she'd be more demanding," Pope said.

Kindle took my hand and kissed my knuckles. His gaze never left mine. "You don't know her very well, Pope. Go gather our things and I'll get the horses ready."

"You *are* leaving. I knew it."

"Come on, Pope. If you want our story, you've got to do something for us."

The two men walked off and I heard Pope say, "Isn't having the whisky enough?"

"No," Kindle said.

I shook my head at the two men. Kindle tried to act gruff with Pope but I knew he liked him. I did, too. Against my better judgment. I wasn't entirely convinced he wouldn't betray us once we got closer to civilization, but I trusted Kindle thought the same thing and had a plan.

We had few belongings to gather. I pulled out my breeches and shirt to change into my men's clothes and stopped. I smoothed the front of my dress and turned from side to side in the mirror. It was a horrible dress, plain gray muslin with a round neck. As unflattering as it was, it made me feel more like myself than the breeches. Still, riding in pants was preferable to a dress. I put the pants on beneath and lifted the front of the skirt up and under. I tucked the hem of the skirt into the waistband of the pants and let the folded material fall in front, showing half of my pants-covered legs. I adjusted my holster so I could pull the gun across my body.

I drew the gun and checked the rounds. Four. I supposed Kindle had reloaded it after the Bell raid. I paused. Should I call it a massacre? I shuddered and holstered the gun, determined to do everything in my power to never fire it again. I considered taking it off and dismissed the idea as quickly as it came. Out here only a fool wouldn't show she had the means for violence, even if she didn't mean to use it.

There was a quick knock at the door. "Charlotte?" a female voice called. Most like Meg coming to check on me.

I opened the door. Deborah stood in the hall with a worried expression, when her gaze dropped to my half skirt and her eyes widened. "What on earth?"

"The gun or the skirt?"

"The skirt."

I released the skirt and let Deborah in the room. "Have you ever heard of pit girls?"

"No."

"Women who sort coal in the north of England. They are quite scandalous. They posed for pictures wearing their outfits like this, and sold them for a pence on the London streets. The girls tuck the skirt up to give them more freedom of movement when they work. I was merely playing around." I stuck my shirt into my saddlebag. "What can I do for you?"

"Are you leaving?"

"We are."

"Now?"

I put my saddlebag over my shoulder and Kindle's over my left arm, forgetting it was burned. I winced and switched the bag to my right. "When the allotment is done. Why?"

"There's a man here, wants to see you."

"Me?"

"And Mr. Oscar. A Pinkerton detective from New York."

Kindle's saddlebag fell to the floor.

Deborah's expression changed to understanding. "It's true, then."

"That my husband sent a Pinkerton for me? Yes."

Deborah narrowed her eyes. "He's from New York."

"I hear they have offices in many cities."

289

"Are you the doctor who killed her lover?" By the expression on her face, Deborah, for all her progressive ideas about slavery and women's suffrage, drew the line at murder.

I turned to the mirror and smoothed my hair back behind my ears, hoping to make it look as feminine as possible, and hoping Deborah saw my unconcern as innocence. "Heavens, no. Though I'm not surprised you'd think so. What bad luck for me there's another woman running from a man in the Territory. Would you do me a favor, darling? Would you take Mr. Oscar's saddlebag to him? He is with Tall Buffalo's tribe. We are going to ride with them for a while. Safety in numbers, and all." I held the saddlebag out. Deborah looked at it like it was a snake. "Don't be nervous, darling. Oscar will be easy to find on his big gray. Tell him I'm saying good-bye to Isabel and will be along shortly."

"You want me to lie to him?"

"A little one. If he comes to talk to this man he'll stand there with that terrifying eye patch and scowl and think he's protecting me. No, better for me to talk to this man alone. I predict I'll be done before you find Mr. Oscar."

I held out my hand. Despite Deborah's distaste for murder — and who can blame her? — I rather liked the girl. "You have the intelligence and fortitude to make a real difference in the world, Deborah."

Her face cleared and she held out her hand. "I wonder if coming out here was the right thing to do."

I shrugged. "I don't know. But, you will do much more than this in your life."

"You think so?"

I nodded. "Absolutely. I hope we meet again someday."

She squeezed my hand. "As do I."

I squeezed her hand, smiled, and went to meet my past.

The Pinkerton sat at Isabel Darlington's kitchen table eating leftover cobbler drowned in cream. His auburn hair was finger combed back from his tall freckled forehead. A long string of hair fell from his widow's peak across his left eye. His face below his peeling nose was noticeably redder than above. With his pale, Irish complexion, he needed a wider brimmed hat than the brown felt John Bull sitting on the table next to him.

I arranged my face in the most vacuous expression I could and thought, Charlotte Martin, don't fail me now.

"Is that not the most heavenly dessert

291

you've ever tasted?"

The Pinkerton looked up at me and stopped chewing. He appraised me from head to toe, and took his time about it. When his eyes finally found mine, my bravado slipped a fraction. The bottle-green eyes that stared back at me were calculating, intelligent, and dead.

He ate another bite and watched me. After he swallowed, he wiped his mouth on the cloth napkin next to the plate and said, "I don't have much to compare it to. Not much dessert being served where I'm from."

The quiet kitchen added to my unease. "Where's Isabel?"

"I asked her for privacy."

I clasped my hands together. "What can I do for you Mr. . . . ?"

"Reed."

"Mr. Reed. Did my husband send you?"

He settled back in his chair, splaying his long legs and resting his hands lightly on his thighs. His long coat gaped open, revealing a holstered gun. "Mrs. Darlington mentioned a husband. In Sherman?"

"Yes."

"You left because he beat you?"

"Yes. Choked me. Almost killed me."

"That's why your voice is so deep."

"Yes."

"And your hand?"

"He broke it months ago."

Mr. Reed nodded and pursed his lips. "And a man named Oscar took you away."

"Mrs. Darlington filled you in admirably. You've never answered my question. Are you here on my husband's behalf?"

He removed a folded piece of paper from his coat pocket and laid it out on the table. "You can drop the act, Catherine. I recognized you the moment you walked in the door."

I picked it up and unfolded it. Pinpricks of light shone through the tiny holes in the creases of the dingy paper. I held the top and bottom of the paper to keep it from folding back on itself and stared at the photo. A proud, arrogant stranger stared back, sure of herself and her talent. Her future. Completely ignorant of the mess her life would become. Of a man halfway across the country who would become more important to her than herself, or her safety. I sniffed, refolded the paper, and tossed it on the table.

"I'm offended. She looks nothing like me."

"You do look a mite harder now."

I narrowed my eyes at the Pinkerton. "You have no proof I'm this Catherine Bennett person."

"I'll admit I'm shocked you've been able to pull off the ruse for as long as you have. You've left a swath of death and destruction behind you, Catherine. You were ridiculously easy to track. You might have made it out of Indian Territory if you hadn't dressed like a man. Everyone knows Catherine Bennett's war story. With the voice and the hand?"

Footsteps sounded in the hall. I would have known that tread anywhere. I guess sending Deborah to Tall Buffalo's tribe instead of the stables hadn't wasted as much time as I wanted. I turned slightly as Kindle's bulk darkened the door. His expression was as I told Deborah it would be. If things hadn't been so dire, I would have laughed.

Reed laid his gun on the table with a *thunk,* and kept his hand on the grip. "Hello, Mr. Oscar."

Kindle stepped forward and slightly in front of me. "Who are you?"

"Lorcan Reed. A Pinkerton sent to retrieve one Catherine Bennett and return her for trial to New York City."

"This isn't Catherine Bennett."

"Right. She's Charlotte Martin. And you're John Oscar, her savior and champion." Reed licked his teeth and leveled the

294

gun at us. "Take off your belts and lay them on the table."

"We'll do nothing of the sort," Kindle said. "We're leaving."

Reed cocked his gun. "I have no compunction about killing you, Captain Kindle. The Army's going to hang you anyway. But, I did enjoy Mrs. Darlington's cobbler and think it a poor thank-you to spill blood all over her freshly scrubbed floors."

I unbuckled my holster and put it on the table, but Kindle didn't move.

"You say she's not Catherine Bennett. Prove it," the Pinkerton said.

"We don't need to prove it. You have to prove she is."

"Why, when you can prove it for me?"

Kindle's eye narrowed, trying to find the trap he knew Reed was laying. "How?"

"Take off your eye patch."

The muscle in Kindle's jaw pulsed.

"It's a good disguise. It almost fooled Sergeant Jones." Reed leaned his chair back on two legs. "So you don't think Jones turned you in, I overheard him talking at Sill to someone who knew you from Saint Louis. Their tongues were loosened from some whisky they'd confiscated. Neither one could believe you threw away your career for a woman. They seemed to think you liked a more sporting woman." Kindle stepped forward, but I grabbed his arm. Reed smirked. "Go on. Take the eye patch off. I bet it itches like the devil."

More footsteps outside. Reed leaned over to look around Kindle to the door. "Mr. Pope! Good to see you again." Reed rose from the table, holding his gun at his waist, and walked to Kindle. Staring Kindle in the eye, Reed took one gun, then the other from Kindle's holster and put them on the table. He pulled the eye patch from Kindle's eye and stuffed it into Kindle's breast pocket. "Never know when you might need it again. Pope?"

"Yes."

"See the bag by the door? There's a pair of irons in there. Get them out and put them on Mr. Kindle here."

"I don't think that's necessary," Pope said, licking his lips, eyes darting between Reed's gun and Kindle.

"Would you rather me put a bullet in his head?"

"No." I stepped forward.

"Stay back, Catherine. No one will get hurt if you all do what I say."

"Are you alone, Reed?" Kindle asked. Neither man had taken their eyes off the other.

Reed smirked. "I was until Pope showed up."

"I'm not going to help you," Pope said. Everyone's eyes fell to the irons he held. "Well, I mean. I'm doing this so you won't kill him."

"Put them on the captain here."

Henry pulled Kindle's right arm behind his back. "Sorry, Captain."

Kindle's expression morphed into one of smug amusement. "Anything for a good story, right, Pope?"

"You understand."

"Perfectly."

"Toss me the bag, Pope," Reed said.

When Kindle was bound, Pope handed Reed the carpetbag, into which the detective placed my holster and Kindle's two guns, but kept his own on Kindle. "I only have one set of irons, for obvious reasons. I'm trusting you to be on your best behavior for a while, Catherine, or I will kill your lover."

I didn't respond.

"We're going out the back around to the stables. No need to draw attention to ourselves."

"Are you taking us to Sill?"

"I want to get closer to New York, not farther away. We're going to the nearest railroad. If I never see another horse in my life, it will be too soon."

CHAPTER 22

The wagon wheels squeaked and groaned across the vast, flat prairie. A relentless wind pushed against our backs and tossed tumbleweeds across our path. Blowing dirt stuck to our sweat and settled into the creases of our skin, tattooing our faces and arms like the Tonkawa. I thought of Little Stick, dead by the cold spring, and wondered if the buzzards had picked his body clean by now.

I pulled on the left rein to steer the oxen around a hole ahead. To my left, Henry Pope rode Kindle's gray. Reed sat on the buckboard to the right, holding his gun in his lap. Kindle sat in the back of the wagon, hands cuffed behind him, head down so his hat protected his face from the sun. Or maybe he was asleep. He hadn't spoken since we left Darlington.

Reed wiped his face with the cloth napkin he'd stolen from Isabel Darlington and squinted up at the sun, his ruddy face twisted into a miserable mien.

"Wrap the napkin around your face," I said. Reed stared at me. "To keep the sun off."

Reed folded the napkin and shoved it in his front pocket. "No wonder they gave this land to the Indians."

"Not much to look at, is there?" I said. "The sunsets are magnificent, though."

"How far to the railroad?"

"I have no idea."

Reed looked questioningly at Pope who shrugged. "How would I know?"

Reed turned to Kindle, who didn't answer. "Kindle," Reed growled.

"Two hundred miles, maybe."

"How long?"

"At this pace? Ten days. Assuming we don't run across angry Indians. Hope you're a good shot at a distance, Reed."

"We would move faster on horses," Pope said.

My sorrel and Pope's horse were tied to the back of the wagon. Reed had sold his horse and tack in exchange for a box of supplies: jerky, beans, flour, and salt. He'd forgotten to buy a pot to cook in, but the three of us remained silent on his omission. He'd figure it out soon enough.

"We only have three horses," I said.

"He has no intention of taking me all the way, do you, Reed?" Kindle said.

"Smart man."

My insides twisted with fear as my mind struggled to come up with a way out of this mess. Reed had the gun trained on me, Kindle was bound, and Henry Pope gave no indication he was here for anything other than his own self-interest. He might help if I instigated something, but I couldn't count on it.

The right front wagon wheel hit a large hole, jolting Reed out of his seat. He yelped in surprise, but regained his balance as the back wheel hit the hole. He gripped the buckboard and yelled, "Watch where you're going."

"I couldn't see it for all the nettles."

"Get out of them."

"Look around. We're surrounded by them. See the yellow-topped plant over there? That is a thistle. They're wonderful for healing burns, Mr. Reed." I lifted my bandaged arm. "You make a tea out of it."

"I'll keep it in mind if I run across any thistles in New York City."

"How much are the Langtons paying you?" I asked.

"Why? You want to match it?"

"If I can."

He wiped his mouth with the back of his hand. "I wasn't sent out here to take you back."

"What? The reward is for her alive," Pope said.

"Not my reward."

My stomach clenched. "Beatrice wants me dead? But, why?"

"I didn't ask, and I don't care."

"I didn't kill George Langton."

"The people who matter say you did."

"You promise to let us go, to stop following me, and I will give you close to five hundred dollars."

"No." He grinned, showing a mouth full of crooked, dirty teeth.

The wagon hit another hole and Reed popped off his seat. Kindle pounced on the Pinkerton before he could regain his balance, sending them over the side of the wagon and into the patch of nettles.

I pulled back on the oxen, set the brake, and jumped into the back of the wagon while the sounds of fighting went on below me. Reed screaming in pain. The thud of fists. The crack of bones. Hissing and rattling. Grunts of exertion. Kindle's growl that escalated into a roar and Reed's scream spoke of excruciating pain. The irons with the key in the lock lay forgotten on the bed of the wagon. I grabbed the first gun I found, stood in the wagon, and turned my attention to the men on the ground. I cocked the gun, ready to shoot Reed if need be. My arm drooped as I saw Kindle straddling the Pinkerton, shoving his face into a nettle with a free hand while squeezing his neck with the other. Reed's visible eye was full of terror. A dozen rattlesnakes squirmed around them.

"William, don't move!" He either didn't hear me or ignored me. His shoulders shook from the exertion of strangling the Pinkerton.

Instead of slithering away from the men in terror, the snakes moved closer. "You're going to kill him and yourself!"

Kindle kept his hands on Reed and looked up at me in astonishment. "You're in the middle of a snake den," I said, my voice coarse with fear. Kindle relaxed his grip and noticed the snakes for the first time. He lifted his hands slowly, but it was enough to entice the nearest and largest snake. In a blink, it reared back, struck Kindle on the hand, and held on. Yelling, he stood and tried to shake the snake off, which only made it cling the harder.

I cocked my gun. "William, don't move."

He stopped and looked at me, understanding crossing his face as I shot. The bullet cut the snake in half. Blood dripped from the half connected to Kindle's hand. Kindle's expression was one of shock, horror, and appreciation.

"Nice shot, but a little more warning next time."

"Goddamn, you're a fine woman," Pope said.

Kindle grabbed the dead snake below its head and tried to pull it off. Snake blood splattered on his pants as he worked his fingers beneath the jaw of the snake and pried its mouth from his hand. He threw the half body away and stared at the back of his hand for a moment, before pulling his gun, cocking it, and aiming it at Reed, who was prone on the ground.

"No!" I yelled.

I jumped from the wagon, away from the snakes that were thankfully slithering away. The wind blew Kindle's hair into his face, obscuring his expression, but not enough that I couldn't tell he was flabbergasted. "What the hell are you doing, Laura? He was going to kill me, probably Pope, too, and do God knows what to you before killing you."

"No more killing."

Pope watched us from the back of the horse. "He's no threat now."

Lorcan Reed's body convulsed on the ground. A snake slithered from beneath him. I stepped back.

"I hate snakes," Pope said.

Kindle holstered his gun and climbed up in the wagon seat. He took the reins and released the brake.

"We aren't leaving him here to die," I said.

"He may live. Live to keep chasing us," Kindle said.

Reed's arms seized up across his chest and his convulsions increased. "Come on, Pope. Help me get him in the wagon," I said.

"Are all the snakes gone?"

"Henry, get down here, now."

Pope was off the horse and beside me. I grabbed one arm and pulled Reed onto his side. A snake hissed and rattled. With his head half-turned away and a grimace on his face, Pope stomped on the snake's head with his boot heel until it was flattened and bloody, though the tail spasmed and rattled. "Get his shoulders," I ordered, and went to the Pinkerton's feet. Pope did as told.

I ignored the painful nettles poking into my hands and struggled with Reed's feet. Kindle jumped from the buckboard, pushed me aside, and helped Pope throw the man into the wagon. Kindle moved around me to get to the buckboard. I grabbed his arm to stop him.

"Let me see your hand."

He held it out. The punctures from the fangs were between the metacarpals of the left index and middle fingers. I lifted the hand closer to my face. "Is the fang in there?"

"Yes." I jumped into the wagon and got my saddlebag, ignoring Reed's obvious pain for the moment. I pulled out my leather pouch containing my medical instruments and returned to Kindle. I lay the instruments out on the back of the wagon.

"Pope, give me your flask."

Already mounted and ready to go, Pope walked his horse to me and handed the flask down. I uncorked it with my teeth and poured whisky on Kindle's hand and my scalpel and tweezers. I pushed the tweezers down into the puncture to get a grip on the fang and pulled the almost-inch-long fang out. Kindle never flinched.

"Jesus," Pope said.

I tossed the tweezers and fang onto the wagon bed and picked up my scalpel.

"Any tips, Kindle?"

"This all is vaguely familiar," Kindle said. I was relieved to see a modicum of humor in his expression. "Cut across it."

I put the tip of the scalpel against Kindle's hand and paused. "Ready?" He nodded and I cut a gash across the wound. He brought his hand to his mouth and sucked out the blood and venom and spit it out. He repeated the action two or three times and wiped his mouth with the back of his other hand. I inspected the hand, which was swelling.

"Did we wait too long?"

Kindle sucked and spit two more times. He shrugged. "We'llsee."

I splashed some whisky on the wound and wrapped it with one of the strips of cloth I'd cut from our sheets at Darlington. I suppose part of me always expected the worst to happen.

"Can you drive?"

"Yes."

"I have to help Reed."

I climbed into the back of the wagon and took quick stock of Lorcan Reed. His entire right side was punctured with nettle needles and his face was swelling alarmingly. I needed to get the needles out of him as quick as possible, but first I had to see if he was snakebit.

"Pope, tie your horse to the back. I need your help."

I had to hand it to Henry Pope, he had zero qualms about taking orders from a woman. His horse was tied to the wagon and he was by me waiting for instructions when Kindle slapped the reins against the oxen's backs and turned the wagon to the north and the Canadian River.

Henry and I sat across the wagon from each other, Lorcan Reed between us, unconscious and barely alive. I'd sucked the venom from two bites on his back and removed fifty nettle needles from his face and neck. Half of his face was swollen and deformed and he was having trouble breathing. I was wracking my brain to figure out what I would use as an airway if I had to perform a tracheotomy when Pope spoke.

"Why are you helping this man?"

I sighed. "I'm so tired of death, Henry."

"Chose the wrong profession, then."

"No, actually. I've lost only three patients in my career. Two at Richardson who were so far gone when I got there I hardly take the blame for their deaths." I tried to smile. "I haven't lost my arrogance, have I?"

"It's not arrogance if it's true." He leveled his gaze at me. "Whose deaths are you talking about, then?"

"Maureen. Everyone on the wagon train.

The soldiers killed when Black had me kidnapped. Little Stick."

"Who's Little Stick?"

"Our first guide." I stared at Lorcan Reed, thought of the five other men who'd come after us since Jacksboro and had died as a result. "The bounty hunters." The Arapaho. Bell, Tuesday, Kruger, and Cuidado. I rubbed my head. The list seemed endless.

The wagon bumped over a hole. Kindle swayed in the seat. "William? Are you all right?"

He nodded, but didn't answer. I stepped over Lorcan and onto the seat. Kindle's head had shrunk into his shoulders and his face was pale and sweaty. Dark circles rimmed his bloodshot eyes. His whole body shook. "William!"

He slumped against me, burning with fever. "Henry! Come take the reins."

Pope wedged himself onto the seat and took the oxen in hand while I tried to hold Kindle upright. Kindle's glassy eyes met mine. "I think one bit my leg."

"Oh, why didn't you tell me?"

"When I realized," he wheezed, "it was too late."

"Too late? What do you mean?"

"He means once the venom gets in the bloodstream, there's not much you can do,"

Henry said.

"No." I pulled Kindle's knife from his boot. "Which leg?" Kindle stared blankly at me, his mouth moved, but no words came out. "Which leg!" I yelled. Blood pounded in my ears, tears pooled in my eyes.

I put the blade of the knife between my teeth and felt Kindle's legs above the knee, assuming his leather riding boots had protected the bottom. He flinched when I touched his right knee, which was warm and straining against his pants. I cut through his pants and saw two tiny punctures in the middle of his kneecap, which had swollen to twice its normal size. I gasped, and for a long moment, was transfixed by indecision and ignorance. My mind was wiped clean of all the knowledge and experience I'd soaked up over the past ten years. My eyes went from Kindle's flaming red knee to his pale face. His eyes met mine and I knew he was resigned to his fate.

Anger spurred me to action. "Goddammit you aren't going to die on me, William Kindle." I pressed the knife tip to his bulging knee and was readying to cut when Pope stopped me.

"Laura, look!"

A line of tipis stretched out on the horizon as far as we could see. I dropped Kindle's knife, lay him out on the buckboard, his head in Pope's lap. I brushed Kindle's hair from his face. "You're going to live, William." I kissed his temple, climbed over the buckboard and around Reed, who was unconscious and breathing laboriously. I untied Kindle's gray from the back of the wagon and with agility born of desperation, jumped on the horse. I kicked him into a run toward the village, praying all the way it was a Cheyenne village, and I could find Falling Stars Woman before it was too late.

CHAPTER 23

I sat out of the way and watched through tear-filled eyes as Falling Stars Woman and Aénóhé'ke tried to heal Kindle. He lay on a buffalo robe at the back of the tent, naked and unconscious, his scars and injuries stark against his pale skin. His head jerked forward and vomit bubbled from his mouth. I reached toward them, but couldn't get out the order to turn him on his side before the women had done it. I settled back on my heels, hands in my lap, and made myself consider what I would do if Kindle died. Where I would go, yes, but mostly how I would live with myself knowing my inattention had killed him.

If I'd let Kindle put a bullet in the Pinkerton none of this would have happened. I would've thought to inspect all of Kindle — he'd fallen in the middle of the rattlesnake den as well — instead of being so worried about saving a man who would most likely do to me what the Comanche had on the Canadian River.

"What about the Pinkerton?" Pope had asked when Kindle was being taken from the wagon and into Falling Stars Woman's tent.

A fly buzzed around Reed's slack face and landed on his eyelid.

"He's dead."

I walked off, tears pooling in my eyes. It had all been for nothing. I'd risked Kindle's life to save a dead man.

Falling Stars Woman held her hands over the smoking fire and brought them toward her, directing the smoke over her body, and did the same for Kindle's knee. It was a routine she'd done four times now. Singing would come next, along with shaking a rattle, followed by biting the afflicted area to suck out the illness, and ending with smoking a pipe that sat between the fire and Kindle's body, with the pipe stem pointing toward the door.

I had little faith in the efficacy of the ceremony, which seemed to be based on spirituality instead of science. I'd always inwardly scoffed at people who put so much faith in prayer and God to save their afflicted kin instead of trusting medicine and my skills as a doctor. Since I had nothing to offer Kindle by way of healing, I was in no position to ridicule. Instead, I remained silent and observed the ritual. The calmness with which it was performed managed to quiet my spiraling mind.

Aénôhé'ke handed Falling Stars Woman a cup. They lifted Kindle up and put the cup to his lips. He sputtered, drank, and was laid down again.

Aénôhé'ke came to me, and as she'd done with most of Falling Stars Woman's actions, explained. "To make him cold."

Falling Stars Woman chewed a root, spat it into her hands, raised it in ceremony to the four cardinal directions, and rubbed the poultice on Kindle's knee. Aénôhé'ke sat next to me. "Medicine root," Aénôhé'ke said.

I wanted to know specifics: How does it work? What is it made of? Where do you find it? But I didn't ask. Their medicine wasn't based on facts, but rather spirituality and knowledge passed down through the years. They didn't concern themselves with the why or how, only knew it effective more often than not. Whether it worked was up to the spirits.

Falling Stars Woman sat down and smoked a pipe as food was brought in. After she finished her pipe, cleaned it, and set it back down with the stem facing the door and the bowl directed toward Kindle, she placed five pieces of meat in her hands and presented them to the sky, earth, and four cardinal directions. She left the tipi and returned a few minutes later with one remaining piece of meat, which she placed between the fire and the door. She returned to her place and we ate. Though I had no appetite, I knew to refuse food was to give the highest offense.

"Will he live?" I asked, after the silence became oppressive.

"He is strong," Falling Stars Woman said. "He wants to live."

The relief that washed through me was short-lived. Aénohé'ke looked to Falling Stars Woman, who nodded. "The poison is strong as well," Aénohé'ke said.

"What can we do?"

"We will give the medicine time to work."

"Wait, you mean. How long?"

"The night. When the sun rises, we will know what to do."

I wanted to lash out at her cryptic mumbo-jumbo, to force her to give me a straight answer to the question. Didn't she realize what was at stake? Couldn't she try harder? Do more? Why did she sit there so calmly, eating, talking quietly to Aénohé'ke, while Kindle lay behind her on the precipice of death?

Aénòhé'ke left the tent. Falling Stars Woman leveled her steady gaze at me and I knew she'd heard every angry thought I'd hurled her way. "Tell me."

"Tell you what?"

"Why your spirit is broken."

"The man I love is dying."

Falling Stars Woman shook her head. "Death follows you."

"Yes, I know."

"It is your companion."

"My companion?"

"You understand each other. He knows you will fight him. He enjoys the fight. As do you."

"I do not enjoy death. My life has been about banishing death."

"And you will always lose. It is why if Spotted Beard Man dies you will mourn, but you will move on."

I shook my head vehemently. "No."

Falling Stars Woman watched me complacently. I wanted to jump across the fire and rip her face off, to take a hatchet to her jaw as the Kiowa had done to Maureen. "How dare you sit there and pretend to know me. You know *nothing* of me. Of what I've been through — at the hands of your people."

Falling Stars Woman raised her eyebrows. "Yes, I know the line. *Your people are the true People.* They are the ones trying to make peace. I saw what those warriors paraded around the bonfire the other night. The blond pigtail? It was obtained through butchery. You cannot deny it." She didn't try. "You sit there and entreat me to heal when my wounds are the direct result of people like you." As the words were leaving my mouth I knew the hypocrisy of them. Hot shame mixed with a determination to hold on to my anger, to direct it at her, at anyone but myself.

I walked around the fire and knelt by Kindle. I took his hand in mine and stroked his long, thin fingers, remembered them massaging my broken hand patiently, gently bringing it back to life. I closed my eyes and saw him sitting at a piano, dressed for dinner, his hair brushed back, accentuating his clean-shaven face and the scar that had brought us together all those years ago. He looked up at me and his eyes sparkled with good humor and happiness as Bach turned into a country jig. My hand, which had been resting on his shoulder, moved to ostensibly rub his neck, but truthfully to feel his silken hair beneath my fingers. A child laughed and I was caught around the legs by small arms, jostling me into Kindle. The piano keys clanged a jarring chord.

"Laura."

My eyes opened to a dim, firelit room and the aroma of burning sage and sweetgrass. Smoke curled and danced through the hole in the ceiling, first obscuring, then revealing a full moon amid a sea of stars. My gaze traveled down to Kindle, hoping he'd spoken my name. His breaths were small and sharp, like the last gasps of a dying man.

I placed my hand on the center of his chest and watched it rise and fall. I could hardly bring myself to look at him fully, to see what throwing in with me had wrought on him physically. His body was a riot of contrasts between the healthy man he had been and the wasted version he'd become. A pelt of dark hair covered his chest and stopped where his ribs protruded like a cliff above his flat stomach. His left leg was noticeably thinner than the right, due to atrophy from the arrow wound, which would be exacerbated by the snakebite on his knee. My vision blurred and a great sob escaped my throat. I blinked and tears fell onto my lap. "The bite was so small," I whispered.

"The smaller the snake, the more dangerous they are." Aénóhé'ke sat across Kindle's body from me. We were alone in the tent. I hadn't noticed or heard Falling Stars Woman leave.

"If I lose him, I lose myself." I laughed, wiping away the tears running down my cheeks. "God, Catherine Bennett would be appalled at the sentiment." I inhaled and exhaled deeply. "The hope of a future is the only thing keeping me sane. Every day, multiple times, I remember what happened to me. How it felt. Physically." I fought against the memories that had become clearer and clearer the further in the past they were. The lone whisker on the chin of one warrior. The smell of mud and dead fish. The pain as they drove themselves deep within me. The sticky blood between my thighs as I curled into a ball during their breaks. My legs being pulled apart and it starting over.

I stared at Aénóhé'ke. Only a yellow bruise around her eyes remained of the beating she took at the hands of the whisky traders. "Help me," I pleaded. "If he dies, I won't ever leave the bank of that river."

Chapter 24

On shaking legs and wrapped in a buffalo skin, I ducked beneath the door of the sweat lodge. Falling Stars Woman, Aénóhé'ke, and Bob Johnson were arranging Kindle's unconscious form on the floor on the opposite side from the door, in the same position he'd been in during the medicine ceremony. I walked clockwise around the lodge and sat near Kindle's head, as Aénóhé'ke had instructed outside while the lodge keeper smudged me with smoking sage and sweetgrass. I sat cross-legged and wrapped the animal skin tight around me as four other Cheyenne entered and took their places.

Using forked tree limbs, the lodge keeper brought hot rocks into the lodge and placed them in the rectangular hole in the center of the area. Finally, the hole was full and she returned with a bucket and a buffalo-tail brush, which she dipped in the water and swept over the hot rocks. The flap over the door closed, throwing us into near darkness. Steam rose and soon surrounded us.

The stones hissed and popped in the silence. The chant started low, and though I didn't understand a word, I knew it for a prayer. I let the rhythm of the words soothe me. My skin was soon slicked with sweat. Rivulets ran down my cheeks and dripped off my chin. It trickled between my breasts and down my spine. The air was heavy with water and the smell of sage. I inhaled the scented air in great gulps and a sense of great calm settled over me. My mind quieted and the world dropped away.

I walked across the plains, humming as my hands skimmed along the tops of the tall buffalo grass. I passed one buffalo, and another, and another, until the beasts roamed around me, occasionally looking up, before returning to their grazing. The grasses evaporated and were replaced by a landscape of low scrub and cacti. Red boulders dotted the ground, but as I got closer they were revealed to be the carcasses of dead, skinned buffalo. Flies buzzed around the carcasses; a buzzard landed on the mound of stinking meat, pecked at its dinner, and fought off others who got too close.

A large cone-shaped mountain loomed

before me. I followed a well-worn hunting path across the foothills to the mouth of a cave, where I paused. The familiar smell of Irish stew and the sound of a woman singing floated from within. I stepped inside.

The cave was roughly ten feet in diameter, with a large, well-scrubbed wooden table and four chairs in the center. A fireplace was set into the back wall, in front of which a woman stood, stirring the contents of a large cast-iron pot.

"Maureen?"

She turned and smiled. "Katie, my girl, I've been waiting an age. Sit down, stew's almost ready."

I glanced around. From the corner of my eye the cave was bursting with items, foreign and familiar: my father's favorite wing chair, my medical bag, a smoldering wagon wheel, a trunk overflowing with colorful silk gowns, Kindle whittling a stick. When I tried to look at the items straight on, they disappeared, leaving only the bare cave walls covered in primitive drawings that seemed to spiral out from a central point. With my finger, I traced the nautilus from its beginning image: a man, woman, and child; man and child; the child on a ship; lines of men aiming guns at one another, a caduceus. When I saw the woman running from a hangman's noose I realized I was reading the story of my life. I carried on with equal parts dread and anticipation, realizing this wall would foretell my future. The images spiraled on up into the dark roof of the cave, but the ones of the future were blurred and jumbled, indistinct, but clearly there.

Maureen was at my elbow, wiping her hands on a towel. "You will have a long life, Katie Girl."

"I'm not sure I want a long life."

" 'Course you do."

The images on the wall came alive, and with jerky, awkward movements replayed what I endured on the Canadian. I watched, rapt, with tears streaming down my face, until a hand reached out and wiped the images from the wall.

"Enough."

I turned. Maureen was gone, replaced by a beautiful woman in a pale green silk gown, her strawberry-blond hair pulled to the side and cascading across her heaving bosom. "Dwelling on it won't change it," Camille King said.

"Don't tell me to move past it."

"You're already past it."

"I'm not."

She grabbed me by the arms and shook me, her eyes steely. "You are. You survived,

Catherine." She released me and lifted her chin to look down her nose at me. "You *want* to play the victim."

"I am not a victim."

"Then stop acting like one."

I heard a clap behind me, then another, and another, and realized it was applause. I turned and found Cotter Black sitting at Maureen's kitchen table, feet kicked up, applauding. There was a large hole in his forehead and dried blood and dirt caked his face.

"Honest to God," Cotter Black said. "I can't believe you and Billy made it this far."

I lunged across the table, grabbed Black by the throat, and squeezed. His faced puffed and turned purple. Blood filled his eyes and the left one popped out and rolled onto the floor. I released him and jumped back, staring at the eye, which looked up at me accusingly, blaming me for its fate.

"Laura."

It was the Kindle from my dream. Dressed for dinner, sitting at a piano, playing Bach. He nodded for me to join him on the bench and I did. He continued to play, softly, beautifully. I was mesmerized by his dancing fingers, until his hands smashed the keys down.

I looked up. Camille, one eyebrow arched

and an amused expression on her face, sat across the table from me.

"I never knew you were so spiritual, Catherine."

"I'm not."

Camille looked around the cave and settled her gaze back on me with a wry grin. She leaned forward and took my hands. "Remember what I told you?"

"You told me quite a lot I'd rather forget."

"My bedroom advice will come in handy, and soon enough. But, that isn't what I'm talking about, and you know it."

"Don't play the victim."

She shook her head. "Men are savages. White, red, black, yellow. Doesn't matter. They're all the same, in the end. They're driven by power."

"Not Kindle."

Her expression turned to one of pity, as if I had failed a test she expected me to pass with flying colors. She squeezed my hand. "They only have power over you if you give it to them." She sat back. "Men are pathetically easy to manipulate, to control." She dipped her head and stared at me with eyes glittering with malice. "It's the women you need to worry about."

"Laura," said a man's voice behind me.

I turned and opened my eyes. The cave

was gone, replaced by a dim lodge, empty save a hole full of steaming rocks and Kindle, sitting hunched beneath an animal skin next to me. I reached out and touched his pale face. "Are you real?"

He grasped my hand and kissed my palm. "Yes."

"Are you well?"

"I'm awake."

The flap of the sweat lodge opened and Aénôhé'ke ducked into the room. "Come."

She and I helped Kindle stand, walk around the stones, and outside. Aénôhé'ke led us to the river and took our skins from our shoulders. Naked, we stood in the moonlight, the night air chilling our sweat-covered skin. Four or five Cheyenne men and women who had been in the sweat lodge with us were in the river. They beckoned for us to join them. Leaning heavily on me, Kindle walked with me to the river and I made sure he was safely settled before crouching down and letting the cool water envelop me. I lifted my head and stared up at the blanket of stars above us. With a deep breath, I closed my eyes, submerged completely, and let the Canadian River wash my past away.

CHAPTER 25

We stayed with the Cheyenne for a month to let Kindle recuperate. Falling Stars Woman took me under her wing and taught me as much as she could about the roots and plants they used as medicine. I begged some paper and a pencil from Pope so I could draw the specimens, and dried what I could to take with me. Pope wrote feverishly in his notebooks from sunup to sundown, and refused to show us what he was writing so adamantly and often that we finally gave up asking. Kindle spent most of the time with the old warriors. He was a fair way on to speaking Cheyenne well enough we wouldn't need a translator when we met other tribes who used the Algonquian dialect in the future.

The three of us shared a tipi, which wasn't as uncomfortable a situation as one would have thought. Kindle was too weak to want to do more than to hold me as we fell asleep, and Pope was so distracted by his writing he barely acknowledged us before bed and fell asleep almost instantly. He snored like a foghorn, which kept me and Kindle awake and gave us hours of opportunity to talk. Over the weeks, we had experimented with all manner of distractions and nothing had moved Pope. I suspected he would sleep through a hurricane.

We took to spending mornings by the river, before we went off to our daily routine with the Cheyenne: Kindle hunting and smoking with the men, me digging roots with Aénóhé'ke and learning as much as possible about their healing practices, and Pope sitting by the river, scribbling away.

"What do you think he's writing?" Kindle whispered, nodding at Pope sitting against a tree nearby.

"I tried to nick it today but he caught me," I said.

"I have corrupted you completely, haven't I?"

"Yes. It is all your fault."

Kindle held my hands between his. "How is your hand?"

I flexed the fingers. "Much better, thanks to you." Kindle massaged my hand every morning by the river.

"Could you perform surgery?"

"If I had to."

"Let's hope you never do."

"Most importantly, I can draw and write."

"That's not the most important thing you do with your hand." He moved my hand down to his groin.

I raised my eyebrows. "You always have been a quick healer."

"I'm motivated."

"Are you?" I rubbed his erection through his breeches.

He inhaled deeply and settled back. I removed my hand and whispered in his ear, "Not in front of Henry." I pulled out the straight razor and strap and had Kindle hold the thick leather while I sharpened the blade.

"It's time we got married."

"How romantic you make it sound."

"I want it to be true when I call you my wife."

My hand stopped. "Do you need approval from the church? Because I do not. I feel more connected to you than I have any other person in my life. A ceremony won't change it."

"But, in the eyes of the law and society, we are not married. Marriage gives you a level of protection you do not currently have." He brushed a strand of hair from my face. "Do you not want to be married?"

"Of course I do. It's only, I feel we are."

He kissed my hand. "As do I. But, I want the church to know it as well. Besides, I feel well enough to travel and we need to put as much distance between us and any other Pinkerton who might be on our trail."

I took the razor strap from Kindle and placed it on his saddlebags. "I wonder how many she sent after me?"

"I wonder why she sent Reed to kill you instead of take you in."

"I've been wondering the same thing."

Pope spoke up. "She knows you didn't do it. If she has you come in for trial, the truth will come out."

Kindle and I stared at each other. "He's right," I said. "That means we should go back. They don't have the evidence. I know they don't. I can clear my name and we won't have to worry about being chased for the rest of our lives."

Kindle pursed his lips and shook his head. "No."

"No? Why not?"

"You said her family is powerful."

"Her father is on the state supreme court and her father-in-law is one of the richest men in the country," Pope said.

"I don't want to take the chance you'll

330

lose. I couldn't bear it. Don't ask me to. We'll find somewhere quiet to live. They won't find us."

"He's right, Laura. Don't take the chance."

I sighed, letting go of the dream of having a normal life. I picked up the cup of soap and handed it out to Kindle. "Are you ready?"

"Ready," Kindle said.

"Will you shave me next?" Pope asked.

"I will."

"You will?"

"Don't act so surprised. You are letting us borrow your tools. It's the least I can do."

"I'll see how well you do on Kindle first."

Kindle twirled the brush in the cup of soap I held and lathered his face. "I'm offended, Henry," I said. "You forget I'm a surgeon. I am an expert with knives."

"She is," Kindle confirmed. "But, take comfort in the knowledge that if she cuts you, she's even better with a needle and thread."

I punched Kindle in the shoulder. He dropped the brush in the mug and I pushed it into his chest. "Hold this while I take a sharp razor to your throat."

I lifted Kindle's chin, ran the blade up his neck, and wiped the soapy whiskers on the blanket across his shoulders. "On second thought . . ." Kindle said.

"Too late." I shaved another strip.

Pope sat with his back against a tree, one knee propped up so he could write.

"Are you ever going to show us what you're writing?" Kindle asked.

"I will. When it's done."

"Going to have a tough time selling a newspaper article as long as a novel," I said.

Pope merely smiled. "How long will it take us to get to Independence?"

"A week?" Kindle said.

"Why Independence and not Saint Louis?"

"More choices. Train east or west. Oregon Trail, river."

"Are you going to tell me where you're going?" Pope said.

"No," Kindle and I said in unison.

"Don't trust me?"

"No," Kindle said.

"How reassuring," Pope said.

"I don't think you would turn us in, Henry," I said.

"But, when your article publishes, the Pinkertons will descend on you. Best you not know our plans," Kindle said.

"Good point," Pope said.

I ran the razor down Kindle's cheek,

revealing the scar I had stitched up at Antietam. I leaned down and kissed his bare cheek, getting soap on the corners of my mouth. "I've missed your cheek."

"You two are nauseating," Pope said.

I laughed and finished shaving Kindle. When I'd wiped all of the soap off him I held up Pope's tiny mirror. Kindle turned his head from side to side and rubbed his smooth face. "Much better."

I traced the stark line between his pale and tanned skin. "You'll need to wear a kerchief for a while." Kindle grabbed me around the waist and pulled me to him. He lifted his face for a kiss. I gladly obliged.

"Hmm," I said. "I don't know. I think I miss the beard." Kindle swatted me on the bum and I skirted away with a laugh. "Your turn, Henry."

"Are you going to kiss me like that when you're done?"

"If you let me read what you're writing."

"Excuse me?" Kindle said.

I lathered Henry's face. "I suppose I should kiss you for slipping Kindle the key to Reed's irons. That was very quick thinking, Henry."

"I do have my moments of brilliance," Henry said.

"I never thanked you," Kindle said.

"A kiss from Laura will be thanks enough," Henry said.

"I think a handshake and a sincere thank-you is enough." Kindle held out his hand and Henry took it.

"You're welcome," Henry said.

I finished shaving Henry's stubble, wiped the blade on the towel across his shoulders, and handed him the closed blade. I took his cheeks in my hands and kissed him on the lips. He was too shocked to reciprocate and the disappointment about that fact became clear on his face. I smiled and said, "Thank you for saving the man I love."

Henry blushed and stammered out a thank-you.

"Did she kiss you?" Kindle said.

Henry cleared his throat.

"Yes, I did." I turned to Kindle, my back to Henry. "He has very soft lips," I said, and winked.

"You aren't trying to steal my woman are you, Henry?"

"Well, I . . ."

"If you keep calling me *woman,* there will be no stealing necessary."

Aénóhé'ke appeared on the top of the riverbank. She waved and climbed down to join us. She carried two rooting sticks. "Time to go to work while you two lazy bums sit around and do nothing," I said.

Kindle took the cup and brush from Pope and went to the river to clean them. "I'm going hunting with Bob Johnson."

Pope chuckled. "Bob Johnson. I can't get over that name."

"You should come with us, Henry. Never know when you'll be on your own and need to know how to hunt and field dress your kill."

"Why do you think I've stuck so doggedly to you, Kindle? It isn't your company, God knows."

Aénòhé'ke stopped next to me and handed me my root digger. "You two stay out of trouble today," I said.

Kindle stood and flicked the excess water out of the mug. He turned and limped toward us, smiling, looking more like himself than he had since Fort Richardson. I inhaled deeply and let the happiness and contentment wash through me. He came to me and kissed me. "Don't work too hard," he said with a sly grin. "Keep an eye out for a long stick. I want to whittle a cane for myself."

"Whittle? You're a whittler?"

"Not a good one." Kindle's brows furrowed. "Aénòhé'ke, are you feeling well?" The Cheyenne stared at Kindle with a

335

confused expression. Kindle rubbed his bare cheeks. "I don't think she likes it,"

"No," she said. "It is nice." She turned and walked up the bank. Kindle watched her go, his brows furrowed much as Aénòhé'ke's had been.

"What's wrong?" I asked.

He smiled down at me. "Nothing. Go find me a stick, woman."

I kissed him on one cheek and gently slapped the other. "Don't overdo it today, Major."

He rolled his eyes and I walked up the riverbank to catch up with Aénòhé'ke.

CHAPTER 26

It was the most uneventful week of my acquaintance with William Kindle. We traveled light, and as a result, were able to make thirty to forty miles per day without blowing our horses. Bob Johnson scouted ahead while one of his helpers scouted behind and returned to the camp each night to help with the watch. Aénóhé'ke hunted small game and cooked at night. Kindle and I helped as much as possible, and Henry continued to write feverishly, as if on a deadline.

As we drew closer to Independence, we encountered more people, whites and Indians, as well as Army columns marching from Saint Louis to various forts on the frontier. Trash littered the land, evidence of the hundreds of people who'd passed on their way to better lives. I could feel the pull of civilization, and thrilled at it. Aénóhé'ke, however, got more withdrawn as evidence of white encroachment increased.

We camped under a large willow tree beside a rushing creek. Firewood was sparse on the ground, due to heavy traffic, so Aénòhé'ke climbed a tree and was cutting small, dead branches with a hatchet and throwing them down to me. She straddled a thick oak limb and reached out for a branch. Her legs dangled down, exposed, and I noticed the scars I'd seen on her legs the night I saved her from Tuesday.

"Aénòhé'ke, how did you get those scars?"

She held the dead limb in one hand, as if it was going to run away, and the hatchet in the other. She seemed to consider my question before cutting the limb with one quick hit, and tossing it down to me. "It is our way, when a loved one dies, to mark yourself with grief. Kiowa and Comanche cut their breasts. We cut our legs and leave them bare while we mourn." She put the hatchet in her belt and climbed higher.

"Oh, be careful!"

Aénòhé'ke grinned at me. "This is nothing, Motse'eoo'e."

I smiled at the name. It was a fair sight better than Talks Like a Man Woman. When I told Aénòhé'ke and Falling Stars Woman of my vision inside the cone-shaped mountain, they said I had been visited by Sweet

Medicine, their holiest of holy men. They told me he visited very few people and his fortunes always came to pass. When word spread across the tribe, people looked at me with more curiosity, and a good deal of awe. Tall Buffalo summoned me and we smoked a pipe while I told him my vision. When I finished he was silent for a long time. He named me Motse'eoo'e — Sweet Medicine Woman — and gave me a medicine bag to wear around my neck. He said I would always be welcome by the Cheyenne and Arapaho, I had only to show them the bag I wore. He entreated me to never remove it, and I had not. Nor had I opened it.

"Who did you lose?" I asked.

"My son." She chopped more dead limbs until I had a nice little pile to take back to the camp. She climbed down the tree and jumped from the lowest branch, landing lithely on the ground. She studied me, waiting for the question she knew would come.

"What happened?"

"He was killed by a soldier at Washita."

I placed my hand over my heart and another on her arm. "Aénóhé'ke, I am so sorry." Her face remained blank and I dropped my hand from her arm, wondering if every time she looked at me, Kindle, and Pope she saw the anonymous soldier who had killed her son, as I had seen the Kiowa and Comanche every time I looked at her. I knew there was nothing I could do, no solace I could offer for her lost child. I tried to smile encouragingly and said, "Let's get this wood back to the camp. Hopefully Henry caught a fish."

Henry was not an outdoorsman, and though he paid attention and tried hard, nothing ever seemed to come together for him. Surrounded by capable people it was endearing, but if I were alone with him in the wilderness, I would survive better on my own.

That night around the campfire everyone was subdued except Henry, who was so excited about catching a small fish one would have thought he'd birthed a baby. Aénòhé'ke stared into the fire and I wondered if her distance was due to my bringing up the death of her son.

"In the morning, we can part," Kindle said. Aénòhé'ke and Bob Johnson looked up from the fish bones in their hands. "We're less than a day's ride from Independence, and seeing more and more people along the way. We can find our way easy enough. I will trade horses with you in the morning, Aénòhé'ke, and you can go on your way."

I'd forgotten about Kindle's horse trade with Aénòhé'ke, and based on her expression, she had as well. Bob Johnson looked to Aénòhé'ke, who stared at Kindle. She nodded and went back to her fish.

I slept soundly, with my saddle as my pillow, and dreamt of Kindle playing the piano in my aunt Emily's parlor and a child running in to say good night, wrapping little arms around my legs, jostling me into Kindle, and a discordant chord. I looked down at the child and saw Aénòhé'ke's face. She opened her mouth, but it was Kindle's scream I heard.

Strong hands grabbed me and dragged me away from the fire. I woke to a chaotic, senseless scene. Bob Johnson sat on Kindle's chest, blocking my view of his face. Aénòhé'ke watched, holding a knife in her hand. My scream pierced through the grunts and groans of Kindle's struggle. Bob Johnson lifted his arm, the hatchet Aénòhé'ke used to cut firewood earlier glowing in the low firelight, and brought it down.

"NOOOOOOOO!" I struggled against my captor, knowing full well what came next. Pope, inconceivably asleep until now, woke and sat up with a dazed expression. Another Indian walked up and put a gun on him.

Pope didn't move.

Kindle had stopped struggling. I sobbed as the realization hit me. Kindle was dead.

Bob Johnson stood, pulled Kindle's arms over his head, and tied them. Another Indian did the same with his feet. I forced myself to look at Kindle's face. It wasn't bloody or broken. Still, I didn't understand.

Aénóhé'ke came to me and stopped an arm's length away.

"Why are you doing this?" I said. "I thought —"

"We were friends?" Aénóhé'ke said. "I like you, but we will never be friends as long as the white men kill and torture our women and children."

"So you're going to kill and torture us as retribution? We haven't done anything!"

Aénóhé'ke glanced over her shoulder at Kindle. "I would not have known him if you hadn't shaved his beard." She paused. "He killed my son at Washita."

"No." The denial was automatic, before I remembered Kindle's story of the boy he'd killed reflexively after an arrow had knocked his hat off. "It was an accident. He didn't realize it was a child."

There was triumph in Aénóhé'ke's eyes. If she'd harbored any doubts about Kindle's identity, she didn't now. "Aénóhé'ke, please.

342

I saved you from the whisky traders."

"It is because you saved me I am not going to kill him. But, he will pay."

She walked to Kindle's unconscious body. "Aénóhé'ke, please. Stop. You don't have to do this. An eye for an eye never ends." She straddled Kindle's chest. "It has to stop somewhere. Please! Stop! I'll do anything!" I was sobbing now. Pope's face was pale and full of horror. I struggled against the man holding me. Aénóhé'ke lifted the knife. "Please, please, PLEASE, DON'T!"

Aénóhé'ke's body shielded me from seeing what she did. Kindle's body bucked. Bob Johnson and the other Indian pulled at the ropes tying his arms and legs, keeping him from fighting back against Aénóhé'ke.

Kindle's scream was inhuman. It reverberated around us, trapping us in a waking nightmare. Pope, who had a clear view of what Aénóhé'ke had done, turned away and vomited. Aénóhé'ke stood, a bloody knife in one hand, the other hand bloody and closed into a fist. She walked to me and opened her hand. "An eye for a life." She dropped Kindle's eye onto the ground.

"NO!" I screamed and went limp as sobs wracked my body. Aénóhé'ke walked off and the man holding me let go. I fell forward onto my hands and knees. Bob Johnson and his accomplice had untied Kindle, who was screaming and writhing on the ground, covering his face where his eye used to be. I crawled to Kindle and tried to calm him, but he was too lost in his pain to respond.

"Pope, come here. Help me hold him."

Pope wiped his mouth and came. We grabbed at Kindle, but he was too strong to subdue. "Sit on him," I told Pope.

Pope sat on Kindle's chest like a cowboy trying to break a colt. "William, stop. Be still so I can help you." I knelt at the top of Kindle's head and put my hands on his cheeks. "Shh, shh, shh," I said.

Blood oozed between Kindle's fingers. His remaining eye was wild with fear and shock. It moved around its socket, trying to focus and make sense of the new, foreign perspective.

"Look at me," I said, in the calmest voice I could muster. Focusing on helping Kindle was the only thing keeping my horror at bay.

Kindle's eye settled on me. "Good. I'm here, and I'm going to help you."

"Laura?" His voice broke, and he cried.

"I know, William. You need to let me see it so I can help you." I grasped his wrists and pulled his hands away from his eye. He fought me and when I got a good look at his wound, I wished he'd won.

Aénóhé'ke had taken his eyelid as well as his eye, leaving a gaping hole pooling with blood.

"Oh, God," Pope said in a strangled voice and turned his head away.

"Pope." My voice held a clear warning for Henry to hold it together. He nodded but kept his head turned and his eyes closed.

Kindle was quietly sobbing, his good eye watching my reaction. I smiled encouragingly at him, though I wanted to sob as well. "Are you going to be still so Henry can get off?"

Kindle nodded.

"Pope, go saddle the horses. Leave your whisky."

Pope shot up, handed me his flask, grabbed my saddle, and headed for the picket. I retrieved my saddlebag and pulled a shirt out of it. I tore strips, doused them with whisky, and packed Kindle's eye socket with it. He screamed and bucked.

"I know," I said, trying to subdue him. "It's almost over."

I tore the sleeves from the shirt and wrapped it around Kindle's head to hold the bandage in place. I helped him sit up and tied the fabric at the back of his head. I handed him the flask. "Drink."

Kindle tilted the flask back and gulped

the rest of the contents. He wiped his mouth with a shaking hand, and tentatively touched the bandage over his eye.

"Try not to touch it."

He nodded and dropped his head. His shoulders shook and full-throated sobs broke from him. I pulled him into my arms and swallowed the lump in my throat. "We have to get to Independence. Can you ride?"

He pressed his forehead against my shoulder and nodded. I stroked his hair. Pope was back for Kindle's saddle. "She left the gray," he said.

I pulled Kindle away from me. "I have to help Henry. Stay here, but don't touch your bandage."

Henry and I saddled the horses and packed up in record time. We helped Kindle onto his gray and rode hard for Independence beneath a full moon.

■ ■ ■ ■

PART THREE:
INDEPENDENCE

■ ■ ■ ■

CHAPTER 27

From the bow of the stern-wheeler we watched the scenery change from farmland to neighborhoods to a bustling, compact business district of redbrick buildings set in the curve of the Mississippi River. Our riverboat cut back its engine to maneuver in and around the other boats vying for their own piece of water.

My hand was nestled in the crook of Kindle's arm, ostensibly to pull myself nearer to him, but in actuality ready to grip him if he swayed in the slightest. He held himself rigid, his head high in defiance, but willpower alone wasn't enough to put color in his cheeks or to banish the dark circles beneath his eyes. We'd planned to stay on in Independence for a week so he could re-cover from his injuries but Kindle had insisted on leaving on the third day, saying he could lie in bed as easily on a steamboat as he could in town.

Kindle's hat was pulled low, throwing half his face in shadow, but not enough to mask the dark bruise beneath Enloe's eye patch, the bottom edge of which bore an uneven stain from the pus seeping from Kindle's eye socket. A bead of sweat ran down his temple despite the breeze coming off the river. I gripped his arm tighter and said in a light voice, "I've never been to Saint Louis. Tell me about it."

He swallowed. "What would you like to know?"

"How long were you stationed here?"

"All told, three years. Every soldier in the West goes through Saint Louis on his way to his post. The first time was on my way to Fort Lyon. I was here long enough to lose all my money on the riverboats."

"All of it?"

"Yes. It happened only the once. Ever since, I've secreted half of my money, pretended it didn't exist." I thought of him sewing up my mother's jewelry into the saddlebag at Darlington. "It's also a good rule of thumb because the river is full of thieves. Of course, a secret pocket in a saddlebag is easy enough for them to discover. But, I felt better having it."

"And, the second time?"

He pressed his lips into a thin line.

"Look."

Two enormous columns stuck out of the middle of the Mississippi and two others nearer the shore were half the size. "What in heaven's name?"

"A bridge, I suppose."

"Indeed it is." Henry Pope walked up, cheeks and nose rosy from drink. "Designed by James Eads."

"Eads?" Kindle asked.

"You know him?"

"I knew him briefly while I was here. He made his fortune salvaging sunken riverboats. A good business on the Mississippi."

"He says his expertise in the shifting riverbed gives him the knowledge to build this monstrosity. Most people think it will collapse, but Eads is confident."

"Most people being the ferry operators?" I asked.

Pope touched his nose. "How are you feeling, Major?"

"Fine, thank you."

"You look green around the gills. Would you like a nip?" Pope held out his flask. Kindle glared at him with his one good eye. Pope corked the flask and said, "No, of course not. You don't want to be drunk when you say your vows."

"Maybe we should find a room and wait a

351

couple of days, for you to feel better," I said.

"No. We are getting married as soon as we get off the boat."

I lowered my voice and leaned near him. "William, I would much rather wait a couple of days than have you collapse at the altar before you say *I do.*"

Kindle whispered in my ear, "We will be at my sister's by the end of the day, I promise. The feather bed awaits."

I blushed and glanced to see if Henry had heard.

"Henry," Kindle said. "Can you do me one last favor?"

"Ask and ye shall receive."

"Take Laura to buy a dress."

"Oh, William, I don't need a dress."

"I'm not marrying a Quaker. Nothing too ostentatious," he said to Pope. He lifted my hand and kissed it. "Make sure it's blue. She looks lovely in blue."

"Will do."

I caressed Kindle's cheek. "And, what will you be doing?"

"Making arrangements."

The steamboat slid into its berth and we disembarked onto a wharf teeming with humanity. I stopped on the wide cobblestone road shared by wagons, people, vendors, and longshoremen. Kindle walked on a couple of steps before realizing I wasn't by his side. He turned with a questioning expression. "It reminds me of Galveston," I said.

The six months since I'd disembarked from the *Dorothy Rosine* with Maureen seemed to have passed like the blink of an eye as well as a long nightmare. Now though, the nightmare was over. Kindle and I were together, starting a new life. I smiled, took his arm, and we walked up the wharf stairs to the city above, with Henry Pope following along like a loyal pup.

Kindle parted from us at the corner of First and Morgan, our saddlebags slung over one shoulder. We watched him limp up the street using the cane he'd never finished whittling, until he turned a corner and was gone.

"Do you think letting him go off by himself is a good idea?" Pope said.

I shrugged and checked the contents of the purple velvet bag I used as a purse. My mother's necklace and the money for a wedding dress were where they should have been. "I suppose we shall see. Where are we going to buy a dress?"

"How am I supposed to know?"

"You've been to Saint Louis before, haven't you?"

"I wasn't frequenting dress shops, I can tell you that."

"I suppose the houses you did frequent would know where a dress shop might be."

Pope's head went back so far his chin melted into his neck. "What are you saying?"

"Henry, go ask a whore where to buy a nice dress."

Henry and I walked in the opposite direction of Kindle. He shook his head and mumbled, "I don't know why you think I know where whorehouses are."

He parked me in the tearoom of a hotel with a full pot of Earl Grey and a plate of tiny sandwiches and left. I stared in disbelief at the china pot and delicate sandwiches for so long a waiter inquired if I was quite well. I smiled, said I was, and picked a sandwich from the plate.

The cucumber was paper-thin and the bread smeared with a hint of soft cheese. My mind drifted to my aunt Emily's house in London: the afternoon tea, vacuous conversation, strict rules of propriety. I sipped my tea and imagined the horror on Aunt Emily's face if she were to see me at this moment, dressed like a Quaker and with hair too short to pull back into an appropriate feminine style. After her initial horror had worn off, and she'd said *I told you so* in thirty different ways, she would spring into action and turn me into a respectable woman again. *Your hair is hopeless, but a nice dress will distract your visitors.*

I was well into my second pot of tea when Henry Pope returned, more red-faced than when he'd left. I glanced at the clock on the wall and sipped my tea without comment. He ran his derby around in his hands. "I've the name of a nice dress shop."

"You look tired. Was it a long walk?"

"Not terribly."

"Sit. A nice cup of tea will rejuvenate you."

"I'm well enough, Laura, thank you. Time's a-wasting."

"Please, sit. I want to talk to you."

Pope sat and placed his hat on the chair between us. I called for another cup and poured his tea.

"Can I trust you, Henry?"

"You have to ask that, after all we've been through?"

"This is a different kind of trust. A long-term trust."

"A take-it-to-my-grave trust?"

I touched my nose.

He considered for longer than I'd thought he would.

"Would you like to hear what I will ask of you?"

He shook his head. "You can count on me, Laura."

I cleared my throat and pressed my hands on the tabletop. "As I waited for you, I realized this" — I motioned to the tearoom — "will probably never be a possibility for me and Kindle. Normalcy." I smiled. "I never wanted to be normal, now I long for it."

Pope nodded along with me, waiting for what I would ask.

"I need you to kill me, Henry."

Pope stared at me uncomprehendingly, then laughed so loud the other diners took notice. I motioned for him to quiet down. He leaned forward. "Goddamn, Laura, you're a clever woman."

I sat back with what I was sure was a smug expression. "Yes, well, I do try."

"You want me to kill you in my story. And, Kindle, too?"

"It would be preferable. Especially before anyone knows about his lost eye. Keep that out."

"How do you want to die?"

I waved my hand. "I leave that to your imagination. Though I suppose you should include Lorcan Reed in your story so no one goes searching for him."

Henry rubbed his hands together. "Oh, this is going to be wonderful."

"Henry," I said in warning. "Whatever story you tell you have to stick with. Forever. You can't get drunk and start spouting another story. Or, God forbid, telling the truth."

"The truth?" Pope laughed again. "I'm a newspaperman, Laura, or have you forgotten?" He reached across and patted my hand. "Don't you worry. It would be my honor to kill you and Kindle. Especially Kindle. I've had a few ideas about that already."

"I thought you like him."

"Oh, I do. I do. But, I hate him a little for winning you." Henry leaned forward. "If you ever get tired of that brooding cavalryman, you come find me." He winked at me broadly, and I knew he was mostly teasing.

I laughed. "I will, Henry."

I paid for our tea and followed Pope to the dress shop his *friend* had suggested. If Pope had been awkward in a tearoom, it was nothing compared to his embarrassment at being in a dress shop. "You may wait outside, Henry," I said as the dressmaker showed me her ready-made dresses. "I assure you I've bought dresses before."

357

His relief was palatable. "Remember, Kindle wants blue."

"I remember."

"I'll nip into the pub down the street."

When Pope left, I told the dressmaker, "We had better complete this quickly. Henry Pope and a pub is a dangerous combination."

"What is the occasion?"

A grin broke across my face and I blushed. "My wedding."

The woman's eyes lit up, no doubt hoping for a large order. She snapped her fingers and an apprentice dressmaker materialized. "You cannot wear blue to your wedding," the woman said. "The only blue I have is more appropriate for mourning."

"Show me what you have on hand, please."

"But, ma'am, it would be much better to have a dress custom made. I have a wonderful azure silk that would look stunning on you."

"Thank you, but I do not have time. We are getting married today, you see."

The woman's brows furrowed, immediately suspicious. "My trunk containing my dress was misplaced on the New Orleans dock, it would seem. The date and time have been fixed with the church for weeks and my fiancé is loath to change it. I would like two dresses, one more formal and the other an everyday dress. I will wear the formal one out of the store and would like to leave this one with you so you can make it look not quite so austere?"

"Of course."

I pulled my mother's necklace from the bag and held it up. The woman's eyes lit up. "I would like a neckline that will show this to its best advantage. And one more thing: I need a man's cane."

When I arrived at the pub an hour later, Pope was in the middle of a serious game of poker with a man who was too well dressed to be a regular at the dingy pub. He wore a white linen suit and a flat-billed straw hat at a cocky angle. His relaxed posture contrasted with his shrewd blue eyes, which surveyed his opponents while appearing to not move in the least. The pile of coins and paper in front of him was significant, but only in comparison to the other players. I'd seen much more money exchange hands in London drawing rooms.

"Call," the man said in a voice devoid of accent.

Pope, the last man playing, lay his cards down. Two nines against the gambler's straight flush. I shook my head. Why Pope had played the hand through, I didn't understand.

The gambler raked the pot and jerked his chin in my direction. "I believe your friend has arrived." His gaze traveled to me and landed squarely on my necklace. I knew he'd taken my measure in as soon as I walked through the door and had valued my necklace with one glance. Now his expression said he was looking past my clothes and to the woman beneath. I felt a flush creep up my neck and turned my focus to Henry. I tapped him on the shoulder with the silver handle of the cane.

"Mr. Pope, we'll be late."

The chair scraped against the raw wooden floor and almost tipped over. With a faraway look in his eyes, Henry searched around his chair and the table.

"Your hat is on your head, Henry," I said.

He touched his derby and nodded. "So it is."

"Pope, aren't you going to introduce us to your friend?"

"What?" Pope searched around his chair, most likely hoping to discover a dropped coin so he wouldn't be completely destitute.

The gambler touched the brim of his hat. "John Lyman, at your service."

I nodded. "Nice to meet you. Henry, William is waiting."

Pope patted his pockets and moved away from the table.

"Pope," Lyman called. Henry turned and caught a chip Lyman tossed to him. "Bring it to the *Grand Republic* for a chance to win your money back."

Pope turned the shiny metal chip over in his hand. He touched a finger to his derby in acknowledgment and followed me out of the pub.

"Give me the chip," I said.

"What? Why?"

"Henry, he is conning you. He took all your money so you will go to the boat tonight and lose more."

"I don't have any more."

"Then he will loan you the money at an exorbitant rate."

"How do you know?"

I sighed. "Let's say I've a bit of experience with confidence men. Give me the chip."

Reluctantly, he placed it in my hand. I tucked it into the sleeve of my dress. "Now take me to the church. I am ready to pledge my troth."

It was as if giving me the chip had broken through the spell Pope had been under. He looked me up and down appreciatively.

"It's not blue."

I rolled my eyes. "It was the best I could do. I refuse to get married in a mourning dress."

Pope cocked his arm for me to take. "Some say marriage is a bit like dying."

"I'm sure it's a wonderful metaphor, Henry, but could you save it until after the wedding?"

He grinned the gap-toothed grin I'd become quite fond of and escorted me to the church.

My first thought when I saw Kindle standing at the altar with a priest was, *Kindle's Catholic?*

The floral scent from the small bouquet of flowers Henry had bought for me from a street vendor contrasted with the cool, mossy smell of the stone church. The ceiling soared above me. Multicolored light from the sun shining through stained-glass windows danced on the flagstone floor. A woman lit a candle and knelt in the transept to pray. A door banged shut somewhere. Henry's footsteps echoed in the cavernous room, while my slippered feet scraped softly as I walked closer and closer to an institution I had thought I would never be a part of.

Kindle left the altar and walked down the aisle toward me.

I focused on him, whose resemblance to a pirate didn't diminish by standing in the house of the Lord. He'd changed into a nicer suit, I noticed, with a white neck cloth. Pus seeped from beneath his eye patch and his scar was stark against his pale face. I worried for a moment this might be too much for him, that he should probably be lying down instead of standing in a damp church. He lifted his right hand to his face and wiped the pus away with a handkerchief.

"You look lovely," he said.

"It isn't blue."

"Emerald suits you as well." He reached out and touched the sapphire pendant around my neck. "Ravishing."

I held out the ebony cane topped with a silver handle. "Your wedding present."

He took it and pursed his lips in approval. "A damn sight better than the one you gave me at Richardson." He dipped his head. "Thank you."

He offered me his arm, which I took, but I kept him from walking me the rest of the way down the aisle. "Kindle," I whispered, "I'm not Catholic."

"Don't tell Father Ryan. Have you ever

been to a Catholic wedding?"

"Once, when I was a child."

"Follow my lead."

I remember nothing about the ceremony, other than how my stumble over the word *obey* caused the priest to pause for a long moment, until Kindle nodded, and the man continued. We were walking to the rector's office, with Pope following as our witness, when I said, "I thought we agreed about the vows."

"We did."

"I think we're lucky he continued with the ceremony."

"If it would have been anyone else, he wouldn't have. Patrick is my cousin."

We signed Father Ryan's book and he poured glasses of wine for each of us. "To the new couple, may God bless your union with happiness and many children."

I sipped, though I wasn't sure I wanted to acknowledge the second part of the toast.

"Kindle tells me you met after Antietam," Father Ryan said. He was about Kindle's age, I guessed, with thinning dark hair and kind brown eyes.

"I told him everything," Kindle said.

"Then I suppose you shouldn't have been surprised at my stumble during the ceremony." I smiled sweetly and sipped my wine.

Father Ryan inclined his head with a rueful smile. "Only temporarily."

"Thank you for continuing," I said. I stopped, my throat thick with emotion. "We have traveled some way to arrive here, together."

"So I hear." He placed his empty glass on his desk. "What you have been through shows a level of dedication to each other much deeper than one small word can convey."

"I thought the love of a man was lost to me long ago, when I chose to pursue medicine. Imagine my surprise when I met William and he loved me because of my mind, not despite it."

"Do not sell yourself short, Catherine. It isn't only your mind Billy loves."

I blushed at the priest's audacity. Pope choked on his wine, and Kindle laughed. "Really, Pat."

"I am sorry. You can take the man out of the Army, but you cannot take the Army out of the man." He slapped his hands together and walked around the desk. "So, where to now? Mary's?"

Pope clapped his hands over his ears and started humming. Father Ryan looked at him as if he was insane. "What the hell are you doing, Pope?"

"He can't know where we're going," I said.

"Afraid he's going to betray you?" Father Ryan said.

Pope removed his hands. "No. I'm going to kill them."

Kindle put his hand on his gun.

"Metaphorically, William," I said, resting my hand on Kindle's.

I sketched my and Pope's plan to a skeptical Kindle and a curious Father Ryan. "It's not a bad idea, Billy," Father Ryan said. "You can visit Mary for a couple of weeks, let the story play out, and leave with a little bit of security."

I nodded to Kindle and squeezed his arm. "It will be a clean break from the past."

Kindle studied Pope. "What do you get out of it?"

"Another story."

"Another one? What the hell have you been working on for the last month?"

"I have decided instead your story will be more believable as a penny dreadful."

Father Ryan laughed. "And, more lucrative."

"Much," Pope said. "I see you and Kindle, with different names, of course, being the heroine and hero of a string of novels about your exploits across the West. The first one is called *Sawbones*. I'll make a fortune."

366

I laughed. "Penny dreadful. I can't imagine a more appropriate vehicle for our story."

"I'll write the story of Laura's demise at the hands of the Pinkerton — don't worry, you'll come off as a tragic heroine — and Kindle's mortal revenge. It will be the West's version of *Romeo and Juliet*."

Kindle looked to the heavens. "God Almighty."

Father Ryan and I couldn't stop laughing. "It sounds brilliant, Henry." I hugged Henry and whispered in his ear. "Thank you. For everything."

He patted my back awkwardly. He reached into his coat and pulled out a flat square package tied with a string and handed it to me. "Your wedding present, madam."

I untied the string and unfolded the plain brown wrapping paper to reveal Soule's glass negative. Kindle and Aénoóhé'ke stared stoically at the camera. My face was blurred and unrecognizable, as I wanted it to be. I showed the negative to Kindle. His face lost its good humor as he stared with his one eye at the woman who'd mutilated him. He took the glass plate into his hand and stared at it for a moment before walking to Father Ryan's fireplace and throwing it inside, shattering it into a hundred pieces.

He turned to Pope. "Was there a paper copy?"

Pope shrugged. "I barely had time to nick the negative."

Kindle nodded and limped over to Pope. He held out his hand. "Thank you."

"The least I could do."

"Oh, do you want your chip?" I asked, reaching inside my sleeve.

"No. You keep it. As a good luck charm. Lord knows you need them."

"Are you ready?" Kindle said, holding out his arm for me.

"Yes."

"Pope, stay and help me finish this bottle of wine," Father Ryan said.

"Well, I need to start the story of their demise, but if you insist."

"Have you ever thought of having a priest as the hero in one of your stories?"

"No, Father, but it's your wine. Fire away."

Kindle and I walked out of the rectory arm in arm, leaving the two men to their sensational, wine-soaked stories.

CHAPTER 28

After we left Father Ryan and Henry Pope
to their wine and lies, Kindle hired a hack
to take us to his sister's orphanage. As we
left the city behind, the forest thickened and
civilization thinned; a bit of trepidation
snuck into my breast. I hadn't realized until
that moment how crowds of people had
made me feel safe since we'd arrived in
Independence a week earlier.

The hack pulled into a driveway bordered
on each side by tall oaks that canopied the
road in darkness. Wild honeysuckle grew
between the trees and filled the air with
their sweet scent. A smaller, somewhat
overgrown lane broke off from the main one
and disappeared into dark woods. In the
distance, I heard children's laughter.

The drive opened up to a semicircle in
front of an old plantation house that was
pockmarked with bullet holes and on the
seedy side of good repair. Girls ranging in

ages from babies to young women stopped their play in the side yard and watched the hack stop at the front door. Kindle jumped down. The driver got our bags and placed them on the ground next to Kindle, who paid him.

A woman in a light gray habit walked out the front door and stared at us. Her expression was serene and without question, as if strange people driving up to her house was an everyday occurrence. I took Kindle's hand and had barely disembarked when the driver slapped the reins against the horses' backs and the hack lurched forward, and was on its way back to Saint Louis.

With our saddlebags in hand, Kindle climbed the steps. The nun furrowed her brow at Kindle's eye patch, which made him look more dangerous than he was. If Kindle noticed her expression, he didn't let on. Instead, he smiled and said, "Don't tell me you don't recognize your favorite brother."

My head jerked to Kindle. *His sister is a nun?*

Her eyes widened and her face cleared. "Billy?" She threw her arms out and Kindle picked her up in a big hug. "What in heaven's name happened to your eye?"

Kindle set her down and held her at arm's length. "Don't you like it?"

"You look infamous."

"Precisely the look I was going for."

"Why are you out of uniform? Are you on leave?"

"Of a sort."

"Stop being enigmatic." The nun remembered I was there and stared for a moment. Her eyes flickered to my décolletage and a shadow of disapproval crossed her brow. "Introduce me to your friend."

Kindle stepped aside and pulled me forward. "Sister Magdalena, this is my wife, Laura Kindle." The nun's eyes widened again and she covered her mouth in surprise. "Laura, this is Sister Magdalena, nee Mary Margaret Kindle. My older sister."

"Oh, Billy." I stood dumbly while Sister Magdalena embraced me. She held me at arm's length. "She's lovely," she said, though her eyes and expression told of deep-seated reservations.

"It's nice to meet you," I said. "He didn't mention you were a nun."

Sister Magdalena leaned toward me and whispered, "Billy always did like his surprises. Come inside. I'll put a pot of tea on."

We followed Sister Magdalena inside and through the entrance hall. A staircase swept up the left side of the wall and around to the landing above. A young mulatto woman

371

walking through stopped upon seeing us. Her mouth gaped open in astonishment. "Mr. William?"

Kindle looked at the girl in puzzlement, before his expression cleared. "Sophia?"

The girl blushed and dipped her head. "Yes, sir."

"But, you're all grown up."

Sophia smiled, shyly. "I'm almost sixteen." Her gaze landed on me. I stepped forward and held out my hand.

"I'm Laura. William's wife."

The girl was too young and inexperienced to hide the emotions that flickered across her face, but she had enough composure to shake my hand with a strong grip. "It's nice to meet you."

"Sophia is one of our longest wards," Mary said. "She will be ready soon to leave us." The proclamation was welcome on one side, but not the other. "Will you bring us a tray of tea, Sophia?"

"Yes, Sister Magdalena. Sister Mauriela Joseph sent me to find you. She's in the chapel."

"Billy, you know where the library is. Excuse me." She and Sophia walked off on silent feet.

Kindle motioned for me to precede him through a door set under the stairs into an airy room with tall ceilings. One wall was taken up entirely by floor-to-ceiling windows that looked out on a vegetable garden in the distance. The other three walls were bookshelves bursting with books. I went to the nearest shelf and ran my hand along the spines.

"Impressive, isn't it?" Kindle said.

"Yes."

"I tried to read my way through it when I was here."

"It would take decades."

"I managed one row of one shelf."

"I'll have to see how many I can read while we're here."

"You'll be too busy to read, Slim."

"Hmm," I said. "So you're Catholic and your sister's a nun?"

"I told you she ran an orphanage."

"Nuns aren't the only people who take care of orphans."

"Does it matter?"

"No. It would have been nice to know. I should have probably told you: I'm not particularly religious."

He pulled me into a light embrace. "I'm not much of a Catholic. Mary got all of the spirituality in the family." Though Kindle was paler than the vibrant, healthy cavalry officer I'd met four months earlier, the ride from Saint Louis had put some color back in his cheeks, and diminished the starkness of the bruise under his missing eye.

"You also didn't tell me you had an admirer here," I teased.

He rolled his eyes. "Sophia was a sweet-tempered girl and uncommonly intelligent. I started practicing Latin with her. By the time I left, she was correcting me. I'm surprised she's still here."

Magdalena breezed into the room, sat behind the desk, and motioned for us to sit. Kindle removed a letter from Father Ryan from his inside pocket and gave it to his sister. Her eyes brightened, which she quickly masked behind indifference. "I suppose Patrick married you?"

"Two hours past," Kindle said. He settled into his chair, stretching out his bad leg and holding his cane across his lap.

Magdalena raised her eyebrows. "Indeed?" She sat back. "This should be an entertaining story."

"First, may I ask, what is this place? I gather it's a home for girls?" I said.

Magdalena nodded. "It began as a home for girls orphaned by the war. Over the years, those girls have aged out. We receive orphans, but the majority of our girls have been arrested for various crimes, indigence mostly, though some for theft and prostitution. They come here instead of prison, and we teach them useful skills so they may support themselves, or find a husband."

"And, this house?"

"Was a plantation. Most of the family died in the war. The remaining son is an inveterate gambler, and a poor one. He put his birthright up and lost. His loss was the church's gain. Ah, here's the tea."

Sophia carried the tea tray in and set it on the desk in front of Magdalena. She curtsied as if she was about to leave, but stopped. "What happened to your eye?"

"Sophia, that is none of your business. I'm sure you have tasks that need to be completed. Please see to them," Magdalena said.

Though Sophia hadn't been able to quickly disguise her surprise and jealousy of me, she was able to extinguish the brief flash of disdain for Sister Magdalena that flashed through her eyes. Sister Magdalena had dismissed Sophia from her notice when she dismissed her from the room and was ignorant of the young woman's reaction. Sophia caught my eye as she turned to leave, and I arched my eyebrow to let her know I'd seen all. She lifted her chin and left the room silently.

Sister Magdalena poured the tea and

handed me my cup. "Impudent young girl."

"It seems a natural question," I said.

"But, inappropriate for a servant to ask." She served Kindle.

"I never understood why she wasn't adopted," Kindle said.

"Unfortunately, few families want a mulatto girl, and then only for a servant. Sophia has been placed and returned twice for just such breaches of propriety." Sister Magdalena sipped her tea as if for fortification and sat back, holding the teacup lightly between her hands. "I'd like to know the answer to her question."

Kindle told our story in great detail, but with noticeable gaps.

When he told about their brother's role in our saga, Sister Magdalena paled, reached into her desk drawer, pulled out a flask of whisky, and fortified her tea. She offered me some, which I refused. I glanced at Kindle, expecting him to blanch at not being offered a drink, but he continued with the story as if the flask had never appeared. Sister Magdalena's hand shook when she lifted her cup.

"John is dead by your hand?" she said, looking directly at Kindle.

"Yes."

She took a shaky breath and smiled

weakly. "Please, continue."

Kindle elided over the bounty hunters killed during our flight, and downplayed Aénoóhé'ke's attack, but the evidence of its violence was clear by the eye patch and the pus that continued to seep from beneath it, which his sister could hardly stop looking at. When Kindle finished, silence fell. A clock ticked on the fireplace mantel and a gray tabby cat jumped onto Sister Magdalena's lap, startling me, but comforting our hostess.

"You told Pat everything?"

Kindle nodded. "I doubt he would have married us so quickly if I hadn't."

"No." She turned her attention to me. "Did you kill the man in New York City?"

"Mary!" Kindle said. "Of course she didn't."

Sister Magdalena didn't acknowledge her brother's exclamation of my innocence, but waited for my response.

"It's fine, William. If she's going to shelter us — me — she has to ask. The answer is no. I didn't kill George Langton."

"Why did you run?"

"I thought it was the right decision at the time. It was a bold, somewhat impulsive decision, I grant you. But, the specter of the noose was too strong to deny."

"And what you've been through since. I cannot imagine."

"Please, do not try. I know how it must seem, knowing Kindle for such a short period of time. Knowing we would marry at the end of my journey is, truthfully, the one thought that got me through."

One corner of Sister Magdalena's mouth quirked up. "Wait until you live with him for a while."

"If I didn't know I was your favorite, I would say you're not very charitable," Kindle said.

"He snores like a locomotive."

I feigned surprise. "Does he? I don't suppose you have wax I can shove in my ears?"

"I do, as a matter of fact, in the kitchen. You are welcome to go ask the cooks to help you. I would like to speak with Billy alone, for one moment."

"Of course," I said easily, though I was taken aback. I stood and put the cups on the tray. "Let me take this on my way."

"No need," Sister Magdalena said. "Sophia will clean it up."

"It's the least I can do."

I lifted the tray and shot Kindle a look when I turned my back to his sister. His face remained placid, but the corner of his good eye twitched, slightly. I wondered if

378

Sister Magdalena was going to lecture her little brother. Or ask him for more details about John Kindle's death. As I closed the door behind me, I hoped it wasn't the latter.

Sophia stood at the stove, absently stirring something in a pot and staring out the window.

"Hello," I said.

She jumped, turned, and hurried to take the tray. "Let me, ma'am."

"I've got it." I placed it on the counter next to the sink and gazed around the kitchen until they fell on what I needed. I smiled at the young woman. "My husband speaks highly of you."

She blushed, prettily, and dropped her hazel eyes to the floor. It was a coquettish mannerism which certain men would read as purposefully alluring. I suspected Sophia had no notion of her natural attraction, or the effect the mannerism would have on people.

"He was kind to me."

Emotion swelled within me. Of course Kindle would be kind to children. I moved close to Sophia and dropped my voice. "Would you like to know how Kindle lost his eye?"

"Yes."

"You cannot tell anyone you know. If you do, Sister Magdalena will find out."

The same flash of disdain shot through her eyes. "I can keep a secret."

The girl's skin was flawless, her lips full and pink, her eyes full of intelligence and wariness. "An Indian woman cut his eye out in retribution for the death of her son."

Sophia's eyes widened to an alarming degree, then narrowed as quickly. "You're making that up."

"Would you like proof?"

She nodded and I reached into the neck of my shirt and pulled out the small leather pouch hung around my neck. Sophia reached out and touched it in awe. "What is it?"

"A medicine bag. A Cheyenne chief gave it to me after a vision I had."

"An Indian? But, one took Mr. William's eye."

"I was given this before." When Sophia looked skeptical, I said, "They're a complicated people. Just as white men are."

She lifted her chin and narrowed her eyes. "White people aren't that complicated to me."

"No?"

She seemed to consider for a moment before dropping the subject and saying,

"What's inside?"

"I don't know. I haven't opened it."

"Why?"

"I'm afraid it will lose its medicine if I do."

"Medicine? You mean like quinine?"

"No." I chuckled. "It's spiritual medicine. It is supposed to protect me from evil spirits."

Sister Magdalena called out for Sophia from the other room. "Can one protect me from nuns?"

I laughed, and tucked the pouch into my shirt. "I don't know." I grasped Sophia's arm as she started to leave. "Remember, this and what happened to William is our secret." The girl nodded and left.

I walked to the pantry, picked up a small, corked bottle of oil, and slipped it into the pocket of my skirt.

"Do you realize it's been almost a week since either of us have been stabbed, shot, beaten, or abused?"

"Is that all?" Kindle said.

I lay on my side next to Kindle, our naked legs entwined, my head pillowed on his bare chest. I traced the scar on Kindle's thigh with my finger and lightly brushed past the hair around his groin before repeating the circuit.

Since my cleansing in the sweat lodge we had regained the connection we found the first time we lay together, much to our great relief. The events on the Canadian and in Palo Duro now seemed like they had happened to another person, a woman only slightly connected with the one who lay in a secluded groundskeeper's cabin for a Catholic orphanage in the Missouri woods. This disconnection made it easier to push away the memories sparked at random by a scent or a sound, but at times physical touch was still a struggle. What Kindle thought of as me being sexually adventurous was really my attempt to not be pinned beneath him. As a result, our lovemaking was passionate and, at times, playful. It was so different from what had happened to me it was easy to separate one act from the other and allow myself to be lost in the pleasure it gave me.

I lifted my head from Kindle's chest. His eye was closed. "Kindle, are you asleep?"

"Hmm?"

I pushed against his chest. "Wake up."

He opened his eye. "Why?"

"Because I want to talk."

He inhaled and pulled me closer. Rubbing his hand up and down my arm, he closed his eye. "You talk. I'll listen."

"Why didn't you tell Mary I killed your brother?"

"I wanted her to like you."

"She was close to him?"

"No, she hated him as much as I did. But, she would never be able to understand a woman killing a man."

"What did she talk to you about when I left?"

"Nothing important. Sibling stuff."

"You're lying to me."

His eye opened and fixed on me. "No, I am not."

"I should go see her."

"Why?"

"Because we haven't left this room in three days. It's unseemly."

"There's nothing unseemly about newly-weds being alone."

"But, she's a nun. She's probably judging us."

"Mary isn't judging us."

"How would I know? I didn't know until three days ago your sister was a nun."

I disentangled myself from Kindle, rose, and walked to the dresser. I brushed my hair and watched him in the mirror, felt the almost ever-present tug of desire at the sight of him. He put an arm behind his head.

"You're angry."

"Not angry, precisely. It feels as if there are large chunks of your past you haven't told me about."

"There are. As there are large chunks of your past you haven't told me."

"Nothing interesting, I assure you."

"The London scandal?"

I set the hairbrush down. "It seems so ridiculous now. I went on a carriage ride unchaperoned."

"That was the scandal?"

"He *was* a rogue, and I had done very little to conform to the ladylike activities Aunt Emily wanted me to perform. I was more interested in attending talks by Florence Nightingale and reading Charles Darwin. That is the extent of my mysteries. Now you know all. Do I know all about you?"

"No. It isn't as if we've had time for those types of conversations. We've been too busy trying to survive. We will spend the rest of our lives telling each other stories."

"Let's start now."

"Okay."

"Tell me about the woman you brought to meet your sister before me."

Kindle paused. "What do you mean?"

"Don't be dense, Kindle. You saw the

expression on Mary's face when you introduced me. Who did she think I was?" I'd
thought more about Mary Kindle's initial
expression at the sight of me than I should
have.

"I didn't see the expression on her face. I
remember the way she embraced you and
said you were lovely. Which you are. Come
back to bed."

"You're trying to distract me."

"Yes, I am."

"Which you've been doing nonstop for
three days."

"You haven't complained before."

"I am not complaining now. But, I do
wonder why you're so interested in not talking."

Kindle laughed. "I know of no man alive
who would rather talk than fuck."

"Kindle!"

"It's true."

I picked up my thin gown from the floor
and put it on before cracking open the door.
No one in sight, but a tray of fruit and a
carafe of wine sat next to the door. I picked
it up and shut the door.

"I suppose she isn't judging us."

"She's taking care of her baby brother."

"There's nothing baby about you." I
placed the tray on the dresser and poured

two glasses of wine. "Do you think this is sacramental wine?" I teased, and handed it to Kindle.

He drank. "It's watered-down wine."

"Are you committing some sort of sin drinking a nun's wine while stark naked and smelling of sex?"

"All sins are equal in the eyes of God."

"Hmm." I made no secret of letting my gaze roam over Kindle from head to toe. I rubbed my hand across his chest, my fingers leaving lines in his dark chest hair like furrows in a plowed field. His upper arms were hairless and white, his forearms muscular, brown, and covered with dark hair. I stood and returned to the dresser.

"Watered-down wine and she didn't offer you whisky when we arrived." I stared at him in the mirror. "Why is that?"

"Mary was an abolitionist."

"Like your wife."

"Mary introduced me to Victoria, as a matter of fact. When the slaves were free Mary was a crusader looking for a cause."

"Seems like that was going around at the time." I pulled my gown over my head and let it fall to the floor in a heap of white cotton. "Mary chose temperance?"

"And orphans. Come back to bed."

"I thought we were talking."

"You cannot stand in front of me like that and expect conversation." I felt a tug of pride at his obvious arousal, and so soon after a long, energetic bout of lovemaking.

I picked up the small bottle of oil I'd filched from the kitchen, sprinkled a couple of drops in my palm, and rubbed my hands together. I crooked my finger at him.

Kindle rose from the bed and stopped before me. We stared at each other while I stroked him with my oiled hands. His moan vibrated through his body. I turned and leaned forward on the dresser. He settled his hands on my hips, pulled me to him. In the mirror, I watched him close his eyes and smile in satisfaction.

"Are you going to tell me where you learned this?"

"I didn't think you wanted to talk."

His gaze met mine as he pulled away so I would feel the void he left.

"You're a tease, William Kindle."

"As are you." I pushed back against him, but he moved away. "Tell me."

"When I opened my practice in New York, only whores would let me treat them. I learned quite a lot."

He gripped my hips almost painfully and pulled me back against him hard. I gasped with pleasure. "So it would seem."

"Though I never thought I'd get to use my knowledge."

"Is there more?"

I grinned. "You have no idea."

CHAPTER 29

I found Mary in the garden with the children, picking strawberries.

"Can I help, Sister?"

Sister Magdalena straightened and put her hand to her back. "You're a Godsend. My back is killing me." She wiped her brow with the sleeve of her habit. "In private, you can call me Mary."

"Mary. I've never picked strawberries before. Is there a secret?"

"If it's red, it's ready."

I picked for a while before Mary spoke. "Will you and Billy join us for dinner?"

"Us?"

"Patrick is coming to visit."

My stomach growled. As much as I appreciated the fruit, cheese, and bread Mary had left, I longed for a proper meal. "We'd love to. Thank you for leaving food and wine for us."

"You're welcome. I thought you could use

some time alone. Though I wasn't expecting it to last three days."

I blushed, thinking of my most recent interlude with Kindle, but was luckily faced away from Mary. I straightened and dropped a large strawberry in her basket. "Nor did I."

"Where is Billy?"

"He walked off toward the stables."

She nodded as if it was the most natural place for him to go. "He left a trunk here last time he went West. Though, I suppose he could be bringing manure for the garden. Billy is quite the farmer."

"Is he?"

"I've never been able to replicate the size of his fruits and vegetables."

"He told me he hates farming."

"He does. But he's good at it."

Grasshoppers chirped and jumped as we walked through the strawberry plants. I smelled the pepper plants before I saw them.

"Caroline! Come take this basket and bring me an empty one for the peppers, please," Mary called. "That one there, see?" She pointed to a large, green pepper hiding beneath its foliage. "That's what to look for."

I picked the pepper, straightened, and placed my hands at my back as Mary had.

"Not a task I would want to perform every day," I said.

"You get used to it." Mary shielded her eyes from the sun. "You don't seem to know much about my brother."

"Why do you say that?"

"You have known my brother since May, yet you didn't know I was a nun?"

"I asked William the very question. We fell in love amid — how should I say this — quite a lot of drama. We have not had the opportunity to have deep conversations about our pasts."

"What about your future?"

I chuckled. "We've talked of the future but little, though I am confident our ideas align."

A small, smug smile played on Mary's lips. "What makes you think so?"

I turned to pick another pepper, in hopes Mary wouldn't see my expression. At Richardson, Kindle had asked me to consider giving up medicine for my and his safety, but we hadn't spoken of it since. I faced my sister-in-law. "What makes you think our ideas are different?"

"You are nothing like Victoria."

"I've been told I'm remarkably like her."

"By William?"

"No."

"John?" Mary laughed. "I suppose he would think so. Victoria was strong-willed about things she cared about, abolition mostly, but she was traditional in every other sense of the word. She was content with her role as a wife and mother, and William was as well. Somehow, I doubt you will be."

"You think William expects the same of me?"

Mary shrugged. "Most men do. He let Victoria have her cause, but he had clear expectations about her role. Don't be surprised if he has the same expectations for you." Mary gazed past me and waved. "Speak of the devil."

I followed her gaze to see Kindle smiling and striding toward us, hand upraised, happier than I'd ever seen him. I waved back. "He doesn't look as disreputable when he smiles."

"He looks like our brother."

"I know."

Mary's gray eyes met mine. "As long as he doesn't act like him."

"How are my two favorite women in the entire world?" He kissed his sister on her forehead and leaned down to kiss me. I turned my head so he kissed my cheek. No need to rub our physical affection in the nose of a woman sworn to celibacy. Kindle seemed to understand, and put his arm around my waist. He inspected the garden. "I see you are struggling to grow peppers."

"My peppers are fine, thank you very much."

"But, they could be so much better."

"Why don't you earn those three days of leisure by rolling up your sleeves and weeding and fertilizing the garden."

"I thought we were your guests."

"Not anymore. This orphanage won't run itself. Laura, you may either help Billy or help in the kitchen."

"I believe I'll help my husband."

Mary nodded. "See you at dinner."

We watched her walk to the house and didn't speak until she was inside. "I can't decide if she likes me or not," I said. I held my hand up to shield my eyes from the sun and squinted at Kindle. "What were you doing in the barn?"

"Looking for something."

"Did you find it?"

"Yes."

"Aren't you being enigmatic?"

"Yes. Come on. Let's haul manure." He held out his hand and I took it.

"You can't be serious."

"I am. We have to earn our keep."

"I think I will go to the kitchen." I tried to pull away but Kindle held firm and wrapped his arm around my waist.

"Don't you want to spend time with your husband?"

"We've spent three days together."

"Tired of me so soon?"

"Don't be absurd. But, this is my only work dress and I don't want it to smell like manure."

"It won't. You'll watch me while I work."

The stables were housed on either side of a wide center aisle in a large barn. Kindle opened the tack room, removed a stool, and set it down for me before returning to roll out a wheelbarrow with a shovel and pitchfork sticking from its empty tray. He stopped in front of the first stall, opened the door, ushered out a Jersey cow, and released her into the pen off the back of the barn. He went into the empty stall and shoveled.

I thought of my conversation with Mary, and for ten minutes thought of different ways to broach the subject, until I realized what was keeping me from asking outright was fear of Kindle's answer.

"How long were you here before?" I asked.

Kindle dumped manure into the wheelbarrow and leaned on his shovel. I thought he was going to deflect the question, but he answered. "Six months."

"Six months?"

He leaned his shovel against the stall wall, got another stool from the tack room, and sat next to me. "After Washita, I was transferred to Saint Louis. A desk job in the quartermaster's office. It was easy and dull, which meant I had too much time on my hands, an itch to cause trouble, and every vice available to choose from."

"Which vice did you choose?"

"All of them." I knew full well what he meant. I'd treated whores for years and had come to understand it was a profession undertaken as a last resort. It was either sell your body or starve. But, I'd never felt so benign or forgiving toward their customers. The news certainly put a new light on his enjoyment of my actions of the last few days.

I stood and paced the barn aisle. "That explains the watered-down wine."

"Mary's always thought drink was my biggest weakness. Patrick was able to keep me in line for the most part. He traveled to New York, and I was left to my own devices for too long. When he returned, I was in the brig."

"What did you do?"

"I was organizing fights between my men, mostly Irish street toughs who thought the

Army's twelve dollars a month was better than starving on the New York streets. They were only too happy to oblige and make extra cash."

"Pope was a fighter. Is that how you two met?"

Kindle nodded. "Somehow, Patrick convinced Ranald Mackenzie to get me out with a slap on the wrist, and a six-month leave. Patrick sent me here to my sister to pull myself together."

I faced him and crossed my arms. "To get you away from the drinking, gambling, and whores?"

He didn't flinch or move. "Yes."

"Who did you bring to meet your sister?"

Kindle sighed. "A woman named Rosemond."

"A whore?"

He nodded.

"That explains Mary's reaction to me as well as your obvious enjoyment of the last few days. She must have meant a lot to you, this Rosemond, if you brought her to meet your sister who's a nun."

"She didn't."

"Why would you bring a whore to meet a nun? To rub it in one or the other's face?"

"Yes. Mary's. I was drunk and high off a recent win. The last time I'd seen Mary she'd played the pious judgmental nun to the hilt. I was being petty and stupid."

The man Kindle described with such candor resembled the man I fell in love with not at all.

Kindle rose and took me in his arms. "Laura, I am not that man. He was an aberration born of grief, anger, and loss of purpose. You don't need to worry about his return."

I stroked Kindle's clean-shaven face and broached the real subject I wanted to talk about. "William, what kind of marriage do you want?"

"What?"

"Do you expect me to stay at home and darn your socks?"

"You *are* good at sewing."

I hit him on the shoulder. "I'm in earnest."

"Is this about practicing medicine?"

"Yes."

Kindle sighed. "You know it won't be safe for you to practice medicine. Why won't you let me take care of you?"

"I don't want to be taken care of. I want to be respected."

"You know I respect you."

"Then you wouldn't ask me to become a housewife. Do you think cleaning and cooking is the best use of my time?"

"What do you want to do? Surgery?"

"Yes. But, I've resolved myself to the idea of midwifery."

He chuckled. "You've said you hated the idea of delivering babies all the time."

"Yes, well, it would be more than that."

"Of course it would." He released me, picked up his shovel, and returned to the stall.

I took a few deep breaths before I spoke, to calm my anger and prevent my voice from shaking. When he dumped the manure into the wheelbarrow I said, "I am giving up surgery because it is the safest thing to do, and it is hypocritical of me to pretend to follow my oath when I have killed men, and stood by and let other men die. You told me our first night together you did not care if I practiced medicine. Did you say it to hook me? Did you think once we married I would come around to my traditional role?"

He leaned against his shovel, met my gaze directly, but didn't speak.

I gasped. "My God. You did."

"Does this rejection of your *traditional role* include children?"

"*Traditional role?* Your sister was right."

"What did she say?"

"That you let Victoria have her cause, but expected her to toe the line otherwise. And that you would expect the same of me."

"You didn't answer the question. Do you want children?"

"Do you?"

"I want to have a family with you. I assumed you did, as well."

"Why have you never mentioned your child with Victoria?"

"What?"

"At Fort Richardson, your nephew told me you lost a child in the carriage accident. Yet, you've never mentioned it to me. So why would I think you would like to have children?"

"Victoria never carried a child to term. She lost two early in her pregnancies and was pregnant when she died. Do you think I would be so callous as to never mention a born child?"

I rubbed my forehead. "No. I apologize."

"Do you not want children?" His voice was strained, as if it was a difficult question to ask.

"Of course I do." I clutched my stomach, roiling against voicing my fear for the first time. I inhaled the sweet and dusty scent of manure and straw and met Kindle's gaze. "I'm not sure I can have children."

The question of why died on his lips when he saw my expression. He swallowed and pursed his lips, as if fighting the urge to scream or vomit. I turned my head to keep him from reading too much in me. It had been six weeks since the abortion and my menses had not come. Since my courses had never been regular, I didn't know if this was due to an irrevocable internal injury, if I was pregnant with Kindle's child, or if my body was rebelling from my poor diet and the physical strain of the last few months. All I could do was wait for pregnancy symptoms to occur, or bleeding to start.

"You should have told me."

"When? I'm not sure even now."

"Before we said our vows."

"What?" The word came out as a gasp. Was he truly implying . . . ? I stepped back and ran into the stall wall. "My God, what are you saying?"

He stepped close, towering over me. "I'm saying I want a real marriage, one that includes a wife who at least occasionally pretends to respect me as a man."

I felt betrayed, as if everything Kindle had told me in the previous months had been a ruse to trap me into a traditional marriage I did not want or agree to. To believe that version of events I had to believe Kindle was a master manipulator, that his respect of me had been feigned, a complicated ruse, and for what? He didn't need to marry me to get me into bed. Did his honor and guilt at what his brother had done to me extend so far he would abandon the Army, travel across Indian Territory and into the camps of the Indians who bore him the most ill will, lose an eye, and marry me? No. Love, or at least a deep affection, had to underpin his actions.

"And I want a husband who treats me as an equal, not as a second-class citizen. Or a broodmare."

"You want a husband who will let you be in charge, in bed and out. There's a limit, Laura. And I've reached it." He picked up the wheelbarrow and rolled it down the aisle.

"Where are you going?"

"To fertilize the garden."

"We're not finished talking about this."

He stopped, set the wheelbarrow down, and returned. With great control he said, "Are you sure you want to finish this now? Do you think we can have this conversation without irreparably wounding each other?"

I wiped tears from my cheeks. I knew Kindle loved me, as I loved him. What we had was real. Unique. I knew it from the moment I had taken the straight razor to his beard one late night at Fort Richardson.

But, was it enduring?

I lifted my chin. "If we cannot, then our marriage is doomed."

Kindle crossed his arms and waited.

"Did I ever misrepresent myself to you?"

He paused, as if searching for a trap. "Besides lying to me about your name and waiting until I declared myself to you to tell me who you are and what you were running from? No."

I narrowed my eyes at him. "I told you everything at Richardson so you could choose, leave before it turned to more. You chose not to."

"Because I loved you."

I hesitated to give him the opportunity to change his verb tense and ignored the jab of fear when he didn't.

"I've given up everything for you. My career, my family, my name," he said.

"I've offered more than once to give it all back, to turn myself in. You refused, every time. So it will do you no good to throw up everything you've lost. We've both made sacrifices."

"What have you given up? You lost your medical career when you killed that man in New York."

I shoved him. "You know I didn't kill Langton." We glared at each other, breathing heavy. In that moment, I hated him. "There's one thing you need to remember, *Billy:* everything done to me on the Canadian was done in your name by your brother's allies. Five savages pinned me to the ground and raped me repeatedly because you didn't kill your brother at Antietam when you had the chance. They violated me with my own gun, loaded and cocked. Can you imagine what that felt like? To wonder if each thrust would be the last, begging it would? Don't preach to me about what you've *lost*," I spat. "You'll get no sympathy from me."

I was sick with fear I'd gone too far, that Kindle would walk out of the barn never to return. But, there was also a lightness of heart, a relief that came with the unburdening of the very last vestiges of my ordeal.

Kindle turned, screamed, and slammed his fist into the wall.

"William!"

He stopped, resting his forehead against the wood with his fist pressed to the wall as if glued. "I knew you blamed me, and you should. I suspected my brother was out there, waiting for his moment. I knew I should have kept my distance from you, but I couldn't." He turned and slid down the wall until he sat on the floor, his injured hand resting on his bent knee. "How could I stay away from the woman I'd been waiting for my entire life?" Kindle stared at his bloody knuckles, flexed his fingers, and grimaced.

"Here, let me see." I knelt next to him. I felt his knuckles and was surprised they weren't broken. They would have a healthy bruise and very soon. I lifted his hand and kissed it. "Oh, William."

He intertwined his good hand in my hair and pulled me forward. His lips rested against my forehead. "Forgive me."

"For what?"

"For loving you."

I looked up at him.

"For being the cause of . . ." He swallowed and continued, voice hoarse, his one eye searching my face. "We can't have this between us anymore. I take responsibility, but you can't throw it up to me in every argument we have."

I sat back on my heels. "I wouldn't do that."

"Do you forgive me?"

"Yes, of course."

"Promise me."

I opened my mouth to say, *I'll never mention it again,* but stopped. I couldn't promise that. As much as I wanted to move past the events of the Canadian, and had in many ways, it was part of me. There could come a time when I'd need to speak about it, for my own sanity.

"We will never argue about it again."

Kindle nodded and sighed in relief. He stood, held out his hand to help me rise, and pulled me into a long, strong embrace. His bruised hand moved to my stomach. "Do you want children?"

I covered my hand with his. "I never thought so. But, I've been having dreams."

Kindle's hand caressed my stomach. "What about?" he whispered.

"You're playing the piano. Bach." His eyebrow raised. "Dressed very smartly, I might add. I'm turning the pages for you, and a child runs up to me and hugs my legs."

"A boy or girl?"

"I never see them. Only hear the laughter." I smiled. "Yes, I want to have your child."

"You're unsure if you can because of what happened?"

I inhaled a shaky breath. "That, and . . ." Kindle's brows furrowed, and I continued. "Ezra didn't know about us, and assumed . . ."

"You were pregnant?"

"I would have asked him to if he hadn't. I

couldn't have borne the nine months of uncertainty."

Kindle shook his head. He knelt in front of me and placed his forehead against my stomach. He kissed my abdomen, letting his lips linger as if saying good-bye. "We have each other. That's all I need."

I knelt down and took Kindle's face in my hands. "And, the rest?" I whispered.

"I want the woman I fell in love with, God help me. Even if that means eating cold cheese and bread for every meal."

"It won't be that dire." I laughed, and kissed his lips, his cheeks, his forehead, and started back to his lips. "I love you, William Kindle."

He kissed me long and deeply. When he pulled away, I tried to rise but he kept me in place.

"What is it?" I said.

He cleared his throat. "When I left Maryland, I took little. I didn't want to be reminded of my family or my childhood. With one exception." He reached into his vest pocket. Between his long fingers he held a thin silver ring. "It was my mother's. After my father broke her hand, my mother's slave managed to remove it before her fingers swelled too much. She never wore it again." Kindle grimaced. "Part of me hates to give you anything associated with my father, but this is the last connection I have to my mother." He caressed my face. "She would have loved you as much as I do."

The depth of emotion I saw in him at that moment took my breath away. I knew that no matter what happened in our future, the fights we would have, the disagreements, that William Kindle loved me as much as I loved him.

Kindle slipped his mother's ring onto my finger and I pulled him into a strong embrace that wasn't broken until Sophia walked into the barn.

"Mr. William? Sister Magdalena told me to fetch you and your wife for dinner."

"Thank you. We'll be up shortly."

Kindle tucked my hair behind my ear. "I'm a mess, aren't I?"

Kindle smiled. "Do you expect me to answer that honestly, Slim?"

"No, actually." Kindle helped me stand. "I'll go to the cabin and splash water on my eyes."

Kindle pulled me to him and kissed me gently, letting his lips linger. "Don't be long."

He wheeled the manure-filled wheelbarrow toward the garden while I took the path to the groundskeeper's cabin. Inside I quickly washed my face and was patting my skin dry with a towel when I saw an open book and small jar of greenery on the kitchen table. I half expected a Bible opened to a passage relevant to a woman's role in marriage courtesy of Sister Magdalena. Instead, I was pleasantly surprised.

It was the best of times, it was the worst of times . . .

I grinned. A more apt description of the last six months, I couldn't have imagined.

Kindle handed me a newspaper when I arrived for dinner. "Pope's story made the front page." Father Ryan and Mary watched for my reaction.

The photo that had haunted me across Texas and Indian Territory was printed above the fold with the dramatic headline: THE MURDERESS AND THE MAJOR DIE IN EACH OTHER'S ARMS.

I folded the paper and set it aside. "Good heavens, Henry."

"Aren't you going to read it?" Kindle said.

"Maybe later."

"The purple prose will be just the thing to rehabilitate your reputation," Father Ryan said.

"Little good it will do me now that I'm dead."

Sophia entered the room carrying a large tray with four bowls and a basket of bread. She placed it on the sideboard and served us steaming bowls of vegetable stew.

"From your garden?" I asked Mary.

"Yes."

I glanced up to thank Sophia and saw her gaze settle on the newspaper next to me, where my picture was clearly visible. Her pause was almost imperceptible. She finished serving, asked Sister Magdalena if there was anything else, and was dismissed.

"Billy, Mary and I were talking . . ." Father Ryan started.

"Would you call him William, please?" I interrupted. "Or Kindle? Hearing him called Billy reminds me of Cotter Black."

The three of them looked at me in silent astonishment. Kindle recovered himself first, knowing full well what I had endured at his brother's hand. "Yes, I agree," Kindle said.

"It's a force of habit," Father Ryan said. "I apologize."

I waved my hand. "I understand. You were saying?"

"I know your plan is to stay for a couple of weeks to allow the story to die down, but what if you stayed longer?"

"It would be much safer for the two of

you if you did," Mary said. "Very few people visit us out here, so you would be perfectly safe."

"What of the nuns and students who were here before? They know William is your brother."

"We are a retired community," Mary said, "and don't concern ourselves with the news. The only people who know of your story are the four people in this room."

"And, Sophia," I said. "She saw the headline and my picture."

Mary smiled. "Do not take this the wrong way, but that picture resembles you very little. Besides, Sophia will be leaving us within the week to take up a position with a family in Chicago."

"Chicago?" Father Ryan said.

"Her reputation as a troublemaker has prevented me from being able to place her with a respectable family in Saint Louis. She leaves on Monday. Back to the original subject, Patrick and I think you should stay on here through the winter. Remain until the spring and the story of the Murderess and the Major will be completely forgotten. You will be able to travel much safer then."

"We cannot live off of you for six months, Mary," Kindle said. "And, we don't have the money to pay."

410

"William, as you probably noticed, the building and grounds haven't been maintained as well as the diocese would like since you left. We were going to hire the work out, but since you've returned you can manage it. Repair what you can and hire out workers for the rest," Patrick said.

"And, plant the fall garden," Mary said.

"What about me?" I asked.

Patrick smiled. "You would earn your keep by teaching our girls about midwifery."

"You do not teach it?"

"We do, but being a trained doctor, I'm sure you would have a depth of knowledge we do not. One of the sisters would assist you and learn from you, so she can continue when you leave," Mary said.

I could tell the idea appealed to Kindle, and staying in one place, setting down roots, even if they were shallow, appealed to me as well. But, it wasn't the kind of decision that needed to be made by silent eye contact and assumptions.

"We will surely consider it," I said.

Father Ryan's brow furrowed in consternation at the wife speaking up for the husband.

"Yes, let us talk about it," Kindle said. "I'm eager to meet Laura's Aunt Emily."

Mary took the answer in stride. "Are you

411

staying the night, Father Ryan?"

"No, I must return. I leave for Rome in a fortnight."

"Rome?" I said.

"Yes. I will be gone for a year."

Mary's serene smile tightened, but she remained silent.

"What an opportunity, Father," I said. "Congratulations. I guess the winter storms in the Atlantic aren't obstacle enough for the work of God," I said.

Patrick laughed. "You've caught me out. I came to bid Mary good-bye. I doubt I'll have the opportunity to visit again before I leave."

Mary smiled at Patrick and dipped her head, a blush creeping across her complexion. There was no denying the undercurrents of tension and affection running between the nun and the priest. I had a similar relationship once; one borne of years of familiarity with a good dose of sexual attraction. Once we consummated our attraction the relationship had fallen apart. Patrick and Mary obviously hadn't — couldn't — but it was obvious one of the two wanted to.

CHAPTER 30

Kindle did not return to his garden fertilization. Instead, we returned to our room to cement our new understanding by attempting a rather risqué position Camille had explained to me over a glass of sherry one afternoon in the parlor of Joe Fisher's boardinghouse. I'd told her it sounded not only disgusting, but highly improbable.

Johns pay extra for it, but good luck getting a husband to do it.

She didn't know Kindle. After his initial shock at the request, he acquiesced, eagerly and enthusiastically. Turns out, it was neither disgusting nor improbable, once we found the most comfortable position.

We were sweaty and naked, chests heaving, staring at the ceiling of our cabin. "My God," Kindle said.

"What?"

"If you ever anger me in public, I merely

413

need to think of you in private to forgive you."

"You do know we won't be able to keep this pace up forever."

"Why not?"

"Some doctors think too much sex is bad for your humors."

"They're clearly insane."

"They've clearly never had good sex." I placed a hand over my heart and felt it beating slow. "So, tell me: do you want to stay?"

Kindle looked down his body at me. "Do you?"

I nodded. "I'm tired of moving."

He ran his hand up and down my bare thigh. "So am I. It will give us time to settle in with each other."

"To get to know each other, you mean?"

He smiled and nodded. "It's obvious we need to, don't you think?"

"What if we find we don't like each other unless we're in mortal peril?"

"Then we'll go West and become outlaws, of course."

I nudged his shoulder with my foot. "I guess I'll be the gunfighter since I'm a better shot than you."

"I'm better with a knife."

"Which makes us the perfect outlaw pair. We already have the name."

"That we do. I doubt it will come to that. Remember, we fell in love before everyone started trying to kill us."

"True."

"Staying here will give me the chance to fatten you up a bit," he said.

"I thought you liked me svelte."

"I need a little something to hold on to right here," he said, squeezing my hipbone. "Don't fret. I'll still call you Slim."

"What a relief." I took Kindle's hand and intertwined our fingers. "What did you do here before?"

"Much of what Patrick suggested tonight. A steward, essentially. I took the property management off of Mary's shoulders, allowing her more time to focus on the girls."

"Did you enjoy it?"

"I did. More than I expected. John was brought up to run the plantation. I was destined for the Army from the cradle, but I couldn't help but learn some of what my father did. He was a cruel master, but adept at management and accounts. I was shocked with the amount of money left after my father died."

"What happened to it?"

Kindle gestured to the air. "I gave it to the church, and this is the result."

I sat up. "Your inheritance bought this

415

orphanage?"

Kindle nodded. "Patrick brought it to the church and they gave him a portion to do with as he saw fit. This is the result."

"Did he do this for Mary?"

"Why do you say that?"

"It's obvious they're in love, or once were."

"Perceptive woman."

"For how long?"

"Since childhood. My father arranged a marriage for Mary with a neighbor. A rich old man whose wife died without giving him children. Of course, half of the slave children were his, but everyone overlooked that. No white children to inherit, so my father offered Mary." Kindle pillowed his head on his arm. "She was sixteen. Father knew Mary and Pat were in love and didn't approve."

"Why?"

"Because he wouldn't benefit from the marriage. Pat was my mother's sister's boy, and they had no land. My father planned Mary's marriage for after Pat went off to West Point and wouldn't know until it was over."

I lay down on my side and propped my head on my hand. I'd never had such a view of his feet before. I wrinkled my nose. "Your toenails are obscene, William. Do you ever cut them?"

He playfully stuck his foot in my face. I pushed it away with a disgusted scream, sat up, and lay my head on the pillow next to him. "Finish your story. Maybe it will help me forget the disaster that is your feet."

Kindle stared at the ceiling as if the story was written there. "My mother seemingly went along with my father. She and Mary left for Washington to get her wedding clothes but instead of shopping, Mother took her to a convent in Pennsylvania. My father was too afraid of hell to go against the church. But, he wasn't too afraid of hell to make my mother pay. It didn't help I chose the week they left for Washington to help Cotter Black escape."

"What did Pat do when he found out?"

"Nothing. He finished West Point, then took orders. Became an Army chaplain."

"Tragic lovers thwarted by families and circumstances. How very Gothic."

Kindle chuckled. "I've never thought of Mary and Patrick as tragic lovers."

"Kept apart by family, now they're kept apart by pride and solemn vows. They're a textbook case." I rolled on top of Kindle and straddled him, raking my fingers through his thick chest hair. "So we are

417

decided: stay here until the spring."

"Yes."

"I would like to write to my cousin, to tell her I'm alive and happy."

Kindle ran his hands up my hips to my waist. "Are you?"

"Immensely."

"She will keep your correspondence secret?"

"Oh, yes. I will write the letter in one of our old secret codes. She'll be thrilled. It'll add a nice bit of variety to her routine."

Kindle sighed and dropped his arm to the bed. "Damn."

"What?"

He flipped me onto my back and kissed me quickly. "I forgot the cow."

"What?"

He rose and pulled on his pants and boots. "I left the cow outside."

"It will be fine until the morning."

"She needs to be fed and watered so she'll be ready for Sophia to milk in the morning. And, the horses need to be tended to."

"Starting your job already?"

"I guess so." He pulled his shirt over his head and put on his vest. He leaned down to kiss me. "I won't be long."

"I'll be asleep."

"I'll wake you up."

"Are you ever satisfied?"

"Not yet." He winked at me and opened the door. Sophia stood outside, arm raised to knock, a startled expression on her face. Over Kindle's shoulder she saw me sprawled out naked on the bed. She blushed, turned, and fled.

Kindle glanced at me. "Do you want me to go after her?"

I rose and started to get dressed. "What would you say? *I apologize for you seeing my naked wife?* I'll go. I have a feeling I know what she wants to talk about."

The house was dark, with only the small glow of light visible in Mary's study. I walked up the stairs of the porch and followed it around the house, expecting to find Sophia at every turn. It was silent and empty. She'd either gone inside to bed or was somewhere on the grounds. I didn't know the grounds well enough to search in the dark and I didn't want to risk walking through the dormitory and waking up the children. Whatever Sophia had wanted to speak about would have to keep.

I walked back to the cabin and found Sophia waiting. She rose when she saw me. When I was close enough to make out her face, I saw the slight blush on her features.

"Come inside, it's chilly," I said.

The newspaper I'd left on the table next to *A Tale of Two Cities* had been refolded incorrectly. "Did you enjoy the article?" I nodded to the paper.

"It's about you and Mr. William?"

"Yes."

Her head jerked back, as if surprised I'd told her the truth. "You're a doctor? I thought you were a whore."

"A whore? Why would you think that?"

"You were in there for three days, and noisy about it."

"You delivered the food and wine?"

She nodded.

"You thought I was a whore because I enjoyed being with my husband?"

"I heard Sister Magdalena talking to Mr. William. She thought you were, too."

"I'm not."

I would speak with Mary about that later, but at the moment I was more interested in the fact Sophia had focused on a throwaway detail about my profession at the beginning of the story instead of the purple prose about bounty hunters, whisky traders, and Indians. "I'm a doctor, but it's not safe for me to practice."

" 'Cause there's not many woman doctors."

420

"Precisely."

"Are you going to stay and teach midwifery?"

I narrowed my eyes at the girl. "How do you know that?"

"I overheard you talking."

"You mean you eavesdropped, as you eavesdropped on Mary and William. It's a nasty habit, Sophia, eavesdropping." Sophia lifted her chin in defiance but I could see embarrassment around the edges of her expression. "You want to learn midwifery?"

"No. I want to be a doctor."

My mouth opened and closed like a beached fish as I tried to find the words to respond. Sophia's defiance expanded, filled the room, covered me with shame. I looked away and said, "How long have you wanted to be a doctor?"

"I didn't know it was possible until I heard you were one."

A germ of pride swelled in my breast. I'd always hoped my accomplishments would inspire other women to follow my footsteps. Here I was, confronted with the first, and all I could think of were the obstacles in her way. "Sophia, deciding to be a physician isn't something you do on a whim. Do you realize how difficult it will be?"

"You saying I'm not smart enough?"

"I hardly know you well enough to make that determination. But, I'll assume you are. I'm not speaking of the coursework, though it will be difficult. You are a woman, and a Negress. It's difficult enough for women to be accepted into the proper schools. It will be nearly impossible for you."

"I cannot go back into service."

"Is it you don't enjoy the work —"

"Of course I don't enjoy carrying people's piss-and-shit pot down the stairs every morning, noon, and night."

I couldn't fault her for that. "Do you know you've been placed with a family in Chicago?"

She nodded. "I'll run away the first chance I get. Chicago is as good a place as any to start out."

I massaged my right hand and considered the young woman. Her near future scrolled in front of my eyes: Sophia stealing a small valuable from her employer to fund her escape, being found, arrested, and thrown into jail or even hanged if she was too greedy. If she survived, she would be turned out onto the streets and most likely end up selling her body to survive.

Kindle spoke highly of Sophia's intelligence, and she had a streak of independence and defiance critical to succeeding in a field such as medicine. And, I liked her.

"I'll speak to Mary in the morning. I cannot promise anything, but I will try to convince her to delay your departure for a month to learn midwifery." Sophia opened her mouth to protest, but I continued. "In that month, you have to prove yourself to me that you truly want to be a doctor. And, you have to prove to Sister Magdalena you deserve the opportunity to be more than a maid."

"How do I do that?"

"Work hard and perform so brilliantly she can't deny you the chance."

"Why do I need her? You can help me."

"Only to a point. I'm dead, remember? If you want to go to medical school, Sister Magdalena and Father Ryan will be the ones to get you in. Not me."

Sophia chewed her bottom lip.

"This is the first and easiest obstacle you'll face. Giving up already?"

She straightened. "No. I'll do whatever you say."

CHAPTER 31

I knocked on the library door, and after a pause and the sound of a chair scraping across the floor, Sister Magdalena called out, "Yes?"

I opened the door and poked my head through. "Is now a bad time?"

"No." She sniffed and turned away from me, but not before I saw her swipe at her cheeks. "Come in." When she turned back, she'd regained some of her composure, but her eyes were red. "Have you come to tell me you've decided to stay."

"Yes."

Mary clapped her hands together. "Oh, I'm so pleased." She walked around the desk and hugged me, which I returned. "It will give us the opportunity to get to know each other better."

"I'd like that."

Mary released me. "Would you like some coffee?"

"Yes, thank you."

"I won't be a moment."

I perused the shelves of books while she was gone. It was an impressive library with titles on a wide range of subjects. I was flipping through a volume on entomology when Mary returned. "Sophia is bringing it directly. You're welcome to any book you want to borrow."

"Thank you for *A Tale of Two Cities*."

"You're welcome. The opening came to mind after hearing about your journey."

"I understand why."

Mary motioned for me to sit. Once we were both settled into our chairs, I said, "There are a couple of things I want to talk to you about, clear the air, so to speak."

"Such as?"

"I learned what you thought of me when we first met. A whore, Mary? Truly?"

Mary's face flamed. "Did William tell you?"

"I wasn't sure it was true. Thank you for confirming it."

"William should have never told you —"

"He didn't. He wouldn't want me to think less of you. Just as he didn't tell you I was the one who killed your brother. He wants us to like each other. To be friends. Sisters."

Mary smiled and nodded. "I wondered

which one of you would tell me the truth about John."

"You knew?"

"Yes, and I never thought you were a prostitute. But I knew the accusation would make Billy indignant." She shrugged one shoulder, and one corner of her mouth quirked up into a mischievous smile. "I'm his big sister. I can't resist needling him when the opportunity arises. As to John, Beau wrote to me. Told me he was mustering out of the Army and that you shot his father in the back."

I blanched. Though Beau Kindle had been present when I killed Cotter Black, I wasn't sure he knew the full story of his father's role in the abuse I suffered. Would he look on the act with more compassion if he did? I doubted it. The shock of losing his father mere moments after learning he was alive, along with Beau's youth, most likely led to his simplified explanation.

"Black could have stopped me. I was weak, trembling. Instead, he mocked me, my courage." I reached back and tapped the base of my skull. "I placed the gun against his head and pulled the trigger. If he sat right there" — I pointed to the chair next to me — "I'd do it again. Without hesitation." I inhaled and released the breath slowly, the memories of that time threatening to derail my thoughts. "Before the massacre I would have never imagined myself capable. An old Texas Ranger told me everyone has killing in them, most haven't been driven to the point yet. I thought it was absurd at the time, but he was correct."

"Murder is a mortal sin."

"I am not Catholic. I didn't come for absolution. I wanted to make sure if you disliked me, it was for a pure reason, a truth, instead of a lie. William and I have been forced to lie about who we are for weeks, and will most like have to lie for the rest of our lives. I want to have one place, one person besides William who knows who I am. Who will not judge me."

Mary raised her eyebrows. "You *do* realize I'm a nun."

I laughed. "Yes, but I think you are more forgiving of other people's faults than other religious people I've known."

Mary studied me for a long time. "I don't dislike you, but as William's sister, it is my job to be protective. To make sure you are worthy of his loyalty and devotion. Coming to me, telling the truth about killing John, took great courage. It's a quality I admire in people, because I so rarely see it." She cleared her throat and busied herself with straightening papers on her desk. "As to forgiveness, the world is a better place without John Kindle, or Cotter Black, terrorizing and killing innocent people."

Sophia knocked and entered on Mary's command, releasing the tension in the room. She placed the tray on a table and started to pour. "I'll serve. Thank you, Sophia," Mary said.

The young woman nodded, then glanced at me with a questioning expression. I shook my head slightly and winked. Mary handed me a cup. "Is there something else, Sophia?"

"No, Sister."

"Thank you."

She closed the door quietly behind her. "Kindle said Sophia is uncommonly intelligent," I said.

"She is."

"Yet, you've turned her into a kitchen maid."

"As opposed to what?"

"Letting her teach the other children, and finding her a teaching position when she ages out."

"Who, precisely would she teach? White communities wouldn't want her. Negros can't pay her."

"She's been released from two positions.

What makes you think this one will be successful?"

"I hope she realizes it is her last chance, and that she will be turned out if she fails."

"If she goes to Chicago she will end up on the streets," I said.

Mary narrowed her eyes at me. "How do you know that?"

"She told me she plans to run away as soon as possible. She's a pretty girl. I would hate for her to be ruined at such a young age."

"When she was a child, I hoped she would have the temperament of a sister."

"She asked me to teach her midwifery."

Mary sighed and looked to the heavens. "This is precisely why she keeps getting turned out. She doesn't know her place. She should have come to me."

"I think she knows her place perfectly well. She wants to better it." A sharp pain penetrated my abdomen. I gripped my stomach and grimaced. "I want to help her."

"What's wrong?" Mary said. "Are you ill?"

"I'll be fine. Thank you. Sophia can't go to Chicago."

"It's all arranged."

"She knows who I am. She read the article."

Mary swore under her breath, but not

quiet enough that I didn't hear her. I moved around the desk and whispered in her ear. "It hasn't occurred to Sophia that she could turn me in for the reward and not have to worry about service or selling herself on the street. If you send her to Chicago, she'll figure it out quickly."

Mary studied me and I saw her consider turning me in herself.

"If I am exposed, Kindle will be as well. The Army will try him, and possibly execute him."

Mary looked down and rubbed her forehead and didn't see me grimace in pain. I balled my hands into fists to keep myself from clutching at my stomach.

"Let her stay. I'll take her under my wing, teach her about midwifery and nursing. If she doesn't make a good midwife, you can place her. She knows you'll be watching. One month. Give me — her — that at least."

"One month. If she steps out of line at all, she goes into service."

"Thank —" I gasped and doubled over as another pain shot through me and I felt a warm trickle of blood slide down the inside of my thigh.

CHAPTER 32

My menses returned every month like clockwork, and with the same vengeance as the first time, incapacitating me for at least two days each time. Strong doses of laudanum and a hot stone clutched to my stomach were the only things that brought me relief. I longed to get pregnant, if for no other reason than to keep the monthly pain at bay. At my lowest points, I wished my womb to be removed from my body by any means possible.

Aside from a few dark days per month, we were happy and content throughout the winter and early spring at the orphanage. Regular meals and physical activity worked wonders on Kindle and me, letting us heal from our various injuries and regain the weight we'd lost. Kindle's limp had almost disappeared, relegating his wedding present to the bottom of the coatrack he made for the cabin. His injured eye had stopped seeping, and he said the discomfort had abated. I knew better. During my physician's training, I had worked with soldiers who had lost their limbs in the war and knew the phantom limb was always physically felt, whether through pain, itching, or spasms. Discomfort made all the worse because there was no way to relieve it. I was confident the loss of an eye was the same, but Kindle assured me it was not. He was a terrible liar. At least to me.

When the movement in my right hand stopped improving, Mary gave me a needlepoint hoop and said, "You have two hands, don't you?" My progress was written across the canvas. My stitches were still atrocious, but they were getting better. The burns on my arm healed so well that the scars were almost imperceptible, though I had little sensation there. My hair grew long enough I could almost pull it back into a bun, and Kindle complimented the growing flesh on my hips each time we made love, which was almost as often as our first days at the orphanage.

Any reservations Mary had about Sophia's ability to be a midwife were put aside almost immediately. When I collapsed in the library, Mary had called out for help and Sophia had responded, following Mary's orders without question or comment, and nursing me through the worst of the first, most painful, menses. I was never sure if Sophia's motivation had been to prove worthy of the opportunity Mary gave her, or if she was afraid my death would mean her immediate placement. Regardless, from the first moment of her apprenticeship, she had proved to be able, eager, intelligent, and most important to Mary, tractable. The other orphans would be serviceable midwives and nurses; Sophia proved to have a talent even Mary couldn't deny. If a place in a medical college could be found, she would make an even better doctor.

One day in late March, I was sitting in a lawn chair watching Kindle hoe the garden in preparation for planting when Sophia came up with a letter.

"From Charlotte?" I asked, rhetorically. She was the only correspondent I had, by necessity. I'd considered writing Harriet Mackenzie to let her know we were alive, but decided against it. I didn't know what repercussions she'd faced for helping us and didn't want to take the chance she wasn't at the New York address she'd given me and the letter might be opened by someone on her behalf. I thought of Harriet often, hoping she was well and happy.

Sophia sat down on the ground next to me and waited for me to parse the code and read the letter to her. It had become something of a routine. Sophia was fascinated by the life of leisure Lady Charlotte MacUspaig led as the mistress of an estate in Scotland. It took reading a few words to realize Charlotte hadn't written the letter in code and wonder why, when I hit upon the critical sentence.

Mother and Father died within days of each other. Father took ill with the flu and Mother would let no one but herself nurse him, confident as always that she was the only one who could do a thing right. Father's weak heart meant he died quickly. Mother suffered for five days more. Mother had insisted I not come to London and risk my unborn child, a piece of advice I'm relieved and pained to have taken.

As you know, after the accusation against you last year Mother insisted Father remove any mention of you from his will. Since we agreed it wouldn't be safe for more than me and Edwin to know about your adventures, Mother and Father died without knowing the truth of your innocence . . . .

I dropped the letter into my lap, tears making it impossible to continue reading. Kindle and Sophia stopped talking. "Laura?

What's wrong?" Kindle said.

I held the letter out to him. He read in silence.

"What happened?" Sophia asked. "Is Lady Charlotte well?"

"Aunt Emily died?" Kindle said, voice filled with regret.

Sophia gasped, having heard enough Aunt Emily stories from me and from Charlotte's letters to feel the shock.

I nodded, but couldn't speak. As much as I'd enjoyed being at the orphanage, the idea of sailing to England and reuniting with my family had gotten me through many dark days. With the loss of Aunt Emily and Uncle Robert, my blood relations consisted of Charlotte and her brother, Charles (who'd never liked or approved of me).

"How far did you read?" Kindle asked.

"They died without knowing the truth."

Kindle folded the letter, put it in his pocket, and helped me stand. "Let's get you to the cabin."

"Do you need my help?" Sophia asked.

"No, thank you. Tell Mary we'll be up for lunch."

Once in the cabin, Kindle pulled me into a strong embrace. "I'm so sorry."

I cried into his shoulder for a long while. Finally, I pulled away and sniffed loudly.

Kindle pulled a kerchief from his pocket and handed it to me. I dabbed my eyes and blew my nose. "What did the rest of the letter say?"

"Charlotte had hoped her father hadn't ignored her mother's entreaties to leave you a small income, but you weren't mentioned."

"I don't care about that."

"No. Though Charlotte cares very much. She is prepared to give you a gift to make up for it, but there's a condition."

"What?"

"You sail to Scotland to visit her."

"Me? I'm not going without you."

Kindle smiled. "She invited me, too. She's booking passage for us on a steamer out of New Orleans. She says she will cable the details to my sister when she has them."

I covered my mouth with my hand. "My God. She's turned into her mother." I burst into hysterical laughter, which turned into tears. Kindle brought me into his chest again while I apologized for being a blubbering mess. Heightened and fluctuating emotions always preceded my menses. "Dark days are coming."

Kindle grimaced. He hated seeing me in such pain and being helpless to fix it. I'd discovered in the previous six months that

Kindle got great satisfaction from fixing things and took it as a personal affront to his masculinity when he couldn't.

"Maybe it won't come this month," he said.

"Maybe." I stroked his hair, which he'd let grow long to further alter his appearance from his days in the Army. Between the eye patch and long hair, he looked nothing like Captain William Kindle of Fort Richardson. But, I'd come to like this version very much. Kindle was more relaxed, had a ready smile, and was a voracious flirt.

"Do you want to go to Scotland?"

"I assumed we would go sometime this summer. Now is as good a time as any."

"But the garden, and trying to find a place for Sophia."

"They've done the garden without me for years. And, Sophia will be here when we return. Unless you think we won't."

"Of course we will. Although, if Charlotte has grown accustomed to everyone doing her bidding without question, leaving may be a challenge."

"I can handle Lady Charlotte MacUspaig," Kindle said. He hugged me again. "I'll go tell Mary. Rest." He kissed me on the temple and left.

I waited for the knock I was sure would

come and opened the door to Sophia's stricken face. I stepped aside and she walked into the cabin.

"You're leaving?"

"You need to stop eavesdropping on people. I love you, but it's a reprehensible habit."

Sophia dropped her eyes to the ground. "Yes, ma'am."

"Yes, we're leaving. My cousin wants to see me, and meet Kindle."

"How long will you be gone?"

"I don't know. If we leave soon, we can be back before the winter storms in the Atlantic."

"But, it could be longer."

I took Sophia's hands. "You'll be fine, Sophia. You've almost surpassed me in midwifery skills."

Sophia scoffed at the idea.

"I said almost," I teased. "It's time you worked on your own."

Sophia shook her head.

"Yes, you know it is. I was never going to be here forever. Going to my family was always our plan. It's just been moved up a couple of months."

"She'll put me in service, I know she will."

"If she was going to put you in service she would have done it months ago. You've

438

proved yourself worthy of more a dozen times over."

Sophia was openly crying now. I hugged the young girl. "There's no reason to be frightened. You'll stay and teach the younger girls what you've learned while Sister Magdalena works on getting you a position at a medical school."

Sophia pulled away, her face full of astonishment. "What?"

"I didn't want to say anything until something was settled."

"I'm going to medical school?"

I sighed. "I don't know, Sophia. I honestly don't. We're going to try, but there's a lot against us."

The resistance that was integral to Sophia's personality reared its head. "Because I'm a Negro."

"Yes. Unfortunately, you're too dark to pass for a white woman." At Sophia's expression of wonder, I said, "It would have been the easiest solution. We will figure something out. You're only sixteen. You have a few years before college is an option. What you have to do now is prove you can stand on your own two feet. That your success isn't because I'm here holding your hand."

"You mean I have to prove myself to Sister Magdalena all over again."

I placed my hands on Sophia's shoulders. "Sweetheart, you're going to have to prove yourself over and over to people throughout your life. That's women's lot in life, especially women who want more than home and hearth. Are you up for it?"

Sophia straightened her shoulders. "Hell yes, I am."

"Good girl." I reached inside my shirt, pulled out my medicine bag, and placed it around Sophia's neck. "Keep this for me while I'm gone."

"But, it's your protection."

I patted Sophia's cheek. "I'll be fine. I have Kindle."

CHAPTER 33

Black smoke belched out of the smokestacks as the *Grand Republic* steamed out of Saint Louis and down the Mississippi. Kindle and I stood at the aft railing, watching Saint Louis disappear around a wide bend in the river. Everything had happened quickly after Charlotte's letter. A telegram had arrived within a week, with the sailing date from New Orleans two short weeks from then. Kindle and I owned little enough that our possessions fit into one trunk, but it was the separation from people we'd grown fond of that was the most difficult part of leave-taking.

Mary and I had fallen into a routine of sitting down to coffee in the late afternoon after my classes were over and before she made her rounds to check on the other nuns and their charges. During our last meeting, Mary had seemed to steel herself for a dreaded conversation and said, "I would like to thank you."

"Heavens. What for?"

"Thank you for seeing what I did not in Sophia. When I think of what kind of life I was sentencing her to, the lost possibilities . . . Sometimes, it's enough to make me consider resigning. If I did that with her, how many other children have I misread?"

I sipped my coffee. "Sophia's afraid you're going to place her in service when we leave. I assured her you wouldn't."

"No. I expect the orphanage to make a little money from her midwifing skills. She will get a portion, of course."

"Don't be afraid to give her responsibilities. It will give her purpose and importance. She thrives on both."

"I will. I expect she's going to be quite worthless for a few days after you two leave. We will be here when you and my baby brother return. Maybe with a niece or nephew in tow."

"We'll see."

Now, the day after our parting, I shielded my eyes against the Western sun and squinted up at Kindle, debating whether to tell him the dark days hadn't come that month. In the whirlwind of getting ready to leave, we'd both forgotten about it. It wasn't until Mary mentioned it the day before that

I realized I was a week late, and that my breasts were tender. It was too early and there were too many possibilities for disaster to tell Kindle and get his hopes up. I determined to remain silent, and felt guilty for it.

"What is there to do on a steamboat besides watch the world go by?" I said.

"Gamble. Eat. Socialize."

"I don't think socializing is in our best interest."

Though months had passed since Henry's story of our deaths in Indian Territory at the hands of Lorcan Reed, Kindle and I decided it was best to be as inconspicuous as possible.

"I suppose that means we will have to spend most of our time in the cabin."

I shook my head and chuckled. "You do realize we have the rest of our lives to discover new and interesting ways to copulate?"

His one eye raked over me in the most inappropriate way. "Have you tired of me already, Slim?" He squeezed my hip.

"Never." I caressed his arm.

A cabin boy holding a footstool walked by. I stepped away from Kindle a little. The boy lit the nearest gas lamp, picked up his footstool, and moved to the next. A few couples walked by arm and arm, taking the air before dinner in the long salon.

"Do not forget how thin our cabin walls are," I said. I pulled Henry Pope's gambling chip from my purse.

"Where did you get that?"

"From Henry all those months ago. I wonder what Henry's doing."

"Probably losing every dime he makes off *Sawbones* in the gambling halls and the whorehouses."

"Don't forget the pubs. I miss Henry."

"So do I," Kindle said. "You trust me to gamble?"

"I want to see you glare at your opponent with one eye, and put the fear of God in them."

Kindle laughed. "What a picture you paint. Too bad they don't let women in the gambling rooms."

"What?"

"They don't let respectable women in."

"I'm not respectable."

Kindle drew me to him and kissed my forehead. "Yes, but I'm the only one allowed to know that. You must know sashaying into a gambling den on my arm would bring unwanted attention to us."

"I've never sashayed in my life."

A nearby boat's horn sounded a warning

to a small flatboat struggling upstream against the powerful Mississippi current. Laughter and voices from a steamboat docked nearby carried across the water. There was a shot, then a cry followed by a *plop* into the water.

"Was that a gunshot?" I looked around.

"Most like."

"Good heavens."

Kindle laughed heartily. "After all we've been through, a gunshot on the river is scandalizing you?"

"I suppose I've gone soft these past few months."

"This is the river, darlin'. Danger at every turn." Kindle gave me his arm and we started down the starboard side of the boat. "There's probably a bridge game in the women's salon you can get in."

"I'd rather be on the receiving end of that bullet. I prefer faro," I said, expertly flipping the coin between the fingers of my left hand. "I'm quite good."

"I have no doubt."

"Are you good at poker?"

"I know to quit when I'm ahead. I prefer gambling on events. Fights, races, which fly will alight first."

I handed him the coin. "Don't lose it all on the first hand."

Kindle palmed the chip. "I will do my best," he said, and kissed my temple.

"I don't like you going without me."

"Why?"

"I don't think you realize how appealing that eye patch makes you to a certain type of woman."

"Rest assured, you are the only type of woman I want. Let's eat."

We asked for and received a table in the far corner of the long salon, hoping to avoid prying, curious eyes. Kindle's eye patch drew attention wherever he went, so he sat in the chair facing away from the other diners.

The salon was lavish almost to the point of bad taste. The walls were painted with a large mural depicting the story of the United States, from the founding of Jamestown to the final spike driven for the transcontinental railroad. I studied the mural while Kindle ordered for us.

When the waiter left, I said, "Did you know our great country was founded without one woman contributing? An astonishing feat."

Kindle glanced at the mural and reached for my hand. "It seems the artist had an affinity for wars and exploration."

I shook my head. "We're going to be

wiped from history."

"What do you mean?"

"I mean, look." I waved my hand at the mural. "Men are writing the history. They give no due whatsoever to the women who are beside them." I leaned forward. "I know I agreed to become a midwife when we finally do settle down one day, and I'm not going back on the promise. But, it pains me to think that there will be one less woman breaking through into a man's field. It's almost enough for me to return to New York and clear my name."

Kindle dipped his chin and glared at me. "We've killed too many people to go that route."

The waiter brought a bottle of wine. I removed my hand from Kindle's and sat back while the waiter served the wine to him. He was right, of course. The list of dead we'd left in our wake scrolled through my mind. Every one would be brought up in my trial and used against me as proof of my character and my ability to take a man's life. The familiar sensation of loss returned. Whenever I thought I was finally resolved to giving up my profession, grief overcame me.

Kindle approved the wine. The waiter poured a small portion in my glass and a

447

larger one in Kindle's.

"Excuse me," I said. "Please fill mine equally." With a frown, the waiter looked at Kindle. "You don't need his approval," I said. "Fill my glass."

"Fill it, please," Kindle said.

I inhaled and glared at the waiter while he obeyed. Almost before he finished pouring, I took the glass and drank deeply, keeping my eyes on the waiter, who left in a huff.

"So much for being inconspicuous," Kindle said.

"Thank you for allowing me to have more wine," I said.

"It's not like that, Laura. I didn't want to cause a scene."

I breathed deeply a few times. "I know. I just feel so helpless at times, restricted by other people's expectations, and it angers me."

"And, you're used to barreling through and getting what you want."

"I rarely get what I want. But, I always make my point."

Kindle lifted his glass. "To my beautiful, strong-willed, fiercely intelligent wife."

We drank and Kindle waited. He raised his eyebrow. "This is where you say something complimentary about me."

"Yes, I know. I'm trying to find a way to

say it so I won't scandalize our fellow diners if I'm overheard."

"Why don't you save it until we're alone?"

"With pleasure."

The waiter brought our first course,
refilled our wineglasses, and left. Kindle and
I ate, occasionally catching the other's gaze
and smiling amid the *clink* of silverware on
other diners' plates, the murmur of conversation, and occasional laughter. "Do you
remember —" I started.

"Yes."

We laughed quietly together, reminiscing
about the conversation about memorable
meals we had during the first night of
Kindle's convalescence. "Who would have
imagined what we would have to go through
to get here?" I said.

Kindle lifted his glass. "Here's to a lifetime
of quiet dinners."

I leaned forward. "Though probably not
this lavish."

"No, probably not." He finished his salad
and wiped his mouth. "Do you really not
know how to cook?"

"Sophia offered to teach me, but I turned
her down."

"Why?"

"I know my limitations." I drank my wine
and didn't meet Kindle's eye, afraid he

449

would read my real reason: a stubborn determination not to be sucked into a life of domesticity. "I can make biscuits. I watched Maureen make Irish stew enough that I might be able to recreate it."

"I can make beans."

"Frying an egg can't be too difficult."

"I suppose wherever we end up we'll have to have chickens."

"I draw the line at wringing one's neck and plucking the feathers."

"You can amputate a leg, but don't want to wring a chicken's neck. You're full of strange contradictions."

"Admit it. It's one of the things you love most about me."

Kindle's eye raked over me in that familiar, inappropriate way. A tingle of anticipation shot through me. I absentmindedly looked over Kindle's shoulder and saw a handsome, well-dressed man being led by the waiter to a nearby table. The man nodded at me absently, before recognition lit his eyes. He spoke briefly to the waiter and walked toward us while the waiter unfolded the extravagantly arranged napkin and laid it over the back of the chair.

"Oh, no."

"What?"

It was too late to warn Kindle, or tell him

about the meeting that had been so inconsequential I'd forgotten about it until that moment. The gambler was beside our table, smiling at me in a friendly way that didn't meet his eyes.

"We meet again."

"Do I know you?"

Lyman's brows furrowed slightly, but his smile never wavered. "I believe so. Last summer in Saint Louis."

I shook my head and arranged my face in a puzzled expression. "No, I don't believe so."

"Hmm," Lyman said. "My mistake." He held out his hand. "John Lyman."

"I'm Sophia Ryan. This is my husband, William."

Lyman turned to Kindle and held out his hand, barely disguising his surprise at Kindle's eye patch. Kindle stood and took the gambler's hand. "Pleasure to meet you," Kindle said.

"Likewise."

"How do you think you know my wife?" Kindle asked. He was taller than Lyman by a good five inches, and with his eye patch and scowl most men would have faltered at the gruff question. Not Lyman. His full mouth curled into an amused smile and his eyes sparkled with mischief.

"Saying would hardly be complimentary to either of us."

Kindle's mouth hardened into a thin line.

"However, since you seem like reasonable man, and I was obviously mistaken, I thought I met her with a man named Henry Pope. Have you heard of him?"

"No."

"Interesting man, Henry Pope. Lots of stories. Mostly lies, I imagine, like any newspaperman. Are you a gaming man, Mr. Ryan?"

"I play."

"Join me for a game after dinner."

"I don't think —" I started.

"I'll find you," Kindle said.

Lyman looked between the two of us with an amused expression and nodded. "I look forward to it." A woman dressed in an expensive green silk dress with a plunging neckline entered the dining room. Lyman lifted his hand in acknowledgment. She nodded and let the waiter seat her. "My dinner companion has arrived. Enjoy yours."

I steamed while we were served our entrees. When we were alone, Kindle spoke before I could. "Do not speak for me like that."

"He is a professional gambler, William."

"Who did you think I would be playing

on a boat like this?" Kindle said. "I've gambled for years, Laura. I know how to handle men like Lyman."

I sighed. "Of course you do."

"You met him with Henry?"

I told him about the brief meeting and Henry losing his money to Lyman. "What if he puts together who we are?"

Kindle reached across the table and took my hand. "He won't. No one knows about William Kindle losing his eye. You don't resemble your Wanted poster." I bristled and tried to remove my hand. Kindle squeezed it. "You don't resemble the stiff, serious, uncomfortable woman who sat for that picture."

"But he suspects I know Henry."

"Don't worry. I can bluff and lie with the best of them."

"I hope so."

Kindle left with assurances he would play long enough to not raise suspicions and return to test my ability to restrain myself when surrounded by thin walls, something neither of us had to do while living in a secluded groundskeeper's cabin.

I pulled a shawl from our trunk. My saddlebags and two extra dresses, Kindle's clothes, and a few books he had taken from his family home in '65 was the sum total of our worldly possessions. It wasn't much, but somehow looked more diminished than when we packed it earlier that morning. I picked up my new medical bag and sat on the bed. Kindle had ordered the bag and had a tanner in Saint Louis put an extra layer of leather on the inside bottom to hide my mother's necklace and money, if needed. He'd sewn the necklace in before giving it to me, and there it was still, beneath all the medical instruments and medicines necessary for a career as a midwife.

As thrilled and touched as I was with the present, a small part of me grieved for the absence of surgeon's tools. Kindle was right when he alluded to the danger I would put myself — and him — in if I tried to expand my future practice beyond midwifery. I feared I would never lose the longing to return to my true profession. However, working with Sophia, seeing her blossom into a confident midwife and nurse had opened up a new idea for my future: I could help women just as well in the role of teacher and mentor as a physician and surgeon. Would my pride let me revel in others' successes and not my own?

Out of the trunk I pulled a needlepoint hoop Mary had given me. I stitched until my fingers were sore and my eyes burned from fatigue, then threw the hoop aside. Where was Kindle? I'd long since lost my father's pocket watch and had no way to know what time it was, but estimated hours had passed. He should've been back by now. What if something had happened to him? I thought of the gunshot and the sound of splashing water from earlier. I adjusted the shawl around my shoulders and left the room.

The splash of the paddle wheel drowned out the sounds of the river, but it couldn't mask the mingled scent of mud and fish. The shore was a dark lump in the distance, too far outside of the gaslight thrown off by the riverboat to make out clearly.

The long salon was empty save the tables set with cloths and china for the next morning's breakfast. I walked around the front of the stern-wheeler and down the port side to the main cabin. Men sat in groups at the low tables smoking cigars, talking, and laughing. A quick glance through the window showed Kindle wasn't among them. The far wall of the main cabin was interspersed with curtains, one of which was partially open and showed a card game in the hidden room. I steeled myself for ridicule, found the door to the cabin, and entered. I went to the first curtain and pulled it back. Empty. I was able to pull two more back before the cigar-smoking men realized what I was doing.

"I say, you there!" one red-faced fat man with a walrus mustache called out. I opened the fourth curtain and surprised a faro game. No Kindle. The fifth compartment was behind the partially opened curtain and defended by four men, including the Walrus. I walked purposefully through and pulled back the curtain.

Kindle lay down his cards with a grin and raked the pot toward him. Lyman's dinner companion sat on the arm of Kindle's chair, ran her hand through his hair, pulled his head back, and kissed him deeply. To my astonishment, Kindle didn't resist.

"William?" His name tumbled from my lips in a strangled cry. I hated myself for the desperation and uncertainty in my voice.

He glanced up in a distracted manner, and saw me. His expression flickered through so many emotions at once it was difficult to know which one to believe.

John Lyman sat next to Kindle. "Your wife has come to take you home." His thin mustache quivered with amusement. The woman appraised me with a cool look of superiority.

456

A pair of strong hands grabbed me by the upper arms and pulled me out of the room. The curtain closed and the waiter who held me by the arms frog marched me out of the cabin. "Women aren't allowed. Unless you've got something to sell. Do you?"

I glared at the man and returned to my cabin to wait for Kindle, sure he would be on my heels.

CHAPTER 34

I spent a sleepless night waiting for Kindle to return. My shock at what I had witnessed evolved into anger as my imagination ran rampant and the minutes ticked into hours. When the sun rose and I was alone still, I calmly rose, donned my wedding dress, and went in search of my wayward husband.

John Lyman sat in the long salon drinking coffee. He saw me and stood. "Would you like to join me?"

I didn't hesitate. Lyman held out the chair for me, and scooted it in when I sat.

A waiter brought me a cup, served coffee from the silver pot on the table, and left. Lyman sat down, put his napkin in his lap, and said, "I apologize in advance for the coffee. I've told Captain Theigen to invest in better for years."

I sipped mine and placed the china cup back on the saucer. "I've had much worse."

The gambler raised one eyebrow. "Have

458

you? I'd like to hear that story."

"Some other time, perhaps."

"You have no idea how persuasive I can be."

"Oh, I think I do, Mr. Lyman."

Lyman wiped his lips with a napkin. The waiter returned with a plate of bacon, eggs, and toast. I declined when asked if I wanted breakfast.

Lyman salted his eggs generously. "Your *husband* took quite a bit of money from me — money I intended to win back." The emphasis on the word *husband* was slight, but significant. "You must have made him feel guilty. He left right after you and didn't return. Did you sock away his winnings?"

When I didn't answer, Lyman's pencil-thin mustache twitched. "He didn't return?" Lyman buttered his toast and said, "I'm sorry to hear it, but I'm not surprised. Rosemond can be very persuasive."

My cup clattered in the saucer, but Lyman continued as if he hadn't noticed. "I got the impression they were acquainted. Do you know Rosemond?"

"I haven't had the pleasure."

"I'm surprised, considering the circles you both run in."

I hardly heard a word he said. I stared out the window and tried to keep my emotions from showing on my countenance. My imagination had been bad enough when I thought Kindle was with a random whore. Knowing it was Rosemond reignited my anger into a roaring bonfire. How he could stay with her for the entire night was incomprehensible.

The hum of the boat's motor dropped to a low rumble, the silence highlighting how loud the motor had actually been.

"We're pulling into Cape Girardeau," Lyman explained, "to take on more fuel and passengers." Lyman lifted the coffeepot on the table between us and poured more into my cup. "You look pale, Mrs. Ryan. Are you feeling quite well?"

"No, actually. I've been slightly seasick since we boarded." I lifted my cup. "The coffee is not helping."

In truth, I'd felt the first stirrings of the dark days coming in the middle of the night, feelings that I attributed to the nausea I felt at seeing Kindle kiss another woman. Even now, I wasn't sure if it the uneasiness in my stomach was physical or emotional sickness.

Lyman wiped the corners of his mouth with his napkin, folded it, and placed it next to his plate. "I have an errand to run in the cape. Would you like to join me? Walk on solid land for a while?"

460

I opened my mouth to instinctively demure, knowing full well it would be unseemly for a married woman to go ashore with a strange man. Knowing full well Kindle would be livid.

I smiled and batted my eyes. "I would."

"Wonderful." Lyman's knowing smirk faded as his gaze traveled over my shoulder. "Speak of the devils."

I plastered a smile on my face and forced it to stay natural as the shock of seeing Kindle with Rosemond on his arm flooded my veins with cold water. I felt Lyman's eyes on me, waiting for what kind of scene I would create. I widened my smile and said, "Well, there you are, darling. Mr. Lyman and I were talking about you. He's sore you didn't return to the game last night so he could win back his money."

There was a certain amount of satisfaction in the glare Kindle shot Lyman. "But, when he told me your . . . companion . . . was Rosemond, I wasn't surprised at all." I held my hand out to the tart. "I'm Sophia Ryan, as I'm sure you know."

"Rosemond Barclay."

"Barclay? Are you related to Lord Barclay?" I turned to Lyman. "I met him when I lived in London. A randy old fellow, but perfectly harmless, really." I turned back to

461

Rosemond with a questioning expression.

"If I am, it is a distant relation."

I flicked my eyes up and down Rose-mond's length, before settling pointedly at her low-cut neckline. "Yes, I imagine it would be," I said wryly to Lyman before turning a beaming smile on Kindle. "Well, darling, Lyman here has offered to take me ashore so I might get my legs under me again. You know, my stomach hasn't sat well since we boarded and I'd love to stand on solid land for a bit. Is there anything you need me to pick up for you while I'm ashore?"

"I'll go with you."

I flicked my hand in dismissal. "I wouldn't want to tear you away from your old friend. Did you have a nice, long visit last night?"

"It was divine," Rosemond said. She smiled up at Kindle and ran her hand up and down his arm. "Just like old times."

"Well." Lyman rose from the table. "As entertaining as this is, I must be off." He held out his arm to me. "Sophia."

I stood and waited for Kindle and Rose-mond to move out of the way. Kindle glared at me.

"Why don't we all go?" Rosemond said.

I inhaled and placed my hand over my chest. "Excellent idea! Lyman, I must go to

462

the cabin first."

He bowed slightly. "Of course. I will meet you at the top of the gangway."

I smiled. "Perfect." Rosemond stepped back to let me pass. "Thank you, Rosie."

"Rosemond."

"Such a mouthful. But, I'm sure you've heard that before."

Rosemond laughed, and though I was trying to goad her and insult her, I feared she liked me. I supposed I would have to be more directly hateful.

I walked off without acknowledging Kindle, but heard his tread behind me before he grasped my elbow. We turned the corner and I ripped my arm from him and kept walking. "You're hurting me."

"What in the hell are you doing?"

"Going to the room."

He grabbed me, spun me around, and pulled me close. "You know what I'm talking about." A couple stared at us as they walked by. I smiled sweetly at them. When they were out of our vision, I dropped the smile and glared at Kindle.

"Let's have this conversation in private, shall we?" I jerked my arm away and walked to the cabin.

When the door closed behind him I turned around and slapped him across the face. He grabbed my wrists and pulled me close. "*Rosemond,* of all the whores on the Mississippi." I tried to twist my wrists from his grasp but couldn't. He pulled my arms behind my back and held me tight.

"Jealousy doesn't look good on you, Laura."

The more I twisted my hands, the more he tightened his grip. My breathing quickened and my heart pounded in my ears. "It didn't look good on you, either. Or were you recovering from reliving old times? Tell me, did she remember what you like? Did she remind you of me?"

He pushed me backward against the wall, still holding my hands behind me. "If you'd give your wit a rest and think for a Godamn minute, you'd realize Rosemond recognizing me is a nightmare for us." My eyes widened and I stopped moving. "There it is." Kindle released me and walked to the center of the room. He ran his hand through his hair.

"Rosemond is not a charitable woman. She won't let us go out of the goodness of her heart." I covered my mouth with my hand. Kindle rounded on me. "I might have been able to buy our freedom cheaply if you hadn't been so rude to her."

I dropped my hand. "Forgive me for

bristling at the sight of my husband walking arm in arm with the whore he spent the night with. Does she know who I am?"

Kindle shook his head. "She believed Henry's newspaper story about Catherine Bennett dying in Indian Territory. I told her you're a hired companion."

"You did *not*."

"Laura," Kindle said in warning, "shut up and listen for a minute. I'm trying to save your life."

"And yours. She could turn you in to the Army."

"She won't turn me in."

"Oh, but she'll throw me — a stranger — to the wolves."

"She will if she thinks there's more between us than paid companionship. I'd hoped to get to you before you left the room, to get our stories straight," Kindle said.

"Did you tell Lyman the same?"

"Yes."

I grasped the bedpost and lowered myself down on the bed to keep my legs from buckling beneath me. "I waited for you until dawn."

"I wanted her to believe you were a paid companion, not my wife."

"How far did you take the ruse, William?"

He at least had the grace to look abashed. "Not that far. I feigned drunkenness and passed out."

I studied him for a long moment. I wanted him to beg, plead with me to believe him. Instead, he defiantly held my gaze, challenging me to question his honor. With horror, I realized I didn't believe him, but I didn't want to know the truth, either.

"How long will we have to play this charade? All the way to New Orleans?"

"No. We'll get off at Cairo."

"What if we miss our ship?"

"We built in time before it leaves. We'll make the ship."

I stood and almost reached out to Kindle, but pulled my hand back. "Let's go ashore."

"What will you give Lyman as the reason for coming to the cabin?" Kindle asked.

"Nothing. The fewer specifics we use the better. Let him use his imagination."

CHAPTER 35

Conning Lyman and Rosemond was more difficult than I had anticipated, especially since Kindle took my advice to heart and said little. Lyman seemed to find Kindle's taciturn demeanor amusing, but being the student of human nature he was, knew better than to rib Kindle directly. Instead, he slowed our pace so we fell behind and aimed his barbs at me.

"I do hope he is paying you handsomely. What torture it must be for a woman like you to be with a stick in the mud such as him."

"He has his charms. You don't mind that Rosemond prefers him to you?"

"Not when I have you as consolation."

"Do you know her well?"

"We have a history."

"Should I be worried?"

"That she will steal your John? I suppose it depends on how well you are satisfying

467

our swain."

I wasn't about to be pulled into a conversation about having sex with Kindle, even if it was playacting. "I am sure he would detest being called a swain."

"He probably doesn't know what it means."

I glanced up a street in Cape Girardeau. It was moderately better than the small towns I had passed through in Texas, owning to the river business, no doubt. The streets were muddy, though these false-front buildings were bricked and somewhat had a sense of permanence. "What is your business in town? We've almost run out of street."

"I need a new hat."

His derby was perfectly fine. "What is wrong with your hat?"

He stopped and took it off. "It's not mine. I won it from a man. Your friend, as a matter of fact."

"What friend?"

One corner of Lyman's mouth curled up. "Of course. My mistake. I won this from a man named Henry Pope." Lyman flipped the hat onto his head and grinned. Kindle and Rosemond had turned back and were walking toward us. "Ryan, come help me buy a hat."

"No, thank you."

"You'd rather stay out here with the women?" Kindle narrowed his eye at Lyman and didn't reply. Lyman threw his arm around Kindle's shoulder. Kindle visibly stiffened. "Come now. It will be worth your while. I promise." Kindle went with him and Lyman called back, "You two ladies go have lunch. We will meet you in an hour."

A bell rang over the door of the haberdashery shop as they entered, and they disappeared.

"They aren't going to buy a hat, are they?" I said.

"No. There's a poker game that's been going on in the back of the store for three years."

"You're joking."

"No. I played in it once. They kicked me out after an hour."

"You were winning that much?"

She shrugged noncommittally. "Do you play?"

"Faro, now and then."

"Are you any good?"

"I won more than I lost."

"Hmm. Are you hungry?"

"No."

"Me, neither." She put her arm through

mine and pulled me along. "Let's go for a walk."

We walked down an alley and through the backstreets until we were out of town and at the start of a trail that wound through the woods and disappeared. I slowed and tried to turn back. "Should we go so far away?"

"It isn't far." She released my arm and appraised me. "Don't you trust me?"

"No."

Rosemond laughed and put her arm through mine again. "As well you shouldn't."

Her eyes were a deep brown, the same color as her hair. A generous amount of powder covered the smallpox scars dotting her face, an adequate disguise in low light, but obscene in the bright light of day. Her features were pleasant enough, but what made her striking were her clothes and her confident carriage.

"You're staring," she said, but kept her eyes forward.

"How long have you known William?"

"Five years, I suppose. Sometime after the war. And, you?"

"We met a week ago, when he obtained my services."

"Hmm." She pulled her arm from mine

470

and pushed a low-hanging tree limb out of the way for me to pass through. It was like walking into a different world.

Large lily pads with white flowers rimmed a small pond. Frogs splashed into the water, and the ducks, which had been serenely floating in the middle, took flight at our arrival. Pine trees fenced the pond in from the rest of the world and shrank the sky to a jagged blue circle dotted with clouds shaped like bolls of cotton. The scent of pinesap, moss, and mud mingled in the air. It was an enchanting place. I turned to say so to Rosemond, but the comment died on my lips at her expression.

"Let's cut the bullshit, *Sophia*. You aren't in the trade any more than I'm related to an English lord."

"I don't know what you mean."

She stepped close and stared at me levelly. We were of the same height and build. "If Kindle had wanted a paid companion in Saint Louis, he would have come to me."

The jab hurt because I knew the truth in it.

"Which leads me to believe you're the woman he threw his career away for. The Murderess who was supposed to have died in Indian Territory."

"I don't know what you're talking about."

471

"You're a serviceable liar, but you're no match for me."

I glared at Rosemond. She knew who I was. The charade was up and I could treat her with all the hatred and disdain I wanted. "Kindle won't need your services ever again."

Rosemond laughed. "Don't fool yourself. Most of my customers are married men, unhappy with their wives. After last night he should be satisfied for a while, at least. Lay with him whenever he asks and he might not stray too often. He's more honorable than most."

My breathing turned shallow and I hated my body for betraying my mortification and anger. I kept my voice level and said, "Thank you. I will give the advice of a whore all of the merit and consideration it deserves."

She smirked. "I have more experience pleasing men than you do."

"Yes, but very little in getting a man to the altar." Her smirk faded. "Was Kindle one of your targets? A dashing young officer with a plantation in Maryland. I imagine landing him as a regular was quite a coup for a pockmarked whore such as you. You must indeed have hidden talents. Or was it your personality and conversation that secured him?"

"You'd be careful to not alienate me."

"Or what? You'll turn me in? I imagine you will regardless. Turn me in and you can have Kindle yourself, yes?"

"I can offer him something you cannot."

I crossed my arms. "Oh, this should be rich."

"His name." She raised a thick, but expertly groomed, eyebrow at my reaction. "I've serviced enough officers at Jefferson Barracks that it would be easy to get his desertion charge dismissed. Or a dishonorable discharge, at the least."

I turned away and thought of our argument at the orphanage, when Kindle had detailed everything he'd given up for me. His name had been at the top of the list.

"What do you offer, Sophia? Or should I call you Catherine?" I looked over my shoulder at her.

"I prefer Laura."

"Laura. I followed your story quite closely. I admired you. You accomplished so much. As much as I hate to admit it, I still admire you." Rosemond walked around and stopped in front of me. She laughed. "Don't look so terrified. I don't want Kindle."

My head jerked up. "Then why offer this?"

"I like him enough I don't want to see

him wasting his life running from the law for you. If you truly loved him, you wouldn't either."

It was my turn to laugh. "You expect me to believe you've got only Kindle's best interests at heart? I've known my share of prostitutes and few do anything out of the goodness of their hearts. What do you want, Rosie?"

"Five hundred dollars."

"I don't have five hundred dollars."

"You either give me five hundred dollars in cash or I turn you in for the money."

"Kindle would never forgive you."

"Kindle would get down on his knees and thank me for freeing him from you."

"What's Lyman's role in this?"

"What?"

"Lyman. Is he in on your little scam?"

"No, and you better hope he doesn't figure out who you are."

"Why?"

"Lyman is a snake. I wouldn't trust him with a plugged nickel."

The limb blocking the trail was brushed aside and the topic of our conversation walked through. "Now, Rosemond, that hurts my feelings. After all we've meant to each other."

Rosemond's initial shock at Lyman's appearance turned into a coy smile. "Lyman, you know better than to eavesdrop on women's private conversation."

Lyman walked forward and put his arm around my waist. "Don't believe her, Sophia. She's jealous."

"I can't imagine of what," I said, trying to disentangle myself from Lyman without seeming to. He tightened his grip on my waist.

"Of you, of course. She and I had a — what would you call it, Rosemond?"

"Business arrangement."

"Oh, it was more than that."

"Maybe to you," Rosemond said.

Lyman grinned, but dropped the subject. "Come, Sophia, I have a business proposition for you." He held the bough back and I walked through, but not before glancing back at Rosemond, who shook her head at me in warning.

"Where's Mr. Ryan?"

"I left him at the game with a full house and a jug of whisky. There was room for only one player and I graciously gave him my seat."

"How kind of you."

"I thought so." Lyman placed his hand over my hand, which was resting in the crook of his arm. "I have a proposition for you."

"Mr. Ryan has paid for my services for the entire trip. I couldn't possibly go back on our arrangement."

"I wouldn't dream of asking you to."

"Then what are you asking?"

He stopped at a curve in the trail and pulled me close. "For a few hours."

I tried to twist away but his grip tightened. "Mr. Lyman, really."

"Why are you fighting, Sophia? You're a professional. I would think you'd be anxious to make a bit of extra money. Ryan never need know. I'm sure Rosemond won't mind keeping him occupied for a few hours."

I stopped struggling and stared up into Lyman's eyes. They were calculating, prescient, and teasing. He was testing me. Did he merely suspect I wasn't a working woman or did he suspect I was Catherine Bennett? Kindle hadn't acted like he knew Lyman, but if Lyman'd been working the river for years, and in Saint Louis, there was a possibility he'd known of Kindle. I glanced back the way we came. Rosemond and Lyman shared a history. What were the chances she'd told him about a former client who'd been the subject of Pope's article?

They were working together.

476

I lifted one corner of my mouth and ran my fingers up and down the lapels of his coat. "You make an excellent point."

Lyman didn't try to mask his surprise as he bent his head to kiss me. I turned away. "We should talk numbers. You might not be able to afford me."

"Oh, I'm sure I can."

"Three hundred dollars."

Lyman laughed. "Don't be absurd."

"If Ryan finds out he will put me off the boat at the next port without the other half of my fee. You have to make the chance worth my while."

"A hundred dollars an hour?"

"Trust me, I'm worth it." I almost gagged on the words, at the proposition I was making this man. Instead, I thought of Camille, how she would react, manipulate him into doing precisely what she wanted.

"What's your specialty?"

My specialty? "Whatever you want."

He removed the combs from my hair, running his hands through it. "Do you pretend to be a boy?"

"If that's what you want."

"And, you'll let me bugger you?"

I swallowed my disgust. "It'll cost double."

"Deal."

I leaned away from Lyman and held out

my hand between us to shake on the deal. Lyman smiled and said, "A kiss would be more appropriate, don't you think?"

I wanted to argue, was readying to, when I realized I couldn't if I wanted to get out of this forest without arousing Lyman's suspicious. I leaned forward and kissed him. He gathered me closer, dashing my hope of a quick kiss. I shuddered in disgust, though Lyman responded as if it was from desire. With great subtlety and skill, Lyman coaxed my mouth open and deepened the kiss before I realized what was happening.

The sound of a gun's hammer being cocked stopped us.

"Get your hands off my whore or I'm gonna put a bullet in your head."

I tried to get free of Lyman's grasp but he held me close. I could see only the left side of Kindle's face and couldn't read his expression. His voice, controlled and quiet, told of the depth of his anger. "Come, now, Ryan. It was an innocent kiss."

"There was nothing innocent in what I saw."

"How did you find us?"

"I've brought him back here," Rosemond said.

Now she shows up.

"Let me go, please."

Lyman released me and I walked to Kindle. I smoothed my mussed hair. Kindle's jaw was clenched so tight the muscle in his cheek pulsed.

The gambler faced Kindle with a smile. "She's something else." He wiped the corners of his mouth, which I was mortified to discover were damp. "And, game. Why don't we share her? She might be willing to do us at the same time."

Kindle punched Lyman in the nose with the butt of his gun. The crack from the cartilage breaking was quickly covered by his scream. Kindle grabbed my hand and dragged me down the trail, as Rosemond moved to help her former, and I suspected current, business partner.

I knew better than to speak, and let Kindle pull me through town, up the gangway, and down the hallway to our room. As he opened the door, the idea I might not leave the room alive flashed through my mind. He pushed me through the door and slammed it behind us.

"Did you enjoy it?" Kindle said.

"Enjoy what?"

"Laura."

I cleared my throat and glanced away. I'd never been able to lie to Kindle, but I knew the honest truth would not serve me well.

"Lyman seemed to know what he was doing."

"Why were you kissing him?"

"He was testing me. A paid companion would have no objection to the proposition, would she? So thank you for telling such a stupid lie that you compromised me with a snake like Lyman."

"What proposition?"

"He wants me to service him on the side — pretend to be a boy, specifically, with all that entails. I can make six hundred dollars for three hours. We'd be able to pay Rosemond off and be one hundred dollars in the clear. She's figured out who I am, by the way."

Kindle moved forward and towered over me. "You are not servicing Lyman."

"Why not? It's no less a sacrifice than you spending the night with Rosemond, is it? You did that to protect me, right?" The thought of Rosemond's taunt about pleasing Kindle emboldened me. "Did you fuck Rosemond last night?"

"I told you what happened."

"Why should I believe you?"

He dipped his head as if to kiss me, but I turned my head away.

"Because I'm your husband and I said a vow I intend to keep."

I glared at him. "It's a simple yes-or-no question."

His hand went to my hip and slowly pulled up my skirt until he found the waist of my bloomers. He slid his hand beneath the soft cotton and onto my bare skin.

I grabbed his wrist to stop him, my desire for him warring with my dislike of his patriarchal attitude, just as my need to carry every argument contradicted the thrill I felt when Kindle wouldn't back down.

"Does knowing that another man wants me excite you?" My breathing quickened in anticipation. "Or does it scare you?"

He jerked my bloomers down and lifted me onto the edge of the dresser. His mouth found mine as his hand moved between my legs. I opened up for him, gasping as his fingers plunged deep inside me.

I pushed his shoulders back. He stared at me, eye hooded with desire. "Swear to me you didn't fuck Rosemond."

"I swear."

CHAPTER 36

The stern-wheeler left Cape Girardeau but we hardly noticed. The rest of the world faded into nothingness. Our lovemaking was passionate and rough, as if we were punishing each other for our fears and the guilt of what we'd done. That night we understood that with great love came an even greater ability to inflict pain, to dole out cruelty when we felt threatened. The only solace, if you could call it that, was the knowledge this wasn't one sided, that neither of us would cower at the other's anger. A true marriage of equals.

Our fiery arguments were rare, but when over and resolved, our marriage was stronger for it, and this one was no different. We lay in our small bed, listening to the sounds of the boat on the other side of our thin cabin wall, and finalized our plan. We would give Rosemond my mother's necklace, sneak off at Cairo, take the first stagecoach south, and make our way to New Orleans in the least logical way possible to throw off anyone who might follow. Rosemond didn't know the name of the ship we were booked on, nor did she know the date, so neither would Lyman, if they were working together. Kindle was skeptical they were, but I didn't want to start another argument so soon after our most recent one.

There was a knock at the door. "Who is it?" Kindle called.

"Message for Mr. Ryan."

"Slide it under the door."

"I'm supposed to deliver it in person."

"Then you won't deliver it."

After a moment's hesitation, the note slid beneath the door and stopped in the middle of the room. Kindle rose, picked it up, and opened it. "It's from Lyman. He apologizes for his proposition. He's inviting me to a game so he can win his money back. He says it's the least I can do after breaking his nose." Kindle smirked and tossed the paper on the dresser and reached for his discarded pants.

"You aren't going."

"Of course I am. I'll apologize for his nose, lose a little money to him, and come right back."

"What if Rosemond's there?"

Kindle bent over and kissed me. "You have nothing to fear from Rosemond, Slim."

"I know that. What if she told Lyman who we are?"

"She wouldn't take the chance of Lyman getting the reward."

"I think they're working together."

Kindle chuckled. "Rosemond isn't working with Lyman."

"How do you know?"

"She warned me about him last night, told me their history. She has no love, or respect, for John Lyman."

My stomach churned at the mention of their night together. "You trust her," I said, astonished.

He hesitated. "I do. She's self-serving but she keeps her word."

He counted out half of the money in his pocket. "You keep half of the cash. Free the jewels while I'm gone. We'll give them to Rosemond and get off this damn boat at the next port, before she changes her mind." He winked at me broadly as he left.

I held my mother's sapphire-and-pearl necklace up to the dim cabin lamplight. I expected to feel a pang of loss, or remorse, at the imminent loss of the last connection to my former life. Instead, all I felt was wonder it had been a part of my life at all. Somehow it had safely traveled beneath a basket of produce, across the ocean, and over the vast Texas plains and Indian Territory to arrive here on the muddy Mississippi, outside Cairo, Illinois. Where it would go from here, I had no idea. It would either be worn on the bosom of a prostitute or be gambled away by a confidence man. My mother and father would never have imagined the fate. Maureen would have been appalled.

I put the necklace in the purple pouch, its home on its long, twisting journey, and brushed my hair. My combs were somewhere on the wooded pond path, I supposed. I wondered what kind of reception Kindle and I would receive when we brought the necklace to Rosemond.

The sharp pain I'd been dreading ripped through my stomach. I fell to my knees. "No, no, no. Not now."

I pulled my medicine bag from the bed, spilling the contents all over the floor, and found the green bottle of laudanum. I uncorked it and took a long, bitter swig. I coughed, felt the opiate ooze through my body, and took another sip. I corked the bottle and clutched it to my stomach, waiting for the numbness to take away the pain.

The motors cut back and the stern-wheeler slowed. We were probably getting ready to make the sharp turn to port before Cairo. Kindle had told me earlier that after Cairo the river bent back and forth on itself for the remaining trip. Fifty miles turned into seventy. The trip would slow considerably. Another reason to get off the boat as soon as possible.

A muffled voice called out, as if from another boat, and the stern-wheeler cut its engines altogether. Sweating and breathless, I dragged myself onto the bed and pulled back the curtains covering the cabin's window. I opened the window and peeked outside to the lower deck where our second-class room was located. Negro cabin boys ran past toward the main deck. Snatches of conversation from other passengers floated on the breeze.

"Why are we stopped?"

"Someone wants to board . . ."

"US Army . . ."

". . . Prisoner . . ."

". . . Deserter onboard . . ."

The sound of boots hitting the forward deck made me jerk my head inside and close the curtains. "Kindle."

I stumbled outside and into the middle of a mass of onlookers. A few glanced at me with curiosity, but the unfolding events were too interesting to keep their attention for long. I sidled up to the nearest couple and asked, "What's the commotion?"

"We aren't sure," the woman said, excitement in her voice. "I think there's a killer onboard."

"Nonsense, Eloise," her husband said. "It's an Army deserter. An officer, the scoundrel. You expect it from the Irish and the niggers, but not the officers. I don't know what the world's coming to."

I went back into the hall to the stairs leading up to the first-class deck. This was all Rosemond's doing, I knew it. The very woman rounded the corner at a trot, spotted me, and sped up. "Which is your room?"

I stepped forward. "You have some nerve —"

Rosemond turned me around and pushed me down the hall. "Where's your room, Catherine?"

"Here." I opened the door and we entered in a rush. She closed it and leaned against it.

"Lyman turned Kindle in."

"You told him!"

"No. Lyman is a clever man. He connected you and Kindle to the newspaper story by Pope." She shoved a dark cloak at me. "Put this on."

"What?"

"Once Kindle is out of the way Lyman is going to take you to New York City and get the reward."

"Isn't that what you're going to do?"

"Not today."

"Why are you helping me?"

"Kindle asked me to."

"He would never do that."

"Yet, here I am." When I didn't move, Rosemond rolled her eyes. "Suit yourself. I'll tell Kindle I tried." She went to the door.

I doubled over in pain again. "Wait."

She placed a hand on my back. "What's wrong?"

"Menses." I knelt on the floor and with shaking hands scooped my instruments and medicines into my bag. I dropped the purple pouch inside and snapped it shut. I was in too much pain and confusion to think to get my holster from the bottom of Kindle's trunk.

Rosemond peeked out of the cabin and nodded for me to follow. We hurried quietly down the hall toward the stern.

We made our way to the stern ladder and Rosemond stopped at the top. A flatboat was tied to the bottom.

When safely aboard I heard voices across

the water. In the distance, I saw a boat being ferried to shore. A lamp hung on the bow of the boat, illuminating Kindle sitting rigidly, his hands tied behind his back.

"William!"

Kindle turned toward my voice, as did the soldiers. "Who's there? Is it the woman?"

"Shut her up." Rosemond's voice was flinty with hatred. I turned in time to see the dripping boat paddle rushing toward me.

CHAPTER 37

"Sleeping Beauty awakes."

I lay on a bench in a second-class compartment, my head hitting the wooden wall with each sway of the train. Rosemond watched me from the bench opposite.

I rubbed my face and winced in pain.

"Sorry about the shiner," she said, "but you almost got us found out. It'll heal soon enough."

With shaky arms, I pushed myself into a sitting position. "What's going on? Where are we?"

"Somewhere west of Independence."

"West?" I was moving backward.

Disjointed images flickered through my mind. Being carried by a large, dark-skinned man. Sleeping in a soft bed. A warm stone. My undergarments being changed. Laudanum and whisky being forced down me.

Bile rose in my throat. I jumped up from the bench, slid open the door on the second try, and stumbled down the hall and out onto the small platform between the trains before wretching over the side. I leaned my head on the iron rail and spit. I took a couple of deep breaths to settle my stomach, but vomiting seemed to make me more nauseated. I wretched over the side of the train again, tasting laudanum. I wiped the back of my mouth with my hand and returned to the compartment. I fell heavily into my seat and leaned my head against the glass, completely exhausted.

"Kindle told me you had a penchant for the dramatic."

I stared at the whore. "Where are you taking me?"

"To a new beginning."

"Where?"

Rosemond clicked her tongue. "So many questions." She tilted her head to the side and seemed to make up her mind. "It's harmless for you to know. We're going to Boulder. To start a new life. If you're lucky, you might be able to start a medical practice there. We'll have to check the lay of the land, first."

"Kindle knows where we're going?"

"It's not safe for you if he knows. When he's acquitted, I'll telegram him."

My eyes settled on my mother's necklace

hanging around the whore's neck. She touched it and said, "It's too much, I know. But, I thought you would appreciate it."

Kindle putting me in the hands of this whore was incomprehensible. He'd trusted my life to a woman who'd tried to blackmail me hours earlier? She watched me with a curious expression, as if she knew precisely the route my thoughts were taking. One corner of her mouth quirked up when I realized I knew very little about the depth of her relationship with Kindle.

My head pounded and my mouth watered with a craving for laudanum. My tongue was thick when I spoke. "If you're lying to me, I'll kill you."

Rosemond grinned. "I'd be disappointed if you didn't try."

Out the window I watched the eastern horizon darken and finally go black as the train rolled west, away from the man I loved.

ACKNOWLEDGMENTS

Without the support and encouragement of the following people, *Blood Oath* would have never been completed: Alice Speilburg, Susan Barnes, Lindsey Hall, Jennifer Mason-Black, Brooke Fossey, Mark Hoover, Jenny Martin, Kendel Lynn, Tex Thompson, William Penn, everyone at DFW Writers' Workshop, and the entire Redhook team.

As always, special thanks to my friends and family for your unwavering love and patience.

ABOUT THE AUTHOR

Melissa Lenhardt is the president of the North Dallas chapter of Sisters in Crime, as well as a member of the DFW Writers' Workshop. She lives in Texas with her husband and two sons.